Praise for Ann's

JACKRABBIT JUNCTION JITTERS

"Ann Charles's *Jackrabbit Junction Jitters*, book two in her Jackrabbit Junction mystery series, is a fast, fun, sexy ride with spunky lovable Claire. We find Claire ensnarled in all sorts of drama including dealing with horrendous storm to getting caught up in a treasure hunt—all the while trying desperately to finagle the wacky characters in her life. Ann has made me a fan of hers all over again. Put *Jackrabbit Junction Jitters* on your must read list."
~Lois Lavrisa, Bestselling author, *Liquid Lies*

"Where there's trouble, Claire's not far behind … but with loyal friends and luck like the Irish, Claire always comes out on top. What a book! Ann's books are always a treat!"
~Natasha Jennex, A Great Book Is The Cheapest Vacation Reviews

"We're not in Deadwood anymore, but fans of Ann Charles's Deadwood series will still recognize her keenly crafted sense of place in her Jackrabbit Junction series. For readers who enjoy the fast-paced dialogue that propels them through her romantic mysteries, *Jackrabbit Junction Jitters* will not leave you jilted."
~C.M. Wendelboe, Author of *Death Along the Spirit Road* and *Death Where the Bad Rocks Live*

"Ann Charles does it again with *Jackrabbit Junction Jitters*. This book has all my favorite things—sassy, real characters, laugh out loud dialogue, a twisty, compelling mystery, and sizzling romantic chemistry. Can't wait for the next installment."
~Terri L. Austin, author of *Diners, Dives and Dead Ends*

"A mysterious murder, car crashes, and sex—you'll find them all in *Jackrabbit Junction Jitters!*"
~Jacquie Rogers, Author of the Hearts of Owyhee Western Romance Series

Dear Reader,

I wrote the first draft of *Jackrabbit Junction Jitters* in 2006, after my son was born. Because I couldn't finagle a trip to Arizona at that time, I did the next best thing and read books about Southeastern Arizona geology, fauna, and flora. I scoured the internet for write-ups about the area from other travelers. I watched movies set around Tucson.

The result was a very long sequel to *Dance of the Winnebagos* with a few too many details about rocks, animals, and plants. But it was written. And then it was shelved after publishers rejected the first book in this series time and again. When was I going to learn that mixing my genres would not land me a publisher?

Apparently, I was too hard-headed to accept that because at this point in my writing career I wrote the first in my award-winning Deadwood Mystery series, *Nearly Departed in Deadwood*, which mixes mystery, romance, humor, and paranormal.

Last fall, Corvallis Press published *Dance of the Winnebagos*, the first book in the Jackrabbit Junction Mystery series. I was thrilled for many reasons, especially since I knew that Claire's second book in the series would see the light of day. So, off the "shelf" came the book in your hands.

As I began to read through and make edits on this story, I realized that what the book and I both needed was a trip to Southeastern Arizona to really soak up the setting and give the book a desert polish. Well, that's the excuse I gave to my family when I was talking them into going with me on a road trip "to the desert."

Fourteen days and five-thousand miles later, we returned home from our Arizona 'research' trip, covered in dust and filled with wonderful memories of cacti and sunshine, wild flowers and tamales, frybread and canyon-filled landscapes. I had stood at the location where I'd placed my fictional town, Jackrabbit Junction. I had looked over the huge open pit mine that I'd used as a basis for the Copper Snake Mining Company. I had found the ravine where Ruby's Dancing Winnebagos R.V. Park was located. Finally, I could hear and smell and see the setting for this story and could smile wide at the knowledge that all of my previous research had paid off—I'd gotten it right.

Now, it's finally your turn to read Claire's continuing story and return to the Southeastern Arizona desert, where the Grackles chatter, the coyotes howl, and the monsoons thunder.

As always, beware of deadly critters, including over-bearing mothers whose good intentions are delivered via razor-sharp tongues.

Welcome back to Jackrabbit Junction!

Ann Charles

www.anncharles.com

JACKRABBIT
JUNCTION JITTERS

ANN CHARLES

ILLUSTRATED BY C.S. KUNKLE

CORVALLIS PRESS

JACKRABBIT JUNCTION JITTERS

Copyright © 2012 by Ann Charles

Cover Art by C.S. Kunkle (www.charlesskunkle.com)
Cover Design by Sharon Benton (www.q42designs.com)
Editing by Mimi the "Grammar Chick"
(www.grammarchick.com)

ISBN: 978-0-9850663-4-5

Corvallis Press, Publisher
630 NW Hickory St., Ste. 120
Albany, OR 97321
www.corvallispress.com

Dedication

To my sisters …

For taking care of me and teaching me so much.
For helping me learn how to lose and still have fun.
For sharing life's highs and lows.
For guiding me through motherhood and more.
For keeping me laughing through it all.

I'm lucky to have so many wonderful women in my life.

Also by Ann Charles:

Dance of the Winnebagos
(Jackrabbit Junction Mystery Series: Book 1)

Nearly Departed in Deadwood
(Deadwood Mystery Series: Book 1)

Optical Delusions in Deadwood
(Deadwood Mystery Series: Book 2)

Dead Case in Deadwood
(Deadwood Mystery Series: Book 3)

Coming Next from Ann Charles:

Better Off Dead in Deadwood
(Deadwood Mystery Series: Book 4)

The Great Jackalope Stampede
(Jackrabbit Junction Mystery Series: Book 3)

Acknowledgments

I could fill a short novella with pages thanking all of the people who have helped me in myriad ways throughout a book's creation and long after it is pushed out into the world, but my publisher informs me that books full of personal thank you messages don't sell very well. So, I'll keep this short and sweet.

I want to thank the following kind and generous folks:

My husband for far too much to write down. You help me from the first story idea through "The End" and long after.

My family for putting up with my characters hanging out with us at the dinner table, in front of the TV, during teeth brushing, on trips to the store, and more. The characters won't leave us alone anymore.

Corvallis Press for allowing me so much freedom in my storytelling.

My agent, Mary Louise Schwartz, for all of your support.

My brother, Charles Kunkle, for your awesome cover art and illustrations, and for overlooking the fact that I never paid up on that *Mrs. Frisby and the Rats of NIMH* bet.

My good friend and graphic artist, Sharon Benton, for jumping onboard without hesitation and working hard to make my covers for this series look amazing. *Peaches* is happy.

My publicist in the Black Hills (and mom), Margo Taylor, for pushing as hard as you have over the last year and a half to make my books fly high and to my brother, Dave, for making sure Margo stays fed and rested and raring to go again. Thanks also to my aunt, Judy Routt, and her family in Ohio for all of your publicist work around my home ground.

My advance readers, editors, and critique helpers—Wendy Delaney, Beth Harris, Jacquie Rogers, Marcia Britton, Mary Ida Kunkle, Paul Franklin, Jody Sherin, Renelle Wilson, Sue Stone-Douglas, Marguerite Phipps, Denise Garlington, Stephanie Kunkle, Sharon Benton, Carol Cabrian, and Cammie Hall.

My Beta Readers for your help finding those final errors—Cheryl Foutz, Kathy Hunter, Betsy Helgesen, Brad Taylor, Carrie Zito, Denise Keef, Marnia Davis, and Toni Mortensen.

My smart and talented editor, Mimi "The Grammar Chick," for always having my back. You keep the world from seeing my screw-ups and then some.

My wonderful reviewers and the amazing authors who gave their valuable time to reading my books and sending me quotes to help introduce more fans to the series.

My goal buddies Gerri Russell and Joleen James who crack the whip weekly to keep me on task.

My career coach and incredibly positive friend Amber Scott for sharing that delightful laugh with me on several occasions. I can't wait to hear it again!

My coworkers who never look twice when I walk in to work all red-eyed and crazy-haired wearing socks that don't match. Your support over the years has been extraordinary.

My family for putting up with my sorry ass for so many years and helping every time I come for a visit.

My fans for all of the cheers and support. Some of you have been there from the start, and I can't thank you enough times. Some are new, and I'm grateful that you gave my books a chance and joined the party.

My brother, Clint Taylor, for letting me convince you into taking that entertaining plunge down the rocks into the Devil's Bathtub. You always were such a good sport about having to ride home in the back of the pickup because you were too wet to ride inside.

JACKRABBIT
JUNCTION JITTERS

Chapter One

Wednesday, August 11th
Jackrabbit Junction, Arizona

Sometimes life tossed Claire Morgan a bone—other days it walloped her upside the head with it. Today was turning into a real knockout, the flat tire on the old Ford pickup the final bonk on her noggin.

Claire dragged her ass out of the passenger side of the truck, joining her grandfather who stood grimacing at a front tire that appeared to have melted under the desert's sun.

"What do you mean we have to hoof it, Gramps?" she asked. "Can't you just throw on the spare so we can get out of here before the storm hits?"

She fanned her T-shirt and squinted through her sunglasses at the cumulus cloud puffing like a microwaved marshmallow as it raced toward her. Lightning lit the inside of the cloud in paparazzi-style.

Harley Ford reached for the grocery bags in the pickup bed. "The spare is flat."

Of course it was. Claire swiped at the sweat dripping down the side of her face. The August sun and gravy-thick humidity had liquefied her modicum of makeup hours ago.

Across the valley, just past the dusty pit-stop of Jackrabbit Junction, a towering vortex of dirt churned. Gusts of sun-baked air whooshed past her, pelting her cheeks with invisible grains of sand, garnishing the barbed-wire fence with plastic bags and tumbleweeds trying to escape from impending doom.

"Maybe we should just wait this out," she said. "Sit in the cab and watch the storm pass."

Monsoon season in southeastern Arizona offered trial and tribulation in biblical fashion: floods, sandstorms, and lightning.

Throw some locusts into the mix, and it would be a plagues of Moses tailgate party.

Gramps passed her one of the grocery bags. "Next you'll want to hold hands and sing campfire songs."

"Is that how you wooed Ruby?" Claire grinned, referring to her soon-to-be step-grandmother. "Serenaded her with 'Kumbayah' and 'Do Your Ears Hang Low' until she agreed to marry you?"

Thunder rumbled across the valley, sounding an early warning. A violet curtain of rain draped from the colossal cloud, veiling the mayhem behind it.

"My love life is off-limits to you this visit, wiseass," Gramps grumbled. "Go roll up your window and grab your stuff. It's not even a mile to the R.V. park. Besides, I have something to tell you, and I'd rather not be within arm's-length when you hear it." He raced toward the Dancing Winnebagos R.V. Park as fast as a seventy-year-old with a trick-hip could skedaddle.

Claire frowned after the ornery goat. The last time he'd spread some joy with one of his announcements, she'd needed a six-pack of Dos Equis and a box of MoonPies to find her happy place.

This called for an emergency fix. She leaned into the cab and popped open the glove box. Scrounging through the nest of ink pens and fast-food napkins, she grunted in satisfaction when her fingers touched the pack of menthols she'd stashed.

Her flip-flops slapped the asphalt as she followed him, the back of his green shirt patchy with sweat by the time she caught up. "All right, Gramps. Let me have it."

His forehead wrinkled in a disapproving scowl at the lit cigarette dangling from her lips. "I thought you'd quit."

"I did." But that was before her love life had been sucked into a huge, panic-inducing maelstrom. "This is just a figment of your imagination, so stop stalling and spill."

"Remember I told you somebody broke into Ruby's place through the office window last month?"

"What?" She stopped in the middle of the road, momentarily forgetting about the thunder, the wind, and the sore spot between her toes where her plastic thongs rubbed.

Ruby's office was practically a museum, full of expensive antiques collected not-so-legally by her first husband Joe. Years ago he'd overdosed on potato chips, Marlboro cigarettes, and stress and had been taking a dirt nap ever since.

To Claire's knowledge, only four people had any inkling of the treasures hidden in Ruby's basement, and two of them were about to be drenched with Mother Nature's dirty bathwater.

"I remember you mailed me a new key, no explanation included." She couldn't believe he was just now telling her this.

Gramps glanced over his shoulder. "You'd better move your butt, girl, before a bolt of lightning zaps it."

She jogged up next to him. The wind whistled around them. "What got stolen?"

Personally, she would've grabbed the first edition copy of *Moby Dick*. No, *Treasure Island*.

"Nothing."

That made no sense. "Anything get destroyed?"

"Nope."

"Then why did they break in?"

"We've been wondering that ever since it happened."

She took a drag from her cigarette, savoring the cool, cough-drop taste before blowing smoke into the wind. "What makes you so certain it was a break-in?"

"Crowbar dents in the window sill and a busted lock."

"Did you call Deputy Sheriff Droopy?"

"Yep. Ruby insisted since Jess lives there, too."

On the threshold of her sixteenth birthday, Ruby's daughter Jess was at that know-it-all, boy-crazy age that caused her mother to fluctuate between loving her unconditionally and wanting to ship her to the nearest convent.

"But since nothing's missing," Gramps continued, "the deputy's hands are tied."

"His hands aren't tied. They're super-glued to a cheeseburger."

"Don't start again, Claire."

She had trouble biting her tongue when it came to the sheriff's choice for a second-in-command. "You think the burglar was after the money?"

A few months ago, Claire had found a wad of cash in Ruby's office, stuffed in an antique desk—a goodbye gift from Joe.

"Ruby doesn't, but I do. Jess doesn't keep secrets well."

The National Enquirer kept secrets better than Jess. Ruby needed to deposit the cash somewhere safe, but her hatred of banks and bank vice presidents, especially Yuccaville's one and only, rivaled Willy Nelson's sentiment about the IRS.

Lightning flashed to their left. A resounding crack of sky-splitting thunder followed within a couple of heartbeats. The smell of rain and wet earth hung in the air.

Claire winced and flipped-flopped faster. "So, what's Plan A? Track down the burglar? There has to be some clue left behind."

Gramps groaned. "That's why I didn't want to tell you."

"Did Deputy Droopy check for fingerprints?"

"I knew you'd go off half-cocked."

"All you need is one hair for a DNA test."

"You'll end up getting into trouble again."

"That guy with the mullet and Care Bear tattoo who works thirds at Biddy's Gas and Carryout is up to something shady, I'm sure of it."

"But Ruby wanted you to know since you and Mac are running the R.V. park while we're on our honeymoon. When is Mac getting here, anyway?"

Thunder boomed again.

Claire leaned into the wind, protecting her cigarette with her body as she took another drag. Now was not the time to mention that her relationship with Ruby's nephew Mac was on the rocks—well, more like on the pebbles, but there were some definite rocks ahead. Maybe even boulders.

"Friday night." Mac had been working four-tens at his engineering firm, Tuesday through Friday, for the last month.

"We've set you two up in my Winnebago."

"What's wrong with the spare bedroom?"

"It's occupied." Gramps's face looked pinched, like he was sucking on an unripe grapefruit.

"Ruby has family coming for the wedding?"

"No."

Was it Claire's imagination or was Gramps walking even faster? "Then who's staying in the spare room?" Gramps and Ruby had been sharing a bed for months, so unless they had decided to spend a little time apart before the big day, the spare should be available.

"That's the thing I needed to tell you."

"I thought the break-in was the bad news."

Gramps shook his head. "Katie is coming for a few weeks."

Lightning flashed nearby.

Claire chuckled. "Come on, Gramps. Kate isn't that bad."

As far as younger sisters went, Kate was the typical spoiled favorite who hid her dirty laundry behind a sweet smile and sugar-coated lies.

"I agree. Katie is an angel."

He would say that. Kate was taller, thinner, smarter, and never mouthed off to Gramps.

"But she's not coming alone." Gramps was practically running now. "She's bringing your mother."

"What?!" Claire skidded to a stop on the asphalt. The cigarette slipped from her fingers.

Thunder crashed and then the sky fell.

Chapter Two

Thursday, August 12th

Someone was in bed with her.

Claire opened her eyes.

Someone whose snores could not be muffled by the two fans that had barely kept her from melting last night.

She rolled over and came nose to snout with Henry, her grandfather's beagle. His pink tongue lolled against the white pillowcase. His breath rustled from between his black lips, smelling like a week-old chili bean and onion burrito. Her stomach lurched. She sat up and glared at the dog.

Henry's sudden need to get cozy made her wary. His world revolved around licking the calluses on Gramps's feet and cleaning himself. Unless she was holding an Oscar Meyer wiener in her hand, he usually hovered just out of grabbing distance.

A glance at the clock had her scrambling from the sheets.

Henry awoke in mid-snore. He rolled onto his stomach and barked at her.

"Can it, mutt." Claire stepped into a pair of jean shorts. "You'll have to eat breakfast at the store, because I'm late." Again.

Good thing her boss was marrying into the family, or Claire would be out of her second job this month—one more after that and she'd have a new record.

She shut off the fans, grabbed yesterday's bra from the floor and her Speedy Gonzales T-shirt, and dashed into the Winnebago's closet-sized bathroom.

If R.V.s were human, Gramps's Winnebago Chieftain would be a cantankerous old warrior, raisin-wrinkled from the sun, donning a brown polyester leisure suit and red faux alligator shoes. Back before the plaid curtains had faded and the ceiling had yellowed with cigar smoke, the R.V. had made heads turn. Now the only thing turning was the odometer.

Claire put on her bra. She winced at the sight of herself in the mirror, but there was no time for fluffing now. She'd take care of that before her mom crossed the threshold.

Oh, God, Mother's coming.

Her gut churned with dread at the mere thought of talking on the phone with the woman, let alone sharing the same square mile for the next few weeks.

While brushing her teeth, she brainstormed escape plans. By the time Claire had rinsed the minty paste from her mouth, all she'd come up with was that Mac needed her back in Tucson.

Henry barked behind her.

"I know," Claire told him as she shelved her toothbrush in the medicine cabinet. "It's a lame plan, but until I score some nicotine and caffeine, it's the best I can do."

He barked twice more, wiggling his butt as he stood next to the accordion-style door.

"What now?"

He whined and looked at the toilet.

"Fine." She lifted the toilet lid, teasing him. "Have at it."

He yipped and circled, whining some more, running toward the front of the R.V. and back. Henry preferred to take care of business behind the bushes without onlookers present. Gramps called it "shy bladder syndrome"; Claire dubbed it "spoiled dog disease."

"All right, you big baby. Let's go." She pulled her T-shirt on over her head on the way to the door.

The sound of laughter outside the kitchen window made her pause. She grabbed her Mighty Mouse baseball cap and covered her messy hair.

With Henry's leash in hand, she opened the door. The dog dashed down the steps and across the dry grass toward Jackrabbit Creek.

"Henry, wait, damn it!" She scooped up her cigarettes, stepped into her flip-flops, and slammed the door behind her.

Hot sunshine smacked her in the face. The thermometer showed eighty-four degrees, but the heavy air made her skin

sticky. The monsoon season had a firm grip on the southern half
of the state, torturing it daily with raging heat, humidity, and
thunderstorms.

A wolf-whistle drowned out the woodpecker rat-a-tap-
tapping away on one of the cottonwood trees behind the
Winnebago. Old Spice aftershave tickled her nose.

"Buenos dias, cupcake," said a deep, silky voice. "Ay yi yi! I
love the sight of a woman's legs first thing in the morning."

Claire grinned. Manuel Carrera, one of her grandfather's old
Army buddies, lounged at the patio table under the awning of
Gramps's Winnebago. Manny was perpetually "sixty-nine,"
single, and oversexed. He looked like a well-aged version of
Jimmy Smits and chased women like Casanova.

"Quit blocking the view, Claire." Chester Thomas, the third
member of Gramps's war vet musketeers, waved her aside.
Where Manny was velvet, Chester was steel wool, from the top
of his spiky gray hair to the bottom of his bowed legs.

Chester lifted a pair of binoculars to his eyes.

Claire moved out of his field of vision. "What are you guys
doing?"

"Watching birds," Chester said.

Following his line of sight, she zeroed in on his prey. Across
the campground, two women sunbathed in lounge chairs next to
a pop-up camper.

"Let me see those." Claire grabbed the binoculars from
Chester.

"Hey!"

She peered through the eyepieces. Judging from the color of
their hair and the wrinkles under their chins, both women had to
be flirting with retirement. One slept, while the other read a book
with an eagle on the cover. Neither should've been wearing
bikinis, but modesty didn't deter them—nor Chester and Manny
from openly drooling over both birds.

"You two need professional help." She handed the
binoculars back to Chester.

"You're right, Dr. Ruth." Manny wiggled his eyebrows. "I'll
cough while you hold my thermometer."

Chester wheezed with laughter. "Good one, Carrera."

Claire shook her head, grinning. Growing up around Manny had taught Claire long ago not to take the old flirt seriously.

Chester lifted the binoculars again. "Shit, Carrera. We've been having our reunion down here during the wrong season all these years. I always figured bird-watching women wore support socks and hair nets, not Coppertone and red nail polish."

"Speaking of nails," Manny said, looking up at Claire. "I hear your *madre* is coming for the wedding."

Claire groaned and fished a cigarette from her pack. She'd sooner deal with a life-ending asteroid headed straight for Arizona than her mother's visit. There had to be some lie that would get her out of this.

"Well, Lord love a duck, here comes a third little bird." Chester handed Manny the binoculars. "Take a look. She's definitely Viagra-worthy."

"Don't you two have something better to do than ogle women this morning?" She stuck the cigarette between her lips.

Chester settled back in his seat with a cock-of-the-walk grin. "For your information, we're working on official pre-wedding business."

"Let me guess," Claire said around her cigarette as she pulled a book of matches from her back pocket. "You're picking out bridesmaids for Ruby so neither of you have to dance alone at the reception?"

Sighing, Manny lowered the binoculars. "Ah, always the groomsman, never the groom."

"No, Miss Smoker." Chester snatched the cigarette from her lips and broke it in half.

"Damn it, Chester. Those aren't free."

He waved away her scowl. "We're planning Harley's bachelor party."

Uh, oh. This couldn't be good.

"What do you think of bikini mud wrestling?" Manny asked.

"Too slippery," Claire said. "Somebody will break a hip."

She fingered another cigarette. If she wanted a hit, she needed to do it while walking to work. Gramps had forbidden her from lighting up in Ruby's place, even though he and the boys filled the rec room with cigar smoke on a nightly basis.

"Good point," Manny said. "How about a wet T-shirt contest?"

Chester nodded. "Or a game of naked Twister?"

And that was Claire's exit cue. "I'll talk to you two later." She glanced one last time at the three women they were wet-dreaming about. "Stay out of trouble."

She headed toward the General Store at an almost-trot. While jogging to work was a surefire way for her to catch a ride in Yuccaville's only ambulance, the scorching sunshine punished dawdlers. Humidity rippled the air in front of her as sweat soaked into the waistline of her shorts. Any urge to smoke evaporated under the skin-blistering sun.

Henry sat in the shade on the General Store's porch, panting at Claire as she climbed the steps. He must have followed the creek to the store. She made a grab for his collar, but he darted out of reach.

Crossing her arms, she leaned against the porch rail. "I guess last night didn't mean anything to you after all."

Henry yawned and watched a grasshopper bounce across the drive.

"Typical male." She tossed the leash onto the floor next to him and stepped through the front door into the combined campground store and house.

A breath of cool air fanned her warm cheeks. The scent of freshly brewed coffee beckoned. Jess sat on a stool behind the counter reading a book. A faded, olive green curtain divided the aisles full of camping whatnot from the rest of the three-bedroom house.

Jess looked up from her book and smiled. "Mornin', Claire."

With her shoulder-length, curly red hair pulled back in a ponytail and her freckled face free of makeup, she looked twelve, not two weeks away from sixteen.

The wooden floorboards creaked as Claire strolled down the aisle that featured potato chips and pretzels on one side and boxes of candy on the other. The buzz of the overhead florescent lights nearly drowned out Emmylou Harris singing "Two More Bottles of Wine" on Ruby's old clock radio above the cash register.

"Hey, Elvis." Claire patted the life-size cardboard cutout of the King wearing his white jumpsuit, holding a can of Diet Coke. She grabbed a can of soda pop from the wall-length cooler at the back of the store. Hot coffee would come later, after she'd stopped sweating. Her breakfast of champions needed a serving of grains according to the good old USDA, so she plucked a pack of Twinkies from the shelf on her way to the counter.

"What are you reading, Jess?"

Jess flipped the book over long enough for Claire to read the title, *Today's Job Market.*

"Is that for school?" Claire dug a couple of dollars out of her back pocket to pay for her meal.

"School hasn't started yet."

"Then why are you reading that?"

Why was she reading at all? Jess wasn't really the bookworm type of girl. Her nose was usually busy rummaging through somebody else's business, and most of the time that somebody else was Ruby.

"I need a job."

"I thought you were babysitting the Franklin triplets this summer." Claire would rather hammer nails through the tips of her fingers than spend four hours with those three little hellions. They made Chucky-the-doll seem like Winnie-the-Pooh.

"I am, but I need more money."

"Why?"

"To buy a car."

Jess had made it no secret that she would be tearing up the roads in a few weeks. It was practically the front-page story in the *Yuccaville Yodeler.*

"Maybe your mom will let you drive the old Ford to school."

Jess glanced at the curtain that separated them from the rec room. "It's not for school," she whispered. "I need it to drive to Cleveland."

Oh, Cleveland. Right.

Claire mentally shook her head at the girl's naiveté. Jess's father lived in Cleveland with his new wife and kids. According to the last letter he'd sent, he had no room in his home or his life for Jess—not that he ever had. The piece of shit only paid child support because Ruby had dragged the Arizona courts into the mess.

Jess wasn't the only one who'd rather be a thousand miles away from Jackrabbit Junction today. Claire was tempted to offer the kid a ride to Cleveland right this moment. Although, she didn't really buy that Jess would run away from her mother, the only sure thing the girl had had since sticking her head out of the womb.

"When do you plan on leaving?" Claire took a bite of a Twinkie, chasing the sweet cake with a swallow of soda.

Jess shrugged. "Soon. After Mom marries Harley, she's probably not going to want me around here anymore."

A tried and true drama-princess, Jess could make flossing her teeth a three-act play with a curtain call to boot. "You think Ruby will be so busy throwing parties and tasting expensive wines that she won't have much time for you?"

"Probably." Jess leaned toward Claire as if she had inside information on Area 51. "She's already making me go through my old clothes and box up the stuff I don't wear anymore."

"Ah, she has a hidden agenda, huh?" Ruby was undoubtedly trying to make room for Gramps and the seventy years of accumulated baggage that came with him.

"Why else would she want to get rid of my old toys? Shouldn't she want to keep them around to cry over after I go off to college?"

"Sure. Most mothers love to sit around and cry over their children." Claire bit back a grin. "So, when are you leaving?" she asked again, hoping like hell that Jess didn't decide to take off on Claire's watch. She didn't need any extra stress over the next few weeks. Her mother would provide plenty, free of charge—if Claire decided to stick around, that was.

"I probably shouldn't tell you."

"Why not?"

"You'll just tell my mom."

"Have I ever spilled one of your secrets to anyone?" Claire often straddled the fence between Ruby and Jess, sometimes so much that she felt saddle-sore for days.

"Well, no." Jess's eyes narrowed. "Not that I know of."

"Gee, thanks for the vote of confidence."

"It's not that I don't want to tell you. I mean, I'd really like you to go along. We could be like those two old women in that movie my mom loves—the one the Lifetime channel plays over and over—where they picked up Brad Pitt, back before he got old, and then drove off the edge of the Grand Canyon. Only we wouldn't drive off the edge of a canyon or anything, just cruise together all the way to Cleveland; that is if Mac doesn't mind you going with me. Do you think he would let you go with me?"

Claire blinked, then blinked again, momentarily baffled by Jess's lung capacity.

"Go with you where, honey?" Ruby asked in her soft, Oklahoma drawl as she breezed through the olive curtain. Like her daughter, her red ringlets were pulled back in a ponytail, but Ruby had bangs, the uncooperative curly kind. "Mornin', Claire. Your grandfather is looking for you."

"Why?" Claire crammed the last of the Twinkie in her mouth, chewing over the possible reasons Gramps might want to see her.

She couldn't help but be suspicious after the bomb he'd dropped on her yesterday. If he wanted help making a Welcome Wagon basket for her mother, he'd better think again. Claire hoped to be halfway to Tucson when her mom crawled out of the car.

As Ruby walked past Claire, Jess stuffed her book under the counter. With her suddenly red cheeks, the kid was the poster girl for Guilty Teens Anonymous.

Ruby paused in mid-stride. "What are you hiding, child?"

"Nothing." Jess inspected a scratch in the counter.

"Dang it, Jess. If you're gonna lie, at least make it believable." Ruby leaned over the counter and pulled out the book.

"Mom!" Jess's voice reached decibel levels that would make Henry howl.

Ruby's face clouded over as she read the title. She tossed the book on the counter, glaring at Jess. "How many times do I have to tell you that I don't want you getting a job right now? I need you here, helping with the store until school starts. After that, you need to focus on your homework."

"I can do what I want! I'm almost sixteen, you know, old enough to earn more than just an allowance for working here. It's time you started treating me like an adult."

With tears clinging to her eyelashes, Jess stomped off, plowing through the curtain so hard that one side of the rod pulled free.

Groaning, Ruby rubbed her forehead. "That girl is going to land me in a straitjacket, I swear."

Claire walked over and snapped the rod back into place. The soft curtain brushed against her bare arms, the velvet smelling like cigar smoke and the wax Ruby used to polish the wood floor.

"Do you want me to take her back to Tucson for a week?" *Or three?*

"Thanks, but no. I need your help here, patching up my back fence and convincing your mother that I'm not fixin' to steal your grandfather's money."

Claire turned around. Behind Ruby's half-hearted smile, worry etched her face. Guilt warmed Claire's ears at her plan of leaving Ruby alone to face off with the Wicked Witch of the West, but her feet still itched to run—fast and far.

"Is Deborah really as bad as Harley and you make her out to be?"

"Of course not," Claire lied with a straight face.

From what Claire had witnessed since her arrival yesterday afternoon, wedding preparations and Jess's threat to find another job had Ruby's head spinning. She didn't need to know that Claire's mother was more dangerous than a belligerent mother bear when it came to protecting Gramps's money.

"Good." Ruby's smile looked fragile. She placed her palm on Claire's arm and squeezed gently. "I can't tell you how glad I am to have you here with me while your mom is in town."

Claire's heart plummeted. "Yeah, about that." She tried to think of a way to let Ruby down easily.

"I wanted you to be my maid of honor, but Jess would turn me in to child protective services if I didn't choose her."

No fair! Claire wanted to cry, feeling like she was being tied up and left on the railroad tracks. "Oh. Well, I, uh ..."

"I couldn't ask for a sweeter granddaughter." Ruby's green eyes welled.

Claire abandoned all plans of escape at the sight of Ruby's tears. She'd never seen Ruby cry, not even when Jess accidentally slammed the pickup door on her finger. The woman had a backbone made of titanium.

"Ruby, you're exactly who our family needs," Claire said, thinking of her mother's lack of a human heart.

She was going to see her mother. Shit. Claire needed a cigarette. "Weren't you saying something about Gramps looking for me?"

"Uh-huh." Ruby opened the cash drawer and grabbed several twenties. "He wants you to ride with him to Yuccaville to get front tires for the old Ford." She handed Claire the cash with a grin, all signs of tears gone. "He's so funny."

Gramps and funny were not two words Claire usually included in the same sentence. Maybe sarcastic. Definitely argumentative. "What makes you say that?"

"Last night, he bet me that you'd scurry back to Tucson before mornin' light to keep from seeing your mom."

"That Gramps." Claire stuffed the bills in her back pocket, realizing she'd just been royally conned into staying. "He's a real cutup."

* * *

"Come on, Mom," Kate Morgan said as she waited alone in her black Volvo outside of Biddy's Gas and Carryout.

The air conditioner protected her from the waves of heat rising from the asphalt, but the noontime sun blazed through the windows, threatening to melt her steering wheel.

Across the parking lot a building with Wheeler's Diner painted on the sign overhead stood empty, fading in the sun. A raven picked at the remains of something furry that had been flattened and then dragged through the gravel.

On the other side of the road sat what must be a hardware store and feed store all rolled into one. Bulging burlap bags, wood-handled pickaxes, and green wheelbarrows lined the sidewalk under the Creekside Supply Company overhang. The store next to it must have gone out of business. The big plate glass windows were empty except for the real estate sign taped to one of them.

Jackrabbit Junction lived up to its name. Kate expected to see a jackrabbit hop by any moment.

Movement at Biddy's double doors drew her gaze back to the carryout. A cowboy walked by her front bumper, a grocery sack in one hand, a bag of potting soil in the other. His suntanned arms were chiseled, but not bulging. His cowboy hat sat low on his forehead, his face carved by the sun and wind. Reddish blond hair ended at the collar of his navy T-shirt. As he passed her window, his dark blue eyes caught her staring. His lips creased in a smile and he gave her a quick nod.

Kate looked away, her cheeks warm despite the cool air blowing from her vent. In her side mirror, she watched him stride across the parking lot: his long legs covered in jeans, his boots worn at the back of the heel, his butt ...

Someone rapped on the passenger side window.

Kate jerked, knocking her knee on the underside of the dash. "Ow, damn!" She rubbed her kneecap.

"Unlock the door, Kathryn. Hurry up before I wilt!"

Kate hit the button that unlocked the door. She grimaced at the gush of heat that whooshed into the car, along with an eye-watering whiff of sandalwood and jasmine as Deborah Morgan dropped into the passenger seat.

"What did you do in there, Mom? Bathe in your Chanel No. 5?"

"That was one of the most disgusting bathrooms I've ever seen." Deborah's nose wrinkled as she fished a Kleenex from her purse. "Apparently, they haven't heard of bleach in this part of the country."

Kate rolled her eyes. After driving over 1000 miles cooped up with her mother, who had bitched non-stop about the cost of gas, Kate's need to speed, and Gramps marrying some floozy, Kate couldn't wait to drown her sorrows in a big bottle of vodka.

"You could've waited until we got to Ruby's place. It's just a couple of miles up the road." Kate shifted into reverse, looked in her rearview mirror, and watched the cowboy jaywalk across the highway.

"That wouldn't be very polite, now would it? Introducing myself and then immediately asking to use her facilities." Deborah sniffed and adjusted her silk blouse. "Besides, I doubt her restroom is any cleaner."

Kate sighed. "Mom, we talked about this already."

"What? That wasn't an insult. It was just speculation."

"Quit splitting hairs. Why can't you just keep an open mind about this woman? She might actually be in love with Gramps."

"I seriously doubt that. She's almost twenty years his junior, you know."

"So you've said." *Over and over again.* With her jaw clenched, Kate rolled onto the highway.

What had she been thinking when she volunteered to drive her mother to the wedding? Deborah's exaggerated fear of flying and night blindness claim had played major roles in Kate's self-imposed guilt trip. But after the first few hours of her mom ranting constantly about Gramps's fiancée, Claire's boyfriend, and Kate's canceled engagement to the man Deborah had hand-picked, Kate had made the steering wheel lopsided from squeezing it like a vice.

She had a feeling that her mom was focusing extra hard on what was wrong with everyone else's life so that she didn't have to think about her own failures and the divorce papers she'd signed last week. Fortunately, her mother didn't know Kate had quit her job as a teacher last month, or she would've been the only one roasting on the end of a stick for most of the miles.

Hitting her blinker, Kate stopped at Jackrabbit Junction's only intersection. Off the side of the road, a billboard advertised the Dancing Winnebagos R.V. Park.

She idled, waiting for a semi to pass from the other direction, and noticed the cowboy crossing a parking lot filled with a handful of dusty cars and pickups in front of a cedar-planked building. The sign out front read, THE SHAFT. Kate watched his long legs, chewing on her lower lip, remembering how blue his eyes had been.

"Kathryn! What are you waiting for?"

Kate blinked and hit the gas.

"You remind me of your father—speeding all of the time and not paying attention to others on the road."

One more complaint about her driving from the woman next to her and Kate was going to park the car and make her mother walk the last mile to the R.V. park—pleated pants, Gianfranco Ferré pumps, pantyhose, and all. With any luck, her mom would melt before reaching Ruby's place and the wedding would go off without a hitch.

Silence broken only by the whir of the air conditioner filled the car for the next several minutes.

The need to escape her mother's presence made Kate's legs ache, while giddiness at seeing her grandfather and sister made her fingers and toes tingle. Without the two of them living close by over the last few months, South Dakota had seemed washed out, lifeless.

As they drove under the Dancing Winnebagos R.V. Park sign bridging the drive and crossed over a creek lined with willow trees and cottonwoods, Deborah flipped down the visor and checked her appearance in the mirror. Kate watched out of the corner of her eye as her mom added another coat of red lipstick.

She parked in front of the General Store, leaving the car idling so the air conditioner kept running, and turned to her mother. "Okay, Mom. Remember the promise you made as part of the deal of me driving you down here? You swore you'd be on your best behavior for the next few weeks."

Deborah nodded, her smile wider than normal as a red-haired woman walked out of the store and onto the porch, followed by Gramps. Kate waved through the windshield at the two.

"I'm well aware of what I said, Kathryn," Deborah said through gritted teeth and reached for the door handle. "Now let's go talk some sense into your grandfather before that little gold digger gets his ring on her finger and her hands in his bank account."

Chapter Three

"Claire, get your ass up here!" Gramps yelled from the top of the basement steps, his tone downright grumpy.

Claire frowned at the open doorway of Ruby's office. What had she done now? Then it hit her.

Mother! Oh, God, Mother!? Norman Bates's voice echoed in her head.

Claire's stomach cramped in anticipation. All hell was about to break loose, and here she sat in Ruby's office, right in the middle of ground zero.

After a half-hour of searching for clues that would explain why someone would break into Ruby's office and leave thousands of dollars' worth of rare antiques behind, she had nothing. Nada. Zilch. And now her mother was here, who would undoubtedly make her feel even more like a loser.

She glanced around for a place to hide. The window caught her eye. Could her butt squeeze through that little rectangle? Whoever had broken in through it couldn't have been packing any extra pounds around the middle.

Grabbing the desk chair, she rolled it below the window. Her flip-flops squeaked against the leather as she tried to balance on the chair, which kept reclining.

After nearly falling ass-over-elbows for the second time, she kicked the chair to the side and pulled the metal trashcan out from under the desk. She dumped the trash on the floor, flipped the can upside down, and crossed her fingers it would hold her weight—plus the three fudge brownies she'd had for a late brunch. Ruby really needed to find another therapeutic release for stress besides baking.

The new window latch unlocked with a click, but when she tried to swing open the hinged window, the sucker refused to budge. She locked and unlocked the latch again, pushing hard on the handle, but the window still wouldn't open. Gramps must have sealed the window shut after the break-in.

"Shit!" She hopped off the trashcan and ran over to the door, listening for the screeching of fingernails on chalkboard, the sound she associated with her mother's yelling.

Silence issued from overhead.

Her mother must not have breached Ruby's sanctuary yet. Maybe she could escape out the back door at the top of the steps.

Claire had one foot on the bottom step when she heard her sister's forced laughter. Sweat trickled down her back.

Tiptoeing back into the office, she shut the door and looked over at the floor-to-ceiling bookcase filled with first edition books and antique box cameras.

Katy, bar the door! Only in this case, her sister would be on the outside.

What the hell. It was worth a try. She could hide out in Ruby's office until her mom went to sleep, then run like the wind.

She tried to pull the bookcase in front of the door, but it wouldn't budge thanks to the stupid shag carpeting. Moving around to the other side, she shoved it with her shoulder, the oak cool against her damp skin.

The bookcase slid toward the door several inches, rocking and teetering in the process. Claire caught an Eastman Kodak Brownie camera mid-fall as it slid off a shelf. Placing the camera on Ruby's desk, she returned to the bookcase, dropped to her knees, and shoved with her shoulder again.

A couple of grunts later, she'd gained almost a foot with four to go. Sweat trickled from her hairline.

The damned bookcase wasn't going anywhere in a hurry unless she gutted the books and collectibles lining its shelves. She leaned her head against the wood, defeated.

"What are you doing?" Jess's voice interrupted her pity party.

Claire squeaked in surprise. She frowned at Jess, who stood in the now-open doorway. Damn, she should've locked the door.

"I'm just making sure this thing is stable," she lied. "You never know when an earthquake might rattle this place."

Jess's eyebrows arched. "An earthquake? In Arizona?"

"Sure. Fault lines can be found throughout this whole state. Just ask Mac." As a geotechnician, scientific crap like range-bounding faults and topographic contours were Mac's idea of breakfast chatter. "Earthquakes happen all of the time. They're just too weak to be felt."

Claire grabbed the trashcan and started sweeping the crinkled papers and dust bunnies back into it while avoiding Jess's gaze. "Did you need me for something?"

"Harley sent me down here. He says you're supposed to get your butt upstairs right now."

Claire curled her lip at Gramps's bossiness. Picking up a partially-wadded letter, she paused when she noticed the gold embossed heading.

Leo M. Scott, Attorney at Law
1435 Chuckwalla Wash Dr.
Tucson, AZ 85520

The greeting was addressed to Mrs. Ruby Martino.

Now what? The woman had been badgered by creditors ever since Joe had died and left her in a landslide of debt without a shovel in sight.

"What are you looking at?" Jess bridged the distance between them.

"Nothing." Claire shoved the wrinkled letter into her back pocket. Jess had enough angst in her life with hormones kicking in, boys snapping her bra, and the hardware store no longer carrying her favorite sparkly lip gloss. She didn't need to learn about sharp-toothed lawyers today.

Claire motioned toward the door. "Let's go."

Jess sighed. "Grownups suck. They're always hiding stuff from us teenagers." She tromped toward the door.

"We live to torture teens."

Jess paused in the doorway, looking at the bookcase. "Are you going to put that back?"

"Oh, yeah." The letter had distracted her.

As Claire gripped the side and prepared to lift, she glanced at the wall behind the bookcase. Her breath caught, and not because of the scorpion carcass lying on the carpet. A white metal door, three feet high by three feet wide, had been fitted flush, hinges and all, into the wall.

She leaned down and ran her palm down the smooth surface of the door. Her heart thrummed in her ears. Knowing what she did about Joe's crooked wheeling and dealing, the goods from King Tut's tomb could be on the other side of that door.

"What is it?" Jess's question made her snap upright.

"Just a scorpion carcass."

With Joe dead, Claire was pretty sure she was now the only one who knew of the door's existence. Jess didn't need to be her partner in crime. A hernia-inducing lift and tug later, Claire had the bookcase back in place.

"All right, let's go see my mother."

Ruby's rec room looked like an acid flashback of the 1970s. Yellow cinderblock walls fenced in burnt-orange shag carpet worn flat in traffic areas. The room still smelled of stale cigar smoke thanks to last night's Euchre game.

Jess led the way into the room and plopped into one of the two beanbags clustered in the far corner. Claire hesitated at the threshold, wanting to test the water before jumping in with the shark.

The head of a ten-point buck hung on the wall above where Gramps glowered from the avocado couch. He looked like he was sitting on a patch of Prickly Pear cactus. Next to him, Ruby balanced on the front edge of a cushion, her face slightly flushed.

Across the room, Kate occupied one of the barstools at Ruby's bar, inspecting her fingernails.

Claire's mother stood center stage, her freshly painted lips pinched, her blonde hair perfectly coifed, her designer clothes somehow crease-free in spite of the long car ride. All she needed was a spotlight and a microphone.

"Claire, darling!" Deborah rushed over and enveloped Claire in a Chanel No. 5 perfume-laced hug. "I've missed you so much."

Dear Lord! Roll out the red carpet for the drama queen. It wasn't as if Claire had joined the Peace Corp and spent a year in some ape-filled jungle. It'd been only three months since her last face-to-face confrontation with her mom.

Claire shot her younger sister a what-the-hell frown over her mom's shoulder. Kate nudged her head toward Ruby, and Claire caught on immediately.

Her sinuses burned from an overdose of perfume by the time Deborah released her. "How was your trip, Mom?"

"Wonderful," Deborah answered too quickly. If she smiled any wider, her ears were going to cave in. "The scenery was breathtaking, and Kathryn is such a good driver. Traveling with her was a treat."

Kate coughed out what sounded vaguely like "bullshit."

Claire seconded that cough. The last time she'd ridden with her sister, Claire had left imprints of her size eight shoes in Kate's dashboard.

After snaking a glare at Kate, Deborah turned back to Claire with another lip-splitting smile. "I was just telling Ruby and your grandfather how excited Kathryn and I are to be joining them for their special day."

"And we're so happy you could join us." Ruby's voice was warm and sweet, like frosting on a freshly baked cake.

Claire wanted to run over and shield Ruby with her body.

The sound of the bell jingling over the store's front door had Ruby eyeing the curtain.

"Sounds like we have a customer."

When nobody moved, Ruby cleared her throat and stared pointedly at Jess.

"Okay, okay," Jess said, trudging across the room and disappearing through the curtain.

Silence, soupy thick, filled the air.

Claire wondered if anyone would notice if she slipped out the back door and left the state.

"You have a lovely daughter," Deborah said.

"Thank you." Ruby smiled back. "And you do, too. Both of them. I mean, I really know only Claire, but I look forward to getting to know Kate. I've heard such good things about her from your grandfath—" Ruby's cheeks reddened even more as she stumbled. "I mean your father."

Again, heavy silence.

The bar stool squeaked as Kate crossed one leg over the other.

Gramps scratched the back of his neck.

The clock cuckooed once, announcing the half-hour.

"Mom!" Jess hollered from the other side of the curtain, snapping the silence like a dry twig.

Deborah and Kate both jumped. They'd need a couple of days to get used to Jess and her propensity for yelling instead of talking.

"I'll be right back." Ruby stood, her whole face now the same shade as her hair as she strode across the room.

As soon as the curtain stopped swaying from Ruby's exit, Gramps jumped up from the couch. For a seventy-plus man, he could sure hit the turbo-boost when needed.

"Deborah Lynn Ford! I don't know what game you think you're playing, but you'd better stop it right now."

"What?" Deborah said, all wide-eyed. "I'm merely trying to make a good impression. Unlike Kathryn with her swearing and Claire."

"What did I do?" Claire asked.

Her mother sniffed. "You could have at least worn socks and shoes to greet me. I didn't raise you in a barn." She glanced around the room, her flawless face crunched in a sneer. "Although, judging by Ruby's lack of interior design, I can see why you'd think thongles were appropriate attire."

Covering her eyes, Kate said, "They're called thongs, Mom."

Claire wanted to walk over and pinch Kate for bringing the she-devil to her dusty paradise. They were all damned now. Not even an exorcism would save them.

"Thongles, thongs, whatever." Deborah pointed at the shelf of German beer steins over the bar. "Just look at the dust on those mugs. And I bet this ceiling hasn't been washed in a decade."

"Mom—" Kate tried to interrupt.

"This carpet probably hasn't had a good raking since Carter was President."

"Mother, stop." Claire crossed her arms. Not everyone idolized Martha Stewart and her housekeeping skills. Some people actually had lives to live.

"Are those cigar butts in the ashtray? What kind of woman allows—"

"Deborah!" Gramps broke up Deborah's monologue. The top of his bald head glowed branding-iron red.

"What?"

"Shut up or get out."

"I'm not leaving without you and Claire."

"Me?" Claire took a step back.

"Yes, you. It's time you realize that while MacDonald is a nice enough boy, he's just too lenient with you. You need someone forceful. Someone who will push you to finish school, to make something of your life and be more like Kathryn."

Claire's cheeks burned as if Deborah had reached out and slapped her—twice. She stuffed her hands in her pockets to keep from strangling her mother. She should have broken the office window Gramps had sealed shut.

"Mom." Kate stood up. "Don't start with this again."

"You know I'm right. You said the same thing last week."

"I did not."

"Yes, you did. You said that MacDonald seems like a toe-the-line type of man, and Claire's toes only touch the line if they are super-glued to it."

Kate's forehead and nose reddened. She'd never quite got blushing down right. "True, but that's not even close to what you just said."

Claire smirked at both of them and leapt into the ring. "Oh, and you guys are such experts on relationships, what with the ink still drying on your divorce papers," she said to her mother before turning on her sister, "and you dating every other convict in the South Dakota prison circuit."

Gramps patted Claire on the shoulder. "Claire has a point, although you probably shouldn't talk to your mother that way."

"Claire, honey, you know I love you." Deborah used her super-sweet voice—the one that made Claire's eardrums throb. "I just want what's best for you. You should try wearing nicer blouses, maybe some silk, and pleated pants to hide your tummy. You'd be so pretty with the right accessories."

Claire looked at Gramps and then Kate with raised eyebrows, wondering if they'd object to her tackling Deborah and cramming her chandelier earrings and other "accessories" down her throat.

"That's it." Gramps grabbed Deborah by the shoulders and pushed her toward the back door. "Katie, put your mother's bags back in the car. She's going home."

"Come on, Gramps," Kate whined. "That's not fair. She drove me nuts all of the way down here. Make Claire drive her home."

Deborah pulled free of Gramps's grip. "Nobody is driving me anywhere. I told you, Dad, I'm not leaving until Claire and you come to your senses. This foolishness has to stop."

"If by 'foolishness' you mean me marrying Ruby, then you're wasting your time here. Nothing and nobody is going to stop me from marrying that woman."

Deborah's nostrils flared. "I didn't want to have to say this, but—"

"Mom, don't." Kate grabbed Deborah's arm.

Shaking off Kate's hand, Deborah continued. "What are you thinking, marrying some woman who is younger than—"

"Claire?" Jess poked her head through the curtain. Her eyes shined with curiosity as she gaped at the group of them all clustered in the center of the room. "Mom needs you to fix an overflowing toilet in the men's restroom by the tool shed."

"I'll be right there." Duty called, thank God! Claire couldn't wait to answer.

She flashed her mother a fake smile. "Always good to see you, Mother." With a nod to Kate and Gramps, she practically sprinted out the back door.

As soon as she fixed the toilet and checked off all the tasks on the To Do list Ruby had given her this morning, Claire was history.

She'd call from Tucson with her string of excuses.

* * *

Crack!

Kate awoke to the sound of the sky shattering into pieces.

She sat up quickly, blinking at the digital clock in the shadows of Gramps's bedroom—almost dinner time. Her head throbbed, her mouth tasted like stale cheese, and her shirt stuck to her back. The bedside fan blew hot air on her skin. Another thirty minutes in this oversized aluminum roasting pan and she'd be well-done.

Someone sneezed.

She flicked on the bedside lamp and peeked over the edge of the bed. Henry stared up at her.

"Henry!" Kate giggled as Gramps's beagle jumped onto the bed and tackled her with licks. He smelled like dirt and dog breath, but Kate nuzzled his head anyway. She'd missed the furry little yapper. "It's good to see you, too, boy."

Henry wiggled his body, his tail bouncing and waving.

"Even the dog likes you better," Claire said from the bedroom doorway. "It has to be the hair. Dolly Parton paved the way for all you blondes."

She reached into the coffin-sized closet and pulled out the Betty Boop bag Kate had given her for Christmas two years ago.

The pounding in Kate's head spread to her chest as she watched Claire open the top drawer of the built-in dresser and throw her underwear into the bag. "What are you doing?"

"What does it look like?"

"You're not leaving me here with *her*."

"Watch me."

"Claire, come on." Kate placed Henry on the bed next to her and scooted to the end of the mattress. "Ruby and Gramps need you here. You're supposed to watch Ruby's kid while they're on their honeymoon, remember?"

Claire stuffed her socks into the bag. "You can watch Jess. You're the teacher. You have loads of experience with kids."

"Well, yeah, but ..." Kate gulped. Nobody in her family knew her dirty little unemployment secret—yet.

Lightning flashed outside the window. Thunder rumbled an encore seconds later.

Henry whined, burying his nose in Kate's ribs.

Claire tucked a few T-shirts into her bag. "Besides, Jess is easy."

An easy teenager? That was laugh-out-loud funny.

"You just need an ear to listen to her troubles and a shoulder for her to cry on. She'll take care of the rest."

Kate grabbed her sister's hand as she reached for another drawer. "Claire, you can't leave me here with her."

"Come on, Jess isn't so bad." Claire's grin didn't quite reach her eyes. "She's a real sweetheart when she's not yelling at her mom."

"I'm talking about *your* mother, not Jess."

"My mother, huh? At least she likes the way you dress." Pulling away, Claire opened the next drawer. "I'm getting out of here before she has me wearing frilly dresses and pajamas with footies again."

"Claire, I need you here."

"Ha! You just need someone to run interference."

"No, there's more to it than that." Kate squeezed the bridge of her nose and took a deep breath. She was going to have to spill the beans.

"Let me guess." Claire turned toward Kate with a small stack of jean shorts in her arms and a grin on her lips. "You're engaged to another klepto, and this one stole your half of the his-and-hers heart pendant you bought."

"That's real funny coming from a woman who can't even commit to a hair appointment."

Henry barked at the rude gesture Claire gave Kate. Kate patted his head, earning a few licks in return.

Grumbling under her breath, Claire tossed the shorts into the bag.

A cool breeze ruffled the faded brown curtains covering the window, sweeping Kate's hot skin. Two flashes of lightning followed, then a drum roll of thunder.

Taking a deep breath, Kate laid her cards face-up on the table. "I quit my job. I don't want to be a teacher anymore. In fact, I don't want to have anything to do with public education at all. But don't say anything to Mom; I haven't told her yet."

Claire's brown eyes widened. "You're kidding me. When did you quit?"

"Last month. I couldn't stand it any longer." It had been her mom's dream job, never hers.

"Mom's going to shit ostrich eggs when she finds out. This isn't in the ten-year plan she has mapped out for you."

Beads of sweat coated Kate's upper lip at just the thought of telling her mom. "Well, she forgot to ask me about my plan."

"So, what job do you have lined up?"

"None."

"Wow, that's ballsy for you." Claire plopped onto the edge of the mattress next to Kate.

"I know, right? But I don't want to tell Mom until I figure out what I want to do. That's why I need you to stay."

Claire jumped up like Henry had bitten her on the butt. "No way. I'm not going to be your fall guy."

"That's not what I was thinking. I want to pick your brain." That wasn't entirely true, but it sure sounded legit.

"Pick *my* brain? You've been smoking that weed that grows behind Gramps's house again."

"I'm serious. You have more college credits than anyone I know." Claire had more schooling under her belt than most doctorate holders. Unfortunately, the content of her classes spanned the spectrum, and she had yet to find a degree program that held her interest for more than a year. Kate had lost count of the number of jobs listed on her sister's resume.

"I'm also the family joke."

Kate sighed. This was going to take some arm twisting. "Please stay. If not for me, then for Ruby. You know how Mom can be when she's got her sights set on something, and she is hell bent on keeping Ruby from becoming one of the family."

Groaning, Claire banged her head against the wall. "Fine, but you have to sleep on the couch—and the dog, too." Claire pointed at Henry, who growled in response. "This is my bed, and I'm the only one who gets to snore in it."

"Okay." The couch couldn't be that bad. Anything was better than sharing the queen bed at Ruby's house with her mother.

"And you have to help out at the store for free."

It wasn't like she had papers to grade. The only thing she'd intended to work on this trip was her tan. "No problem."

"And you have to help me figure out who broke into Ruby's place last month and why."

A little summer mystery could be fun. "Sure, as long as I don't have to do anything illegal."

Claire licked her lips. "Define illegal."

"As in forbidden by law." Kate glared at her sister. "I still haven't forgiven you for our last trip to jail."

"Fine, I'll do the illegal stuff on my own. But it's going to cost you a sandwich and a drink at The Shaft. We'll drop off Henry at Ruby's on the way."

Henry whimpered and buried his snout under his paws.

Kate's headache dulled at the thought of throwing back something mixed with alcohol. She slipped on her sandals. "Just one drink?" That didn't sound like her sister.

"You're right. We're talking about defending Ruby from *your* mother. Bring your credit card." Claire smiled at her from the doorway. "And grab Gramps's spare keys from the bed stand drawer. We're taking his car. He owes us both."

* * *

The Shaft bustled—well, as much as a small-time bar in a two-bit former railroad stop can bustle. With Happy Hour still at full throttle, miners and cowboys took turns cuing up at the pool table, shoving quarters in the old jukebox, and shooting at Bambi's folks with a plastic rifle on the Big Buck Hunter video game. The artificial plants swayed to the music and the peanut-shell-covered floor crackled underfoot as Hank "Bocephus" Williams Jr. sang about giving some guy an attitude adjustment.

Claire tapped her cigarette on the lip of the ashtray, ignoring the disapproving frowns Kate kept sending her way. If she was sticking around to deal with her mother, she deserved a reward. Or two. She took a swig of her Corona.

Despite the thunderstorm that had blown through town a short time ago carrying cooler breezes in its one-two punch, the air in the bar felt steamed-towel hot and made everything sticky.

Across the room, a lovesick cowpoke strutted around like a peacock with its tail feathers spread, casting glances at Kate as he hooted and hollered over the twang of Hank's guitar. Claire expected him to start shaking his ass and flapping his arms any minute now.

Kate seemed oblivious to the mating ritual display as she sipped her favorite drink, a Fuzzy Navel, and stared out at the rolling sea of cowboy hats.

"Do you know most of these people?" she yelled to Claire over the ruckus.

"Nope, just Guillermo over there by the Strip Poker video game. Oh, and Butch, of course."

"Who's Butch?"

"The bartender."

"You mean the guy behind the bar with the Coke-bottle glasses?"

"No, that's Gary. He's Butch's pinch hitter. Butch must be in his office in back."

Kate took another sip. "When's Mac going to get here?"

Too soon. "Tomorrow night."

"What's going on with you two?"

"Nothing much." Just some boat rocking, and not the fun, under-the-covers kind.

"I'm sorry about what I said to Mom about you two." Leaning closer to Claire, Kate lowered her voice to a public speaking level. The scent of peach schnapps was heavy on her breath. "It's just he's not at all like the other men you've dated."

Kate was dead-on there. Mac had not only turned Claire's nice little snow globe of a world upside down, he'd shaken the shit out of it, too. In the four months they'd been together, she'd lost track of which way was up.

"I mean, for one thing, he's intelligent."

"Hey!" Claire sat up straight. "I've dated smart guys before. Remember the chemist?"

"Claire, he mixed paint at Sherwin Williams." Kate stirred her drink. "Mac also has a steady job."

An accomplishment Claire had yet to attain. What was the big deal with being employed? As if a job defined the person.

"Plus, he has a house."

He sure did, all set up and ready for a wife and two-point-five kids. He probably had a timeshare already rented at Disney World, too, knowing Mac and his organizational skills. Claire finished off her beer and set the bottle down with a thud.

"And he really cares about you."

So he'd said Wednesday morning, smack dab in the middle of back-arching, blow-her-socks-off sex. Claire took a hit from her cigarette, remembering the icicle of panic that had stabbed her in the chest after he'd driven off to work.

In the two days she'd been in Jackrabbit Junction, she'd buried her head in the sand and avoided dealing with the insecurities Mac's words had stirred up. But tomorrow night, Mac would be sharing the same bed with her. She couldn't hide forever.

Kate finished her drink and pushed it aside. "So, how soon until you freak out and leave him?"

Claire did a double-take. "What are you talking about?"

"Come on, Claire. I've known you my whole life. All of those things I listed smell of commitment, and you and I know that at the merest whiff of the "C" word, you run like hell."

Claire hated how well her family had her pegged.

"Good evening, ladies." A tall, blond haired cowboy with the greenest eyes Claire had ever seen pulled out the chair next to her, turned it around, and straddled it. His Hollywood smile and clean-shaven jaw emphasized his strong cheekbones and rugged good looks.

He tipped his white Stetson at Claire. "Don't you work at that R.V. park just up the road?" His slow Texas drawl rounded out the hard consonants.

Claire looked over at her sister, wondering if this Matthew McConaughey look-a-like was just a figment of her over-stressed imagination. But Kate was too busy doing that flirty eyelash-batting, pouty-lip routine she always did when she was trying to catch a man's attention to notice Claire.

"Who wants to know?" She wasn't above being suspicious of a stranger, especially one with whiter teeth than her dentist's.

His smile deepened at the creases. "I forgot my manners. Porter Banks at your service." He held out his hand.

Claire stared at it a few seconds before shaking it, wondering what Porter Banks was up to. If he thought spreading a little charm would get her to agree to spin his spurs, he could climb back on his horse and *vaya con dios* his sorry ass out of town.

His palm was pencil-pushing soft. She pulled her hand free.

"I'm Claire, and this is Kate."

And that was how the song-and-dance usually started. Men approached Claire first because Kate had eye-contact issues. But soon after introducing her blonde sister, Claire was left to drink alone for the remainder of the evening.

Porter gave Kate a quick "nice-ta-meetcha" and a brief nod, then refocused on Claire.

She blinked in the halogen brightness of his smile. Wasn't it against the law for a man to be prettier than a woman? It made all of the shaving and preening futile.

"Would you mind takin' a spin on the dance floor, Claire?" When she hesitated, he added, "I promise not to bite."

What could one dance hurt? "Sure."

Claire stubbed out her cigarette. She shoved a piece of cinnamon gum in her mouth as she followed him. Hank Williams Jr.'s rowdy song ended and Linda Ronstadt's version of *Desperado* filled the bar. One other couple shared the floor, their lips locked so tightly Claire couldn't tell where one started and the other ended.

Porter pulled her so close she could feel the heat radiating from his skin. He smelled of a subtle mixture of vanilla and cedar. They danced for several seconds in silence, his lead smooth, his footsteps sure.

In her pre-Mac days, Claire might have gotten a bit warm and breathy around him. But just one look from Mac sucked the wind out of her sails and lit her fire with rocket fuel gusto. Other men didn't stand a chance.

"How'd you know I work at the R.V. park?"

"Butch mentioned it."

There wasn't much around Jackrabbit Junction that Butch the bartender didn't know.

"Do you live around here?" She hadn't seen this guy in town before.

"Not permanently. I'm renting a double-wide just south of town. I'm here doing some research."

"For what?"

"My next book." He paused, as if waiting for her to ooh and ahh.

"Let me guess, the great American novel."

"Sarcasm, huh? I like that in a girl."

"What are you researching?" Jackrabbit Junction wasn't exactly an eclectic town, although the hardware store did offer a wide selection of deer piss and shotgun shells.

"Mining." He twirled her around and pulled her back against him, even closer.

Claire didn't object, not yet anyway. She could still make eye contact. "How long are you staying?"

"A couple of months, maybe. Then I'll head back to Amarillo and put pen to paper." He glanced over her head.

"How long does it take to research mining in this area?"

"That depends."

"On what?"

"Library hours, company records, people's willingness to share information." He glanced over her head again. "I think your friend is trying to get your attention."

Her friend? "Oh, you mean my sister."

"Your sister? Is she working at the R.V. park, too?"

"No, she's just visiting. She's here for—"

"Excuse me." A very familiar, deep voice interrupted her. "Mind if I cut in?"

Claire choked on the rest of her sentence.

Chapter Four

"You come here often?" Mac asked as he tucked Claire into his chest while swaying to Linda Ronstadt's sappy finale to a perfectly good Eagles's tune. She felt supple and smooth in all the right places, despite the slight tension in her back and shoulders.

"Not often enough." Her breath heated his shoulder through his shirt. "You're early."

Judging from her reluctance to meet his gaze, that wasn't a good thing. His slip of the tongue Wednesday morning seemed to have stuck in her brain and festered. Shit.

"You make it tough to stay away," he said.

He'd pushed hard, working late last night, and left straight from the job site, driving too fast through the rain and wind.

"Did Gramps tell you where we were?"

"No. I haven't made it out to Ruby's yet. I saw Mabel in the parking lot and figured it was you."

Good ol' sleek and sexy Mabel—Harley's chopped top, two-door, 1949 Merc. Dressed to thrill, with her player spoke wheels, skirts on back, shaved door handles, side pipes, and custom flame paint job, she was a hot rodder's pinup. Just the sight of her buxom chrome grill gleaming under the orange parking lot lights had made Mac itch to crawl behind the wheel, hit the open road, and bury the gas pedal. But first, he needed to see Claire naked again.

She leaned away from him, staring up at him with those sexy dark eyes of hers fringed with even darker lashes. "Mac, do you realize we're slow dancing to 'Boot Scootin' Boogie'?"

A couple of girls jiggled and whooped on the dance floor next to them.

"Yes." He pulled her closer and brushed his lips across her temple. A whiff of her watermelon-scented shampoo reminded him of how much he'd missed her in his bed these last few nights, of how bland his life was without her in it driving him nuts.

Claire let out a shaky sigh, the kind she usually saved for under the covers. His body hardened as if on cue, his heart picking up speed.

"Aren't you going to ask me who I was dancing with?" she asked.

"No."

Getting Claire alone, preferably with a bed close by, dominated his thoughts at the moment.

"Why not?"

She'd let her hair down tonight. The dark, wavy tresses shined, curling around her shoulders, softening her usually tough exterior. He wanted to take her somewhere shadow-filled and explore more of her softness. Pushing aside her silky brown tendrils, his mouth found the sweet spot right behind her ear.

"Were you attracted to him?" he whispered against her skin.

He felt her shiver under his lips. "He was very charming."

"Undoubtedly." Charm came complimentary with his white Stetson and ostrich-skin cowboy boots.

"And definitely good-looking. Even Kate was making googly eyes at him."

He dragged his mouth away from her skin and stared into her brown eyes, searching for signs of one of her half-truths. "Claire, answer the question. Were you attracted to him?"

"I might've been if you weren't in the picture." Her voice sounded all husky, like when he joined her in the shower last Friday morning before work and occupied her until the water ran cold.

"But I am in the picture." He slipped his hands under her Speedy Gonzales T-shirt, needing to touch bare skin, settling for her smooth back for now. "And I trust you."

"Why?"

"You know why. Do you want me to say it again?"

"No, don't." She covered his lips with her palm.

How such an intelligent woman could suffer from such acute symptoms of Commitment Phobia was beyond him. They needed to work through this little problem to keep the fissures from spreading, but not in the middle of the dance floor at The Shaft. Maybe later tonight in bed with the lights off—where eye contact wasn't required.

He pulled her hand away and nodded in Kate's direction. "I think your cowboy is hitting on your sister."

"He's not my ... what?" Claire looked at Kate. "That figures. They always go for Kate in the end."

"Not always." Kate might be cute, but Claire burrowed into a guy's head and drove him nuts with hunger for more of her. He tipped her chin up. "Some of us can't get past you."

Claire's gaze met his, her eyes lighting up with wicked promises. She wrapped her arms around his neck and pressed her soft curves against his length, making everything south of his neck rigid.

"You haven't kissed me 'hello' yet," she said, licking her lips.

"Claire," he said leaning down.

"Yeah?" She rose up onto her toes, closing the gap.

He cupped her head, his fingers entwined in her silky-smooth hair. He ran his tongue along her lower lip, teasing her mouth open, then increased the pressure, exploring deeper. She tasted like cinnamon and beer and all things Claire, and he ached to bury himself deep inside her.

They'd danced long enough. He pulled away. "Let's get out of here."

Her heavy breathing matched his. "You read my mind."

She led the way back to the table where Kate and the cowboy were trading flirting glances.

"It's time to leave, Kate," Claire said.

Kate waved her off. "You guys go ahead. I'll follow later in Mabel."

"No way," Claire said. "You know you're not allowed to drive Mabel after the last incident."

Kate rolled her eyes. "Fine. I'll drive Mac's truck back."

"Mac likes his pickup the way it is—dent-free. Why don't you just ride home with me and drive your own car back?"

"Good idea." Kate stood, touching the cowboy's shoulder. "You'll still be here when I get back, right?"

Not interested in hanging around to hear the guy's answer, Mac towed Claire toward the door. It opened from the outside as he reached for it.

Butch, The Shaft's owner, stepped aside to let them pass. "Howdy, Mac. Claire." His smile faltered when his gaze landed on Kate.

"Butch." Mac nodded his hello. "This is Kate Morgan, Claire's sister."

Kate wore a deer-in-the-headlights expression.

"Nice to meet you, Kate." Butch offered his hand.

After a moment, Kate finally shook his hand. She cleared her throat. "You, too."

"See ya, Butch." Claire patted the bar owner on the arm on her way out the door. She grabbed Mac by the shirt as she passed and dragged him with her.

Glancing back, he saw Kate stumble after them, looking like her shoes were tied together.

Maybe Kate driving back to The Shaft wasn't such a great idea. "Claire," Mac started.

"No talking." She hit the remote and Mabel's doors popped open. "No thinking either. Just you and me, naked and sweaty."

His body throbbed in agreement.

"I didn't need to hear that." Kate said, rounding Mabel's grill.

"Get inside." Claire ordered. She fired up Mabel.

Chuckling, Mac climbed into his pickup and shadowed Mabel's taillights to the R.V. park. Claire was opening the camper door when he cut the engine and climbed out.

Behind the R.V., Sonoran Desert toads trilled their mating calls from the weeds that banked Jackrabbit Creek. He smirked in their direction, appreciating the irony.

A breeze with a trace of coolness ruffled his hair. As usual during monsoon season, the storm had sapped the earth of some of its heat. The sun would dish it back out tomorrow.

He glanced at the darkened windows in Chester and Manny's rigs, crossing his fingers they were up to their elbows in beer, cigars, and cards at Ruby's place. He didn't want any interruptions tonight.

Stepping inside the Winnebago, Mac blinked in the light. The place smelled just as he remembered, like stale cigar smoke with an inkling of dog. The only difference was the hint of something flowery on top of it all.

"I need to use the bathroom quick." Kate grabbed her keys from the counter. "Then I'll leave you guys alone for an hour."

Wagging his tail in greeting, Henry looked up from where he lay sprawled on his side on the couch. Mac patted him on the head on his way to Claire, who stood in the darkened hallway, wiggling her index finger for him to join her.

His blood pressure raced. No more dallying.

"Make that two hours, Kate," Mac said. Then he strode over and pinned Claire against the wall, his mouth drinking her in. God, she always tasted so damned sweet.

"Jeez, you guys. You live together, for chrissake." Kate squeezed past them, slapping Mac's shoulder as she passed. "Quit acting like he just came back from the war."

The bathroom light flooded the hall with a yellow glow. Mac caught a glimpse of Claire and him in the mirror on the closed bedroom door, his hands palming her hips through her jean shorts. Her fingers slid under his shirt, her nails scratching down his back. Maybe she had something with that mirror-covered wall idea a few weeks ago.

He pressed harder against her, hungry to tear off her T-shirt and explore his favorite terrain with his hands and mouth. He caught her leg as she rubbed it up and down his pants and slid his hand up the back of her bare thigh.

"Mac." Claire writhed as his fingertips brushed along the soft skin of her inner thigh. "Take me to b—"

The bedroom door hinges squeaked.

"Claire Alice Morgan!"

Mac jerked back from Claire so hard he whacked his elbow on the opposite wall.

Claire gaped at her mother, who stood silhouetted in the bedroom doorway with her pink satin robe cinched around her.

Fuck! He groaned, adjusting his jeans to disguise the tell-tale effect her daughter had on his body. He'd hoped to delay his reunion with the woman who'd made it no secret that she'd rather see Claire join the Ringling Brothers Barnum and Bailey Circus as a tight-rope walker than live with him.

"Mom?" Kate popped her head out of the bathroom. "What are you doing here?"

"Making sure you two stay out of trouble." Deborah sniffed. "And it's obviously a good thing too, judging by the alcohol on your breath, Kathryn."

A growling sound came from Claire. "Here we go."

"And you." Scowling, Deborah pointed at Claire. "What kind of a girl brings a man home to her grandfather's bed?"

Sighing, Mac leaned his head back against the wall. Deborah didn't need to worry about Claire's virtue tonight. After seeing her pinched face, every single flame of desire was now doused, extinguished, stomped out.

"It's Mac, Mom. I live with him, remember?"

"Maybe so, but this is not the time or place for fooling around. It's a good thing I decided to stay here with you two."

"You decided to stay here?" Kate stepped into the hall, an edge of panic in her voice. "What does that mean?"

"It means I'm sleeping in your grandfather's bed. I'd rather sleep in this smelly old beast than at *her* house."

"Then where are we sleeping?" Claire shot Mac a troubled frown.

"Mac is sleeping in his aunt's guest room. You're on the couch with the dog."

Henry barked from the couch cushions.

"No, she's not." Kate crossed her arms. "That's my bed."

"Then she can sleep with me in the bedroom."

Claire shook her head. "I'll sleep wherever Mac does."

"No, you won't. That's irresponsible."

Mac opened his mouth to object, but Claire beat him to the punch. "Irresponsible?" Her tone insinuated Deborah had lost a few marbles out of one ear. He was figuring more like a bagful.

"Yes. What kind of an impression does that make on Kate?"

Claire laughed, short and sharp. "Kate sleeps with guys all the time."

Mac chuckled under his breath.

"Claire!" Kate punched her sister's arm.

"Claire Alice." Deborah cinched her robe even tighter. Mac wondered how much more stress the belt could take. "Do not talk about your sister like that in front of strangers."

"Mac isn't a stranger."

"I'm not talking about MacDonald." Deborah glared past Mac. "I'm talking about those two."

Mac followed her gaze. Manny and Chester stood inside the R.V., watching the fireworks display with beers in their hands and wide-toothed grins on their faces.

Damn. He'd forgotten to lock the door.

* * *

Friday, August 13th

Claire woke up feeling as if a mule train had tromped on her head. She swung her legs over the edge of the foam pad covering the R.V.'s dining table and rubbed the grit from her eyes. Her tongue tasted like sour milk and her teeth felt furry. Henry seemed to be rubbing off on her.

Across the room, Kate let out a soft sigh. Henry snored lightly. All cuddled up on the green cushions, they were a picture of cuteness. Claire whipped her pillow at them.

Henry yipped, bounding from behind the pillow with teeth bared. Kate moaned and rolled deeper into the crack between the back and butt cushions.

Claire slipped into the jean shorts and Speedy Gonzales T-shirt she'd worn yesterday. The Shaft's smoky cologne still clung to them. Her clean clothes were in the bedroom with her mom, and nothing short of a swarm of killer bees would spur her to cross that threshold this morning.

Her ears still rang from all the yelling last night. She thought of Mac, sleepy and naked, all of that lovely male skin entangled in the pale yellow sheets on Ruby's spare bed, and rattled out a string of curses that would have made Blackbeard proud.

"Good morning to you, too, sunshine." Kate stared up at Claire with one eye open and hair plastered flat on the left side of her head.

Claire grabbed her pack of cigarettes from the counter.

"Where are you going?"

"Anywhere but here." She slid into her flip-flops and stepped out into the retina-frying sunlight.

"*Buenos dias, bonita.*" Manny sat in his usual lawn chair.

Nodding at him, Claire dropped into the chair next to him and rubbed her eyes. The sun-steamed breeze made her throbbing head feel like she could dispense cotton balls from her ears and nose. She dumped her last cigarette on the table and swore when she saw it—smashed flat and broken in half. Her fairy godmother must have called in sick today. Maybe it was time to crawl back up on the smoke-free wagon. She eyed the chewed cigar butt in the ashtray. Or maybe not. Desperate times and all that shit, she thought, reaching for it.

"Please, *querida.*" Manny caught her hand and placed it palm down on the table. "That was Chester's. You'd be better off licking the bottom of my shoe."

Closing her eyes, Claire took a deep breath and wondered if she could get away with drugging her mom and shipping her home in a FedEx box. Three-day service would do fine. No bubble wrap necessary.

"How was the table?" Manny asked.

"Hard."

"I'm surprised you didn't sneak up to the house in the middle of the night. I would have."

She squeezed the bridge of her nose. "I tried. She caught me. I swear she's half hound dog."

"You going to sleep on that table for the next few weeks?"

"I don't know." Claire would be damned if she was sleeping on that table again tonight. "Do you know where a girl might be able to buy some hemlock around here?"

Manny chuckled.

"Where's Chester?" She was surprised not to see the old bowlegged boy around this morning.

"I expect he's still in bed."

"It's almost nine." Which meant Claire needed to head to Ruby's pronto. She'd agreed to watch the store this morning while Ruby took Jess to Yuccaville to shop for school clothes.

"He was out late last night, conducting auditions for Harley's bachelor party."

The door to Gramps's R.V. slammed open. Still sleep rumpled, Kate stumbled out, recoiling visibly from the sun. She plopped down in the chair next to Claire.

"Well, if it isn't Katie Morgan, porn star extraordinaire." Manny's grin mimicked the Cheshire Cat's. He never missed a chance to give Kate trouble about sharing a porn star's name.

Kate stuck her tongue out at him, then turned to Claire. "Mom's up. I heard her humming 'The Sound of Music' in the bathroom."

"That's my cue." Claire stood. "I'm off to work." And off to see what was behind that little door in Joe's office.

As she plodded along under the charring sun, her thoughts returned to Mac. Before he'd shown up at the bar last night, she'd been fostering the idea of throwing some water on the fire that had burned between them since they'd met in April. But then he'd appeared, wooed her with his sexy voice and heated touches, and kissed away all thoughts of rebellion.

But now, after a night of tossing and turning, her fears trickled back one drop at a time. What if he grew tired of her job-hopping? What if the flame blazing between them flickered and died? What if, what if, what if? It was hard to think with the damned Energizer Bunny beating that drum in her head.

She took the porch steps two at a time. Maybe her mother was right about not sleeping with Mac. His proximity short-circuited Claire's brain and made her heartbeat erratic. Maybe she should avoid muddling her thoughts even more with sex, at least until she figured out if she was going to stay or run.

As she walked into the store, her steps faltered. Mac stood behind the counter next to Jess. His sandy-brown hair was still damp, curling just above his collar. His faded green T-shirt hugged broad shoulders. A combination of a rugged outdoorsman and a brainy science major, Mac the geotechnician could give Indiana Jones a run for his money.

He looked up from the Volkswagen Beetle magazine ad spread out on the counter in front of him, his gaze raking up and down her before locking onto her face. The blatant lust smoldering there made her mouth suddenly seem too dry, her tongue wooly.

"Morning, Slugger. How was your night?"

"Lonely," she admitted.

"Mine, too."

"Why do you call Claire *Slugger*?" Jess asked.

"Because she throws a wicked right hook." Mac rounded the counter and dropped a kiss on Claire's lips. He smelled fresh—of soap, sage, and something entirely too male that had Claire's pheromones tripping breakers left and right.

She shoved her hands in her back pockets to keep from touching him and her right hand brushed over the attorney's letter she'd found yesterday in Ruby's office. She pulled it out and unfolded it.

Mac caught her free hand and reeled her in. "What are you up to this morning?"

"I'm watching the store."

He ran a finger down the inside of her arm, his hazel eyes burning holes in all of her reasons for staying out of his bed. "We could close the place for a half hour."

Claire grinned. "MacDonald Garner, what are you suggesting?"

He lifted her hand and kissed the inside of her wrist, kick-starting her libido with just a flick of his tongue on her skin. "Just a massage to work out the kinks you probably have from sleeping on that table last night."

"Gawd!" Jess snorted, obviously grossed out at Mac's public display of affection. "You guys need to get a room. Let me know when you're done snogging." She scuffed out of the room.

That left the two of them alone under the buzzing florescent lights. On Ruby's old radio, Patsy Cline sang about falling to pieces. Claire could empathize with the woman.

"Alone, finally." Mac kissed his way up her arm to her shoulder.

Claire shivered, in spite of the sweat trickling down her spine. The throbbing in her head waned. She forced her attention on the piece of paper in her hand.

"Claire." Mac breathed in her ear. "Let's go—"

"Oh, shit." Claire's stomach clenched as her eyes and brain collaborated to make sense of the words on the page.

Mac released her arm. "What?"

"This." She handed the letter to Mac and watched his eyes travel down the letter. His jaw clenched as he read.

"Son of a—" He crumpled the letter. "Ruby!" He took two strides toward the curtain, stopping when his aunt cruised through it.

"What, darlin'?" Ruby dropped her purse on the counter; the keys to her old pickup were in her hand. "Jessica, come on!" she yelled over her shoulder. "We gotta go."

Mac handed the crinkled letter to her. "What's this?"

"What's what?" Ruby smoothed the piece of paper, her gaze moving down the page. Her cheeks blushed as she read. When she looked back at Mac, lines etched her forehead. "Where'd you find this?"

He glanced at Claire. Ruby's eyes followed.

Claire felt her own cheeks redden. "I'm sorry, Ruby. I didn't mean to snoop. I found it yesterday when I was in the office trying to find a reason for the break-in."

"It's okay, hon'," Ruby told Claire and then handed the letter back to Mac. "You know what it is."

"Yeah. Somebody wants the Lucky Monk."

Claire blinked. "The lucky what?"

"The Lucky Monk," Ruby said. "It's one of Joe's old mines."

"Shit." Mac tossed the letter on the counter.

"Now Mac, this is no concern of yours. I can handle it."

He raked his hand through his hair. "Does Harley know?"

"No, and he doesn't need to find out. Deborah already thinks I want him for his money. Him helpin' me out of this mess will just cement that idea in her head."

Last spring, Gramps had nearly bought Ruby's mines in order to give her the cash to dig herself out of near-bankruptcy.

In the end, though, they'd agreed he'd make her a loan, allowing Ruby to keep the mines and her dignity.

Jess pushed through the curtain. "Mom, have you—" She paused. Her eyes narrowed as she studied Ruby, then Mac. "What?"

"Nothin', sweetheart." Ruby's smile looked brittle. She grabbed her purse from the counter. "You ready to go?"

"No, I can't find my library books."

"We'll return them another day." Taking Jess by the arm, Ruby propelled her toward the door.

"Fine, but they're due tomorrow." Jess slammed outside. The bells over the door jingled in her wake.

Ruby turned back to Mac. "Don't worry about this. I have it under control."

Mac dug his keys from his pocket. "Sure you do."

"What are you doin'?" Ruby asked as he walked over and opened the door for her.

"Driving you to Yuccaville. I want you to explain to me how you have this 'under control.'"

"Now, Mac—"

"Let's go. Besides, I want to hear all about this break-in that has Claire digging for bones again." Shooting a wink back at Claire, he said, "Stay out of trouble, Slugger."

Claire watched the three of them rumble off in Mac's truck. In just four short months, they'd become more of a family to her than her own flesh and blood. Leaving them would cut deep, and playing with knives always made her armpits clammy.

Christ, she needed a smoke. She stared at the packs of cigarettes lining the display shelf next to the cash register. Nobody would know if she bought a pack and slipped out back for a few minutes ... Groaning, she grabbed Jess's copy of the latest glam magazine from under the counter and settled onto the stool. She'd picked a hell of a year to try to quit smoking.

Three nicotine-free hours later, Claire looked up as Kate breezed into the store, along with a gust of hairdryer-hot air. "What are you reading?"

Claire lowered the copy of *Ohio: Travel Smart*—one of Jess's missing library books. "A book."

"Jeez, Claire. If you're going to run, don't move to Ohio."

"What do you have against Ohio?"

"Who's moving to Ohio?" Gramps swished through the curtain, wiping his hands on a dishtowel.

"Claire." Kate pointed at the book.

"What?" Gramps snatched it from Claire's grip, holding the copy under his nose. "Why? Is Mac being transferred?"

"No. I was just ..." Claire paused, biting her lip. Gramps didn't know about Jess's Cleveland plans, and Claire didn't want to be the one who let that rattlesnake out of its tank.

"She's thinking about leaving Mac."

Gramps lowered the book, his pale blue eyes frosty. "Damn it, Claire. I knew this would happen. What's wrong with Mac? He has a good job, a nice house, and a savings account."

Claire snatched the book from his hands. "It's not—"

"I told her the same thing last night." Kate lifted her chin like she was a good little girl who deserved a chocolate-chip cookie and a pat on the head.

Claire would give her a pat all right. A solid whack with the library book should ring her bell. "Listen, I never—"

"I know." Gramps said. "You never stay with one man for more than a couple of months. What did Mac do? Ask you to take your coat off, unpack your bags, and stay awhile?"

She slammed the book on the counter. "He said he loves me."

"Oh, well then." Gramps crossed his arms, a smirk on his face. "By all means, you'd better start running, Chicken Little, because the sky is surely about to fall."

Kate giggled.

"Would you two shut up! I'm not leaving Mac." At least she didn't think she was, not yet anyway.

"Then what's with the book on Ohio?" Kate asked.

"It's Jess's." Damn them both for needling her.

Gramps stared at Claire for several seconds, then he sighed and rubbed the back of his neck. "Not that again."

"Yeah, that again."

"What?" Kate's gaze darted back and forth between them.

The phone shrilled on the wall next to Claire. She picked up the receiver. "Yes?"

"Aren't you supposed to say the name of the store when you answer the phone?"

"What do you want, Chester?"

"I need to speak to Harley, Miss Crabby-Ass."

She held the phone out to Gramps.

"I'll take it in the rec room." He pushed through the curtain.

Claire waited to hear his voice on the line and then hung up. Kate flipped through the book on Ohio, whistling.

Claire had been waiting for this opportunity all morning. "Kate, I need you to watch the store for a bit."

"Why? Can't Mom do it?"

"None of your business why, and Mom's taking a nap."

"Claire, I'm in the middle of a good tan. I just stopped in for more lotion."

"Too bad. You said you'd help out if I stayed, remember?"

Kate cursed. "Fine." She rounded the counter as Claire headed for the curtain. "But don't take forever."

Claire tiptoed past Gramps, who had his back to her while he grunted out Yes's and No's into the phone. She crept down the steps and closed the door to the basement office behind her.

Ten minutes later, she had the bookcase partially emptied and light enough to move without hemorrhaging a kidney. As she grabbed the side to lift it, Kate slammed into the room. "What are you doing, Claire?"

Claire stood, wiping her hands on her shorts. "Nothing."

"Oh, bullshit." Kate edged around Claire. "What's that?" She pointed at the door in the wall.

"A door. Who's watching the store?"

"Ruby's back." Kate crossed her arms over her chest. "And don't patronize me, Claire. I know you're up to something. Your eye is ticcing."

Claire touched her eyelid. She couldn't feel it ticcing.

"Ha! Gotcha. Are you trying to sneak into Ruby's safe?"

"It's not Ruby's."

Claire lifted the bookcase out of the way. There was no use trying to sidetrack Kate now. She was like a badger—once she'd sunk her teeth in and locked her jaws, short of cutting off a limb, there'd be no getting rid of her.

"I don't think Ruby even knows it exists," Claire told Kate. "And if you tell anyone about this, I'll play barbershop again while you're sleeping."

Kate shot her a dirty glare. "Touch my hair and die."

"Nobody needs to know about this door, especially Jess." Claire emphasized her point with a finger poke to Kate's shoulder. Jess tended to follow in Paul Revere's footsteps when it came to spreading news. "Got it?"

"Sure, whatever." Kate waved off Claire's warning. "It's Joe's, isn't it?" Kate's knowledge of Ruby's dead husband came from Claire, so she knew all of the dirt and none of the gems.

"Yep." Claire squatted in front of the door. She frowned at the keypad in the bottom left corner. "Shit. We need a code." At least they didn't need a thumbprint. Claire hadn't exhumed a body before, but she was all for learning new trades.

Where in the hell was she going to find the code? Joe wasn't exactly a chatterbox these days, and Johnny Cash, whose profile had been painted on black velvet and hung on the wall next to the door, didn't share secrets.

"Well, that sucks." Kate echoed Claire's thoughts.

"What sucks?" Jess asked.

Claire looked up to see Jess peeking over Kate's shoulder.

"Hey, I bet that's where Mom's keeping that money you found last spring." Jess nudged Kate aside and squatted next to Claire. "Cool, it even has a keypad."

Claire closed her eyes and groaned.

* * *

"I don't know why *you* have to drive me to the Franklin's place," Jess said to Kate as they drove under the Dancing Winnebagos R.V. Park sign and sped toward Jackrabbit Junction.

The tires hummed along the asphalt, not quite drowning out the whir of the air conditioning blowing lukewarm air from the vents. Kate swiped at the sweat beading on her upper lip. The back of her legs stuck to the leather seat.

"I'm perfectly capable of driving myself." Jess popped her bubblegum, polluting Kate's Volvo with the grape scent.

Kate gritted her teeth, not exactly thrilled to be driving Jess anywhere. The girl didn't stop talking long enough to breathe. But with Ruby minding the store, Gramps nowhere to be found, Mac heading to Yuccaville to "take care of something," and Claire trying to fix one of the campground toilets that had overflowed again, Kate had drawn the short straw.

Jess channel surfed on the radio with the same fingers she'd just used to pull and twirl her gum. "Claire says you're a teacher."

Not anymore. Kate fished a napkin from her glove box and offered it to Jess, who stuffed it in her pocket.

"You don't look like a teacher."

Kate wasn't sure if that was a compliment or not. "Really?" She let off the gas pedal as the STOP sign came into view.

"No. You're too young looking."

A compliment, how sweet. She might get along with her soon-to-be aunt yet. "Thank you."

"And you don't have as many gray hairs as Claire."

That was because she didn't land ass-deep in trouble as often as Claire. Besides the occasional rotten boyfriend, Kate's life was relatively stress-free.

"But you really should wax those sideburns."

Kate gasped as if she'd been pinched. Sideburns? She tipped the rearview mirror down and turned her face from side to side. What sideburns?

"Stop! Pull in here!" Jess yelled, pointing at the hardware store's gravel drive they were about to blow by.

Kate swerved into the drive and stomped on the brake pedal. Her anti-lock brakes thumped, while the gravel crunched under her tires. From out of nowhere, a pickup appeared in front of her.

Jess screamed and covered her face.

Kate tromped harder on the brakes. She winced as the passenger side of the truck filled her front windshield right before she crashed into it. The impact slammed her forward. The airbags exploded with a deafening bang.

Then there was silence.

Chapter Five

"I'd like to talk to the president, please, Edith," Mac told the gray-haired receptionist, a name plaque and tall counter separating her from the reception area. He added a wide smile to his request in an attempt to sprinkle on some charm.

Edith was new since March, the last time Mac had stormed into this office. Her perfume reminded him of the rose-shaped soaps his grandma had kept in a basket on the back of her toilet.

On the green wall behind Edith, the words *Copper Snake Mining Company* hung in thick letters, made of the very metal the company had mined daily for the past one hundred and twenty years.

Edith looked up at him, her rhinestone-rimmed reading glasses resting on the tip of her pinched nose. "Do you have an appointment, Mr. ...?" She had a raspy, two-pack-a-day voice.

"Garner. And no, I don't." He hadn't wanted to alert the big tuna until he'd baited his hook and cast his line.

The wrinkles above her upper lip deepened. "I'm sorry, Mr. Garner, but you need an appointment to see Mr. Johnson." She flipped open a small leather book and trailed her finger down one page and then another. "He has an opening next Wednesday at three. Would that work for you?"

"No. I'd like you to call him right now and tell him Mac Garner is here to see him."

"Well." She sniffed. "I can try, but he may still be at lunch. Even if he's not, I doubt he'll be available. He's a very busy man, especially on Friday afternoons." She picked up the phone and punched in three numbers.

Mac glanced around the empty reception room. Things hadn't changed much in five months. The plush burgundy carpet still smelled new and the cherry-wood chairs and coffee table still gleamed under the florescent lights. Sepia-toned pictures of huge, land-moving mining trucks and excavators—machines that made engineers shiver and environmentalists shudder—dotted the walls, along with before-and-after pictures of Roadrunner Mountain and Paloverde Hill, now both vast open pits.

"Mr. Johnson," Edith said. "There's a Mac Garner here to see you."

Mac stared down at Edith, waiting to see if Johnson was going to grant him five minutes of his time or play hard-to-get.

"No, he doesn't have an appointment." Edith lifted her chin, challenging Mac with a glare. "I explained that to him, but he's insisting on meeting with you right now." She listened for several seconds, nodding, smiling in victory. "All right, I'll see what you have available next week."

Hard-to-get it was.

Leaning over the counter, Mac snatched the phone receiver from Edith.

"Hey!" Her face contorted, mottling with a purplish-red hue.

"Listen, Chuck," Mac spoke into the receiver. "I'm here to discuss selling Ruby Martino's mines. This is a one-time deal. If you won't see me now, I'm sure Nick Black down at the Copper Star in Sierra Sol will."

Silence hissed through the receiver for several heartbeats.

Edith, now standing, held her hand out for the receiver, her eyes narrowed.

"Okay, Mac." Chuck Johnson's nasally voice sounded amiable, yet wary. "Come on back. The door is open."

Mac handed the receiver back to Edith with a victory smile of his own and didn't wait around to receive any more glares.

Johnson stood and extended his hand as Mac approached his desk. "Nice to see you again, Mac." His gray eyes contrasted with his white bushy eyebrows and thinning hair.

Mac shook Johnson's hand. "Always a pleasure," he lied.

Following Johnson's lead, he dropped into one of the cushy chairs across from the mining company president.

Johnson's office smelled of well-oiled leather and spoke of a century of wealth built on the sweaty, broken backs of many past and present Cholla County residents. A plate glass window looked out over the town of Yuccaville, mud-brick houses and white-roofed buildings littering the narrow valley below. The black frame on Johnson's desk displayed a picture of a smiling blonde, her arms clutching two miniature poodles.

"So." Johnson steepled his fingers. "Ruby is thinking again about selling?"

Mac nodded.

"Why the sudden change of heart? Last April, she fought tooth and nail to keep those mines."

"Last April, she was teetering on the edge of bankruptcy, about to lose her house and the campground to the bank. The mines were her only lien-free assets."

Not to mention that the mining company's low-ball offer on those mines only added insult to injury after Mac had figured out the estimated value of just two of Ruby's four mines.

"Which mines are we talking about?"

"Rattlesnake Ridge and Socrates Pit." Mac dangled the bait.

"What's her price?"

"That's still up in the air."

"Then why are you here?"

"To test the waters, see if the fish are still biting."

Johnson sat back, his leather chair creaking. He stared at Mac for several seconds. "They're still hungry."

Mac smiled, his chest loosening, relieved Johnson hadn't called his bluff. "I'll let her know." Here was where he might lose his catch. "If you'll give me the names and phone numbers of your attorneys, we'll deal through them from here on and I'll stay out of your hair."

Johnson reached in his desk drawer, pulled out a couple of business cards, and handed them to Mac. "How soon will Ruby be making a decision?"

"I'm not sure, but she seems anxious to get moving on this." Mac glanced down at the names; neither card belonged to Leo M. Scott, the lawyer from Tucson who'd sent the letter to Ruby.

Okay, one more lie. "She's already contacted an attorney out of Tucson by the name of Leo Scott." He studied Johnson's face, waiting for some telltale sign that the mining company had done business with Leo Scott before.

Johnson just nodded and rose with his hand extended. "Great. I look forward to working out a deal this time."

"She does, too." Mac stood, knowing he'd be playing ice hockey in hell first. He shook Johnson's hand. "Thanks for your time."

Mac could have sworn he heard Edith hiss at him as he walked by her desk.

The sight of Richard Rensberg, vice-president of the Cactus Creek Bank, in the reception area stopped him just short of the double glass doors. He was reading some paper from an open folder, his forehead furrowed. Two cardboard mapping tubes leaned against the seat next to him.

If Ruby were with him, Mac would be holding her back from beating Rensberg senseless with the tubes. The asshole had hassled Ruby on a daily basis in April for being behind on her mortgage payments for the R.V. park. Ever since, she'd used a picture of him for dart practice in the rec room.

"Hello, Rensberg."

Rensberg looked up from the paper, his eyes widening as he stared back. He snapped the file folder closed, his right hand touching one of the tubes next to him. "Garner."

"Harassed any widows lately?"

The bank man's ruddy cheeks darkened visibly. "Only those who try to skip out of paying what they legally owe."

"What brings you to the Copper Snake? Chasing ghosts?"

Rensberg's great, great grandfather graced several of the pictures hanging on the reception room's walls. He'd founded the Copper Snake, and along with his son and then grandson, built it into a mammoth monster that had gobbled up most other mining companies in the area.

Then Rensberg's father had taken over and sold off most of the family's shares to support his very young, very beautiful, and very expensive wife, only to kill himself after she left him and his son years later. Last Mac had heard, the only role Richard Rensberg played in the Copper Snake's day-to-day operation was cashing paychecks for the miners at the teller window.

"None of your business, Garner. How's your aunt? Still scraping the bottom of the barrel as always?"

Red-hot fury fired in Mac's gut. He hid it behind a cool smile.

"Mr. Johnson will see you now, Mr. Rensberg." Edith interrupted.

Rensberg stuffed the file folder back in his briefcase and stood. "Thank you, Edith."

"Would you like your coffee sweetened, as usual?"

"Please." He clutched the two map tubes to his chest. "Garner, tell your aunt our refinance rates are at a five-year low," he said, his expression smug. "Just like her paltry savings account."

Mac wanted to scrape the look off the banker's face with his knuckles. "It's always unpleasant to see you, *Dick*."

Without wasting another breath on the son of a bitch, Mac pushed through the glass doors and stepped into the afternoon heat. Coming from the air-conditioned office, he felt like an ant under a magnifying glass.

He climbed into his pickup and fired it up. Next stop, the library. Time to dig through old claims and trace the lineage of the Lucky Monk mine.

Inhaling the hot air blasting from the vents, he wasn't sure if he should be grinning wide or popping antacids. If the mining company wasn't behind Leo Scott's letter about the claim for the Lucky Monk, then who was? And how deep were their pockets?

* * *

Jess plopped down on the curb next to Kate. "Mom said she'll be here as soon as she can find Claire and get her to watch the store." The paper sack in Jess's hands crackled as she pulled out a tube of tangerine lip gloss.

The teenager smacked her grape gum and popped another bubble—a smell and sound Kate would probably always associate with barreling into the broadside of a brand-stinking-new, red Chevy Silverado SS. The damned pickup still had the temporary plates stuck in the window for chrissake.

Every time Kate blinked, dollar signs floated behind her eyes.

She stared across the hardware store's gravel parking lot at the blue-eyed cowboy she'd exchanged stares with outside the mini-mart yesterday, aka Butch the bartender. He stood next to his pickup, giving his play-by-play of the demolition derby to the sheriff. From the easy-going tilt of Butch's white cowboy hat and the quick grins on the sheriff's face, Kate guessed the two had a fishing rendezvous every Saturday morning.

Dragging her gaze away from Butch, she tried to block out the banjo chords from Deliverance that kept repeating in her head. Sweat trickled down the back of her neck. Even the whitish-pink flowers on the prickly poppies growing along the highway's shoulder drooped in submission to the sun's rays.

Lifting her hair from her neck, she fanned herself with the copy of the citation she hadn't been able to wiggle out from under no matter how many times she'd batted her eyelashes. Today was one of the few times in her life that being blonde hadn't earned her bonus points.

If word of this fiasco made it back to her insurance company, the scissor sharpening would commence. After her string of speeding tickets a couple of years back, they'd spare no time cutting her loose, and a year of using cruise control would be wasted all because Jess had run out of lip gloss.

Maybe Kate should just suck it up and pay out-of-pocket for this mess. It would drain a good chunk of her reserves, forcing her to job hunt sooner than she'd planned, but not being dropped by her insurance company might be worth it in the long run.

Batting at a pair of flies that buzzed around her head like it was a control tower, she looked over at Jess, who was busy painting her lips. "You sure you're okay?"

"Yeah. My shoulder is a little sore from the seat belt, but that's it. Those air bags were super coolio. It sounded like gunshots when they popped out."

Her own ears still rang from it.

"I can't believe what a rotten driver you are, though." Jess kicked her coltish legs out in front of her. "Especially after all of the years of practice you've had."

Kate shot the teenager a dirty look. Maybe Ruby should consider boarding school for the little shit.

"Claire is a way better driver than you, that's for sure."

Claire was better at most things than Kate, but she didn't need this pissant reminding her of that fact right now. Kate opened her mouth to tell Jess to go sit somewhere else, preferably on something pointy, but held her tongue when she noticed Butch striding toward her.

Uh, oh.

The scowl was back on his rugged face, his blue eyes practically glowing red. The tendons in his neck strained against the neckline of his faded T-shirt.

Gulping, Kate stepped onto the curb for extra leverage. She brushed the stone crumbs from her linen shorts, straightened the hem of her white, silk tank top, and braced for the storm.

"What in the hell is wrong with you, woman?" Butch's glare rivaled the sun.

Kate lifted her chin. "If you're referring to the possible variance in our reports, I can assure you—"

"I'm referring to the load of shit you tried to slide under Grady's nose."

"Grady?"

"Sheriff Grady Harrison."

Kate was surprised the sheriff's name wasn't Opie, Jeb, or Billy Bob. "Well, I was just relaying the facts as I saw them."

"Really?" Butch's eyes narrowed. He leaned closer, nearly nose-to-nose. "Explain to me how I was backing recklessly into oncoming traffic when I hadn't even left the parking lot."

Kate held her ground, unruffled by his proximity. She'd battled screaming, outraged parents enough times to know a level voice and polite smile were her best defenses. "You were backing up without checking to see if anyone was pulling into the lot."

"And you were the 'oncoming traffic'?"

"Exactly." So she'd been reaching on that one, but it had a grain of sense to it. Unfortunately, the sheriff had only chuckled and kept writing, unlike Butch, whose fists were now clenched.

"And what about the 'failure to use a signal' part?"

That had taken some creativity, but Kate had been spinning the truth since potty training. "Had you used your turn signal, I might've been able to swerve to avoid your truck."

"I was backing up."

"All the more reason to use your signal to indicate the direction in which you were going to back."

Butch opened his mouth, then glanced at Jess and snapped it shut. He shook his head. "Amazing. You crash into me and it's my fault."

Kate smiled politely.

"Woman, they should take your license, cut it into pieces, and spread it over the Sonoran Desert. It's a good thing Grady could see through your bullshit. I'm just lucky you have insurance."

"Umm, about that." Kate almost swallowed her tongue at the death-threat look Butch nailed her with. She took a deep breath and continued. "I'd like to skip turning this into my insurance and just pay for it myself. You can choose which repair facility you'd like to use, so long as the prices are reasonable. I'm sure you 'know a guy,' being a bartender and all, but I'd prefer to stick with legitimate shops. A triple-A mechanic in Yuccaville should do just fine."

Butch stared at her, a muscle in his jaw twitching. "You've got to be fuckin' kidding me."

"Really, Mr. … ah, Butch." She nudged her head toward Jess, who watched them with her mouth open wide. Kate could see the wad of purple gum on her tongue. "We have young ears listening."

Butch's chest rose and fell rapidly several times. "Listen, lady—"

"Excuse me, Ms. Morgan." Sheriff Harrison approached them with an unreadable expression on his face.

"Yes, Sheriff?" Kate beamed at him, relieved to have a referee enter the ring and break up the fight. Maybe good ol'

Grady had changed his mind about the citation she still clutched in her sweaty palm.

"I'm sorry, ma'am, but I'm gonna have to take you in."

Kate blinked. "Take me into where?"

"The police station."

The air suddenly seemed pizza oven hot. Kate's smile faltered. "The police station?" She tittered, sounding like her mother after a martini and hating herself for it. "Is being a victim in an accident a crime in this state?"

"No. But driving a stolen vehicle is."

* * *

Claire and Ruby sat on the General Store's front porch and basked in the warm rays of the setting sun. The early evening storm rumbled its goodbyes as it traveled on to the next valley, a cool breeze its parting gift. The air, washed clean and sun dried, still smelled of wet greasewood and damp dirt.

"So, the sheriff detained Kate for six hours." Claire said.

Sipping from her Corona, she savored the lemony bite on her tongue, and enjoyed a quiet lull before Gramps and Deborah arrived home with Kate and more thunderclouds in tow. The hankering for a cigarette lingered in the back of her mind.

"Six hours," Ruby repeated, whistling.

Staring out over the driveway, Claire watched the sparkles of light reflecting off the quartz mixed with the gravel, looking like a sea of Tinkerbells.

"You think that's normal or a little extra punishment for trying to lie her way out of that ticket?" Claire asked.

"Probably just normal." Ruby's soft, drawl sounded almost musical. "The law takes stolen vehicle reports very seriously 'round these parts, with Mexico being so close and all. If I remember right, Joe mentioned something about the FBI bustin' up a stolen car ring several years ago. He said the roots spread out quite a ways on both sides of the border."

Ruby's late husband's past was more than checkered, it was gingham. Claire wouldn't be surprised if he'd been the ring leader—the master of criminal ceremonies.

Since Ruby had brought up Joe, and Gramps was off collecting Kate, Claire decided to broach the subject she'd obsessed about all afternoon. "Back before Joe had his memory zapped by that big stroke, did he ever mention anything about a safe hidden somewhere in the house?"

Ruby remained quiet for several seconds. The breeze toyed with a red curl that had escaped from her ponytail, while the setting sun lit her freckled cheeks in a yellowish-orange glow.

"No. Never," she answered. "And I was too caught up in runnin' this place to ask." With a sigh, Ruby turned to Claire. "When I think about Jess and me scraping by for the last year with the bank pounding on my door and fixin' to take this place out from under me, I want to dig up Joe and let the coyotes chew on what's left of him."

Claire blinked, stunned at Ruby's fierce tone.

"I used to think Joe was my Lancelot, ridin' in on his white horse and whiskin' Jess and me away from my job waiting tables in Oklahoma City. But when you found that money back in April, I realized what a selfish bastard I'd been married to for the last five years. The man refused to buy health insurance, let alone life insurance, but he had no problem stashin' wads of cash in his office."

Claire shook her head, still amazed the money had been right under Ruby's nose all of that time.

"I was a fool to marry him, and an even bigger fool not to question how a travelin' salesman could afford to buy such expensive toys and gadgets, not to mention the antiques."

"Come on, Ruby, you're being hard on yourself." Claire patted Ruby on the knee. "You were blinded by love." A perfect example of why Claire considered that heart-fluttering emotion another four-letter word.

"Love, ha!" Ruby snorted. "I thought I was in love. Turns out, I was just tired of serving burgers and fries for a livin'. I'll tell you what, if Mac, Harley, and you hadn't stepped forward to help me last spring, I'd be in Yuccaville right now at the welfare office." She squeezed Claire's hand. "Don't think for one second I've forgotten all you and Mac did for me, including risking your lives."

Claire squirmed in her chair, suffering from an attack of the "ah, shucks."

When Ruby said that kind of stuff to her, Claire understood why Mac never hesitated to jump to his aunt's aid. Ruby's gratitude made Claire feel content in a way she hadn't experienced since her grandmother had died.

She made a vow right then to figure out who had broken into Ruby's house and why, come hell, high water, or her own mother's scorn.

Wanting to help Ruby with something that might make life easier financially, Claire came clean. "I found a safe hidden behind the bookcase in your office. It may have more money stashed in it."

"Why does that not surprise me?" Sarcasm weighed heavy in Ruby's drawl. She crossed her arms, scowling. "Joe probably hid gold bars from Fort Knox in there."

"I need a code to open it. Any idea where Joe might've written down those numbers?"

"Not a single clue."

"Do you mind if I dig around in the office some more?"

"Help yourself. You already found my dirty secret."

Claire grimaced. "What're you going to do about that letter?"

"I don't know. Mac is looking into it for me." She shook her head. "That boy just won't take 'No' for an answer. Reminds me of his mother when he gets all stubborn like this."

Claire smiled. Mac's mother had been Ruby's sister. She'd been killed in an accident almost twenty years ago. Shortly after her death, Mac's father had remarried and moved to the Florida Keys, leaving Mac on his own to deal with his grief. Ruby had been the shoulder for him to lean on then. Now, he wanted to be there for her to lean back.

"Did Mac mention what his plans are?" Claire asked.

"No, but you can ask him in a minute. I see his pickup headed this way as we speak."

The sight of Mac's grin as he parked in front of the store and climbed out of his pickup spurred Claire's heart into its usual grand jeté followed by a series of pirouettes that would make a ballerina green with envy.

"Good evening, ladies." He looked finger-lickin' good in his Levi's as he climbed the porch steps.

Claire noticed that his eyes were slightly red when he dropped a kiss on her lips. "Where have you been?"

"I don't kiss and tell."

"If you don't tell, you won't be kissing anymore."

"You drive a hard bargain, Slugger." He eyed Claire's Corona. "Share your beer with me and I'll spill the gory details."

She handed him her drink, which he drained in seconds.

"Did you return Jess's books to the library?" Ruby asked.

Mac nodded. The bottle clunked when he set it on the wood railing. "After I paid a visit to Chuck Johnson."

Red patches appeared on Ruby's cheeks. "Why'd you see him?"

"Just doing some fishing."

That name was new to Claire. "Who's Chuck Johnson?"

"The president of Copper Snake Mining Company," Mac answered, leaning on the porch rail. He gave Ruby a cocky grin. "He sends his love."

"He can kiss my ass."

Claire chuckled. Ruby had plenty of reasons to want to hogtie and torture any of those scavengers from the mining company. When times had been tough, they'd lurked nearby while the bank circled overhead.

"I told Chuck you were considering selling Rattlesnake Ridge and Socrates Pit."

Ruby did a double take. "I am?"

"As far as he's concerned."

"I hope I'm asking for a higher price this time?"

"We didn't get that far."

Claire sat forward. "Why'd you tell him that?"

"I needed a spur-of-the-moment appointment, and his receptionist was practicing her bouncer routine."

"He's still interested, I take it?" Ruby asked.

"Definitely. Rumor around town is that the copper in Roadrunner Mountain has petered out."

"You mean Roadrunner pit," Claire clarified. The mountain part of that name was forever gone.

"The ore in the pit contains less than a half percent of copper now, taking almost as much capital per ounce as it's worth. But copper prices have been up lately, and your mines are ore-rich in comparison. They could keep the company in the black for another decade."

Claire's shoulders tightened. "But you aren't really thinking Ruby should sell, are you?"

Mac and she had had this argument plenty of times last spring. She didn't relish taking up her sword again.

"Hell, no." He winked at Claire. "Don't start rattling your tail again, Slugger. I haven't healed from your previous bites." He turned to Ruby. "I told him your lawyer would be in touch."

"Who's my lawyer?"

"Leo M. Scott, Attorney at Law."

"The guy in the letter." Claire smiled as she caught on to Mac's game. "Oh, you naughty boy." This new risky side of Mac made her want to ogle him in private, preferably sans clothing.

"Claire, quit looking at me like that in front of my aunt."

She dragged her eyes away from his long legs and focused on her own dusty toes. "Did this Chuck guy react to Leo's name?" she asked.

"Not even a little."

"Does that let them off the hook?" Ruby asked.

Claire looked up to catch Mac staring at her tool belt draped over the arm of her chair.

"From the looks of it." He answered Ruby, making eye contact with Claire. The hunger in his gaze made the back of her knees sweaty. They definitely needed some alone time.

"Then who's behind it?" Claire asked.

"I'm still working on that. I hit the library next, intending to dig up details on the history of the claim, but left empty-handed."

"I thought the Yuccaville Library led the state in mining resources," Claire said. "Thanks to that huge grant from the Copper Snake."

"It does. But every single piece of information about the claim has been stolen from the shelves according to the librarian."

"Stolen?" Claire sat forward.

Mac nodded. "I figured you'd pounce on that."

Thumbing her nose at Mac, Claire turned to Ruby. "I bet your burglar and the library thief are one and the same."

"You think so, darlin'?"

"Not necessarily, Claire." Mac crossed his arms. "Ruby's burglar could've been a meth addict searching for easy money. You're adding one and one and coming up with three."

"Come on, Mac." Claire slid up next to him, leaning back on the rail. "You know I'm onto something. If I can find the PIN to that safe, I bet I'll have the proof Ruby needs."

Ruby cleared her throat.

"What PIN to what safe?" Mac frowned. "Jesus, Claire. You haven't broken into somebody's house again, have you?"

"No! Not yet, anyway."

"Claire, the sheriff said—"

Ruby cleared her throat again.

Claire and Mac looked at Ruby, who glanced behind them. Claire followed Ruby's gaze and groaned. Manny and Chester were eavesdropping from the foot of the porch steps. She'd been so engrossed in arguing with Mac she hadn't heard them walk up.

"What safe are you talking about, *querida*?" Manny asked.

"Proof for what?" Chester chimed in.

Chapter Six

An hour and another Corona later, Claire sat slumped at the card table in Ruby's rec room, staring at the cards Chester had just dealt her—nines, tens, and the Queen of hearts. When it came to all-time shittiest Bid Euchre hand, hers earned the first runner-up sash.

She laid her cards face-down on the table.

Wispy contrails of cigar smoke drifted along the ceiling, swirling in the cool air blasting from the air conditioner, softening the flickering glare from the florescent lights.

Popping the lid off her third bottle of Corona, she squeezed a lemon wedge into it. She tore the last bit of lemon pulp from the rind with her teeth and glanced over her shoulder at the curtained doorway leading to the store.

The bell over the front door had jingled moments ago, and Ruby had gone to see if Deborah, Gramps, and Kate were back from the police station. Claire chuckled. She couldn't wait to hear Kate's account of her trip to Yuccaville's version of Alcatraz.

Chester tapped his fingers on the table. "It's your bid, Giggles Magoo. Can we finish this game before I'm worm food?"

Picking her cards back up, she said, "It's called patience, Mr. Antsy Pants." Chester had been growing pissier with each hand that she and Mac won. "Maybe you've read about it in the latest issue of Geezer's Digest or Popular Geriatrics."

Chester puffed on his cigar. "Bid, wiseass, or I'll tell Harley all about that new scratch on Mabel's front bumper."

"Okay, no need to play dirty." Trust Chester to be there to catch her stealing Mabel to run out for a pack of cigarettes. "Three."

"Four." Manny bid next, his smile wide, like he'd jammed a banana in his mouth sideways. He obviously had a hot date after the game, because he smelled as if he'd been marinated in Old Spice.

"Pass," Mac said, watching Claire from where he sat across the table. His hazel eyes traveled down the front of her "Mister Magoo for President" T-shirt, lingering.

Claire fanned herself with her cards. When he stared at her that way, she got all steamy inside and out. She ran her bare foot up his inner calf, her toes rubbing over the inseam of his jeans.

They'd agreed to disagree about the burglar for the moment, calling a truce so that they could pair up for tonight's segment of the Euchre tournament that Chester and Manny had organized as a pre-wedding gift to Gramps. Gramps had lived and breathed Bid Euchre until Ruby had come along. Now he just enjoyed a game any chance he got, and lately that had been every night.

Chester knocked on the table, indicating that he passed, too. He looked at Manny. "What's trump, partner?"

"Spades." Manny laid down the Ace of spades.

Claire glanced at the curtain again.

"All right, Señorita." Manny tugged on Claire's sleeve. "Now that Ruby is out of earshot, tell us whose house you're going to break into."

"I'm not planning to break into anyone's place." Claire turned back from the curtain to find three sets of eyes boring into her. The theme from *The Good, the Bad, and the Ugly* whistled in her head.

Her foldout chair creaked as she shifted on the hard metal seat. "At least not yet."

Mac groaned deep in his throat and shook his head. "You're going to wind up in jail, just like your sister." He tossed the ten of spades onto Manny's card.

Snickering, Chester threw the Queen of spades onto Mac's ten. "Katie's been telling sugar-coated tall tales since she was no bigger than a cricket." He spoke around his cigar. "I'm surprised I haven't seen her profile yet on some of those women in prison websites I poke around on."

Claire grimaced at Chester. "You've been spending too much time on the Internet again." She dropped the nine of hearts onto the pile of cards, grabbed her beer, and frowned at Mac. "You're being overly cautious."

"And you're running around half-cocked again." Mac shot back at her, his grin taking the sting out of his words.

"Speaking of half-cocked." Chester laid his cigar in the ashtray. He wiggled his eyebrows at Manny. "How'd your skinny dipping date with lovely Miss Lilly go this morning? Did you pickle your hide or hide your pickle?"

Claire choked on the mouthful of beer she'd been about to swallow. Beer burned the inside of her nose.

Laughing, Manny patted her on the back. "Both."

Mac raised his cards, hiding his face.

Between coughs, Claire said, "Haven't you two ever heard of the saying, 'gentlemen don't kiss and tell'?"

"We're too old to keep secrets." Manny raked in the cards from the center of the table and threw out the Ace of clubs to start the next round.

Nodding, Chester added, "And I don't have time to waste running the bases anymore. I need to know from the get-go if Lilly's version of the backseat boogie ends with the horizontal bop. Viagra doesn't come with a 'pause' button, ya know."

"So you've mentioned before," Mac said and dropped the Jack of clubs, second only to the Jack of spades in trump suit rank, on top of Manny's Ace.

"Hey, that's trump." Chester slapped his King of clubs on the pile.

"I know my left bower from my right when it comes to Euchre." Mac's poker face gave away nothing.

Claire sat forward, wondering if Mac had something up his sleeve besides a nice bicep. She threw her nine of clubs on the table and grinned at Manny as Mac scooped up the cards and led the next round with the Ace of diamonds.

"Earlier on the porch, you two mentioned something about Ruby and finding some proof," Manny said as Chester played the Jack of diamonds. "Is Ruby in some kind of trouble again?"

Claire's gut told her to lie and she did so without hesitation. "No."

If either Chester or Manny found out about that letter from the lawyer, they'd blab to Gramps, who would burn needless calories cussing and swearing, and then Claire's mom would use her bionic ears to eavesdrop—and *then* all hell would break loose.

Laying her ten of diamonds on the stack, Claire floundered in the pool of alcohol saturating her synapses and tried to think of a believable tale she could float past these two old sharks. "Mac and I were just ..." she trailed off, looking to Mac for help.

"I was just warning Claire not to go spelunking in Ruby's mines on her own."

"Then what was the proof you were referring to?" Chester's tone said he wasn't buying Mac's story.

"Proof that the mines are dangerous."

"You two have to be the worst liars this side of the Rio Grande." Manny tossed the King of diamonds on Claire's ten.

Chuckling, Mac collected the cards from the center of the table. He led the next round with the lowest trump card, the nine of spades, obviously fishing for trump.

Claire gulped some beer to keep from grinning broadly across the table. Judging from the lines wrinkling Manny's forehead, things weren't going as he'd planned this hand.

"What about a PIN for a safe?" Chester asked. "Whose safe?"

These boys did not want to give up this bone.

"Ruby's safe." Claire tossed out her nine of diamonds.

Come first thing tomorrow morning, she was going to pay that safe another visit and start punching in some numbers.

Manny slammed down the Jack of spades, the leading trump card, and scraped the cards over to his win pile. He wore a wary frown as he led the next round with the Ace of hearts. "If it's Ruby's safe, why doesn't she know her own code?"

"She forgot it." Mac remained Fonzie-like cool. "You know how some women get when there are wedding bells ringing." He threw down the King of spades, the last trump card floating around, and smiled wide.

Manny rattled out a stream of Spanish, swearing with both single and double rolled r's.

They'd set the boys, sending them backwards four points and winning the game. Claire leaned across the table, grabbed Mac by the cheeks, and planted a big, wet kiss on his mouth.

"Knock it off, horny toads." Chester grunted and scooted back from the table. "Just because Mac said he loves you doesn't mean you need to give us a demonstration."

Sirens pealed in Claire's head. She fell back onto her chair, her gaze frozen on Mac. As she watched, his jaw clenched, and then a vein began to pulse above his left eye.

"You're just jealous," Manny said, seemingly unaware that Claire's happy-go-lucky world had just been flipped.

"Who's jealous?" asked Gramps as he stepped through the curtain. Ruby followed, her cheeks flushed and her hair a little messier than before.

Mac pushed his chair back and rose to his feet, his lips now thin and tight.

"Mac." Claire scrambled to her feet. "I didn't ..." she didn't know how to finish. Damn Kate and her big-ass mouth! Gramps would have kept this to himself, understanding men much more than her freaking sister.

"Apparently, you must have," Mac said. "Because now it's public knowledge."

Manny grinned at Gramps. "Where's the jailbird?"

"I dropped her and her mom off at my R.V. Deborah was giving Kate the third degree, and I was tired of hearing it."

"So, who won?" Ruby asked Mac, sliding up next to him.

"We did." He turned his back to Claire. "I'm going to hit the sack," he told Ruby, dropped a peck on her cheek, and left, taking the steps two at a time.

"Who plays next?" Gramps took Mac's empty seat.

Claire didn't wait around to hear Chester or Manny's answer. She chased after Mac, catching up with him outside the spare bedroom.

"Mac, wait." She huffed, slightly breathless from racing up the steps with a belly full of beer and pretzels.

He paused in the dark doorway, not looking back.

"It's not like it seems." Reaching, she tentatively touched his back.

His muscles tightened under her fingers. "Really? So you didn't tell somebody else what I said to you the other morning in the privacy of our bedroom?"

"Well, yes, but ..." Her cheeks burned with guilt. She glanced over her shoulder, wondering if Jess was lurking around the corner. "Listen, can we go in the bedroom and discuss this behind a closed door?"

There were too many ears around this place, and Claire was already zero for three on keeping secrets.

Mac's eyes were shrouded when he turned to her. Shadows defined his cheekbones. "I don't think so."

"Why not?"

"Because you have a way of distracting me, especially when you start removing your clothes. Maybe it'd be best if you spent another night in the R.V. with your mom and sister." He flicked on the light and backed into the room. "Sleep tight, Claire. Don't let the bedbugs bite."

"Mac, come on."

"Or your mother." With his lips flat-lined, he shut the door.

* * *

Kate rubbed her eyes and dropped onto the couch. She wanted nothing more than to nestle all snug in her bed while visions of cell bars slipped from her head.

The R.V. smelled like baked plastic. The heat that had built up during the day seeped slowly out through the windows Kate had opened after Gramps had dropped her off. She could hear the tinkling of Manny's wind chimes every now and then above the racket the frogs were making down by the creek.

Ten minutes under Gramps's shower had washed the musty, locker room smell of the police station from her skin and hair, but no amount of water could rinse off the layer of shame and humiliation that now coated her from head to toe. If Kate ever saw Butch again, she'd run and hide under the nearest cactus.

Henry finished chomping down his dinner and walked over to her. He rubbed his snout against her leg and whined quietly.

Smiling, she patted his head. At least someone still liked her. With a grunt, he dropped onto his belly at her feet.

Kicking off her old Snoopy slippers, she fell back onto her pillow. The soft cotton sheet underneath her felt cool against the back of her legs. Kate hummed softly, trying to block out the sound of her mom brushing her teeth in the bathroom.

If she heard one more peep out of Deborah about how embarrassing it'd been to walk into that police station in broad daylight, Kate was going to shave her eyebrows and join a cult.

But worse than the lecture Deborah had been cramming down Kate's throat was the lack of comment from Gramps. The few looks he'd shot her in the rearview mirror on the way home had made her feel nine years old—fresh from the principal's office after fighting on the school bus. With each passing milepost, she had slumped deeper into Mabel's leather embrace, wishing she could slip down between the seats and curl into a ball in the trunk.

Kate couldn't wait to close her eyes and make it all go away. She clapped her hands twice, and the overhead light turned off. Ah, sweet, nonjudgmental darkness.

She heard her mother emerge from the bathroom and shut the bedroom door behind her. Apparently, there'd be no "goodnight, dear" from her mom tonight. Thank God for the silent treatment.

Breathing deeply, Kate focused on relaxing her legs, then her lower back, her arms, her fing …

The front door banged open. The smack of the aluminum into the wall triggered the Clapper.

Kate popped up like a whack-a-mole, blinking in the light.

Henry jumped up, growling.

Claire stood just inside the threshold, her face stony, eyes flaming.

"Christ, Claire." Kate sank back against cushions. "You scared the crap out of me."

"Good!" Claire shut the door so hard that Gramps's singing bass fish fell off the wall and crashed to the floor. The lights went off again.

"What the hell is your problem?" Kate clapped the lights back on. She was the one who'd sat in the Mayberry jail all afternoon while Deputy Dipshit dug the dirt and sock lint out from under his toenails.

"My problem," Claire kicked off her flip-flops, "is your freakin' mouth."

Kate's neck and cheeks warmed. She'd already caught plenty of fire and brimstone from her mom about her fictitious accident report. She didn't need Claire jumping on that bandwagon, too.

"Well, take a number and get in line, because today you're one of many. And while you're waiting, you can kiss my ass." Kate flopped onto her pillow and rolled over, turning her back to Claire. She clapped twice. Darkness surrounded her again.

A pillow hit her in the back.

"Knock it off, Claire. I still owe you for this morning."

One of the rectangular foam cushions from the bench seats smacked her on the hip.

"Don't make me get off this couch and kick your butt."

A balled up dish towel whopped her in the back of the head.

"Damn it, Claire!" Kate grabbed the towel and whipped it back at her sister. "Go sleep with Mac."

"I'd love to, but you screwed that up by flapping your lips."

Kate flipped onto her back, frowning up at the shadows flickering across the ceiling. "How exactly did trying to lie my way out of getting a ticket after slamming my car into Butch's truck interfere with your stupid love life?"

"This isn't about your accident. I'm talking about you blabbing to Chester and Manny that Mac said he loves me."

"And when did I have time to do that?" She looked over at Claire, who sat on the table, her eyes reflecting the light seeping in through the closed mini-blinds. "In case you've forgotten, I was sitting on a piss-stained mattress behind bars most of the afternoon. What do you think? I used my one quarter to call Manny and gab about Mac and you?"

"Well, when you put it that way, no." The fire had fizzled from Claire's tone. Now she just sounded tired. The table creaked. "Damn Gramps. How am I going to fix this mess?"

"Welcome to my world." Kate rubbed her temples. "Hang up your saddle and roll a smoke with me, why don't ya?"

"God, I'd sell a kidney right now for a cigarette." The table creaked again in the darkness. "So what's the story with your car being listed as stolen?"

"Apparently, my ex, Gary—you remember him, the one who tried to shoplift a tennis racket and told the clerk that he wasn't stealing, he was just happy to see her?"

"Yeah, I remember Gary." Claire chuckled. "He five-fingered my snow globe of the Mitchell Corn Palace and super-glued it to the dashboard of his 1975 Pinto to up its resale value."

"Well, he got stopped for speeding while driving my car about nine months ago, but apparently he couldn't find the registration in the glove box. Even though he was let off with just a ticket, the cop listed my car as stolen. Gary was supposed to take my registration in and have the flag removed, but he never did, *and* he never told me about any of this either."

Claire scoffed. "It took six hours to figure that out?"

"Yep. Between miscommunication, no communication, and then an overload of convoluted communication, the sheriff wouldn't let me go until everything came out spot-free. It seems they had some problems with stolen vehicles in the last few months, and now they like to use a magnifying glass when a pair of bifocals would work fine."

Kate let out a dry, humorless chuckle. "First, I smash my car, then I get hauled off to jail for six hours, and as a final reward, my insurance agent gives me my walking papers after hearing about the accident." Butch had insisted she go through her insurance company, damn it.

"Shit. They are going to pay for the damages, right?"

"Yes, but I'm going to have to find a new carrier to cover me for the drive home." Kate sighed. "I picked a hell of a time to quit my job."

Someone clapped twice, and the light flickered on.

Kate shielded her eyes.

"What do you mean you quit your job?" Deborah's voice squeaked like pieces of Styrofoam rubbing together.

Kate winced and slid down her pillow. Damn it. She'd been so focused on reliving the day's events that she hadn't heard the sound of the bedroom door opening.

Deborah marched over to the couch, hands planted on her hips, and glared down at Kate. "Quitting is not part of the ten-year plan we put together."

"You mean the plan you put together," Claire said dryly.

"Don't you start with me." Deborah pointed a well-manicured fingernail at Claire. "You're still in the dog house."

"What did I do?" Claire rose from her seat on the table.

"It's not what you did, but what you haven't done yet."

"Huh?"

"Neither of you realize how important it is to be able to take care of yourself."

Sitting up, Kate frowned up at her mom. "What are you talking about? We've been taking care of ourselves for years."

Deborah sneered down at her. "You call jumping from man to man or job to job taking care of yourself?"

Kate pressed back into the cushions as her mom loomed over her. "Maybe." She shot a help-me glance at Claire.

"Well, it's not. Each of you needs to find a nice man with a good-sized house, a hefty bank account, and a retirement plan that doesn't involve winning the lotto."

Claire closed the distance between them. "Mom—"

"You've both had plenty of time to get your act together and line up your ducks." Deborah's nostrils were flared, her cheeks rosy. All she needed was a pulpit. "But neither of you have paid attention to one word of advice I've given. I can see now that the only way you two are going to have secure futures is with my guidance."

With a groan, Kate buried her face in a couch cushion. The last time she'd seen that determined glint in her mother's eyes, Kate had ended up in grad school chasing a degree she wasn't sure she wanted.

"Listen, Moth—" Claire started again, her tone strong.

"And I'm going to start with you." Deborah whirled on Claire. "First, we need to find you a nice dress, a pretty sunhat, and a decent pair of sandals. Then we'll get to work on doing something with that hair of yours."

* * *

Saturday, August 14th

"Morning, darlin'," Ruby said to Mac as he sat down at the kitchen table. She stood barefoot at the stove in a yellow checkered blouse and faded blue jeans, a spatula in one hand and an oven mitt on the other, her smile welcoming. Eggs spit and sputtered in the frying pan in front of her.

"You hungry?" she asked.

"Definitely." The smell of freshly cooked bacon filled the house. He'd woken up chewing on his pillow.

The dinner plate-sized thermometer nailed to one of the clothesline posts outside the window showed eighty-seven degrees already—a good day to play around in a big wormhole in the ground. Ruby's new air conditioner chugged away in the next room, keeping this part of the house cool.

"Thanks," Mac said as Ruby handed him a plate of fried eggs, buttered toast, and crispy bacon. Taking the chair opposite him, she plunked down two mugs of coffee.

"Where are Harley and Jess?" He splashed some Tabasco sauce on his eggs. Besides the rattling of dishes in the sink, he hadn't heard a peep in the house this morning.

"Harley drove Chester to Yuccaville for parts to fix Chester's generator." Ruby paused to sip her coffee. "Jess is still sleeping; at least she was when I looked in on her a bit ago. She didn't get home from babysittin' last night until two."

Good, both were out of the picture. Mac had spent half the night missing Claire's soft curves and sleepy murmurs, even though he was still ticked at her for running her mouth. The rest of the night he'd tossed and turned, stressing about Ruby.

"I'm worried about your burglar coming back." He dipped a piece of toast in a slightly runny egg yolk.

"Harley and I are, too." Ruby's forehead wrinkled. "We've changed the locks and nailed the basement window closed. Plus, Jess knows to lock up before she turns off the light."

"Good."

"But if someone's fixin' to break in, they'll find a way."

That's what he feared. "Where are the spare keys?"

"There are two sets: one in my nightstand, the other behind the bar."

"Do you still have Joe's old double-barreled 12-gauge and the snub-nosed .357 stashed in your closet?"

She nodded.

"You should probably let Claire know about both guns and where you keep the ammo, since she'll be running the show here when Harley and you are on your honeymoon." If anything happened to Claire and Jess while Ruby was gone, Mac would shift into Dirty Harry mode. "Make sure she knows how to use at least one of them."

"Good idea." Ruby sighed and rubbed the bridge of her nose. "I sure hate living like this. I keep bouncing back and forth between fixin' to form a lynch mob and jumping at every little bump in the night."

Mac hated to admit it, but maybe Claire had the right idea about hunting down the burglar. Playing defense day after day made sleeping soundly a pipedream, which reminded him of another question he'd pondered before the sun crested the horizon. "Where's everyone going to sleep while you're gone?"

"Jess will be in her own bed, of course. Deborah and Kate can choose if they want to shack up here or just stay in Harley's R.V. Claire and you can sleep in our bed."

"Not if Deborah has her way." Mac stabbed at a piece of egg with his fork. He didn't relish the idea of facing off with Claire's mom over the next couple of weeks. "That woman makes Lizzie Borden seem like Minnie Mouse."

"Now, Mac." Ruby patted his arm. "I'm sure her bark is worse than her bite."

"Have you been bitten yet?" He chomped on a piece of bacon, the smoky taste coating his tongue. Ah, bacon. It made everything tolerable, even Claire's mom.

She stopped patting. "Uh, no. At least I don't think so."

"Well, I have, a couple of times now."

He stirred his coffee, remembering the first time he'd met Claire's mom and had listened to her pointed comments about Claire's poor judgment when it came to picking men. Deborah had made it crystal clear that Mac was on the low end of her scale for suitable bachelors.

"She has sharp nails," he warned. "Watch your back."

Jess breezed into the kitchen, her hair pulled back in a ponytail, several envelopes in her hand. Smelling like fruity bubblegum, she flopped onto the seat next to Mac and smiled. "Mornin'. Who has sharp nails?" She turned to Ruby without missing a beat. "Can I have some coffee?"

Ruby pushed to her feet. "You can have some orange juice or tomato juice, but no coffee."

"Come on, Mom." Jess pouted.

"You know the deal, not until you're sixteen."

"That's less than two weeks away. Just let me have half a cup now. C'mon, please."

"Nope." Setting a glass of orange juice on the table in front of Jess, Ruby kissed her daughter on the forehead.

"Fine." Jess let out a long, loud sigh, obviously carrying the weight of the world on her freckled shoulders. She tossed the envelopes she'd been carrying onto the table. "So, who were you two talking about?"

"Nobody. What are these?" Ruby picked up a letter with her name on it, her brows drawn as she tore it open.

"Yesterday's mail. I grabbed it on the way to the Franklin's house and forgot it was in my bag." Jess stole a piece of bacon from Mac's plate. "Who were you talking about when I walked in the kitchen?"

"A friend of Claire's." He lied, watching his aunt. Ruby's cheeks paled visibly then flushed pepper red as her gaze trailed down the page. "What is it, Ruby?"

She handed him the paper. He recognized the letterhead immediately. Ruby's new pen pal, Mr. Leo M. Scott, had written again. Mac scanned the letter, his eyes focusing on the words *deadline* and *court date*.

"Christ!" He tossed the paper on the table. "It looks like we're up shit creek again."

Chapter Seven

"Claire?" Jess called as she burst through the R.V. door.

Claire stood in the hall outside of the bathroom, towel-drying her hair. She placed her finger against her lips and nudged her head toward the closed bedroom door.

Not wanting to wake the beast, she kept her voice low when she replied, "Morning, Jess."

Kate groaned from the couch cushions, rolling so her back was to them. Henry hopped to the floor, stretched, and waddled over to his food bowl.

"Mac sent me to tell you he's leaving," Jess whispered and patted Henry on the top of his butt.

Claire dropped her towel. "What?" She stumbled forward, her feet as surprised as her brain. Last night he'd been pissed at her, but not mad enough to drive back to Tucson. "Why?"

"I don't know. Nobody ever tells me anything."

Claire glanced in the hallway mirror. After a couple of nights of staring wide-eyed at the ceiling with a bunch of "what-ifs" flapping around in her head, she looked scary enough to send Ruby's guests running. But she'd have to forego a brush and makeup for now and just hope for a solar eclipse this morning. She needed to talk to Mac, to stop him before he raced off without hearing her explanation.

Slipping on her flip-flops, she grabbed her sunglasses and Henry's leash from the kitchen counter.

"I brought you some breakfast." Jess offered Claire a MoonPie with a bite-sized chunk missing.

"Thanks." Claire exchanged Henry's leash for food. "Let's go. I want to try to catch Mac before he leaves."

The humidity made the horizon wavy, as if Claire were staring at it through a fish tank. Henry led the way toward the

General Store, straining at the leash, snapping at bees collecting pollen from the clover that lined the drive. They shifted to the shoulder, single file with Jess in front, as a mammoth-sized Fleetwood idled past. The curly-haired blonde behind the wheel waved and smiled, a cloud of dust and exhaust fumes swirling after her.

Jess coughed exaggeratedly and angled back onto the drive. Several steps later, she stopped, balanced on one foot, and took off her sandal, looking like a flamingo with those long, skinny legs of hers.

"Do you think the person who broke into our house was searching for my money?"

What money? Jess blew every penny she had on lip gloss and nail polish. "You mean your babysitting money? Come on, put your shoe on and let's go."

Jess shook a pebble from her sandal and slipped it back on. "No. The money Mom is going to give me when I graduate from high school." She skipped along on the drive next to Claire. "You know. The money you found in Joe's office last April."

Claire's step faltered for a moment. Oh, that money. This was news to Claire. The last she'd heard, Ruby hadn't decided what to do with the cash.

Something smelled kind of anchovy-ish here. "When did your mom tell you the money was for you?"

"A while ago." The girl's gaze darted up, down, and all around—everywhere but in Claire's direction.

Getting the truth out of Jess sometimes took a little arm twisting. "Jess, come clean, or I'll tell Gramps you were the one who dipped Henry's paws in blue paint."

"Paintings by Henry" had been Jess's big scheme back in June for making some quick cash. Unfortunately, Henry had confused the poster board for newspaper, leaving Jess with a dinner-plate sized pee puddle and several blue paw prints running off the edge of the thick paper and across the floor. Jess spent an hour spot cleaning the carpet so when Gramps and Ruby returned from Tucson they were none the wiser—except for the mysterious blue paint around Henry's toenails.

"Darned dog." Jess walked in silence for several seconds, no more skips in her step.

"Mom didn't exactly tell me," she clarified, kicking at a rock. "I overheard her and Harley talking about the money. He wants Mom to put it in some bank in Tucson until I go to college."

"Well, there's a good possibility that whoever broke into your house was looking for money." Claire flip-flopped faster as the General Store came into view, along with the sight of Mac's truck idling out front. "But I'd be surprised if the money from Joe's office was the lure. I'm sure it was just a random hit from some meth-heads looking for quick cash." She stole Mac's earlier theory.

Okay, so she was a liar-liar-pants-on-fire, but she didn't want Jess freaking out about the burglar coming back for the cash, especially with Ruby taking off on her honeymoon soon.

As they neared Mac's truck, Claire noticed the cab was empty. He'd waited for her. The knots in her stomach unraveled.

"Are you sure?" Jess asked as they skirted Mac's pickup. "That's a lot of money. When I move to Cleve—"

"Very few people know that money exists." Claire didn't want to be an ear on Jess's party-line when it came to daydreams about blowing the cash. That was between Jess and her maker— as in her mother.

"And it should stay that way, Jess, if you get my meaning." Claire glanced at Jess, who was busy folding a piece of gum into her mouth. "You do get my meaning, right?"

"Yeah, yeah. What do you think I am? An idiot?" Jess took the porch steps two at a time.

No, just a babbling teenager. Pushing her sunglasses up on her head, Claire followed her onto the porch.

The screen door opened as Jess reached for the handle. "Your mom wants to talk to you," Mac told his cousin and held the door for her.

"Now what?" Jess slipped past him into the store.

Sporting a golden tan, a fresh shave, jeans, and a T-shirt, Mac made her pheromones fly. Claire dropped her sunglasses back down, hiding her makeup-free, shadow-rimmed, bloodshot eyes.

Mac pulled the main door closed behind Jess and let the screen door bang shut.

"Morning, Slugger." He kissed Claire on the lips, his breath minty-fresh.

Claire wished she'd taken the time to brush the fuzz from her teeth. The kiss ended before she had time to settle in and enjoy it.

"Where are you going?" She trailed down the porch steps after him.

He shoved his backpack behind the bench seat and stuffed a jug full of water next to it.

"Up to the Lucky Monk," he said and climbed into his truck, pulling the door closed.

So, he wasn't leaving her here alone with her mother. Relief loosened her shoulders. Claire leaned into the open window. Rolled maps, a hardhat with a light on it, and a collection of flashlights filled the passenger seat.

"Why?" she asked.

"Ruby received another letter from the attorney." Mac adjusted one of the vents so that a cool blast of air whooshed over Claire's arms. "Somebody is officially disputing her claim. She has to go to court at the end of this month."

"Shit!" Claire ran her fingers through her hair. As if Ruby didn't have enough on her plate with planning the wedding, Jess bucking orders, and Deborah just being in the same state. "What do you think you'll find in the Lucky Monk?"

"Copper. Maybe some amethyst. Maybe nothing."

"Then why waste your time in there?"

"I need to assess the value of it. I didn't check out the Lucky Monk last April. I was too busy messing around in the other mines."

She didn't like Mac going up there alone. Cave-ins occurred too often in old mines, especially with the mining company dynamiting out chunks of earth from nearby Roadrunner pit every day.

"Let me go with you."

Mac shook his head. "Ruby needs your help."

"Then wait until I'm free this afternoon."

"I can't. Harley will be back any minute now, and Ruby wants me gone before he gets here and figures out what I'm up to. She doesn't want him to know anything about this."

"She's going to have to tell him sometime. How is she going to hide going to court?"

"That's her problem, not mine." He shifted into gear.

"Mac." Claire grabbed his forearm. After a night of beating herself up for betraying his trust, she wanted a chance to explain. "I need to talk to you."

"Save it for tonight," he said.

"What's tonight?"

"You and me in a queen-sized bed."

The heat in his stare had her fanning her faded yellow Daffy Duck T-shirt. "Oh."

"You can make it up to me then. Bring your tool belt."

Her pulse danced as she remembered the last time she'd joined him in bed in nothing but her tool belt.

"I'll be waiting." She stepped back. "But I'm coming to look for you if you're not back by sunset."

"Deal." He hit the gas, rolling away from her.

Claire watched Mac cross the bridge and speed down the road, her palms clammy at the thought of him alone in the mine. Shaking off all thoughts of doom and gloom, she climbed the porch steps and focused on cracking that damned safe.

The cool air inside the store slid across her skin, soaking up the heat. Ruby stood behind the counter, her arms crossed, a grin on her face.

Manny leaned against the opposite side of the counter, pointing down at the campground map taped there. A six pack of V-8 juice sweated onto the wood in front of him. "I'm just saying that if you cut down these trees here, it would make these sites in the middle more accessible."

"And the drive leading right up to the sites isn't good enough?"

"What's going on?" Claire asked, leaning next to Manny.

"Manny wants me to remove some mesquite and paloverde trees so he can spy on my other campers."

"Ah, *mi amor.*" Manny's voice took on that velvety Latino lilt meant to woo women out of their underwear. "You wound me with your words. I was just trying to help boost your business."

Ruby bent over the counter, resting her elbows on the scarred wood surface, her smile playful. "Sure you were, honey. And I bet it's a pure coincidence that a cute little blonde in a Fleetwood just rented site B15—which sits on the other side of these very trees." Ruby tapped the trees drawn on the map.

"An amazing coincidence." The laugh lines deepened around Manny's eyes. "I'm sure Claire would be happy to clear some brush today."

"Right, no problem." It was supposed to top out at 105 degrees this afternoon. Claire jabbed him with her elbow. "I'll roll around in some zinc oxide and get right to work on that."

"Wear a bikini." Manny wiggled his eyebrows at Claire. "You'll look like a mud-wrestling ghost."

Chuckling, Claire stole one of his V-8s. "You need to seek counseling."

"Without these here trees, loverboy, what would I do for a privacy screen for these sites?" Ruby traced a circle around the small group of tent-only camping sites clustered in the middle of the map next to the trees.

"Who cares?" Manny shrugged. "They are a waste of real estate. When's the last time you rented one?"

"Just last week."

Manny waved Ruby's answer aside. "They aren't even lettered right. All your other sites have an A or B in front of them. These have an I. Makes no sense."

"I agree, but Joe had the maps printed before I came along, so until I have to order new ones, the tent sites stay."

Ruby dropped onto the stool and crossed one leg over the other, kicking her foot. "I have an idea, Manny. Why don't Chester and you just walk over and say 'howdy' instead of eyeballin' my other campers through your binoculars?"

Manny acted shocked—wide-eyed, open-mouthed, and all. "Those are for bird watching."

"Sure, darlin'. But if one of your little birds comes in here squawkin' about a certain skinny dipper and his peepers, I'm sending Harley to take those bird-watchers away from y'all."

The clock in the other room cuckooed to mark the half-hour.

Claire grabbed the small notepad next to the cash register. She'd better get to work opening that safe before the pressure cooker whistle blew outside. Weed-whacking under the noontime sun was about as fun as swimming with electric eels.

"Ruby, do you mind if I take care of some business downstairs before I get started today?"

"Sure thing, honey."

"Take care of what?" Manny eyed the notepad suspiciously.

"Girl stuff." Claire tucked the pad out of view.

"You know I love girl stuff."

"Manny, mind your own business. Claire, take your time. Jess can take over here if I need help."

Claire slipped through the curtain and down the basement steps. Flipping on the light, she locked the door behind her this time. The smell of dust and cement greeted her. She pulled out the bookshelf and dropped onto the hard floor in front of the small door.

She started pushing numbers at random, counting under her breath as she went. When she punched in a ninth digit, the Error light glowed red.

"Eight it is." She hit the Clear button a couple of times.

Leaning the pad of paper against the door, she punched in the first group of numbers she'd asked Ruby to write down—Joe's birthday, including four digits for the year—and held her breath.

Nothing happened. No click, no clunk. The door didn't pop open. She'd figured that was too easy, but she had to try.

Claire exhaled and punched in the next set, this time Ruby's birthday. Nothing again.

Next came Joe and Ruby's wedding day, then Jess's birthday, then the date Joe officially retired. Still nothing, but she had a bunch more possibilities to go, thanks to Ruby and her knack for remembering dates.

Thirty minutes later, Claire was ready to go out to the tool shed and get the sledgehammer. She took off one of her thongs and threw it at the safe. It hit with a soft thwap.

She'd tried every number on the list, then a few more she'd made up. She'd ransacked Ruby's desk, checking every nook and cranny.

She'd entered invoice numbers and dates of purchase for everything from the novelty cannon pencil sharpener on his desk to the SL500 Roadster Convertible he'd totaled when he'd had his stroke.

Someone knocked on the door.

"Who is it?" Claire glanced around the room, frowning at the mess she'd made.

"It's Jess." The girl's voice was muffled by the slab of pine between them. "Mom needs you upstairs."

"Damn!" Claire closed the top desk drawer. "Tell her I'll be there in a couple of minutes."

"What are you doing?" Jess's voice came from the crack in the bottom of the door this time.

"Nothing." Claire scooped up a pile of doctor and lab invoices and crammed them into one of the side drawers.

"Then why are there papers all over the place?" Jess would have made a good Inquisitor General for the Spanish.

"Ummm, I dropped something."

"Where's your other shoe?"

Christ! "I had an itch."

"Are you looking for my money?" Jess whispered loudly.

Claire paused in the midst of trying to close a stuck drawer. Jess was going to have to get off this kick about the money being hers. True or not, she didn't need to be throwing news about Ruby's money around like rice at a reception. It would only attract unwanted attention.

"No." Claire gave up on the drawer and grabbed her thong. She unlocked the door and pulled it open just enough to see Jess with her cheek pressed against the floor.

Rising to her feet, Jess smiled sheepishly at Claire.

"Let's go." Nodding toward the steps, Claire waited for Jess to lead the way.

As she crested the top step, Claire hesitated at the sound of Deborah's voice coming from the other side of the green curtain. After last night's rant, she'd vowed to avoid her mother today.

"You didn't tell me my mom was here."

Jess paused halfway across the rec room shag. "Kate's here too."

Taking a deep breath, Claire followed Jess through the curtain.

"There she is!" Kate stood behind the counter, her smile flashbulb bright, her eyes fifty-cent pieces. She looked like she'd slammed three espressos in a row.

Deborah looked up from the latest issue of *Vogue* long enough to give Claire a frown-filled once over, then returned to flipping through the pages.

Approaching the counter slowly, Claire glanced around. "Where's Ruby?"

Had Deborah eaten her already?

"She's getting her keys." Her mother brushed a nonexistent piece of lint from her peach silk blouse.

"Is she going somewhere?" Running as far from Gramps's family as a tank of gas would take her sounded great to Claire.

"Mom and Ruby are going to Yuccaville." Kate was still grinning as if she'd slept with a coat hanger in her mouth. Her frozen jack-in-the-box expression was starting to give Claire the willies.

"They're going to go shopping." Jess sounded a bit wistful. "And have their nails done."

Claire leaned against the counter. "I don't think that's a good idea, Mom."

"I don't think it's any of your business, young lady." Deborah's pale blue eyes challenged Claire.

Ruby came swooshing through the curtain, her purse in one hand and her pickup keys jingling in the other. "Sorry to bother you, Claire, but your mom insists on kidnapping me for the day."

"Ruby could use some pre-wedding pampering." Deborah's smile was a total forgery. "Coddling for the bride-to-be."

Claire glared at her mom. More like strangling for the bride-to-be if Deborah was allowed to spend the day alone with Ruby. An idea flitted into Claire's head. "You're right, Mom."

"I am?" Deborah did a double-take. "I mean, I know I am."

"And since Jess is the maid-of-honor, she should go with you guys and enjoy the pampering, too. It will be a little event just for the bridal party."

Jess's gaze whipped to Ruby, her mouth open in a half-grin, her eyes sparkling. "Oh, can I, Mom? Please?"

Deborah scowled at Claire, thunder rumbling over her brows.

"That's not up to me, honey." Ruby looked at Deborah.

In a heartbeat, Deborah was all teeth and titters. "Of course you can go, Jessica. It will be fun."

Jess squealed. "Thank you, thank you, thank you!" She skipped to the door behind her mom and Deborah. "This is going to be so cool."

Claire and Kate followed them out onto the porch.

"Do you realize that we're going to be sisters soon?" Jess asked Deborah as she hopped down the steps. "I've always wanted a sister. I mean, you're a lot older than I wanted, but it's not like you're going to die tomorrow."

Claire laughed under her breath at the visible tightening of her mother's shoulders.

"Oh, Claire." Ruby paused as she opened the driver's side door of the old Ford pickup and let Jess slide into the middle of the bench seat. "I forgot to tell you that the toilet in the men's restroom down by site B23 is plugged again."

"Crap!" Claire growled in her throat.

Kate snickered. "Literally."

Ruby shut her door and started the truck. She leaned out her open window. "We'll be back this afternoon."

"Have a good time." Claire waved at Jess and Ruby, avoiding her mother's furious gaze.

As the pickup rattled off down the drive and over the bridge, Kate sighed. "That was close. Quick thinking on your part. I'm impressed."

"You should be. I haven't even had any caffeine yet." The ringing of the phone caught Claire's ear. She rushed inside and picked up the receiver. "Dancing Winnebagos R.V. Park."

"Good morning." A familiar male voice she couldn't quite place came through the line. "Is Kate Morgan there?"

Claire glanced at her sister, who was chewing on her lower lip while staring at the rack of granola bars. "May I tell her who's calling?"

"Porter Banks."

* * *

The late afternoon sunshine reflected off the front window of a shiny blue Ford F250 pickup parked in front of the General Store.

Claire looked across the valley at the violet rain veil that dangled from thick, dark clouds; the whole mess aiming for the Rabo de Gallo Mountains in the distance. Jackrabbit Junction had escaped the apocalypse—this time.

Noticing Mabel's polished black hood as she walked by the old Mercury, Claire wiped her forehead and then grimaced at the coat of grit and sweat on her skin.

Her shoulders drooped after a day of rolling with the punches.

First, she hadn't been able to crack the safe.

Then that damned toilet won round two, at least until she could make a trip to Yuccaville for some plumbing parts.

Next, one of the washing machines choked on a sock and proceeded to leak all over the floor in the laundry room when Claire performed a modified version of the Heimlich on it.

Then, the grand finale—while weed-whacking around the tool shed, a rattlesnake shot out of the knee-high grass, rattled and hissed, and chased Claire up onto a picnic table. For thirty minutes, she baked in the sunshine at what felt close to 450 degrees, and squished roving harvester ants for entertainment until the snake finished sunning itself and slithered away.

She loosened her tool belt and let it hang low on her hips as she climbed the porch steps. A storm-fresh breeze swirled past, tickling the nape of her neck with tendrils of hair that had escaped from her ponytail. With one last glance at the receding squall, she pulled open the door.

The cardboard version of Elvis stood at the end of the chips and pretzels aisle as usual, offering Claire his can of Diet Coke. She tapped him on the nose as she passed by. "Where is everyone, Elvis the Pelvis?"

She grabbed a Hostess Cherry Pie from the shelf and tossed a dollar bill onto the counter. A brochure for Sam's Town Hotel and Casino lay next to the spare change dish. On the radio, Randy Travis sang about being too gone for too long. Claire wished he were singing about her.

Lumbering toward the green curtain, she tore open the wrapper, crammed a third of the pie in her mouth, and groaned as the sweet cherry filling and glazed pastry dough spread over every taste bud.

All she wanted to do was crawl into a tub of cool water and soak her bones, a margarita in one hand and pastrami on rye in the other. Maybe Mac could peel some grapes for her, run a sponge over her back, hand wash her …

As she stepped through the curtain, two things hit her at once.

First, the aroma of vanilla and cedar.

Second, the urge to run.

Across the rec room, Deborah sat on the couch, her back straight, her hands folded and resting on one knee—a Norman Rockwell picture of Ms. Prim and Proper, except for the gape-jawed stare she was giving Claire. Next to Deborah, Porter Banks leaned back against the cushions, looking like he'd just finished shooting a Stetson-for-Men commercial and forgotten to shuck the ostrich-skin boots and cowboy hat.

"Claire!" Deborah's tone was high and screechy.

Claire winced. She'd heard similar sounding shrieks coming from the baboon cage at the Rapid City Zoo last summer. She swallowed the lump of cherry pastry in her throat and waved, struggling to smile politely at the romance novel cover-model now rising to his feet.

"Hello, Claire." Porter's extra white teeth nearly blinded her. His green eyes flirted as his gaze traveled down over Daffy Duck to her grease-smeared jeans.

Kate flounced into the room from the hallway leading back to Ruby and Gramps's bedroom. "Thanks for waiting, Porter."

Her hips swished more than usual under her paisley, sarong-style skirt. Her blonde curls bounced with every step. A sweet-smelling, fruity cloud of Angel perfume followed her into the room.

When Kate saw Claire, a squawk of laughter burst from her mouth, which she quickly covered with her hand. Her shoulders shook under her mint green tank top.

"Oh, can it!" Claire took another bite of her cherry pie. So she was a little dirty, what was the big deal? There hadn't been time to run for cover when that dust devil had swirled along the drive, coating her with sand and dust.

"And that's our cue to leave." Kate grabbed Porter by the arm and tugged him toward the curtain. "Don't wait up."

Claire stepped to the side.

"Nice to see you again, Claire." Porter tipped his hat as he skirted her. He grinned back at Deborah. "I sure enjoyed meeting you, Ms. Morgan. I can see now where your girls get their good looks."

Rolling her eyes at her mother's blush, Claire breathed a sigh of relief after they disappeared through the curtain. Swallowing the last of her pie, she headed for the kitchen. The smell of fried burgers teased her stomach.

Gramps peeked out from the kitchen doorway. "Are they gone?" He didn't even blink when he caught sight of Claire. "Oh, there you are. Did you get that toilet fixed?"

Ruby walked out around him, took one look at Claire, and smiled. "Let me get you a washcloth." She hurried past Claire.

Nostrils flared, Deborah whirled on Claire. "That was rude and disgusting."

"What? I was chewing with my mouth closed."

The back door opened and Chester and Manny barreled inside.

"And when I asked her to blow on my schnitzel," Chester said, "she slapped me." He stopped short when he realized he had an audience. He started wheezing when his gaze hit Claire. "Damn, girl. You look like you crawled out of the back end of a mule."

"Ay yi yi, *mi bonita*." Manny rubbed his hands together, his eyes glued on her hips. "You're wearing your tool belt. I love a woman who knows how to handle a tool."

Claire smirked. Him and Mac both.

"Get your mind out of the gutter, Carrera." Gramps shot Manny a one-eyed glare. "And stop looking at my granddaughter like that."

"Howdy, boys." Ruby handed Claire a wet pink washrag. "Supper's ready for y'all."

Deborah sniffed and wrinkled her upper lip as if Ruby had cooked Lutefisk. She grabbed her Coach designer purse from the bar and started toward the back door.

"Where are you going?" Gramps asked.

"I have some reading to do."

"You can do that after you eat the food Ruby cooked for you." Gramps poured on the guilt, like a true parent.

"Let the games begin." Chester unfolded the card table.

Claire wiped her cheek and looked down at the rag. A brown smudge stained the pink terry cloth. A spit bath with a dainty washcloth wasn't going to cut it. When she was finished, she was going to have to scour the tub clean.

While Deborah and Gramps argued about eating at the kitchen table instead of the card table, Claire slipped into the bathroom and locked the door behind her. The shower beckoned.

A bubble of laughter popped in her throat when she caught sight of herself in the mirror. She looked like she'd been dragged behind a horse across the desert floor.

She pulled her shirt over her head and unbuttoned her jeans. As soon as she'd scrubbed her skin clean and grabbed some supper, she planned on sneaking up to Mac's room and daydreaming about the things she would do to him later tonight.

The lock on the bedroom door would keep her mother out. There was no way she wanted to spend another evening listening to Deborah's lectures on etiquette and morality, not with the Mac-filled fantasies Claire had been stirring up all day.

She paused in the midst of taking her socks off, chewed her bottom lip, and fretted for a moment about Mac being alone up in the Lucky Monk. Cave-ins were always a possibility, as well as crazy bitches with guns, which they'd both learned from experience.

Somebody pounded on the door.

She jumped. "What?"

"What are you doing in there?" Gramps asked in her favorite barking tone of his.

"Knitting you a sweater. What do you think?"

"Well, hurry up."

"There are two other bathrooms in this house."

"You're up next in the tournament."

Claire sighed. "Can't someone sit in for me?"

"No. You've got five minutes."

"Then what? You'll break the door down?"

"I know where Ruby keeps the key. I'll send your mother in there to get you."

Claire grimaced at her reflection in the mirror. Gramps knew how to play dirty. "I thought she was going back to the R.V. to read."

"She did, too. But she can't."

"Why not?"

"Because she's your Euchre partner tonight."

Chapter Eight

"That Porter is a real gentleman," Deborah said as she rearranged the cards in her hand. "He actually asked me what time he should have Kate back here. Can you believe that?"

She looked across the table at Claire, sporting a porcelain smile that barely reached the corners of her lips, let alone her eyes. "Claire, didn't you tell me MacDonald asked your grandfather for permission to date you?"

"No, Mother."

White knuckled, Claire stared blindly at her own cards, her tongue raw from biting it repeatedly while Deborah crowed praises for a man with whom she'd spent a grand total of ten minutes trading weather forecasts.

She tipped back her Corona, barely tasting it. Cigar smoke and Chanel No. 5 swirled around on the air conditioned trade winds that circled the rec room.

"Oh, that's right. I'd forgotten that MacDonald isn't concerned with your family's feelings. My mistake."

With Ruby off to Yuccaville to pick up Jess from a friend's house, Deborah had no incentive to censor her comments about Mac and his so-called shortcomings. But Claire was about to give her mom a reason. She just wasn't sure if cramming a bear claw doughnut in Deborah's mouth and then duct taping her lips shut would be enough.

"Claire, it's your bid." Gramps thumped his fingers on the table, puffing on his cigar. His knickers were wadded up double-knot tight because he and Manny needed only one more trick to win the game. "And that tic is back in your eye, girl."

Closing the guilty eye, Claire shot Gramps a Cyclops glare over the top of her cards. His cheeks creased slightly as he noticeably fought to keep a grin from surfacing.

"Did you see how Porter kissed the back of my hand?" Deborah sipped her second glass of White Zinfandel. "I haven't had a young man kiss my hand since I was in college." She tittered as she lowered her glass to the table.

Claire winced. Whistling tea kettles grated less on her nerves.

"Claire, bid." Gramps nudged her again.

Chester belched from where he sat at the bar watching them play. "Did he kiss your hand, too, Claire?" The smirk on his face said he already knew the answer.

"Of course he didn't." Deborah spoke for Claire, like any good, overbearing mother. "I don't blame him either. You saw how filthy she was."

Her stomach churning with tension, Claire stared down at her cards. She tried to focus on the suits and numbers. Manners instilled back when she wore pigtails kept her from snarling at her mother in front of Chester and Manny, but her teeth were going to crack if she gritted them much harder.

"Seems to me," Manny said, "a gentleman would look past a little dirt to have a chance to touch his lips to the hand of a beautiful woman."

Claire shot him a quick smile.

Gramps slammed down his cards. "Would you quit horsing around and bid already, Claire!"

"Fine! I'm going to shoot." That should shut Gramps up.

The only way to keep him from basking in the spoils of victory was to try to win all of the tricks this hand and steal the game out from under Manny and Gramps.

"Alone?" Manny asked.

"No." Claire laid her worst card face-down on the table and pushed it across to her mother. "Give me your best heart."

Gramps snickered. "I'm not sure Deborah even has one."

Deborah frowned. "Very funny, Dad." She shoved one card across the table toward Claire and pocketed the rest. "Since I'm sitting out this round, I may as well file my nails. That country bumpkin at the Nail Palace turned my fingertips into daggers."

Claire had always thought her mom's nails grew that way naturally.

She picked up her mother's card—the Queen of clubs. What part of "best heart" had Deborah not understood? Claire stuffed the card in between her others.

Straight faced in spite of this chink in her armor, she told the guys, "Hearts is trump," and led the round with the highest trump card—the Jack of hearts.

Gramps and Manny threw out lower-ranking suit cards. One down, five to go.

"Honestly, Claire." Deborah pulled a short nail file from her purse. "If you want my opinion—"

"I don't." Honest opinions from her mother usually burned in Claire's gut.

She dropped the second highest trump card, the Jack of diamonds, onto the table.

"It would do you some good to be a little more like Kathryn." Deborah filed away on her talons.

Gramps tossed out the nine of diamonds. "So, you want Claire to start lying to the cops?"

Chester guffawed.

"I think she means Claire should bleach her hair blonde and wear short skirts." Manny dropped the Ace of hearts on the pile. "And I for one am all for short skirts."

Chester rolled his cigar in the ashtray. "They say blondes have more fun, but I've known many brunettes who could—"

"I'm referring to Kathryn's choice in men." Deborah had stopped filing. She glared at each of the three stooges in turn.

Claire scooped up the cards and replaced them with the Queen of hearts, her penultimate trump card. "Oh, I get it. You want me to start dating petty thieves."

"Don't get smart with me, Claire Alice." Deborah pointed the file at her. "I'm not your father. I don't think it's cute."

"What's your problem with Mac?" Gramps slapped the Jack of spades on Claire's card.

Manny added the Jack of clubs.

Three down, three to go. Claire's nine of hearts came next— the last trump card out there.

"MacDonald needs someone less refined than Claire. Someone more his social equal."

"Have you forgotten Claire's entrance earlier this evening?" Gramps asked. "She looked like she'd been making mud pies all afternoon. And look at her now, sitting there in her paint-stained shirt and torn jeans. She's not even wearing a bra, for chrissake."

"Hey!" Claire pulled Ruby's windbreaker closed over her purple *Deadwood Rocks!* T-shirt. "You guys are the ones who couldn't wait for me to run to the Winnebago for some clean underwear."

The stash of spare clothes she kept in Ruby's linen closet included jeans, shorts, some old tennis shoes, and a couple of T-shirts—extra clothes she didn't care about getting paint or grease on. But no skivvies or bra, and she'd refused to slip back into the ones she'd sweated in all afternoon.

"Claire is not exactly a model of refinement." Gramps placed the King of clubs down. "No offense, kid."

"None taken." She watched Manny place the ten of diamonds on the stack. "Refinement sounds too much like 'confinement'."

"Her outfit tonight is just a minor setback in my plans for updating her wardrobe."

"I swear to God, Mother, if you lay one manicured finger on my T-shirts, I'll tell Kate that you never really took Mr. Bojangles to that 'nice little farm' out on the prairie."

Deborah flashed Claire a narrow-eyed, silent warning. "I'm just saying that you could use someone to guide you here and there."

"What do you think I am? Some ass-scratching ape?" Claire rolled her eyes and threw out the Ace of spades, Gramps the Ace of diamonds, and Manny the Queen of spades. "Besides, Mac has a master's degree. You've obviously never heard him talk about soil types or plate tectonics at the breakfast table."

One to go and she'd be free of her mother for the night. Crossing her fingers under the table, Claire dropped the Queen of clubs in the center of the table.

Manny sighed and threw his King of spades out of turn.

She looked at Gramps. The grin on his face made her swear. He slapped the Ace of clubs down and howled in victory.

Deborah pulled her cards from her pocket and laid them in the center of the table. Claire flipped over her mom's cards. The King of diamonds mocked her.

"Damn it, Mom. Why didn't you give this one to me? We could have won the game."

"No one likes a sore loser, sweetie." Deborah's gaze remained glued on the nail she was filing. "Besides, you shouldn't have shot. It was too risky. One of these days you're going to learn the importance of using caution and not jumping before you've had a chance to plan things out."

"Whatever!" Claire fell back in her chair. She shoved her stack of won tricks across the table, her shoulders drooping in defeat. Partnering with her mom had added several wrinkles on her face. She'd eat a fly in exchange for a cigarette right now.

"Don't 'whatever' me. You're thirty-four years old."

"Thirty-three and a half."

"You have yet to settle down with a good man."

"Have you forgotten that I live with Mac?"

"And raise a family of your own."

"If this is about you wanting grandchildren—"

"No, it's not about grandchildren. It's about you being a responsible, well-groomed woman. Take Kathryn, for example."

"No, you take Kate." Claire had put up enough with her mom raining glory on her younger sister's deeds for this evening. "I'm going to take Henry."

The dog looked up from where he'd been snoozing on the couch. He stood and stretched.

"We're going to go for a walk. And tonight, when Mac gets back, we're going to have wild and wooly sex. The kind improperly-dressed, intellectually-challenged girls like me revel in. So if you don't want to hear it, stay away from the spare bedroom."

Eyes bulging, Deborah gaped at Claire.

Gramps grimaced and puffed on his cigar.

"What do you mean by 'wooly'?" asked Chester.

Henry hopped to the floor when Claire grabbed his leash and stepped into her flip-flops.

"And for your information, Princess Kate hasn't been a virgin since her sixteenth birthday, while I waited until my eighteenth before letting Stevie Logan go cherry picking. So stuff that in Kate's 'Best Daughter' trophy and shove it."

Claire slammed out the back door with Henry in tow.

* * *

Mac pulled up next to the General Store and cut the engine. The rec room lights blazed through the window in the back door. Mabel gleamed under the outside nightlight, but Ruby's truck was gone and chances were, so was Ruby.

After spending the last ten hours inside a hole in the earth, Mac wanted nothing more than to wash the dirt from his body and touch Claire, but if Harley was home, he couldn't walk in the back door looking like he'd been in a mine all day. Claire's grandpa would tie him in a chair and put a spotlight on his face until Mac coughed up all the details and then some about the letters to Ruby.

He stepped to the ground, slinging his pack over his back. The pickup engine ticked as it cooled. The willow tree next to the house quivered in the lukewarm breeze.

He tiptoed up to one of the rec room windows and peeked inside. Harley, Chester, Manny, and Deborah sat at the card table, playing cards, drinking beer—well, except for Deborah, she had a half-full glass of wine in front of her.

Where was Claire? He glanced up at the spare room window. The light was off. Maybe she was with Ruby.

He rubbed the back of his neck, his skin sticky. So much for that shower. Then he remembered Harley's R.V.

Crunching along under the waning moon toward the Winnebago, his thoughts slipped back underground.

The mine hadn't given up its secrets, if there were any. Joe's old maps were outdated—several tunnels not shown, others now blocked by cave-ins. But the maps were all Mac had, since the library's stash had been pilfered. He'd taken his time, noting changes on the maps, inspecting the walls and ceiling for cracks, using spray paint as bread crumbs so he didn't end up lost in the black maze.

The Winnebago's windows were dark, the door locked. Maybe Harley still kept a spare key hidden inside the rear bumper.

Down by Jackrabbit Creek, Chorus frogs trilled their raspy tunes, sounding like fingernails running over comb teeth. High up in one of the cottonwoods, a Western Screech owl greeted him with a soft "cr-r-oo-oo-oo-oo."

Desert summer nights reminded him of a rave party, with hundreds of mammals, amphibians, and insects all clamoring and bumping against each other under the Milky Way.

He squatted next to the back bumper avoiding a patch of rank-smelling clammyweed and reached underneath. His fingers brushed over the magnetic key box.

The hinges creaked as he swung open the R.V.'s door. With two claps the light overhead flickered to life. He trod softly across the linoleum floor even though the place was empty.

Somebody had opened the windows. A breeze rippled the curtains.

Mac didn't waste any time while showering; Deborah or Kate could walk into the Winnebago at any minute and he didn't want to risk seeing either of them, especially the former.

Squeaky clean, still damp around the edges, he slid into his jeans. He grabbed his pack and dug out the extra T-shirt he kept there, slipping it over his head. With one last glance in the bathroom mirror to make sure he'd washed off all traces of the Lucky Monk, he clapped the lights off, swung open the door, and stepped down into the night.

"Come here often?" A soft voice asked.

Mac lowered his pack to the ground and walked over to where Claire stood in the shadows under the awning. "Not often enough."

He ran his hands down her arms, slid his fingers between hers, and sandwiched her against the R.V.'s aluminum siding.

"You're late," she whispered as he nuzzled her neck.

He dragged his lips along her jaw line. "I missed you."

She moaned as his mouth covered hers.

"You taste like chocolate." He released her fingers so he could explore the warm skin under her shirt.

"It's the M&Ms."

He nibbled on her collarbone; his fingertips slid up her smooth stomach and paused. "Hey, you're not wearing a bra."

Her laugh sounded low and husky.

His body hardened, eager to explore further. "Let's go inside."

"We can't." She delved her fingers into his hair, dragging his lips back to hers.

"Why not?" he asked when he came up for air.

"Because my mom could be back any minute, and what I plan on doing to you is going to be loud and take a while."

"Jesus, Claire." Mac pressed harder against her and savored her sweetness, immersing himself in her scent and softness. She filled his palms, so full and inviting.

Her hand pressed his zipper, and he almost hoisted her over his shoulder, carried her down by the creek, and had his way with her on the bank.

Instead, he pulled away from the she-devil's grasp and took several deep breaths. He needed to focus on something besides Claire's body for a few minutes.

Claire adjusted her shirt, her breath as choppy as his. "Did you find anything at the mine?"

Good idea, talk about the mine. "Just some empty ore carts and a dead possum."

"Yuck." She grabbed Henry's leash from the back of a lawn chair. "So now what?"

"Dig deeper. It's an expansive mine with a lot of real estate left to cover."

"Are you going back up there tomorrow?"

"Yes." He stuffed his hands in his pockets to keep from grabbing her and yanking her shirt over her head.

"I don't want you to."

"I have to."

"Is there anything I can do to stop you?"

Mac chuckled. "Tie me to the bed."

"Okay."

"I forgot to tell you this morning that I'm going home tomorrow night."

Her forehead wrinkled. "But you don't have to be back to work until Tuesday."

"I'm going to pay a visit to Leo Scott."

He hoped a little face-to-face exchange would land some answers—like who was so hell bent on taking the Lucky Monk mine from Ruby. Mac would work on figuring out the "why" part on his own.

Claire closed the distance between them. "When are you leaving for the mine tomorrow?"

"Before Harley wakes up."

She ran her fingertip down his sternum. "So, I get you until sunrise?"

He captured her hand at the waistline of his jeans. "Unless you put me in a coma."

"I'll give it the old college try."

Lifting her palm, he kissed the center of it. "Let's go back to Ruby's."

She moaned and curled her fingers, rubbing her knuckles along his stubble-covered jaw. "Let me just run inside and get some underwear."

"You're not wearing underwear either?" Screw the bed, the creek bank would do just fine. A little sand never hurt anyone.

"I'm totally commando, baby." Handing him Henry's leash, she asked, "Will you get Henry? He's down by the creek taking care of doggie business."

Then she took the spare key from him, unlocked the door, and stepped into the darkness. He listened to her footfalls as she walked to the back bedroom.

"Henry?" Mac shook the bell on the dog's leash.

The thick thatch of mesquite behind the R.V. rattled.

Inside the Winnebago, the bedroom light switched on. A soft glow spilled out from the window.

"Henry?"

Something growled from under the thicket.

"Henry!" Mac walked toward the bushes. "Come here, boy."

Hisses came from the brush.

Crap! Somebody's cat was about to tear Henry a new ass. Mac squatted, spreading the low branches, looking for a patch of white beagle fur.

The growling stopped, replaced by a rhythmic thumping.

Thumping? Mac frowned; cats didn't thump. Pack rats thumped their tails. Skunks thumped their feet.

He rose and took several steps back. "Henry?"

Suddenly, something small and black bolted toward him from the bush. Henry chased it, hot on its tail—its long black tail with a white stripe running down the center of it.

Mac leapt aside.

The skunk veered, raced past the lawn table, and dashed up the Winnebago's steps. Henry followed it through the door and into the darkness beyond.

"Oh, shit!" Mac whispered, frozen. He heard a crash.

The lights came on, thanks to the Clapper.

Henry barked.

The skunk growled, thumping again.

Another crash. The lights went out.

A series of thumps and hisses and barks followed, the light flicking on and off. The Winnebago flashed and pinged like an oversized pinball machine.

"What in the hell?" Mac heard Claire yell. The sound of her voice snapped him out of his paralysis. He sprinted to the door.

The light went out again.

Henry howled and Claire screamed.

* * *

Sunday, August 15th

Jess sat behind the General Store counter, twirling her hair. "I can still smell that skunk on you."

Claire stuffed half a Twinkie in her mouth to keep from biting Jess's head off. The sponge cake was tasteless on her tongue. Her sense of smell still suffered from olfactory fatigue.

She swallowed the lump of dough. "Spray some more perfume."

"Where's Mac?"

Claire pulled another handful of Milky Way candy bars from the box and lined them up on the shelf. "You just asked me that a half hour ago and nothing has changed since then."

"I can't remember your answer. I think that skunk smell has zapped my brain."

Only Ruby and Claire knew that Mac had gone up to the mine today. Ruby didn't want Jess knowing because she'd undoubtedly let it leak to Gramps.

Tossing the empty cardboard box toward the trash can, Claire ripped open a box of Baby Ruth bars. "He's gone to Bisbee again today."

"Oh, that's right—to see an old friend."

Worried Jess might be onto her, Claire glanced at the girl. Jess's head bobbed to some tune beating in her brain while she stared into a small mirror, puckering her glossed lips repeatedly. "I hope Mom buys me that mini-skirt we saw in the store window yesterday."

Nope, not a single suspicious thought in that head.

Claire stacked Baby Ruths on the shelf and wondered if Ruby had slit her wrists yet. Since the skunk spray had saturated everything in the R.V., including Kate and Deborah's clothes, Ruby had volunteered to take the two women shopping this morning, unaware that taming hungry lions would have been less dangerous. Unfortunately, being a Sunday, the only store open in Yuccaville was a secondhand one, and Claire doubted they'd find any Ralph Lauren, Abercrombie & Fitch, or Ann Taylor labels hanging on the racks.

Luckily for Claire, she had the spare painting clothes she could wear until Mac returned next weekend with reinforcements. She just needed to find another dress for the wedding, but she had a week to do that.

The bells over the door jingled. Claire winced in anticipation of a skunk-smell comment from another customer.

"Ah, my two favorite *chicas*." Manny closed the door behind him, his smile wide—suspiciously so.

"What are you doing in here?" Claire finished stacking Baby Ruths and tossed the box aside. "You're supposed to be helping Gramps and Chester gut the Winnebago."

After being reminded of all the times during the war that Gramps had saved their asses, Chester and Manny had grudgingly been manipulated to help.

"Woo wee!" Jess spritzed Manny with perfume as he approached the counter. "And I thought Claire was stinky."

Gramps had driven the R.V. to the back of the park next to the tool shed. His insurance company was going to give him some money to pay for a detailed detoxification, but he wanted to gut the Winnebago to remove as much of the stench as possible before driving it to the closest detailer he could find—in Tucson.

"I needed a break from the frontlines." Manny pointed at the guestbook leaning between the cash register and the wall. "Will you hand me that book, *por favor*?"

Her nose pinched shut, Jess dropped the book onto the counter. She hopped off the chair and walked over to the curtain, putting some distance between her and Manny. "Maybe you should look at it outside."

"I'll just be *un segundo*." Manny flipped through the pages.

Claire moved up beside him. "What are you doing?"

"Finding out the name of my future wife."

As if she hadn't heard that line before from Don Juan Sr. Claire leaned against the counter. "How's Gramps doing?"

While she hadn't lured the skunk into the Winnebago, she couldn't help feeling guilty about the whole smelly incident. Gramps loved that R.V., almost as much as he did Mabel.

"I don't know. I couldn't see him through the tears in my eyes." Manny trailed his finger down one of the pages. "Aha!" He grabbed the pen next to the cash register and wrote Rebecca Hawthorne on his palm.

Claire grinned. "When is the wedding?"

"Soon, *mi amor*." He stood back, blowing the ink dry on his hand. The book pages fluttered closed, leaving the inside front cover showing. "I just need to introduce myself first."

With a bounce in his step, he disappeared out the door.

"Ick." Jess slipped back behind the counter and sprayed more perfume. "You guys all need a bath."

After last night, what Claire needed was a long vacation far from the desert. Mac had tried to save her from the skunk, but by the time he'd clambered into the R.V., the skunk had darted back outside, and Claire and Henry were temporarily blinded from the spray. He led them both to a lawn chair and left Claire holding Henry's leash while he ran back to Ruby's to get some help.

Alone in the watery shadows, Claire's sinuses had drained and drained. When the cavalry arrived, the liquid exorcism began. First a vinegar scrub down, then a cold water rinse from the hose. By her third bath, her skin was beyond pruned—closer to raisined. It had taken an hour for the shakes to stop.

Henry hadn't faired much better. The little shit now sat in the shade tied to one of the front porch posts, quarantined until Gramps got back from tearing apart the R.V.

Claire blinked out of her reverie to find Jess doodling on the front page of the guest book.

"What are you doing? That's going to tick off your mom." She pulled the book away and looked down at the sideways eights Jess had been drawing.

"Just drawing the symbol for infinity. I learned about infinity in math last year."

Claire chewed on her lower lip. She'd seen that symbol somewhere lately—in this very store.

"Besides, somebody else wrote on the page first." Jess blew a bubble and let it pop in Claire's ear.

Claire stared down at the word "infinity" written in the bottom left corner of the first page. She recognized Joe's writing. After all of the documents she'd sifted through in his office, she knew his squiggles better than her own.

"Mom should just be happy I'm practicing my math skills."

Why would Joe write that word in the guest book? From what Claire had learned about Joe over the last few months, doodling was not his style. Her gut told her that there was a meaning behind the word, maybe even a purpose.

"Do you think it will come off with an eraser?" Jess pulled the book back toward her, uncovering the campground map taped to the counter below it.

Then Claire saw it. Right there, in the middle of the map, like a flashing neon Vegas marquee—the infinity symbol, in the tent-camping only section. The drive that connected each of the eight campsites looked like a sideways eight, only the corners weren't quite as round.

"Oh, crap. This eraser is all dried out." Jess tossed her pencil aside. "Now I've smudged the page."

Claire rubbed her jaw. That must be why Joe labeled those sites with an I instead of an A or B. I for infinity.

"What's so important about infinity?" Claire asked aloud.

"Infinity isn't a real number, but could be considered part of an extended real number line," Jess recited, as if reading from a dictionary.

Claire looked up at Jess. The last part of what the girl said replayed in her head: *part of an extended real number line.* She slapped her palms on the counter. "That's it!"

Jess squawked in surprise. The pencil and guestbook went flying into the wall behind her.

"Paper! I need paper." Claire grabbed a spare campground map. "Even better."

Jess coughed out her gum into her palm. "You need help. I almost choked!"

"Sorry about that." Claire circled the eight site numbers. "Stay here. I'll be right back." She dashed toward the curtain.

"Where are you going?" Jess yelled after her.

Claire took the basement steps two at a time, nearly falling down the last three. She hit the lights. The bookcase was still pulled away from the wall. She hadn't had a chance to put the office back in order since yesterday morning. Kneeling on the shag carpet, Claire held up the map. Her hand shook as she read the numbers aloud and punched them into the keypad. "5, 3, 8, 2, 9, 1, 7, 4."

Nothing happened. "Shit."

Hitting the Clear button, she reversed the numbers. A clicking sound came from the door.

Her breath caught.

The safe door popped open.

Chapter Nine

Miles away from Claire and Harley's Winnebago, deep in the belly of Wiggle Toe Mountain, Mac could still smell that damned skunk. Short of snorting vinegar, he figured nothing but time would erase the stench from his olfactory memory.

The air in the Lucky Monk mine felt cool and heavy. The light on his hard hat cast elongated shadows that wavered and danced with every step. Blackness pursued him, hot on his heels, always hovering out of the corner of his eyes.

Pebbles crunching under his boots, he navigated the stone tunnels. Every hundred feet or so, he stopped to study Joe's maps and make notes of changes.

The morning had been productive. Several hundred feet back in a side tunnel, the throat of a shaft had been encrusted with ocean-blue chalcanthite, a mineral usually found near the surface of copper deposits. The aggregates glittered like a crystal choker under Mac's flashlight beam.

He plucked a few small samples and doused them with water from his canteen. They dissolved quickly in his palm, turning the small pool murky blue—and poisonous to the last drop.

Further back, a vein of copper on one wall was nearly invisible under a mosaic of quartz mixed with chrysocolla, an opaque greenish-blue mineral that crooked dealers sold as actual turquoise to naïve tourists at the rock and gem show in Tucson.

Now, as Mac continued along the main adit to another unmapped side tunnel he'd found yesterday afternoon, he wondered how Joe had gotten his hands on the Lucky Monk and the other three mines. Had he purchased them legally? Won them in a card game? Inherited them from a long lost uncle?

Mac understood why Joe had wanted them, especially with the racket the guy had been running. The mines offered an excellent hiding place for stolen goods, and the old wagon trails leading up to two of them were wide enough for a four-wheel drive truck to navigate.

But who had owned them before Joe? The original prospectors? Their descendants? And how had the mines evaded the hands of the Copper Snake Mining Company all these years?

Following the adit as it curved to the right, Mac took a sip of water from his canteen. Shadowy amorphous figures slunk back against the walls as he passed, reminding him of the Mine Monk spirit from European folktales he'd read about years ago.

The miners of old Europe were a superstitious lot, which didn't surprise Mac considering they'd used fire to light their way deep into the earth where pockets of methane gas often accumulated. The explosions would either kill them outright or leave them buried, sealed up tight in a pitch-black tomb with suffocation as their only way out.

Stories abounded of ghostly spirits of the earth, the tale of the Mine Monk being one of these. Sometimes benevolent, sometimes not, the monk would make an appearance in black robes, its face hooded. Mac assumed the prospector who filed the original claim for the Lucky Monk mine had heard his fair share of ghost stories.

The tunnel veered to the right; Mac followed. Ten feet in front of him, a paper cup lay on its side on the stone floor.

Litter was nothing new to the underground world. Back before Budweiser cans and plastic Evian bottles, there had been soda pop tabs and Necco Wafer wrappers, rusted tin cans with serrated lids and hand-sewn leather gloves, broken shovel handles and dented ore carts.

Mac squatted next to the coffee cup. The fact that someone had tossed it on the floor of Ruby's mine wasn't what made his hands clammy. What had his heart knocking was that the cup hadn't been here last night when he'd walked along this section of the adit.

He picked up the cup and peeked through the small opening in the lid. A sip of brown liquid still sloshed in the bottom.

Someone had been in the Lucky Monk last night.

Kids trespassed in mines often, especially if the entrances were partially blocked off with "No Trespassing" signs. But kids left broken beer bottles and cigarette butts, not coffee cups.

Maybe it was the Mine Monk.

Mac stood, suddenly feeling like he was in the crosshairs of a scope. He squinted into the thick shadows in front of him, searching for movement, his ears straining to pick up any sound besides his own breathing.

The hairs on the back of his neck prickled. He whirled around, looking back the way he'd come. The darkness at the edge of his vision teased him with glimpses of shifting shapes.

Déjà vu had him wiping his palms on his jeans.

Unlike Claire, his imagination rarely took flight, his preferred modus operandi based on rational, logical planning rather than radical theories or suspicious notions. But after being hunted by a crazed killer through the stone corridors of Socrates Pit and being deliberately entombed in Two Jakes last spring, his pulse often danced the jitterbug when he traipsed through these oversized worm holes.

Mac glanced down at his watch. He'd planned on scouting around in the Lucky Monk for a few more hours, but the sudden craving for sunshine, fresh air, even humidity, changed his mind.

He left the cup where he'd found it and hiked toward the entrance. Speeding up to a jog as he rounded the corner, he expected to hear the sound of boots clapping on the stone floor behind him at any moment.

* * *

The safe door swung open.

Claire dropped onto her butt, legs crossed, and stared at the three shelves lined with violet felt material. She scooted closer, not wanting to touch anything until she'd had a chance to thoroughly inspect how Joe had left the contents. She'd learned over the summer, after watching a season's worth of *CSI: Crime Scene Investigation*, that sometimes placement was as telling as the evidence itself.

A derringer laid on the left side of the top shelf, its stubby nose buried in a miniature holster. A leather strap wide enough to encircle a calf or bicep wove through two slits in the holster. A box of .22 caliber cartridges sat on the other side of the strap, taking up most of the remaining shelf space.

So, in addition to a double-barreled shotgun and a .357 Magnum Ruby kept stashed in her closet, Joe had also had a derringer. Was the tiny pistol just an antique or had he actually carried it? Used it?

She'd always pictured Joe's fingers as fat and stubby, like thick Jimmy Dean sausage links, covered with greasy potato chip crumbs—fingers that couldn't remove such a tiny gun from its elf-sized holster without shooting off a pinkie or a toe in the process.

A pocket watch monopolized the middle shelf, centered as if on display under a spotlight along with the other crown jewels in the Tower of London. The polished gold casing beckoned Claire to pick it up and rub her fingers over the smooth face. Clasping her hands together, she resisted the urge to touch and leaned closer, breathing all over it.

Tiny flowers and ovals rimmed the gold case, raised on the surface rather than carved into the metal. The pastel painting on the cover had pale green trees dotting the landscape. Small indistinguishable buildings rose in the distance. A carriage seemed to be the focal point, with two dark horses hitched to it. Crowds of people filled the foreground—a depiction of a fair or some festival possibly. Whatever the subject matter, the piece shone with nineteenth century European elegance.

Claire chewed on her thumb. Maybe she should show it to her mother.

Deborah glued herself to the television every time *Antiques Roadshow* was on PBS. She'd recorded volumes and volumes of it. Her obsession with the program had been one of the many reasons Claire's father had walked the plank.

Or, maybe Claire should take the watch to Tucson to have it examined, find out the details on its age and value.

Then again, just bringing the piece out into the open could endanger Ruby's welfare, even her life, along with Jess and Gramps's. If Joe had stolen the watch, the police or FBI might come down hard on Ruby, seize her assets, tear her house apart looking for other stolen goods.

Worse, though, would be if word of the pocket watch reached one of Joe's ex-business partners—someone with a grudge or an unpaid debt. Someone who didn't waste time with badges when it came to shooting.

On second thought, Claire would talk to Mac and Ruby. Let them weigh the risks.

Staring at the watch, she could see why someone would break into Ruby's place to steal it. Its beauty alone would certainly lure eager fingers, even without the added value of its legacy.

A bag with a red and black angular design woven into the natural-looking fibers filled the bottom shelf from side to side, its width crammed into the space. Claire had seen similar, but more detailed and sophisticated, versions of the design on some Anasazi and Mogollon pottery at the Arizona State Museum.

The office door hinges creaked behind her.

"Claire?" Jess whispered.

Claire tried to slam the safe door closed before Jess could take full inventory of the pieces inside, but the locking bolts still stuck out, so the door bounced back open.

The bag fell onto the floor before Claire could catch it. She pushed the door shut again and held it there this time while frowning at Jess. "I told you to stay put. Who's watching the store?"

"Nobody. It's been dead all morning."

"Jess, your mom said—"

"I locked the door and taped up a note that we'll be back in five minutes. For all they know, I had to use the bathroom." Jess squatted next to Claire and pointed toward the bag. "What's that? Some old toy?"

A horse made out of bound twigs stuck half way out of the bag.

Claire let go of the safe door, which remained mostly closed this time. She picked up the twig figure. "I don't think it's a toy."

"Are there more of them in the bag?"

Claire laid the figure on her thigh and gingerly reached her hand in the bag opening. Something scratchy brushed her fingertips, some kind of cloth, possibly. She pulled it out and unrolled it.

"Looks like some kind of homemade sandal," she said, brushing her fingers over the rectangular sole made of brittle, woven fibers. There was a hole in the heel where the fibers had loosened or worn away. A strip of scarred, tattered leather hung from it.

"This might be the piece that tied it to your ankle." Several strands of what felt like human hair lay in a flat loop near the front edge. "And this could be for your big toe."

"Cool." Jess echoed Claire's thoughts. "How old do you think it is? All of the drawings in our history books show the native people wearing moccasins."

"I don't know." Claire turned the sandal over, then held it out toward Jess. "My nose is fried. What's it smell like?"

Jess jerked back. "You want me to sniff a shoe that hasn't been washed for like hundreds of years? I don't think so."

"Come on, you big chicken. I just want to know if it smells like grass or straw or what."

Jess shook her head.

"I'll give you a dollar."

"Make it twenty."

Claire laughed. "Dream on. How about five?"

"I won't do it for under ten. I have my standards."

"Fine, ten. Now smell."

Jess leaned down and sniffed the sandal.

"Well? Old grass?"

"No. More like old dirt."

Claire rubbed her brow. Why would something hidden for years in Joe's safe smell like dirt?

Jess nodded at the bag. "It looks like there is something still in there."

Claire stuck her hand in past her wrist this time. There was something in the bottom. The texture reminded Claire of dried leather, the surface bumpy. As she tried to draw it out, it kept getting caught in the fibers of the bag.

"What is it?" Jess leaned close, her eyes wide.

Claire could actually smell the fruity perfume Jess had been spritzing all morning, which meant the kid must be swimming in it. Ruby's poor customers were in for a treat if they popped into the General Store today.

With a gentle, but firm tug, Claire pulled the last item free. She flipped it over and blinked.

Holy shit!

Jess screamed in her ear.

* * *

"I found a hand," Claire whispered to Kate an hour later over a BLT sandwich while the two of them sat on The Shaft's back patio.

"You found a what?" Kate blurted.

"Shhh! A hand." Claire swallowed some sweet, icy lemonade. Finally, her taste buds were coming back online.

Kate pushed her Jackie O sunglasses on top of her head. "You mean the kind with five fingers."

"Four—the thumb's partly chewed off."

"Why are you whispering? There's nobody else crazy enough to sit out here in this sauna."

"I don't know." Claire brushed away a drop of sweat running down from her temple.

The sun blazed all around them, the large overhead umbrella spotlighting them with shade, which did little to quell the pizza-oven heat. The slight breeze barely ruffled the string of plastic Arizona state flags hanging from the gutter, let alone cut the pea-soup-thick humidity. The glass door into the bar was closed, no doubt to keep the cool air inside.

Eating in the heat usually made Claire nauseated, but she needed to talk to her sister in private, and there was no such thing as privacy at the R.V. park—not with Jess and Deborah patrolling the place. And while Kate hadn't been thrilled at the idea of eating at The Shaft and possibly running into Butch again, no pun intended, Claire had assured her the bar owner took Sundays off. So here they were, roasting and bloating like two-day-old road kill.

On that thought, Claire pushed the last half of her sandwich away and focused on her glass of lemonade. It was sweating, too.

Kate swallowed the last of her sandwich. Vertical lines creased the skin between her blonde eyebrows. "A real hand?"

Claire nodded. "Mummified."

"That's disgusting." Kate's nose wrinkled. "Did you bring it with you?"

"Of course not. It's not a rabbit's foot. It's a freakin' human hand."

Claire shivered at the memory of the feel of the hardened leathery skin, similar to the stiff pig's ears Henry liked to chew on while watching Gunsmoke with Gramps.

Jess's reaction still had Claire's eardrums aching. Bribery hadn't been enough to keep the teenager's lips sealed about their find. Claire had had to resort to blackmail, too.

Which reminded her, before returning to Ruby's, they had to swing by the hardware store to buy the pink fuzzy makeup bag on display in the Ladies' Department—aka Aisle Ten: Housewares, Hosiery, and Hygiene.

"Why was Joe keeping it in a safe?" Kate asked. "Who keeps a mummy's hand in their office?"

These were questions that Claire had already asked herself over and over. Where had the hand come from? Was there a body somewhere too? How long did it take for a body to mummify anyway?

First thing tomorrow, she planned to make a trip to the library in Yuccaville to find some answers. "You got me."

"Do you think it belonged to someone he knew?"

"No. I think Joe would have gotten rid of a body, removed all evidence, not kept souvenirs. He might have been a bad man, but he wasn't twisted."

The patio door slid open and Mac stepped out into the sunshine, shading his eyes.

Claire frowned. She hadn't expected to see him for another few hours.

Kate sipped at her water, oblivious that Mac was walking up behind her. "Are you going to show it to Sheriff Harrison?"

"Show what to the sheriff?" Mac pulled out the chair next to Claire. He skimmed her lips with a kiss and then dropped into the chair.

Claire gave him bonus points for not making any skunk comments.

"Claire found a hand." Kate's blue eyes sparkled.

"How'd you know we were here?" Claire asked Mac, wondering if he'd been back to the perfumery, as she now called the General Store.

"I saw Ruby's Ford out front and figured it was you. Harley wouldn't let you drive Mabel in your condition, huh?"

"He said she's off limits until I stop peeling paint from the walls." Claire offered him a drink of her lemonade.

"Tell him about the hand, Claire."

Mac took a big gulp, then set it back down in front of Claire. "What's Kate talking about?"

"First," Claire said, "tell me why you're back from the mine so soon." Mac didn't change his plans on a whim. She had the feeling something had changed them for him.

"I saw something I didn't like," Mac answered, "so I cut out of there early." He nodded at Claire's sandwich, his eyebrows raised. She shoved the plate toward him.

"Claire figured out how to open the safe," Kate said.

"You opened the safe?" He bit into the BLT.

"Yes." Claire waved his question off. That was old news. She wanted to hear his story. "What did you see in the mine?"

Kate grabbed Mac's arm, gaining his attention. "She figured out the PIN based on clues Joe had planted in the campground map."

Mac turned back to Claire. "I saw a cup. How did you figure out the map had the answers?"

"What do you mean you saw a cup? Mac, you're not making sense. Tell me what happened." It wasn't like him to turn tail and run, not even in the face of a pissed off *javelina.*

"Inside the safe was a mummy hand," Kate added.

"A mummy hand?" Mac stopped chewing and leaned toward Claire. "Has Kate been drinking already?"

"Claire, tell him about the hand."

"Okay, stop, both of you." Claire's head spun. The heat wasn't helping matters. Another hour out here and she'd be wringing out her underwear. "Mac, you explain what happened at the mine, and then I'll fill you in on the safe."

Mac swallowed the last bite of her BLT and pushed the plate to the side. "There's not much to tell. Somebody visited the mine last night after I left."

"Could it have been some kids up there partying?" Claire asked.

"I didn't see any beer bottles or roaches, just a paper coffee cup with a few drips still in it."

Claire sat forward, trying to ignore that her deodorant was melting down her ribs. "You think someone from the mining company was checking it out?"

"I don't know."

"What about that lawyer you told me about?" Kate said to Claire. "The one who keeps sending Ruby letters about the Lucky Monk. Could he have hired someone to check out the mine?"

"That's a possibility. Or maybe Joe hid something in there and one of his old cronies is back in town to get it."

Kate was sitting forward now too. "Or maybe somebody went up there last night to hide something in one of the chambers."

"They could have been dumping a body down a shaft!" Claire's voice rose in excitement.

Kate grinned. "That reminds me of when we found that dead porcupine floating in that water-filled shaft in the mine behind Gramps's place."

"Whoa, both of you!" Mac pointed at Claire, his gaze serious. "Listen, Agatha Christie, let's keep to the facts for now. Your wild theories last spring landed you in the hospital."

"Fine." Sighing, Claire crossed her arms over her chest. But she was going to explore this subject more later, preferably in the Lucky Monk's cool interior, possibly without Mac present.

"Now, tell me about the safe." Mac sat back in his chair.

Claire took a deep breath and caught him up on the whole story. Kate listened wide-eyed–some of the tale new to her, some of it a repeat.

"So, why do I have a feeling you're not going to turn this mummified hand into the police?" he asked.

"They'll just put it in a plastic bag and lock it away in a filing cabinet somewhere. This is too important."

"How do you know it's important?"

"Mac, it's mummified. You know that process doesn't happen overnight. Wherever this hand came from, there's probably a body too, and I have a feeling Joe knew where it was."

"I still want to know why he stuffed the hand in his wall safe," Kate said.

Claire shrugged. "Maybe he skimmed the bag and its contents from a shipment of stolen artifacts he was transporting."

Mac crunched on a piece of ice. "I'm sure the state archaeological society would be interested in looking at it."

Maybe Mac knew somebody at the university who could help them. Claire smiled at him, touching his arm, preparing to spread some honey.

Mac laughed and caught her hand. "No way, gorgeous. Don't even ask." He kissed the inside of her wrist, softening the blow of his refusal. "Why don't you just let the authorities figure this out? You have enough to do with running the store and campground while Ruby and Harley are away, plus taking care of Jess."

Kate grinned. "And your mother."

"But what if there are more artifacts hidden around Ruby's place?" Claire tried to ignore the feel of his fingers now tickling her inner forearm. The cheater—he knew that usually made her all breathy and wobbly-kneed. "If I turn these things in and the wrong person catches wind of it, we may have more than a burglar prowling around the place."

"You think that's what the burglar was looking for?" Kate asked.

Claire shook her head. "I'd lay my money on that pocket watch. It has to be worth some bucks."

Kate tucked a curl behind her ear. "You think Joe skimmed that too?"

"Who knows?" Claire pulled her arm from Mac's grasp. She was already hot and bothered thanks to the sun and Joe's shenanigans. Much more of Mac's teasing and she'd melt into a sticky pool of goo on the patio.

"The problem with Joe is he's dead," she continued. "We have no idea how deep his hands were in this shit."

Rubbing the back of his neck, Mac blew out a breath. "Claire, you're endangering everyone staying at Ruby's. If we let the sheriff know, he can provide some security. Possibly have his deputy drive through the R.V. park a couple of times a night—at least while Ruby and Harley are on their honeymoon and I'm in Tucson."

"You don't think we girls can take care of ourselves?"

"There are always Manny and Chester." Kate threw out.

"Those guys are too busy chasing tail," Mac said.

He had a point there. "You're forgetting about Ruby's guns. I'm no stranger to a trigger, Mac." Claire reminded him.

"That's reassuring."

Claire stuck her tongue out at him. "I'm telling you, our best bet is keeping our lips sealed. Right now, we have one burglar. We tell the world what's in that safe, and we could end up with several of Joe's old business associates milling around. It'll be like a modern-day version of the O.K. Corral."

Kate stood, fanning her yellow T-shirt she'd snagged at the secondhand store. "The ladies' room is calling. I'll be back."

"What are you going to do next?" Mac asked as Kate left.

"Visit the library and see if the Anasazi or Mogollon cultures mummified their dead. I'll also see if I can find out more about that pocket watch."

Mac captured her right hand, lacing his fingers through hers. "Why do I have the feeling that by the time I get back Friday night, you're going to be up to your ears in trouble?"

Claire scooted closer to him, wishing he weren't leaving her for five long days and nights. She was going to miss his touch, his scent—well, that was, as soon as her nose started fully working again.

"I'll be good. Kate will keep me out of trouble."

"Right." He chuckled, capturing her chin and drawing her lips toward his. "She's the kettle, and you're black. Just promise me you'll stay out of the mines."

Under the table, Claire crossed her fingers on her free hand. "Sure."

"Claire." His tone warned as his breath brushed her lips.

She crossed her ankles. "I promise. Now kiss me like you mean it."

* * *

Kate wiped her hands on a paper towel and pulled open the ladies' room door. She stepped out into the narrow hallway and collided with a black shirt and a wall of chest.

"Oof!" she said, stumbling sideways.

A pair of hands grabbed her and kept her from hitting the wall.

"Sorry about th—" His voice trailed off as she locked gazes with a familiar pair of dark blue eyes. "Oh, it's you."

Butch didn't sound happy to see her. He looked shorter without his white cowboy hat. His reddish-blonde hair curled at his collar.

"We keep running into each other." Wincing at her own words, Kate tried to laugh off her embarrassment, but it came out high-pitched, squeaky around the edges.

His eyes narrowed. "I suppose you're going to tell me I should've let you know I was walking down the hall before you came busting out of the bathroom and slammed into me."

She deserved that, but he didn't have to glare at her like she'd run over his foot.

She'd screwed up royally when it came to handling that accident. Hours of doodling on the concrete wall in a jail cell had given her plenty of time to realize the error of her ways. It was time to clear the slate and start over.

Lifting her chin, she said, "Listen, I need to talk to you, Mr. … Butch." She had yet to learn the man's last name and she doubted he'd appreciate her calling him Mr. Bartender.

He held up his hand, stopping her. "I'm too tired for this today after being up all night."

Now that he mentioned it, his eyes were slightly bloodshot around the rims.

"I just want to say—"

"I think you said enough last time, Miss Morgan. Goodbye."

Without a backwards glance, he strode past her and pushed through the men's room door, the creaking hinges his encore.

Kate stared after him, her mouth hanging open, stunned by his abrupt departure. So she'd been a pain the day of the accident. That was no reason to be so rude in return. He was going to hear her apology whether he wanted to or not.

She marched to the men's room door and lifted her hand to knock, but halted, her hand in the air. What was she going to do? Talk to him through a slab of wood? Ask if she could join him?

Before she could change her mind, she closed her eyes, pushed open the door, and stepped inside.

The smell surprised her. She'd expected stale urine with a hint of cigarette smoke, or worse. Instead, a fresh pine scent filled the air. The sound of water hitting porcelain made her squeeze her eyelids closed even tighter.

"Butch?" she said too loud for such a small room and jumped at the sound of her own voice.

"Jesus, woman! What are you doing in here?"

"I need to talk to you."

"I'm a little busy right now."

"You can just listen then." She continued with her mission before he could interrupt. "I want to tell you that I'm sorry for my behavior after I smashed your pickup. I wasn't thinking straight and kind of panicked."

"Kind of?" The water stopped. She heard him zip his jeans.

Ignoring his skepticism, she swallowed the nervous fluttering in her throat. "If there's anything else I can do to help get your pickup fixed, let me know."

The urinal flushed. She tried to smile, but it felt stiff on her cheeks, so she dropped it.

"I'd offer to drive you around, but my car is out of commission, of course, and nobody in my family will allow me to drive their vehicle. So, the best I can offer is a ride on the handlebars of Ruby's bicycle while I peddle."

"You can open your eyes now."

She peeked between her eyelashes as he turned on the faucet. He stared back at her through the mirror above the sink, an unreadable expression on his face.

Glancing away, she tried to focus on something else. Her gaze landed on the urinals, and she felt her forehead grow warm. She turned to her right and realized she was staring at a condom machine. Her ears practically burst into flames.

She looked down at her sandals. "Anyway, I don't want you to—"

The door behind her creaked opened, bumping her in the shoulder. She stepped to the side as a short, very chubby, very hairy man in a wife-beater tank top walked in.

"Hey, Don." Butch greeted the guy with a nod.

"Howdy, Butch," Don replied. When he noticed Kate standing there, his smile widened. "Good afternoon, Miss." He touched the brim of his brown, dusty cowboy hat, then headed for a urinal.

Zipppp.

Kate squeezed her eyes closed again.

The door hinges squeaked.

"Come on, crazy lady," Butch whispered in her ear. He grabbed her arm and dragged her into the hallway.

Kate opened her eyes and found herself standing close enough to Butch to count his blond eyelashes. He smelled like soap and something fresh—not strong enough to be cologne.

"Anyway," she said, her voice higher this time.

"Apology accepted." Butch stepped back. "While I'm thinking about it, I need to return this to you." He pulled his wallet from his back pocket and flipped it open.

Kate looked down at his Arizona driver's license stuffed behind clear plastic. He looked rugged in his picture, his hair combed back, his cheekbones and chin chiseled. The name "Valentine" was printed next to his picture, but his hand blocked the rest. As he dug through one of the pockets, a couple of cards slipped out and drifted to the floor.

"Damn," he said under his breath.

"I'll get them." Happy to give her fingers something to do besides twiddling, she squatted down. One of the cards was for a video rental store, the other had Copper Snake Mining Company printed in bold letters on it.

"Thanks." Butch held out his hand.

She stood and gave them to him without getting a chance to see the name on the business card.

"Here you go." He held out her insurance card. "You got hauled off to jail before I could return it."

At that moment, a hole in the floor big enough for her to disappear into would have been appreciated.

"How's the stolen car business treating you these days?" His grin took the sting out of his words.

Wow! She'd forgotten how handsome he could be when he wasn't glaring at her. She tried to think of something witty to say. "Umm, good," was what spilled out of her mouth.

Criminy, she was an idiot.

His grin faltered.

"Hey, Butch." The guy who'd brought Kate and Claire their BLTs stood at the end of the hall. "Your lawyer's on the phone."

"Thanks." Butch turned to Kate. "Duty calls. Run into you another time." With a goodbye nod, he strode away.

Kate watched him go. The sight of his broad shoulders, narrow waist, and long legs made her feel like she'd been sniffing Elmer's glue all afternoon.

The sound of a urinal flushing cleared the fog in her brain. Her attraction to Butch faded with the mist. She must have had too much sun today. Way too much sun.

She headed for the patio and Claire.

The truth hit her like a snow shovel to the head, stopping her in her tracks in front of the glass door. She stared blindly out at Mac and her sister. How could she be such an idiot?

The clues were right in front of her like a police line-up. First, Butch's eyes were red from being up all night. Second, he had a business card from the mining company in his wallet. Third, at this very moment, he was talking to his lawyer.

It couldn't be any more obvious—Butch was the one trying to steal the Lucky Monk mine away from Ruby.

Chapter Ten

Monday, August 16th

"Damn, it's hot in here." Claire wiped her brow with her forearm. Her hands swam inside a pair of yellow rubber gloves, her sweat-ringed, "Mummy Dearest" monster T-shirt clung to her back like a baby opossum. Even the concrete felt warm under her knees.

Ruby needed to install fans in the R.V. park's public restrooms. After spending the last half-hour in this concrete-lined crock-pot, heatstroke was just a hallucination away.

Afternoon sunlight glared through the window, spotlighting the drain in the center of the floor. The florescent light bulbs droned overhead as an incessant memorial to all of the dead fly carcasses littering the windowsill and dark corners.

Sitting back on her heels, Claire frowned at the toilet with the steel "snake" coil still jammed down its porcelain throat. Thank God her nose was still only partially working.

"Here, *mi amor.*" Manny squeezed into the toilet stall with her, patting dry her forehead and cheeks with a scratchy paper towel, and wiping off her chin. "You had dirt on your face."

"Thanks." she blinked sweat from her lashes.

"You sure that was dirt?" Chester's grin was wide enough to have its own zip code.

Claire shuddered. It was going to take two bars of soap to get her fresh and clean again, especially after spending the morning putting out fires—literally.

Some bozo hadn't fully doused a pit fire before hitching up and rolling out of the park. The mid-morning breeze had stoked the smoldering embers and had carried sparks to a nearby knoll covered with grass, aka kindling with roots. Luckily, Manny noticed the smoke while on binocular patrol, and Claire and

Gramps were able to douse the flames before involving Yuccaville's voluntary fire department.

Finished playing towel boy, Manny returned to his seat next to Chester on the sink counter. "You guys still haven't helped me figure out how to get Rebecca to notice me."

Chester lit a cigar, his eyes squinty, thoughtful.

It was hard to conjure romantic ideas while splashing elbow-deep in what Chester kept referring to as "the crapper." Claire pulled the snake from the toilet and tossed it on the floor drain.

"I've tried some of my best pick-up lines on her." Manny continued. "But she won't give me the time of day."

Cigar smoke billowed around Chester's buzz cut. "Just tell her you have less than three months to live."

Using the toilet paper holder to pull herself to her feet, Claire asked, "What happens when he's still alive in four months?"

"Simple—a case of divine intervention. It's a goddamned miracle." Chester waved his hands in the air holy-roller style.

"Maybe." Manny leaned back against the mirror, his lips pursed as if he was actually considering Chester's suggestion. "No. Rebecca is too smart for that one."

Chester smirked. "For all you know, she could have the I.Q. of a dung beetle. What do you really know about this dame?"

"She's blonde." Manny smiled, as if that said it all.

"So was Crazy Carol. Her fetish for sharp knives almost left you singing in the Vienna Boys Choir."

Manny cringed visibly. "I still get asked about that scar."

"What else you got?"

"She has a cute little tattoo of Toucan Sam on her hip, right above her tan line."

Claire peeled off the yellow gloves. She didn't want to know how Manny found out about the tattoo. She had a feeling Chester's binoculars had played a part.

"And she seems really sweet."

A rusty chuckle rumbled from Chester's chest. "So did that Flo dame. Turned out she was sweet like a Pay Day bar—half sugar and half nuts."

Manny's cheeks dimpled. "I'll never play naked leap frog again."

Wincing away the images in her head, Claire tossed the gloves onto the floor next to her toolbox. "Why don't you just start with, 'Hello, my name is Manny'?"

Both men scoffed at her.

She chuckled at their twin horrified expressions. "What's wrong with introducing yourself?"

"That's what you do when you join Alcoholics Anonymous." Chester adjusted himself in front of her as if she were just one of the boys.

She really needed to make some new friends.

"Asking a lady out takes more finesse," Manny explained.

Claire bit back a smile. Yosemite Sam and Elmer Fudd had more finesse than these two circus clowns.

"I know!" Chester took his cigar out of his mouth. "Ask her if she was on a rerun of Baywatch last week. That always makes the ladies smile."

"Hey, that's not bad." Manny nodded.

"And if that gets your foot in the door." A grin split Chester's face. "Ask if she collects birds, because she sure has a nice set of hooters."

Manny's laugh bounced off the concrete walls.

Washing her hands in the sink, Claire groaned. "Chester, I'm amazed you found one woman to marry you, let alone three."

"What can I say? Women want a taste of America's Most Wanted." Chester slid off the counter, shuffled over to the stall, and frowned at the toilet. "So, did you fix the latrine?"

Claire dried her hands on a paper towel. "No. The clog is too deep for the snake. And there isn't an access panel or cleanout anywhere around here, so I'm going to have to remove the whole damned toilet."

On the upside, now she had an excuse to go to Yuccaville. Never mind that Creekside Hardware and Supply had plenty of wax toilet rings.

Her fingers itched to hit the keyboard at the county library and pin down the age of Joe's cache of artifacts. She'd worry about where the pieces had come from in due time—there were only so many plates she could spin at once.

Manny scooted off the counter as Claire closed her toolbox. "Let me know when Act II of Much Ado About Toilets starts." He held out her cap. "I'll bring beer and pretzels."

Slipping on her hat, she said, "Listen, I know Mac told you two to keep an eye on me, but how much trouble can I get into fixing a clogged toilet?"

"Who cares?" Manny's waggled his bushy eyebrows. "We just like watching a woman get all sweaty and dirty."

"Claire." Kate breezed in through the propped open door.

With her hair styled in a sleek chignon, her skin lightly tanned, her lips glossed, and her white tank top and pink mini-skirt freshly ironed, Kate looked like she'd just finished shooting a L'Oréal commercial.

Claire felt like she'd been coughed up by a cat.

She lifted her toolbox. "What?"

"Buck called."

A cricket chirped in Claire's brain. "Buck who?"

"Buck. As in Buck's Auto Oasis."

A second cricket joined the first. Claire blinked.

Kate sighed as if she were trying to explain logarithm rules to a couple of stoners. "The mechanic working on my car."

Her sister must have been painting her nails with the windows closed again, because this was the first Claire had heard of Buck.

"Anyway, I need you to drive me to Yuccaville."

"No." Claire had a hot date with the library computer today. She scooped up her gloves and the snake.

"Gramps said you have to."

"Fine, but we're stopping by the library for an hour or two, and I don't want to hear any complaining."

"Is it air conditioned?"

Claire nodded.

"Okay with me, but ..." Kate suddenly found the paint peeling off the doorjamb extremely interesting.

"But what?"

"Mom's coming, too."

* * *

"Kathryn, did you hear a single word I just said?" Deborah waved her manicured pink nails in front of Kate's face.

Pushing all conspiratorial thoughts about Butch from the forefront of her mind, Kate dragged her gaze from the hypnotic white paint lining the shoulder of the road.

Ruby's old pickup bounced along, the tires thumping rhythmically over the veins of tar patches crisscrossing the asphalt. Warm air filled with the scent of hot tar and baked earth blew in through Kate's open window, tearing at her chignon, whistling in her ears.

According to the mile marker, they were five miles out from Jackrabbit Junction. A storm raged in the east. Dark clouds converged over the mountain range that rimmed the valley, the peaks tinted purple with shadows.

"Kathryn!"

"What?" Kate looked at her mother, who sat between Claire and her.

"I asked when Porter was picking you up this evening."

Crap! Amidst all her plotting on how to catch Butch red-handed, she'd forgotten all about her dinner date with Porter.

She checked her watch. "He's probably waiting for me at Ruby's as we speak."

"I told you we should have left the library a half-hour earlier," Deborah said to Claire, who drove with white-knuckled intensity. "At least we wouldn't have been kicked out then. I still can't get over the way you shoved that poor old lady off the computer. I've never been so mortified."

Claire nailed Deborah with a sideways glare. "She was hogging the one computer with an Internet connection."

Kate smiled to herself, remembering the look of shock on her sister's face when Ma Kettle had told Claire to shove her time limit up her ass and spin on it.

"Like I told that bully of a librarian," Claire continued, "The old bat's time had been up for twenty minutes. And I didn't shove her. I guided her firmly by the arm. She faked that stumbling bit."

"You're just lucky she hit you with her purse instead of her cane." Deborah touched the bruise on Claire's cheekbone.

"Would you stop touching it!" Claire winced away from Deborah's fingertips. "I thought we all agreed not to talk until we got back to the R.V. park."

She cranked up the radio volume. Willie Nelson sang about a good-hearted woman falling for a guy who liked to party a little too much.

Kate grimaced. That seemed to be the story of her life.

Deborah turned down the volume. "I never agreed to anything. You ordered us not to talk, which was very rude considering that I bought you two very nice dresses this afternoon. Of course, they aren't Christian Dior or Donna Karan, but what can you expect for such a ragamuffin town?"

Kate chuckled under her breath at the memory of Claire standing in front of the dressing room mirror while Deborah and the sales lady fluttered around her like Cinderella's seamstress birds.

"The cherry jubilee dress and the matching straw hat covered with fake fruit is my all-time favorite," Kate said.

"You look so pretty in that one." Deborah clapped.

"I'm not wearing that dress, Mother."

"You are, too. Stop being such a fuss-budget about this."

"It makes me look like Carmen Miranda wrapped in a tablecloth." Claire's lips thinned. "Mac is going to laugh his ass off when he sees me in it."

"Well, if that's true, then he obviously got his fashion sense from his aunt. That woman would wear burlap for the Queen's visit. Have you seen the dress she plans to wear for her wedding? It's pale yellow, for heaven's sake. That alone is reason enough for getting this wedding called off."

A muscle in Claire's jaw twitched.

"Mother," Kate warned.

"And if that isn't bad enough, you should see the dress Jessica pick—"

Claire boosted the radio volume again, drowning out Deborah with Willie Nelson.

Deborah frowned, reaching for the volume, but Claire kept her fingers clamped on the knob and shot Deborah a glare hot enough to fuse the pearls in her chandelier earrings.

Neither of them could hear Kate's laughter over the twangy guitar riffs blaring from the speakers.

As the barbed-wire fence posts passed, Kate shifted in her seat. The back of her thighs were damp where her skin touched the vinyl-covered cushions, her skirt undoubtedly seat-wrinkled beyond repair for tonight's date.

She sighed, homesick for her Volvo with its air conditioning and plush leather seats. But judging from Buck the Mechanic's grim predictions, she had another week at least before she'd be reunited with her baby.

Claire slowed the pickup as they approached the road to Ruby's place.

Kate stared out the window at The Shaft.

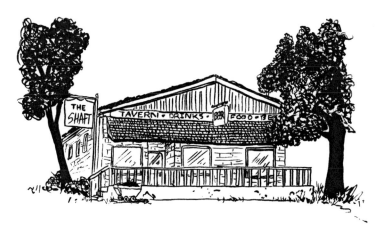

Was Butch inside planning his next move? She needed to talk to Claire about what she'd found out yesterday, drill her sister with some questions about the bartender's personal life. But Claire's friendship with Butch made Kate hesitate.

After Mac had left last night, Jessica had glued herself to Claire's side. Between the Euchre tournament and crowded sleeping arrangements, Kate hadn't been able to catch her sister alone. If only Porter weren't at Ruby's waiting for her, she could take a walk with Claire and test the water.

As Willie's song came to an end, Kate leaned forward. "Claire, I need to ask you something."

There was one thing she wanted to confirm, something that shouldn't raise any hairs on her sister's neck.

Claire turned down the radio.

"What is Butch the bartender's last name?"

Her sister took her eyes off the road long enough to shoot Kate a questioning frown. "Carter. Butch Carter. Didn't you get his name when you traded paint?"

"I was too busy panicking, remember?"

"And lying," Deborah added, her lips pinched.

Kate contemplated guiding her mother firmly by the arm right off the nearest cliff.

She looked back out her window, staring at the glittering bits of broken glass that littered the ditch.

"Butch Carter" was also the name typed on the copy of the police report she'd picked up today, as well as written on one of the clipboards hanging in Buck the mechanic's office, along with Butch's address and phone number. Lucky for her there was only one body shop in all of Yuccaville.

So who was Valentine? Was Butch carrying a fake I.D.? More importantly, why would Butch be carrying a fake I.D.?

Did it have something to do with the Copper Snake Mining Company? An alias he used when performing crooked business deals?

She should have followed Butch yesterday afternoon and eavesdropped on his phone call with his lawyer.

"What's with your sudden interest in Butch?" Claire's question jarred Kate out of her Miss Marple fantasy.

Now was not the time to explain. "I was just curious."

"I call bullshit."

Deborah slapped Claire's hand. "Watch your mouth. That's the exact type of filthy talk I was speaking to you about in the dressing room. Gentlemen don't like potty mouths."

"How do you know what men like, Mom?" Claire downshifted as they approached the bridge into the R.V. park. "You've been out of the circuit for almost forty years now. For all you know, guys like women who cuss like crab fishermen and braid their armpit hair. Look at that guy Kate was dating last year."

"Let's not," Kate said.

"He wanted Kate to—"

"Claire!"

"Didn't you tell Mom?"

"I most certainly did not." There were some things mothers should never know. Kate caught sight of Porter's shiny blue truck in front of the General Store.

"Chicken." Claire grinned at Kate before turning back to Deborah. "Anyway, my point is that maybe instead of working so hard on changing us, you should consider changing yourself."

"Now you're talking nonsense." Deborah collected her purse from the floor as Claire slowed to a stop. "Men haven't changed that much. I'm not a complete recluse, you know. I'm hip with the times. I watch television."

"*Golden Girls* went off the air in the nineties, Mom, and *Antiques Roadshow* doesn't count." Switching off the engine, Claire stared at Kate. "Now what's the deal with you and Butch?"

"Nothing." Sweat broke out on Kate's upper lip. "I just ran into him outside the restroom yesterday at the bar."

"And?"

"There is no 'and.'"

Claire's brown eyes narrowed, searching Kate's face. "You like him, don't you?"

"What? No, of course not." Kate unbuckled her seat belt and shoved open her door. "No, absolutely not."

Well, maybe just the way he filled out his jeans and T-shirt, but that was all. Oh, and his eyes.

"Why would Kathryn be interested in a bartender when she has Porter, a handsome gentleman and successful writer, asking her out to dinner?"

Butch's forearms and biceps weren't so bad either, Kate thought, as she stepped to the ground.

"Butch isn't just a bartender, Mom." Claire pushed open her door. "He owns The Shaft."

He what? Kate eyed Claire. That explained how a bartender in a flea-bitten town could afford a brand new pickup. It also shed new light on Butch's potential as a prime suspect.

"Besides, Kate's never been into handsome and successful men. She's usually drawn to the dark side of the force."

Kate shot Claire a shut-your-big-mouth glare. "Leave it alone, Claire."

"And Butch isn't exactly 'dark,' unless you consider that he works nights most of the time in a shadow-filled bar."

"Now is not the time to discuss this," Kate sang in a sing-song voice, helping her mother out of the pickup cab.

Claire leaned against the steering wheel, chewing on her thumb, watching Kate as if Hydra's nine heads were sprouting from her neck. "You must think Butch is into something shady, otherwise, you wouldn't have been daydreaming about him all of the way home."

"I wasn't daydreaming, I was pondering."

"Pondering what?" Deborah asked, both feet now on the ground.

"Just something I saw yesterday."

Claire climbed from the truck and walked around the front fender. "Keep talking."

"Something I noticed in his wallet."

Claire's brows drew together. "Why were you digging in Butch's wallet?"

"I wasn't. He was."

A drop of sweat ran down Kate's back. She shaded her eyes. Her sunglasses were merely a fashion accessory in this sunshine.

"When he was fishing out my insurance card, which he'd forgotten to return, I saw a fake I.D. with the name 'Valentine' on it."

"Why would Butch have a fake I.D.?"

The disbelief in Claire's voice didn't surprise Kate. She'd been right to hesitate. Clearly, she'd need to find more proof before Claire would jump on board with her theory about the bar owner's part in Ruby's dilemma.

The screen door opened and Porter walked out. He touched the brim of his hat in their direction. "Good evening, ladies. Is that you, Mrs. Morgan? I swear, in this light, y'all look like sisters."

Deborah giggled, tee-heed, and tittered all at once.

Kate glanced at Claire, who rolled her eyes so hard she looked possessed for a split second.

Facing Porter, Kate pasted a smile on her lips as he descended the steps. In his ostrich-skin boots, black jeans, tan shirt, and white hat, he looked good enough to dip in chocolate sauce and lick clean.

So why wasn't she feeling hungry anymore?

* * *

Claire crept barefoot down the basement steps, carrying the two books Kate had checked out for her at the library while their mother had chewed Claire's ass raw in the pickup. She skipped the third step from the bottom, which usually creaked under her weight. With one foot hovering over the bottom step, she froze at the sound of Gramps's voice, loud and close. "I think she went to bed."

Standing there with only her eyeballs moving, she held her breath. If the boys knew she was still awake, they'd drag her upstairs kicking and scratching, plop her in a chair next to her mother, and make her play another game of Euchre.

The tension between Gramps and Deborah crackled and sparked, just like old times. Ruby had gone to bed early, claiming a migraine, but Claire suspected it had more to do with bobbing and weaving Deborah's passive-aggressive jabs all evening.

Gramps's footsteps thumped past the top of the stair and headed down the hall. The bathroom door slammed shut.

Claire gasped for air. Straining her ears, she heard the faucet running in the bathroom and made her break. She pushed into Joe's office without hitting the lights and shut the door quietly.

A flashlight beam nailed her in the face. She flattened against the door with a squeak of surprise. It took her a handful of seconds to extract her tongue from the back of her throat.

"Who's there?" she whispered, and then realized what a stupid thing that was to ask. Squinting, her heart still galloping down the backstretch, she blocked the light with her hand.

"It's me," Jess whispered back.

Claire's peeled herself off the door. "What are you doing down here?" The last she'd seen Jess, the girl had been watching *Friends* reruns in her bedroom.

"Do you promise not to tell Mom?"

"Only if you remove that damned light from my face."

"Oh, sorry." Jess dropped the beam to the tops of her pink slippers. "I'm looking for my money."

She should have known. Jess had the determination of a beaver with a dam to build, especially when it came to money.

Walking over to the desk, she set the library books down. "What makes you think Ruby would hide it in here?"

"Well ... umm ... I don't know. Why wouldn't she?"

"Think about it, Jess." Claire dropped into Ruby's cushy chair and pulled her own mini-flashlight out of her pocket. "Not only is this the room where we found the money, but it's the one room in the house where Gramps found evidence of the burglar. Don't you think your mom would be smart enough to hide the money somewhere less busy?"

"Yeah, I guess." Jess sidled up next to her, sniffing.

"Are you smelling my hair?"

"I'm smelling all of you for skunk. You finally don't stink anymore." She peered over Claire's shoulder as she flipped open the cover of *History of the Southwest: A Keyhole View.* "What are you doing?"

"Trying to figure out how old that mummy hand is."

"Coolio. How are you going to do that?"

Claire turned to the index. "Find out which cultures used to bury their dead instead of cremate them."

"Why are you reading down here in the dark?"

Because it was the only place she had thought she'd find peace and quiet in the house. "Mom's in the spare room, the boys are in the rec room, and I thought you were in your room." She scanned the "B" page.

Jess leaned closer. "What word are you looking for?"

"Burial."

"It's right there." Jess pointed at the word on the page.

Claire glanced at the girl, who seemed oblivious that she was about to get her finger bitten off.

"Do you want me to write down the page numbers?"

"No, thanks." Claire flipped to the first page number listed. "Aren't you tired? It's past eleven, and you were up late last night talking." Talking to Claire that was, about everything from how to tell a boy gecko from a girl gecko to why pink lemonade was her all-time favorite lip gloss flavor. Not even two feather pillows had muffled Jess's voice.

"Nope. I drank one of Mom's energy drinks at supper. I'm good to go until after midnight probably."

Ruby needed to stop stocking energy drinks in the fridge.

"Here." Claire handed Jess *Ancient Southwestern Cultures in a Nutshell* and nodded toward the floor. "See what you can find in there about burials."

Jess dropped to the floor and started fanning pages. "What if there's more than one group of people who buried their dead?"

"Then I'll start comparing basket designs, or see if that twig figurine is unique to a certain culture."

For the next minute or two, the only sound was paper rustling. Claire scanned the pages about the Anasazi death rituals, all of which involved cremation.

"Claire?"

"Hmm?" She turned back to the index, looking for the page number on the Mogollon culture burial practices.

"How old were you the first time you had sex?"

Claire's thoughts screeched to a stop, her finger hovering over *Metate*, the ground beneath her feet suddenly slippery. "Probably too young."

"Was it fun?"

She stared down at the top of Jess's head. The girl was looking at the color pictures in the center of the book. "I wouldn't exactly use the word 'fun' to describe it. Why?"

Jess shrugged. "Last spring, Tammy Mapes was talking about sex in the bathroom. She's done it six times now."

"And how old is Tammy?"

"I don't know. I think she just turned sixteen."

Ah ha! With her sixteenth birthday on the horizon, Jess must be dealing with peer pressure.

"What's sex like?"

"Well—" Uncertain how Ruby would feel about Claire and Jess analyzing Chapter Five of *The Season of Jess's Deflowering* without her permission, Claire hesitated. On the other hand, better Jess come to Claire than Tammy Mapes, the little tramp.

"I mean, I don't want to know what sex is like with Mac, because he's my cousin and it's pretty disgusting that you're exchanging any bodily fluids with him, especially that kind."

Claire opened her mouth only to shut it again.

"What was it like your first time?" Jess blinked up at Claire. "In those romance books Manny reads, the woman sometimes cries afterward because she's happy. Did you cry?"

"Uh ..."

"Did it hurt?"

"I ..."

"Was it smelly?"

"Smelly?" Claire sat back in the chair, fighting a grin.

"Yeah, you know, like the boys' locker room."

"What were you doing in the boys' locker room?"

"Helping Tammy find her kiwi-flavored lip gloss."

"Maybe you should stop hanging around Tammy."

"Yeah, that's what Kevin says."

Claire frowned. "Who's Kevin?"

"He was my lab partner in Chemistry last year."

"Is he cute?"

"He's a total hottie. Without his glasses, I'd give him an 8.5 on the hot-ilicious scale."

"Is he your boyfriend?"

"I wish! I think he's going with some senior girl. Do you think Kate and Porter are having sex tonight?"

Knowing Kate, Claire doubted it. Porter's credentials were too clean—no visible scars, no prison tattoos on his arms. Although, there was something slick about the guy that Claire didn't quite trust, but it was probably something to do with Deborah and her instant approval.

"Kevin is a major hunk, especially when he smiles, even though he has braces, but they are the clear kind, so you can hardly tell he's wearing them. Do you think after Mom marries Harley she'll be able to afford to buy me braces? Have you ever kissed a boy with braces?"

Claire crossed her arms, watching Jess, waiting for the girl's head to pop and shower confetti throughout the room.

"Mac wore braces in school, did you know that? His teeth are almost as straight as Porter's. Mac smells better, though."

And they were back to smells again.

"But Porter's glasses are cooler."

Glasses? "How do you know Porter wears glasses?" Claire hadn't even seen him in sunglasses.

"He was wearing them tonight."

"When?" She'd been forced to sit and listen to her mother fawn all over the man while Kate changed her clothes and fixed her already perfect hair and makeup.

"Before you got home. But he only wears them to read."

"How do you know?"

"Because he was wearing them when he was reading one of Joe's old books." Jess nudged her head toward the bookcase filled with Joe's pricey first editions.

"Jess, you know you're not supposed to take those books out of this office." Ruby had found the first edition copy of *Pride and Prejudice* in Jess's room being used as a coaster.

"I didn't. Porter was reading it down here."

The chair squeaked as Claire sat forward. "You brought him down here?"

"No, silly. I found him in here."

Chapter Eleven

Tuesday, August 17th

"What's that?" Chester leaned over the counter and frowned down at the cell phone in Claire's hand. "One of those electronic blueberries?"

"You mean a BlackBerry." Manny corrected him from where he stood in front of the magazine rack, skimming through the latest edition of *Cosmopolitan*. "You need to get with the times, old man."

From her stool behind the counter, Claire did her best to ignore her two sidekicks, who'd been hanging out inside the cool, air conditioned General Store with her for the last half hour—ever since they'd finished devouring the omelets Gramps had made for them. She scrolled through the list of contact names on Kate's cell phone.

Gramps swished through the green curtain and sidled up next to Chester at the counter, pointing at Kate's phone. "Did you call Mac back last night?"

"What do you mean 'back'? Nobody told me he called."

"Oops," Gramps said. "Oh well, you're supposed to call him back, and when you do, ask him if he got my package."

"What package?"

"None of your business." He glanced at her hand again, his brows knitted. "That's a fancy-looking phone."

Claire knew a diversionary tactic when she heard one. She'd just have to ask Mac about Gramps's mysterious package.

Taking the phone from Claire's hand, Gramps inspected it at arm's length. He must have left his reading glasses in the kitchen. "When did you get that?"

He handed it back to her.

"Umm, not very long ago." Just this morning, as a matter of fact.

"You think Ruby would like one?"

"Would Ruby like what?" Deborah stepped through the curtain, her bright red lipstick matching the shiny red cowboy boots she'd purchased yesterday in Yuccaville. Her boot heels clomped against the wood floor as she approached the counter. Manny and Chester fell back, as if she carried the Black Death with her. A rogue wave of Channel No. 5 slammed into Claire, drowning her still-tender sinuses.

Deborah wrinkled her brow. "What are you doing with Kate's phone?"

"Nothing." Claire avoided Gramps's squint. "I was just checking it out, that's all."

"Then why is Porter's name highlighted?"

"Is it? Oh, hmmm. Would you look at that?" Claire hit the button that turned off the screen and smiled at Deborah. "You look nice this morning, Mother. Where are you off to?"

"Well, I was hoping I could convince Ruby to take me back to Yuccaville. I broke a nail."

Gramps visibly bristled. "Ruby is not your chauffeur. She's a busy woman."

"Where is she?" Deborah arched a plucked brow.

"In Tucson."

"For how long?"

"All day. She had some errands to run."

Claire narrowed her eyes, wondering what Gramps was up to. His story had changed since they'd shared a moment waiting on the coffee maker this morning.

"I thought you said she took Jess shopping." Manny had replaced *Cosmopolitan* with *Vogue*.

"Really? Shopping? Did you sponsor this trip, Dad?"

Gramps turned a dark shade of pink.

"It figures." Deborah tapped one of her long, sharp talons on the countertop. "You see, this is exactly what I was talking about last night. You're so blinded by this woman that you can't see that all she's after is your money. You've been putting out her fires with your cash ever since you stepped into the picture."

Gramps's face darkened even more, now almost as red as Deborah's boots.

"Mom," Claire started, intending to veer her mother off course before Gramps turned purple.

"Stay out of this, Claire Alice!" Deborah practically snarled.

Closing her mouth, Claire touched the top of her head to make sure it hadn't actually been bitten off.

"How many times is Ruby going to have to ask for money before you wake up?"

"For your information," Gramps said, "I sent her to Tucson this morning with Jess."

"Is that what she made you think? Oh, she's good."

"I sent her there to get her away from *you*. And yes, I did give her the money, because whether you like it or not, she's going to be my wife in less than a week." He pushed away from the counter and hobbled toward the front door, his shoulders rigid.

"Have you thought about how selfish you're being?" Deborah threw at his back. "She's young enough to be your daughter. It's only a matter of time until she's left nursing another invalid."

Claire gasped.

"Hoooooo!" Chester shouted, a look of disgust on his face.

Gramps paused with his fists clenched at his sides. His pale blue eyes were mere slits when he turned around. "Nobody invited you down here, Deborah. Go home."

"I'm sorry if the truth hurts, Dad, but somebody has to talk some sense into you, and Claire certainly isn't capable of it. She's too mired in her own mess."

Claire searched the counter for something to whack her mom upside the head with that wouldn't cause permanent damage.

"Hey, guys." Kate breezed in from the rec room, smiling and bouncing with every step—clueless that she'd just walked into the middle of a gunfight. "Have any of you seen my phone?"

* * *

"Just because I'm paranoid doesn't mean they're not after me," Chester told Manny while dealing cards around the table.

The ringing of Ruby's wall telephone interrupted Manny's reply.

Claire looked up from the Jack of hearts and Queen of diamonds in her hand.

Kate stared back at her with raised brows.

"Well, don't any of you get off your butts to get that." Claire pushed back her chair, taking the potato chips with her.

Chester and Manny had moved the card table into the back of the store. This made it so Claire could watch the cash register and sit in for Gramps, who'd grabbed Henry and spun out of the R.V. park after his row with Deborah.

Nobody seemed interested in enlisting Deborah to play, especially Claire. Her mother had returned to her bedroom after the big showdown, probably to file her teeth into sharper points.

Claire picked up the receiver on the fourth ring. "Dancing Winnebagos R.V. Park."

"Miss me yet, Slugger?" The sound of Mac's voice coming through the receiver brought a smile to Claire's lips.

"More than you can imagine." She wiped her greasy fingers on her jean shorts. "Hold on while I switch to the phone in the rec room." She laid the receiver down on the counter. "Kate, hang this up as soon as I pick up in the other room."

As Claire slipped through the curtain, she heard Kate tell the boys, "She's always been that bossy."

Claire picked up the other phone. "Can you take Friday off and come back early?"

"Things that bad there?"

"I'm surprised you haven't been able to see the mushroom clouds from Tucson." The sound of heavy breathing came on the line. Claire covered the mouthpiece. "Manny Carrera, hang up that phone right now!"

"Spoilsport," Manny yelled back, then Claire heard a click.

"Are the boys keeping an eye on you?" Claire could hear the grin in Mac's tone.

"Are you kidding? The only time they leave my side is when I have to use the bathroom, and Manny even tries to follow me in there."

She glanced around to make sure her mother wasn't hovering nearby in the shadows before asking, "So, what did you find out about the lawyer?"

"Nothing."

"Didn't you go to his office?"

"I tried, but I must have the address wrong, because I ended up at a strip mall with a tattoo parlor, a cheap cigarette store, and an adult video mart."

"Sounds like my kind of mall."

"Do you know where Ruby stashed those letters?"

"I think so." Claire circled the bar, taking the phone with her, and started pulling open the drawers. She found the envelopes on her third try. "Here they are." She pulled one out. "Do you have a pen handy?"

"Yep. Shoot."

She rattled off the address.

"Damn, that's what I have. Is there a different address on the other envelopes?"

"No, they're all the same. Maybe there are two streets in Tucson named Chuckwalla Wash Drive."

"I doubt it, but I'll check again."

Claire grabbed a pen from the drawer and drew hearts and smiley faces on the back of an envelope. "Did you go to Phoenix yesterday?"

Mac had mentioned zipping up to the state capitol to comb through public records in the state mining archives for information about the Lucky Monk.

"Yeah."

"What did you find out?"

"Well …"

"What?"

"It seems owning this mine is hazardous to your health." Mac's voice sounded quieter, but closer, as if he were cupping the mouthpiece. "It's passed through the hands of twelve owners, and none of them hung around long enough to receive Medicare benefits. One even disappeared entirely, never to be seen again. Joe has the current longevity record."

"Do you think it's cursed?" she whispered.

"Why did I know you'd ask that?"

"Because you have this bad habit of reading my mind."

"No, Miss Superstitious. I don't think it's cursed. There's probably a logical explanation for each death. But I do find it an ominous statistic considering Ruby is the current owner."

She was for now, anyway, unless Leo Scott's client stole it away. Claire scribbled some sad faces on the envelope. "What else did you find?"

"Several pages worth of information, but I haven't had time to read through any of them yet. I'll bring them on Friday, along with a suitcase full of your clothes. Tell me again which dress I'm supposed to pack for the wedding—the purple one with the low neckline that makes me drool and stutter, or the red one with the thin straps that makes me stutter and then drool?"

"Actually, I was thinking the green striped dress without a back to it. You know which one I'm talking about?"

"Mmmm, I sure do. No fumbling with zippers or buttons on that one. Maybe we should rent a room in Yuccaville that night."

"Lord knows finding privacy around here is nearly impossible. Jess has been glued to my side since you left."

"So I hear. Ruby and Jess met me for lunch today."

"Between Chester, Manny, and Jess, I feel as if I have a car full of paparazzi members riding my ass at every turn."

Claire glanced toward the curtain at the sound of the bells over the front door jingling.

"Can't say I blame them," Mac said. "I'm enthralled with your backside myself."

"Yeah, well you're hopeless."

"I can't help it. I love you."

Claire's blood rushed in her ears. She opened her mouth and then closed it, not knowing how to respond.

They were back to the stalemate they'd reached a week ago, with Mac using the "L" word and her being scared shitless, struggling to catch her breath.

"I know you don't want to hear that, Claire, but you can't avoid it forever."

She cleared her throat. "I thought most guys were happy to have a woman sharing their bed but not their name."

"I'm not 'most guys.'"

No, he wasn't.

"Claire!" Kate pulled back the curtain and stuck her head through. "There's a guy out here saying the toilet in the men's room is flooding."

"Son of a bitch." Claire threw down the pen. "I gotta go," she told Mac. "That damned toilet is overflowing again."

"Okay. I'll talk to you later." His voice sounded stilted, withdrawn.

She didn't want to end the call with him feeling jilted. "I miss you, Mac."

"Good. Happy plunging, Slugger. Stay out of trouble." The phone clicked in her ear.

"Kate, watch the store," she yelled through the curtain. Grabbing her tool belt from the cubbyhole next to the back door, she stepped out into the afternoon sunlight.

She had two hours to take care of this mess and get cleaned up before Porter would be waiting for her at the bar ... well, he'd be waiting for Kate, anyway.

At least that was what his reply had been to her text message invite from Kate's phone.

* * *

The Shaft shook, rattled, and rolled around Claire.

With Ladies' Night in full swing, beer poured from the tap at half the price for anyone sporting a vagina. Outnumbering the women two-to-one, bucks butted heads for a chance to woo any woman brave enough to walk through the door.

Claire inhaled the secondhand cigarette smoke swirling above her head. The hankering to light up made her fingers itch.

She sipped on her Corona instead, savoring the cold bite, wondering if anyone would notice if she slipped the cool, sweating bottle down her shirt. Butch's air conditioner couldn't compete with the heat radiating off so much skin. Another hour in this humidity and she'd be steamed pink.

Across the table from her, Kate kept sneaking glances at Butch, who stood behind the bar, pouring drinks and listening to drunken yarns while sporting his usual friendly grin.

Leaning over her drink, Claire hollered above the din, "Porter is late for your date."

Kate stared back at her for several seconds, her forehead wrinkling. "What date?"

"The date I set up for you."

More wrinkles appeared, these even deeper. Any more, and Claire would expect Kate to start speaking Klingon. "That's why you had my phone!"

"You should be more careful where you leave it."

"Why am I seeing Porter tonight?" Her focus drifted back to Butch.

"I need you to find out why he was in Ruby's office yesterday."

Kate did a double-take. "He was?"

"Yep. Jess caught him down there."

"Doing what?"

"Reading Joe's first editions. I want to know what he was doing looking at those books."

Flicking Claire's suspicions off with a wave of her hand, Kate said, "You're making too much of this. He's an author. First editions of classics are probably his idea of bathroom reading fodder."

"That still doesn't explain why he went down to Ruby's office. That's where you come into the equation."

"Why me?"

"Because he's not trying to get into my pants."

"Porter's not like that. He hasn't even tried to slip me the tongue yet."

"All the more reason to be suspicious of him."

Kate rolled her eyes. "What if I don't want to see Porter tonight?"

"Too late, he just walked in the door."

Amongst the sea of dusty cowboy hats, Porter's white brim stuck out like a pristine sailboat illuminated by a ray of sunshine. Claire beckoned him over.

As he skirted the dance floor, she turned to Kate. "Now flash him those pearly white teeth and get him to spill."

* * *

From the dance floor, Kate glared at Claire, who was chatting with Butch after exchanging her chair for a barstool—the seat where Kate wanted to be sitting, rather than swaying in Porter's arms to the warm baritones of Don Williams.

Porter leaned closer. "I was surprised to hear from you. Pleasantly so." His breath smelled minty, like he had a cheek full of Tic Tacs.

Me, too. Kate just smiled through her frustration.

"What was it you wanted to talk to me about?"

Behind her fake smile, Kate wished a plague of locusts on Claire. Some frogs, too. "That was some storm we had a couple of hours ago. Have you ever seen it rain so hard?"

"Yes. Texas has its fair share of severe thunderstorms, often mixed with hail and tornadoes."

"Have you ever been in a tornado?"

"Sure, a few actually."

Stall, stall, stall, her mind radioed to the frontlines. If she could keep him talking long enough, maybe she'd come up with a plan on how to do Claire's bidding.

"What was it like?"

"Windy." He chuckled. "I know you didn't ask me here to talk about storm cells. What's on your mind?"

She chanced a look at her sister for help, but Claire was too busy grinning at something Butch was saying to notice Kate thrashing around in the water. "Ummm."

"Just spit it out, Kate."

She contemplated throwing one of her sandals at Claire's head, but decided on another course of action. "It's Claire."

Porter looked toward the bar. "What about her?"

"She's very upset."

Right then, Butch finished telling his tale. Claire threw back her head, laughing loud enough to be heard over the music.

Damn!

Porter turned back to Kate. "She doesn't look upset to me."

"She's covering her pain with laughter. It's a common trait of hers."

"Why is she so upset?"

Scrambling, Kate blurted the first thing that came to mind. "It's Mac. He dumped her like a block of Limburger cheese."

Porter grimaced. "That's too bad. He seemed pretty taken with her when they were dancing together last week."

"Mac has a good poker face." As the song on the jukebox ended, Kate stepped back. "Will you do me a big favor and ask her to dance? She could really use a distraction tonight, someone to get her mind off Mac."

Porter frowned over at Claire. "It looks like Butch is already on the case."

"Butch won't do."

"Why not?" Porter's gaze returned to Kate.

She drew a blank and panicked. "He confided in me that he's taken a life-long vow of abstinence."

Porter's eyes widened. "Really?"

"The way he acts around women is just a ploy to keep customers coming back."

"Ah. That explains it."

She started to nod, but stopped. "Explains what?"

"Why he always has women hanging on him, but never takes any of them home."

"He doesn't?"

"Not that I've ever seen, and I've been hanging around here for almost two months now."

Good! Kate shouldn't feel like skipping after hearing that tidbit about Butch, but she did, damn it.

Squeezing Porter's forearm, she asked, "Will you please dance with Claire for a bit? It would mean the world to her."

"And this is why you asked me to meet you here tonight? To dance with your sister?"

"Uh-huh. She's been so depressed all day."

"Okay. But where will you be?"

"I'll just hang out at the bar." And grill Butch.

* * *

Someone tapped Claire on the shoulder.

If one more cowboy asked her to chalk his cue stick, pet his Wookie, or try out his Artificial Insemination Home Kit, she was going to start dumping some beer over heads—and with drinks half-priced, she could afford plenty of glasses.

"Go away!" she barked without turning around.

"Tag," Kate said in her ear.

She frowned at her sister as Kate dropped onto the stool beside her. "What?"

"You're it."

Porter leaned on the bar next to Claire. "Will you dance with me, Claire?"

Kate's eyes sparkled with merriment.

"Uh, sure." Claire kicked Kate in the ankle as she stood.

"Ow!" Kate yelped.

"I'm putting fire ants in your sheets tonight." Claire spoke loud enough for Kate's ears only.

"Try it and I'll pour peroxide in your shampoo bottle. Now get out there; Porter's waiting."

Sure enough, Porter was already on the dance floor.

Claire forced a smile as she slipped into Porter's arms. The scent of vanilla and cedar embraced her.

He led her away from the jukebox. "I'm sorry to hear about Mac and you."

"What do you mean?"

"Kate said that Mac and you are no longer a couple."

Stumbling in surprise, Claire came down on his toes. "Sorry 'bout that. What exactly did Kate tell you?"

"He broke up with you and you needed some cheering up."

Fire ants weren't going to cut it. Claire drilled Kate with a glare over Porter's shoulder.

Kate just toasted her glass of beer.

* * *

Kate emptied her glass in three gulps, partly to draw Butch back down to her end of the bar, but mostly to calm the horde of butterflies bouncing off the walls of her stomach. Interrogating suspects was Claire's forte, not hers.

Butch pointed at her empty glass. "Another?"

She nodded, trying to dislodge her tongue from the roof of her mouth as she watched him pull on the tap. "Uh, Butch?"

He placed a full glass in front of her. "Yeah?"

"How long have you lived around here?" Something about him gave her the feeling he wasn't born and raised in this corner of Arizona.

"Going on eleven years now."

"So, you know this area pretty well?"

"Sure, you could say that. Why?"

Kate licked the beer foam from her upper lip and dove in. "I was wondering if you'd mind taking me on a tour of some of the more interesting places in the area."

The bar wasn't exactly the most private venue to put Butch under a spotlight. She needed to get him alone, so she could slap on some lipstick and wiggle her hips until he spilled the truth.

Butch looked at her for several long seconds, his eyes searching for something, probably her angle after she had tried to screw him over at the accident. Her stomach knotted, then double-knotted, then wound itself into a hangman's knot as she held his stare.

"What about your sister?" he asked.

"Well, I'd rather she not tag along. She's clingy."

A hint of a smile flickered across his lips. "I meant, why can't she tour you around?"

"Oh. She's too busy at the R.V. park, fixing toilets, putting out fires, chasing skunks—you know, typical busy work. She really has very little time to spare most days."

His smile crinkled his eyes. "What about Porter?"

"He's only been here a couple of months. I'm sure he doesn't know this area like you do."

"I know, but how will he feel about you and me spending time together?" He leaned close, his voice lowering. "Alone."

The sudden heat in his eyes along with the spicy smell of his cologne had Kate gulping for air. She coughed, covering her mouth with her hand so her heart wouldn't fly out of her throat and hit Butch in the forehead.

"He, uh …" Her voice squeaked like a rusty hinge. She swallowed and tried again. "He and I are just friends. So, that shouldn't be a problem."

"Okay." He grabbed a towel from behind the bar.

"You mean, 'okay,' as in, 'it's a date'?"

"Well, I wouldn't call it a 'date'—unless you're looking for something more than I planned to give."

"No!"

Butch's eyebrows shot northward.

"Sorry, I mean, no, I'm just looking for a good time—a nice time, not 'good' like 'good-time Saturday night.'" Oh, God, she was botching this up so bad. She took a breath. "I just want you to show me some of the local sights, please."

Grinning, Butch asked, "How about Sunday afternoon?"

"No!"

His smile widened. "Are you always this passionate, Kate?"

Was there a double meaning behind that question? Did she want there to be?

"Not usually, it's just this weekend is Gramps and Ruby's wedding, so that probably won't work. I have tomorrow open, though."

"I forgot about the wedding. Okay, tomorrow it is, but we'll have to go in the morning."

"You name the time, and I'll be ready."

"How about eight?"

"Perfect."

A full-figured brunette wearing a tube-top and shorts that rode low on her hipbones and high on her cheeks placed a plastic pitcher on the bar next to Kate. She batted eyelashes gooped with mascara at Butch. "Will you fill me up again, sugar?"

As Butch took the pitcher, the brunette added, "Could you get me a clean pitcher? Billy sneezed in that one."

Kate watched the bombshell ogle Butch's butt as he turned around and bent over to grab a clean pitcher from a lower shelf. Her fingers itched to reach out and squeeze the tramp's lashes together, gluing her peepers shut.

While Butch filled the pitcher, the tramp asked him, "How's the takeover going?"

"According to my lawyer, we should close the deal by the end of the month."

"Perfect. Give me a call when the dust settles, and we can make a play date."

"Will do." Butch pushed the pitcher across the bar.

"Thanks, sweetie." With a wink in his direction, the tramp bounced back to her table, where two leering cowboys waited.

Kate looked back to find Butch watching her, his gaze narrowed, assessing. Assessing what, she didn't know. Maybe her lack of mascara. She wondered if he liked his women to wear tube tops.

"Kate," he said, leaning closer, his focus now on her mouth. "Tell me something."

She licked her lips, nervous all of a sudden. The flare of attraction she saw in his eyes made her heart speed up. "What?"

"Hey, Butch." A guy wearing a baseball hat backwards over a hairnet peeked out the door leading to the kitchen. "Phone."

"You want to transfer it out here?"

"It's Lana."

"Oh. Can you cover for me for a few?"

The guy nodded.

Butch tapped the bar in front of Kate. "I'll see you tomorrow in front of Ruby's store at eight sharp."

Kate nodded. Watching Butch walk away, Kate wondered who Lana was, what Miss Tube Top meant about playing, and if Ruby was going to be able to save her claim before Butch snatched it away from her at the end of the month.

She also wondered what Butch had wanted her to tell him right before "Lana" had interrupted, and if it had anything to do with the heat still steaming deep inside of her.

Tomorrow, Kate was going to find out some answers.

* * *

Claire's eye began to twitch from glaring at Kate's back for so long.

A sweaty, shirt-covered back bumped against Claire's elbow, making her cringe. This sardine can had too many damp, oily, cologne-dipped bodies wriggling around in it. She huddled close to Porter, earning a couple of raised brows from him.

She smiled, focusing on the task at hand—drilling him for answers. "How's the research going?"

"Good."

"So, is your book going to be fiction or non-fiction?"

"Fiction."

"Do you ever read for fun?"

"Sure."

"Who are your favorite authors?"

He cocked his head to the side. "Dean Koontz and Clive Cussler, for starters. Stephen King and James Patterson, too."

All of those authors frequently bumped into each other on the New York Times bestseller list. She would expect a writer to be more eccentric, to throw out the names of some up-and-comers, or maybe a Pulitzer-Prize winner like William Faulkner or Harper Lee.

Claire continued to smile, wishing she had some Vaseline to make it easier for her lips to slide over her teeth. "Do you like the classics?"

"Of course. What writer doesn't?"

"Exactly." Now she was getting somewhere. It was time for all those English Lit classes to finally pay off. "Mark Twain has to be one of my all-time favorites, along with Jane Austen, of course. What about you? Name five of your favorite classic novelists."

He cocked his head to the other side this time. "Classic, huh? Let's see. Charles Dickens, Edgar Allen Poe, and ummmm … who else is there … Hemmingway and Tolkien and … oh, his name is on the tip of my tongue."

So far, he'd listed only heavy-hitters. Most sixth graders knew those names. "Steinbeck or Crane?" Claire threw out a couple of authors whose names any Classic Lit fan or college English student should know.

"No."

"Verne, James, Alcott." She purposely threw Louisa May Alcott in there, playing the one-of-these-authors-is-not-like-the-others game.

"His name starts with an 'S'."

This time, Claire listed all females. "Stoddard, Stowe, Steedman?"

"No. It's 'Sh' something." He chuckled, the usually charming grin replaced by a lopsided, nervous-looking, upward tilt of the lips. "I must have had one too many beers tonight."

Claire hadn't seen him drink any yet. "Is it Shakespeare?" If he couldn't remember the great poet's name, he must have been sick his whole senior year of high school.

"No, not him. I can't believe I'm forgetting his name."

She tried to think of male authors whose names began with 'sh' and came up blank. "What's the name of one of his books?"

"Frankenstein."

"You mean Shelley?"

"That's it!" His grin was extra-bright and extra-charming, probably meant to blow all thoughts about classical authors from her head. "I can't believe Mac was willing to walk away from such a smart *and* beautiful woman."

Yada, yada, yada, Claire thought.

How could he not know Shelley was a woman? He liked Stephen King and Dean Koontz, for chrissake; he should at least know Shelley's first name was Mary.

She shook off her surprise and threw him another curve. "Being an author, I'm sure you're familiar with Robert Louis Stevenson's work?"

If Porter was really an author (and Claire was beginning to have serious doubts that he was), he should recognize that name because according to Jess, he'd been thumbing through *Treasure Island* when she caught him in Ruby's office last night.

"Sure."

"Which of his stories do you like best? *Jungle Book* or *Gulliver's Travels*?" Neither was written by Stevenson.

The charm in his smile dimmed. "That's tough. Both are great stories, but I'd have to go with *Jungle Book*."

Of course he would, because if Disney hadn't made it into a cartoon, he'd probably never have heard of it.

Claire lowered her gaze, not certain she could keep suspicion from her eyes.

It was apparent that Porter didn't know classic literature from a Chilton's car repair manual, which in itself wasn't a federal crime, but why did he claim to be a fan then? What need was there to lie? It couldn't be to impress her, could it?

Now that she'd discovered his knowledge about classic lit could fit into a shot glass, Claire decided to stop messing around and get to the point.

"Ruby has quite a collection of classics," she said, purposely not mentioning that they were in the basement office, which left Porter the opportunity to come clean about Jess finding him red-handed.

"I know."

"You do?"

Finally, a slice of hope for Matthew McConaughey's twin. Maybe he'd just been trying to impress Claire after all.

"Her daughter showed them to me yesterday before you returned from Yuccaville."

Wowzer. That was a liar-liar-pants-on-fire doozy. While the diameter of Jess's open jaws may be measurable on the big-mouth-bass scale most days, the kid wasn't a liar. Unlike Porter.

Now that she knew for sure he was lying, she needed to figure out why, and that was going to take some help.

Good thing Kate was going to be in town for a couple more weeks.

"Thanks for the dance, Porter." Claire backed out of his arms. "How about a drink? Kate's buying."

Chapter Twelve

Wednesday, August 18th

"Where are we going?" Kate asked Butch's backside as she followed him along a winding trail through a thicket of bushes with hanging yellow flowers, bean pods, and inch-long thorns that kept snagging her blue linen miniskirt. This was so not what she'd had in mind for this morning's interrogation.

Somewhere overhead, a bird screeched, sounding very perturbed at having uninvited guests. Not exactly the bluebird of happiness.

Kate flipped it off.

"It's just a little farther." Butch plowed ahead. "Where that tall cottonwood tree rises out of this bosque of mesquite."

"This what of what?" Kate frantically brushed a cobweb from her eyebrows and chin, worried its creator was now hitching a ride in her now not-so-coiled chignon.

"Bosque is the Spanish word for forest, and mesquite is a type of tree. These are velvet mesquite, to be exact."

Velvet, huh? She rubbed her nose. The way the thorns kept scratching her, they should've been named porcupine trees.

Dust coated the inside of her nose and crusted her dry lips, her sheen of lip gloss long wiped away. She plodded onward and upward as the trail climbed.

Sandals had seemed the best choice this morning, not only to keep her cool, but also to show off her manicured mauve toenails dotted with little white daisies. Had she known she'd be traipsing through a "bosque," she would have donned the hiking boots Ruby had offered.

If this was Butch's idea of a non-date, she could only imagine where he'd take her if it was the real thing. Skydiving? Spelunking? Cow tipping?

The warm breeze she'd felt when she crawled out of Butch's dented old Chevy pickup seemed to have been swallowed by the bramble of trees, leaving an uneasy stillness.

As the trail steepened even more, the trees closed in around her, grabbing at her with their bristly arms. Mottled rays of sunshine penetrated the branches and rows of skinny leaves, alternately highlighting and shadowing Butch's white cowboy hat.

With the only sign of civilization being a wispy contrail high in the cobalt sky, Kate wondered if hiking alone with Butch into the middle of nowhere was the smartest thing to do. Ditching a body would be an easy job in this tangled wilderness.

Clearing her throat, she swallowed what felt like a tablespoon of dirt.

"Is this your land?" She kept her tone extra light and happy, straight out of a Rodgers and Hammerstein musical.

"No, it belongs to old Dick Webber."

She looked up from stepping over a raised root just in time to collide nose-first into Butch's green T-shirt-covered sternum. He caught her by the shoulders as she teetered backward and waited for her to gain her footing before releasing her.

Blushing for absolutely no reason she could think of—except for the fact that she always seemed to have two left feet whenever Butch was within stumbling reach—Kate took a step back to put some much-needed space between her and his dark blue eyes.

"Sorry." She adjusted her perfectly straight skirt. "I seem to have developed a bad habit of colliding with you."

"I don't mind." Holding out his canteen to her, he added with a grin, "Unless you're sitting behind a steering wheel."

Her face burned hotter. Grateful for the shadows cloaking her at the moment, she grabbed the canteen and took a swig, letting the lukewarm water soak into the lining of her mouth before she swallowed it.

She handed the canteen back. As Butch took it from her outstretched hand, his fingertips touched hers and lingered. Kate felt sixteen again all of a sudden, full of silly crushes and raging hormones, her heart beating in her throat.

Then, without wiping the mouthpiece, he tipped the canteen back. As he capped it, he watched her, his eyes narrowed, assessing. She resisted the urge to tuck loose strands back into her chignon.

"Has anyone ever told you that you have cute ears?" he asked.

"Uh, no." She squeezed her right earlobe, realizing that in the midst of trying on six different outfits for her non-date with Butch, she'd forgotten to put in any earrings.

"Well, you do." Without another word, he turned and continued up the path.

She frowned after him. As far as compliments went, she wasn't even sure that registered on the charts.

Butch glanced back. "You coming?"

With a mental slap to knock some sense into the overheated gray matter in her skull, she trudged along behind him.

When she'd asked him to show her the sights around Jackrabbit Junction, she'd figured they'd head to Yuccaville, maybe meander through a mining museum; or drive to the top of one of the mountains ringing the valley and stare out across the endless shades of brown as she cunningly probed him for answers.

Instead, he'd spread out a blanket under a hundred-year-old cottonwood tree and treated her to a breakfast of granola bars, bacon, grapes, and bottled orange juice.

The second stop on his tour had been a huge ocotillo plant sporting more than seventy thorn-laden, green branches covered in tiny leaves. While botany field trips were more Claire's cup of tea, as evidenced by her numerous courses on the subject, Kate had actually enjoyed Butch's explanation on the many uses of the ocotillo, so much that she'd forgotten she was supposed to be playing Mata Hari with him.

Now, as Butch dragged her along to see his "hidden gem," Kate cursed herself for failing to figure out a clever way to prod him about his connection to the Copper Snake Mining Company. Not to mention asking him about Valentine, Lana, and Miss Tube Top.

Further up the trail, Butch paused and waited for her to catch up.

"So," she spoke between heavy breaths as she drew near. "Mr. Webber doesn't mind us trespassing on his property?"

"No, he's my neighbor. I hike up here periodically, checking his fences, looking for stray cattle, keeping an eye out for more coprolites to add to his collection."

Kate choked out a laugh between her parched lips. "He collects petrified shi—uh, dung?"

Butch nodded.

"What does he do with his collection?" She imagined an old guy dusting each piece with a paintbrush, labeling them, and enclosing the whole collection in a glass case.

"You don't want to know." Butch pushed aside a thick jumble of branches. "It's right through here."

Giving him a wary glance, she ducked under his arm. After several steps along what looked like a deer path, she stepped out of the thick brush and into a meadow lined with willows, cottonwoods, and stunted sycamores. Small clusters of vivid orange and red flowers dotted the meadow floor and undulated as the air breathed around her, cooling her sweaty skin. A mourning dove cooed.

Wow! Where were Adam and Eve and the apple tree?

Butch rustled through the trees behind her, joining her.

"What do you think?" he asked.

"It's beautiful. Those are pretty red flowers."

"The Indian paintbrush is nice, but that's not what I'm talking about. What do you think of the ruins?"

Ruins? Until Butch pointed it out, Kate didn't notice the alcove in the cliff to her left.

"You mean that cave?"

"It's not just a cave."

Butch grabbed her hand and led the way toward it, tromping through the grass. She didn't pull away, feeling like an idiot for the rush that came with just holding his hand.

They stopped at the base of a towering cliff. Kate shielded her eyes and peered at the ruins fifteen feet up in the rock wall.

She could see the base of the remains of an adobe structure. "What are those marks on the cave wall?"

"Pictographs." Butch's excitement showed in the slightly higher tone in his voice. "You want to take a closer look?"

Of course she did, but archaeological sites were usually fenced off. "Can we?"

"That depends." Butch let go of her hand and walked over to a pile of cut tree trunks lying in the grass at the base of the cliff and rolled several to the side.

"On what?"

He lifted a wooden ladder that had been hidden under the pile and leaned it against the stone wall. His gaze lingered on her legs before traveling up to her face. "If you can climb a ladder in a miniskirt."

Kate tried to act as if his interest in her legs didn't have her stomach feeling like it were full of bouncing lotto balls. "Sure, but you have to promise not to look up my skirt for London and France while I climb."

His grin spread wide. "How about if I promise to just check for one of them?"

He took several steps back, waving her toward the ladder.

Slipping off her sandals, Kate stuffed them down the back of her skirt inside the elastic of her underwear.

Butch watched, but said nothing.

She grabbed one of the rungs and started up the ladder, making it to the ledge without incident, and then held the ladder while Butch ascended.

"So, what do you think?" he asked as he joined her in the shallow cave.

Kate took in the pottery shards, stone *metates*, stubby remains of four adobe walls, and faded pictograph paintings on the cave walls. "Does anybody else know about this?"

"Just old man Webber and me." Butch extracted a leaf from her hair, letting it drift to the floor. "And now you."

He walked over and leaned against the wall next to the painting of what she guessed was a herd of stick deer. His gaze lingered on her for a moment, before focusing on the valley below.

She gulped. She was supposed to be seducing him, not the other way around. She needed to retreat to Ruby's, clear her head of this damned crush she'd seemed to have developed for yet another sure-to-be criminal, and come up with a new plan of attack—one that involved less bare skin and more technique.

In the meantime, she might as well explore the last stop on Butch's tour and try to keep from making a total ass of herself.

Pebbles dug into her heels as she strolled over next to him. "How old do you think this site is?"

"A thousand years, maybe two."

She started to reach out to touch the painting but stopped, remembering countless museum signs stating the detrimental effects of finger oil. "Why haven't any archaeologists been here to pick it apart?"

"Because Dick is a tried and true libertarian. He doesn't like the government—local, state, or federal—snooping around in his backyard. Plus, he's worried that if he tells anyone about it, he'll have vandals up here stealing artifacts, destroying the site. It's been a family secret for generations."

That reminded Kate of Joe's little family secret, the one about a mummified hand. Could that hand have been from this site? Had Joe known about this place? If not, had Butch found the hand here, along with the woven bag and little stick figure, and sold them to Joe? Maybe Joe and Butch had been working together, selling items on the black market. What did mummified hands go for these days, anyway?

She turned to Butch. "Did you know Ruby's husband, Joe?"

"Sure, why?"

"No reason." Kate glanced away, afraid he'd see more than she wanted him to in her eyes. She tiptoed through a litter of pottery shards over to the remains of the adobe structure. "I just wondered what he was like."

"He was ... interesting."

"Interesting in what way?" She peeked at Butch from under her lashes. He was still watching her, frowning.

"In the patrons that would come into the bar whenever he was in town. I could always tell when Joe was home." Butch glanced at his watch and did a double take. "Damn, we need to head back. I'll hold the ladder for you."

Kate didn't want to leave, not when she was finally making some progress—well, not exactly progress, more like digging her hole deeper.

She climbed down the ladder. Seconds later, he joined her on the ground. They hiked back to his pickup in silence.

Her mind churning, Kate wondered how well Butch had gotten to know some of Joe's "interesting" patrons, if he had ever been involved in any of Joe's jobs, and if those artifacts Claire found in the safe were from Dick Webber's land.

Butch held the passenger door open for her.

"Thanks for the tour," she said and climbed into the cab.

"Tomorrow, I have an appointment in Tucson. But if you'd like, we can go out again Friday morning."

Was his appointment with his lawyer?

"Friday sounds great." This time, she'd don boots, a pair of jeans, and bug spray.

"Great." He shut her door and came around, slipping behind the wheel. "We'll start the tour with the house where your sister got shot."

* * *

"If you two are going to start talking about women again, I need a drink," Claire said, dropping to the ground beside Manny's lawn chair.

Chester handed her a cold bottle of hard lemonade, still dripping from the slushy mix of ice and water in the bottom of the cooler.

She twisted off the bottle cap and washed the inside of her throat with the bittersweet alcohol, then held the bottle against her cheek. Sweat soaked her body, from the rim of her Mighty Mouse cap to the toes of her filthy socks.

If only those dark clouds to the east were drifting her way instead of hovering over the *Tres Dedos* Mountains. The afternoon heat had eased slightly as the thunderstorm cruised by, but the sun had served up a plate of extra hot rays today, and nothing short of an arctic front was going to break the heat's chokehold on the land.

Chester belched. "The fence looks good, girl. You may have a nose for trouble, but you have the hands of a carpenter."

"*Si, bonita.*" Manny lowered the binoculars and smiled at her. "You can't even tell an idiot backed into it this morning, especially since you added that coat of paint."

"Good." Claire took off her cap and shook her damp hair doggy-style. Fixing the fence had been bad enough in the blistering sunshine, but restacking ten-plus cords of wood had her daydreaming about lynch mobs. She wished she'd nabbed the asshole driver before he'd happy-trailed on out of the R.V. park.

The sound of shoes crunching on the drive snared her attention. Tossing her hat on the ground, Claire shielded her eyes at the sight of a pair of ladies approaching in matching red tennis shoes, blue knee-length shorts, and white shirts. Their silver curls gleamed under their identical navy visors.

Claire wondered if the other members of the Fourth-of-July parade float knew these two had escaped.

Each carried one plastic bag from the General Store. The woman on the left batted her eyelashes behind her rose-colored sunglasses. "Hi, Chester."

With a grunt, Chester struggled up from his chair and took the woman's outstretched hand. "Hello, Milly." He kissed her wrist.

"I'm Tilly." The lady giggled.

Chuckling, Chester winked. "I mean, Tilly." He turned to the twin. "Hi, Milly. No hard feelings, I hope."

Milly crossed her arms over her chest and gave him a "hrumph!"

"*Buenos dias, Señoritas.*" Manny's voice was thick with his Julio Iglesias brand of charm. He hovered next to Chester. "My name is Manuel."

Tilly's smile widened. "So you're Manny. Chester mentioned you last night. It's nice to meet you, isn't it, Milly?" She elbowed her pinched-faced sister.

Milly's eyes narrowed. "I suppose you're a two-timer too."

Manny's smile wobbled at the corners. "Uh, no. One woman is all I need."

Right, Claire thought. Make that one woman per hour. According to Gramps, Manny held the record for the most dates in one night. Claire couldn't remember the details, but it had something to do with Dallas, a Mary Kay convention, and a naked bowling tournament. Or did Manny get kicked out for getting naked at the tournament?

Milly grabbed her sister by the arm. "Come on, Tilly. My marshmallows are melting."

As Milly dragged her sister away, Tilly blew Chester kisses and waved at Manny.

"I'd like to melt her marshmallows again myself," Chester said under his breath.

Manny whirled on Chester as soon as the girls were out of earshot. "*Dios, mio.* Please tell me you didn't sleep with Rebecca's friends."

"I didn't." Chester dropped into his lawn chair. The cooler lid creaked as he grabbed another beer. "I just had sex with 'em."

Claire cringed and chugged more hard lemonade to wash away the image of those two and Chester.

Manny rattled out a string of curses in Spanish. "I told you to talk to them, find out what kind of men Rebecca dates. Not play house with them."

"Hey, I can't help it that women find me irresistible."

"What did you do to piss off Milly?" Claire asked.

Chester reddened slightly. "Nothing. We just played a little game of peek-a-boo on the couch, and then she went to the laundromat to get her clothes from the dryer."

Claire didn't buy his act. "So why does she want to string you up by your testicles and bat you around like a piñata?"

Chester smiled from ear to ear. "Tilly came home while she was gone."

Smacking his forehead, Manny said, "Don't tell me you used the same couch."

"Hey, it's not my fault. I offered Tilly some gin and platonic, but she insisted on a little scotch and sofa."

"Let me guess." Claire sat forward. "Milly walked in and caught Tilly and you doing the Poke-a-dance."

Straight-faced, Chester and Manny both stared at her, not even the hint of a grin on their lips.

"What?" Claire chuckled at her own wit. "Come on, you two. That was funny."

"No, that was just plain lame, Claire," Chester said.

"Is that the best you can do, *chica?* Your grandfather would be so disappointed."

"Speaking of Gramps." Claire pointed at Gramps, who was striding toward them with her mother hot on his heels.

Deborah was still wearing those ugly red boots. Gramps was wearing an even uglier frown.

"Uh, oh." Manny lowered back into his chair.

Chester murmured, "Who popped his balloon?"

Gramps stopped in front of Claire, glaring down at her. "Is this what you call working? Lazing on your butt in the shade, drinking beer? What do you think Ruby pays you to do all day?"

Claire sat there in stunned silence, her chin hitting the ground. She couldn't have been more shocked if he'd nested in front of her and squeezed a golden egg out of his ass.

"Really, Claire." Deborah joined Gramps's choir. "If I didn't already know, I'd never even guess there was a girl under all of that dirt. You'll never get a gentleman smelling like that. Oh, my God, is that stubble on your legs?"

Claire sniffed her pits, making sure her deodorant was still fighting the battle. Maybe she still stunk like skunk juice after all.

"Cut her some slack, Deborah." Chester defended Claire. "She'll wash up before Mac gets back from Tucson. Besides, some men like their women a little hairy. It adds friction, if you know what I mean." He waggled his eyebrows at Claire's mom.

While Claire appreciated Chester's attempts to help, the wide-eyed, horrified expression on her mother's face confirmed that he'd only made matters worse.

Ignoring her mother's criticism, Claire frowned up at Gramps. "What in the hell is your problem? You know I spent all afternoon restacking a shitload of wood and mending that damned fence. And while I appreciate that Ruby is helping me out financially, I'm not exactly making union wages here."

Gramps yanked three envelopes from his back pocket. "These are my problem." He tossed them at her. "How long have you known about these? And why in the hell didn't you tell me about them?"

Staring down at the envelopes in her lap, Claire played the clueless card. "What are these?"

"Don't play dumb." Gramps reached down and flipped over the top envelope. "You're the only one I know who draws reading glasses on her smiley faces and rabbit ears on her hearts."

Claire saw the doodles she'd made while talking on the phone to Mac. "Shit."

"Where did you find these?" Claire looked up to find Manny and Chester both leaning down to see what she was holding. She flipped the envelopes over so they couldn't see Leo M. Scott's name, or the letters spelling Attorney at Law.

"Your mother found them on the bar in the rec room."

Claire fell back onto the crispy grass and stared up at the cobalt sky, wishing the U.S.S. Enterprise would beam her up now. Ruby and Mac were going to kill her for leaving the letters out. She'd forgotten all about them when she'd heard that damned toilet was overflowing again.

"Well?" Gramps prompted, bending over her, his head blocking out the sun.

"Did you read them?"

He nodded.

"Then you know as much as I do." That was almost the truth.

"Bullshit!" Gramps squatted, his face close enough for her to see the vein pulsing under his right eye. "Claire, I swear, if you don't cough up the truth right now, I'll …"

"What?" Claire sat upright so fast they almost knocked foreheads. "What are you going to do? Ground me? Give me a time out? Send me to my room?"

"Maybe."

"Here's a novel idea." She pushed to her feet. "Why don't you ask *your* fiancée about the letters?"

"I'm telling you, Dad. This is just the tip of the iceberg. If Ruby's been hiding these letters from you, what else will come out as soon as you slip that ring on her finger?"

Claire reeled on her mother. "You need to keep your big mouth shut! This is none of your business. This is between Gramps and Ruby."

Deborah's cheeks turned a mottled pink at Claire's words. "How dare you speak to me like that, Claire Alice!"

"How dare you speak to your father like that, Deborah Marie!" Claire shot back.

"Claire." Gramps warned, his tone tired. He squeezed the bridge of his nose. "I appreciate your help, but you shouldn't talk to your mother that way."

"Fine!" Claire scooped up her hat and slammed it on her head. "From here on out, I'm done speaking to both of you."

With a nod to the boys, she grabbed another full bottle from the cooler, and strode away, heading for the hills.

Or maybe just the shower.

* * *

An hour later, Claire's temper still smoldered as she minded the store for Ruby.

"Claire, Mac's on the phone," Gramps called from the kitchen.

"I'll take it in the rec room," Claire yelled back, turning to Jess. "Will you watch the store?"

"For a dollar."

Claire growled in her throat, but agreed with a nod.

Jess hopped on the stool behind the counter and proceeded to blow grape-scented bubbles while perusing the latest teeny-bop magazine.

On the other side of the curtain, Gramps stood at the bar, holding the cordless phone toward her.

"I thought you weren't talking to me."

"I'm not." She grabbed the phone. "Starting right now."

He snickered as he disappeared through the curtain.

"Hey, Slugger." Mac's voice sounded slightly tinny through the receiver. "Why aren't you talking to Harley?"

"It's a long story."

"Does it have anything to do with why he asked me what I know about Leo Scott?"

Claire's shoulders scrunched as she braced herself for Mac's anger at her stupidity. "Yes. I accidentally left those letters out on the bar yesterday and Mom found them."

Silence pulsed through the line for several seconds. "And I'm sure Deborah wasted no time showing them to Harley."

"She waited until she could catch him alone—after Ruby left for Yuccaville and Jess was busy minding the store."

Mac sighed. "Damn."

"I'm so sorry."

"You're not to blame for this mess, Claire. We both know Ruby should have told Harley about this as soon as she got that first letter. If only she wasn't so damned stubborn. Has Harley confronted her?"

"No, she's not home yet. But he made sure to roast my ass over the coals until it got good and crispy."

"Is that why you're not talking to him?"

"Something like that. Are you sure you can't get off work a day early and come whisk me away from here?"

"I have a lunch meeting on Friday."

Claire grabbed a can of soda from the mini-fridge Ruby kept behind the bar. She cracked it open and slid down the wall, stretching her tired legs out in front of her.

"Have you found out anything more about the mine?" She kept her voice low, just in case Gramps or Jess had their ears pressed to the curtain.

"Yes, but it opens a door I thought I'd closed."

"What do you mean?"

"Ruby isn't the first owner to have someone use the courts to try to steal the Lucky Monk away. Fifty years ago, the Copper Snake Mining Company alleged that the mine belonged to them, stating that the then-current owner, Levi Taylor, had a forged copy of the claim and they had the original. Unfortunately for them, Levi fought the litigation all the way to the state supreme court, proving in the end that the mining claim was given to him as a form of compensation from the previous owner—an old miner who seemed to have an addiction to poker chips."

"If he had proof of this, why did the case go all the way to the state supreme court?"

"My guess is that the Copper Snake was lining the pockets of the local court justices."

"Does this court document show who owned the Copper Snake at that time?"

"Richard Rensberg Sr."

"Does he still own the company?"

"No. He's long dead."

"Then why does 'Rensberg' sound familiar?"

"Because—"

"I need to talk to you." Gramps's voice sounded loud, like he stood on the other side of the curtain. "Alone."

"Hold on a minute, Mac," Claire whispered, as footfalls clomped across the store's wooden floor. The clomping grew muffled on the carpet.

"Sure, Harley," Ruby said. "What's got you all fired up, honey?"

Claire covered the earpiece with her hand in case Mac decided to get chatty. Crawling across the carpet on her knees, she peeked around the edge of the bar.

Gramps and Ruby stood in the middle of the rec room. Ruby's purse still hung on her shoulder.

"Care to explain these?" Gramps held up the letters.

Claire winced, feeling like a Benedict Arnold.

A red blotch warmed Ruby's cheek as she eyed the envelopes. "No, I sure don't."

"Why didn't you tell me about them?" Gramps's tone was gruff, abrasive.

Ruby lifted her chin. "Don't you scold me like one of your children, Harley."

"I'm not scolding. I'm just wondering why I had to learn about this from my daughter instead of my soon-to-be wife."

Hands on her hips now, Ruby frowned. "I bet Deborah loved playin' show-and-tell with my dirty laundry."

"Well, at least she realized that I needed to be enlightened. Why were you hiding them from me?"

"Because they aren't your concern."

"Aren't my concern?" Gramps's shock resonated in his tone. "How can you say that? We're about to trade rings."

"The Lucky Monk is my mine, Harley, not yours. I didn't figure you needed to know about this."

"Yet you ran to your nephew for help. Do you know how that makes me feel?"

"I don't know. Why don't you spell it out?"

"Foolish and pissed off."

Hold up! Mac had offered to help Ruby only after Claire found the letters and showed them to him. Why wasn't Ruby clarifying that to Gramps?

"Well, get over it," Ruby said. "I didn't want to burden you with this, especially with your daughter here."

"So what were you going to do? Wait until we were married and then burden me with paying for a lawyer?"

Ruby took a step back, the red in her cheeks streaking down her neck. "Is that what Deborah's been whisperin' in your ear all afternoon? That I'm fixin' to marry you for your money?"

Gramps crossed his arms over his chest. "Are you?"

"I can't believe you'd even ask that, Harley Ford."

"What am I supposed to think?"

"How about thinking that I'm tired of takin' your handouts and wanted to try to fix this mess on my own without you throwing more of your money at it?"

That shut up Gramps for several seconds. He reached for Ruby's shoulder. "Listen, Ruby—"

Ruby dodged out of his reach. "Don't you 'Listen, Ruby' me, damn it. I meant what I said. This is none of your concern." She ripped the envelopes out of his hand. "Three days before our wedding and you have the nerve to accuse me of marryin' you for your money, you son-of-a-bitch."

Claire winced again, only this time for Gramps's sake.

"You should have told me about this," he said in defense.

"I'll tell you what I damned well please when I want to."

"Mom?" Jess cruised into the rec room with her usual bouncy step, apparently clueless that she'd walked smack dab into a tornado. "Can I have twenty bucks? I want to buy a—"

"No, you cannot!" Ruby shouted. "Now get back behind that register and earn your money like the rest of us have to."

Jess looked as if her mother had slapped her. Her eyes watered. "I'm your kid, Mother! Not your slave!" she stomped back into the store.

As soon as Jess crossed the threshold, Ruby zeroed in on Gramps. "I'll tell you somethin' else, Harley Ford. Since you like listening to Deborah so much, she can bend your ear all night long while you share the spare room with her, because you're not sleeping in my bed tonight! Or tomorrow night for that matter. Maybe ever!"

Ruby strode off down the hall, slamming her bedroom door behind her.

"There are too many goddamned hens in this chicken coup," Gramps told the walls and crashed out the back door, following his fiancée's lead and slamming it in his wake.

Claire sat there on tingling knees that were working on going numb, her eyes wide, the phone still in her hand.

"Claire!" Mac's said loud enough to travel through the hand she had cupped over the earpiece.

She started to lift the receiver to her ear and froze at the sound of footfalls approaching again. As she watched, Deborah slipped through the curtain, her smile stretched from ear to ear as she headed toward the stair. Claire could hear her mom humming all the way across the room.

Sitting back on her heels, Claire's gut boiled. It appeared she hadn't been the only ringside ticket holder for Gramps and Ruby's fight.

"Claire, what's going on?"

"Sorry," she whispered into the phone just in case anyone else was in earshot. "Gramps and Ruby were just in here."

"What happened?"

Claire dropped onto her butt and leaned her head back against the bar. "Shit just hit the fan."

Chapter Thirteen

Thursday, August 19th

"Lunch time," Ruby said to Kate, who sat behind the counter, working on a crossword puzzle while minding the store for the last hour while Ruby paid bills.

Her young grandmother-to-be carried a plate with two grilled cheese sandwiches on it. Kate was beginning to understand why Claire claimed life at the R.V. park made her clothes shrink. The smell of grilled bread and melting cheese had Kate drooling like a teething baby.

With Claire and Jess running errands in Yuccaville, and Gramps driving the stink-mobile to Tucson to be de-skunked while Deborah followed in Mabel, it was the first alone-time Kate and Ruby had had in days.

"I forgot to ask," Ruby said, grabbing a bag of pretzels from a shelf. She placed the plate and the pretzels on the counter in front of Kate. "How was your date yesterday?"

"Which date?"

"You must be a popular girl," Ruby's grin took any malice out of her comment. "I meant the date with Butch."

"It was … interesting."

So much so that she'd spent most of her evening with Porter thinking about the blue-eyed bar owner.

"Interesting, huh?" Ruby walked over to the cooler and opened the door. "What'll ya have?"

"Diet, please."

The cooler door closed with a thump. "I'd think with a good-lookin' guy like Butch, the date would be more than just 'interesting.'"

"It's not like that. We're just friends." At least that's what Kate kept telling herself every time her imagination started removing his clothing.

"That's too bad." Ruby set the soda on the counter. "Butch isn't only easy on the eyes; he's also a real wiz-bang when it comes to running a business. He turned The Shaft from a stagnant watering hole into a desert oasis."

Maybe Ruby could answer some of the questions Kate was too afraid to ask Butch. "How long have you known him?"

Ripping open the bag of pretzels, Ruby pursed her lips. "Let's see, it must be going on five years now. He's owned The Shaft ever since I moved to Jackrabbit Junction."

"Do you know where he's from?"

"Nope. Joe once mentioned something about Butch tumblin' into town on a breeze and catchin' on a fence, but not where he'd tumbled from."

Kate took a handful of pretzels from the open bag Ruby held out. "Do you know anyone around here named Valentine?"

"Can't say that I do. But there's a girl named Valerie who works at the hair salon in Yuccaville where I took your mother."

Kate shoved a couple of salty pretzels in her mouth, crunching loudly in her head. "Has Butch ever worked for the Copper Snake Mining Company?"

"I don't think so. Morning 'til night most days, his truck sits in The Shaft's parking lot. It wasn't until Wheeler's Diner went out of business a few months ago that he hired himself a full-time cook."

The bells over the front door jingled as Kate took a bite of her sandwich.

"We're back," Jess sang as she be-bopped through the doorway and across the wooden floor. She pulled a folded piece of paper from her back pocket and handed it to Kate.

"Thanks." The sparkle in Jess's eyes gave Kate the sense that the kid had come through with the private investigator work Kate had hired her to do at the Yuccaville library. Jess better have, anyway—she'd charged ten bucks for her services.

Claire came through the door just in time to see Jess pass Kate the note. Her sister stared at the paper, eyes narrowing.

With suspicion plastered across her furrowed brow, she looked up at Kate and kicked the door closed.

"What's that?"

Kate stuffed the paper in her back pocket. "I asked Jess to look up the phone numbers on the Internet for several insurance companies." She lied without skipping a beat.

"I thought you weren't going to mess with that until after the wedding."

"I changed my mind." Kate shoved the rest of her sandwich in her mouth, sparing Claire a cheesy-toothed smile while opening her pop.

"You want some?" Ruby offered to share the other half of her sandwich.

"No, thanks. We grabbed some lunch in town." Claire leaned against the counter. "How was your date last night, Kate?"

"Enlightening," Kate lied again.

She'd spent more enthralling evenings watching infomercials for albums full of sappy love songs from the seventies. Porter had spent the evening talking about two things—writing and Porter. He'd make an ideal Stepford husband.

"Did you ask him the questions I wrote down for you?"

Kate bristled. "No, I did not."

"Damn it, Kate." Claire's tone was full of exasperation.

"Don't you start in with me." Kate chomped on a couple more pretzels, barely tasting them. "I'm sick and tired of you pimping me out to that man. If you want to ask him questions, you go out with him."

Jess tossed a Milky Way bar on the counter. "You can pimp me out. I'll ask any question you want for twenty bucks."

Ruby's nostrils flared. "You'll do no such thing."

"I can't go out on an actual date with him until I turn sixteen." Jess blatantly ignored her mother's glare. "But you could invite him here for supper. Just give me ten minutes with the guy and I'll have all of the answers you need."

"Jessica Lynn, what did I just tell you?"

With a loud sigh, Jessica turned to her mother. "Did you or did you not tell me last night that I have to work for my money just like everyone else?"

Ruby crossed her arms over her chest, her lips pressed tight.

"Now, if you'll excuse me, Mother, I'm in the process of making a deal with Claire." Jess pulled a dollar bill out of her pocket and placed it on the counter next to the candy bar.

Kate wasn't sure if she should take the kid's money or let Jess keep it for bus fare out of town.

Ruby snatched up Jess's candy bar and money. "That's it, you're grounded. Go to your room."

Whirling, Jess cried, "Gimme that back! That's my hard-earned babysitting money. You can't take it from me."

"You wanna bet?"

"That's stealing!"

"No, that's called charging you a dollar for my white shirt, which you wore without my permission and then ruined by washing it with your red shorts."

Jess's eyes widened, then her face crinkled into a sneer. "I hate you!"

"Join the club." Ruby stuffed the candy bar in her shirt pocket. "There are two of you now."

With a war cry Geronimo would have admired, Jess ran from the room. She clomped up the steps and across the upper hall, sounding like a herd of moose sporting wooden clogs.

"Sorry about that." Ruby's voice sounded strained.

Kate patted Ruby on the shoulder.

"When are you going to see Porter again?" Claire asked Kate.

It was none of her business. "We didn't make any plans."

"Come on, Kate. How am I going to find out anything about him if you are too chicken-shit to ask?"

"Why don't you take him out to dinner and ask him yourself."

"Maybe I will. He still thinks Mac and I are splitsville, right?"

"Uh, yeah." Kate swallowed the lump of pretzel mush that suddenly seemed extra dry and thick. She hadn't expected Claire to take her up on her advice.

"Fine, I'll see if he's available tonight."

"You know, on second thought." Kate avoided eye contact. "That's probably not a good idea."

Claire tapped her fingers on the counter. "Why not?"

"Well, I might have let something slip last night that might make him a little closed-mouth around you."

"Damn it, Kate. What did you tell him?"

"Claire, I swear it was an accident." Kate had been so distracted by her thoughts of Butch and a little too loose-lipped from all of the wine Porter kept pouring into her glass, that she'd spoken before realizing what was tumbling over her tongue.

"What did you say?"

"Nothing much really. Just that—"

The phone rang.

"I'll get it," Ruby said, but Kate lunged for the receiver.

"Dancing Winnebagos R.V. Park, Kate speaking." She paused, listening, trying to ignore Claire's glower. "Yeah, sure." She held the phone out to her sister. "It's Mac."

"I'll take it in the rec room." As she backed toward the curtain, Claire pointed at Kate. "We're not finished."

Kate stuck out her tongue. "Catch me if you can."

* * *

Claire cupped the receiver. "You're calling early."

"I'm on my way to a project site about fifty miles south of Tucson." Mac's voice crackled through the phone. The canned sounds of traffic and his pickup engine ran interference. "I probably won't make it home before dark, and I doubt I'll feel like doing much more than showering and crashing, so I thought I'd take a minute to fill you in on the latest news."

There was something about his tone that made her stomach clench. "What's wrong?"

"Is Ruby within hearing distance?"

"Hold on." Claire walked across the rec room with the cordless phone and stepped out the back door, closing it quietly behind her. "Okay. What's going on?"

The smell of barbecued meat wafted under her nose. She shielded her eyes from the sun. Who could cook in this heat?

"I heard back from the Cholla County Recorder's office this morning. There's no proof in their files showing Joe ever owned the Lucky Monk mine."

"What do you mean by proof?"

"Claims or patents in his name."

"How is a patent different from a claim?"

"A mining claim gives the right to mine on federal land. A land patent gives outright ownership of mineral-laden land."

"I thought Ruby owned the land the mines are on, not the federal government."

"So did I, but now I'm not so sure."

"Shit." Claire fanned her T-shirt. The lack of a breeze made it hard to think.

On the southwestern horizon, cotton-like cumulus clouds roiled and swelled, cooking up another earth-shaking round of afternoon thunderstorms.

"Exactly," Mac said.

"What are you going to do?"

"I don't know. I guess I need to start by going through Joe's old files. See if I can find anything proving he owned the Lucky Monk. The problem is that Ruby has that stuff stashed away somewhere, and I'm going to have to ask her where."

"How are you going to do that without explaining why?"

"Lie, probably. I hate to, but with her wedding just days away, she doesn't need to worry about this stuff."

"So you'll dump the truth on her when she comes back from her honeymoon?"

"Hey, I don't like this any more than you do, but there's still time to get to the bottom of this without troubling her."

"What if you can't find anything in Joe's files?"

"I don't know." Mac sounded tired. "Probably contact the ADMMR and try to trace the history of the mine from its inception."

"What's the ADMMR?"

"Arizona Department of Mines and Mineral Resources—the agency that governs all mining activity on BLM land."

"BLM as in the Bureau of Land Management?"

"Exactly. The ADMMR has extensive files on mining in Arizona. It would be like finding a toothpick in a bin of tumbleweeds, but I'm running out of options." Mac's voice grew fuzzy with static. "There are some permit offices I can check with as well, but since Joe never actually performed any mining operations on his property, I doubt I'll have any luck on that score."

Claire held the phone tight against her ear. "What about the other three mines?" she yelled above the static.

"Claims and patents ... *crackle* ... on file under Ruby's name ... *fizz* ... each of them ... *sizzle* ... county recorder's office."

"Mac, you're breaking up." A drop of sweat trickled down her spine. "What if you can't prove the mine belongs to Ruby?"

"We're up ... *hiss* ... creek."

Sudden quiet filled her ear.

"Mac?"

Silence. Claire held the phone to her ear for another few seconds, then disconnected. She punched in Mac's cell phone number and got his voice mail.

"Damn it!" She slipped back inside to escape the heat.

Ruby stood in front of the walnut bar, her arms crossed. "What's goin' on?"

Claire cursed under her breath. Ruby didn't miss a trick.

Plastering a fake, sunny smile on her face, Claire shrugged. "Nothing. I just wanted some fresh air."

Ruby's eyes narrowed. "It's one hundred and six degrees in the shade out there. Why were you talking to Mac outside?"

Panicking, Claire said the first thing that came to mind, "Phone sex." She felt her cheeks blaze at her own lie. "It's been a while since we've uhhh ... been intimate, and we were both feeling kind of ... frisky. I didn't want Jess to hear."

Ruby held Claire's gaze for several agonizing seconds, then sighed and rubbed the back of her neck. "Thanks for considering Jess's ever-growin' curiosity ... I guess."

She glanced down at the phone in Claire's hand. Her lips tilted down at the corners. "There are some disinfectant wipes under the bathroom sink."

Without another word, she headed toward her bedroom.

Crossing the rec room, Claire banged her head on the bar—repeatedly. She needed to work on her lie-on-the-fly skills.

* * *

Sitting at the same Euchre table as her mother was the last place on the planet that Claire wanted to be at the moment.

Dangling from a noose under the starlit sky with hungry wolves nipping at her heels would have been preferable.

"It's your bid, Deborah." Ruby's fake smile shook at the corners of her lips.

Thankfully, Claire had been partnered with Ruby for this round in the tournament, so she could continue giving her mother the silent treatment without much of a problem.

"Thank you for yet another reminder." Deborah rearranged the cards in her hand. "You seem to be in another bad mood tonight, Ruby. Are you still going through 'the change'? Or is this just a case of prenuptial jitters?"

Shooting her mother a scowl, Claire shifted in her seat. The tension crackling in the air tonight had nothing to do with the lightening-filled storm clouds that had rumbled through the valley an hour earlier.

Ruby stared hard at her cards, her hands trembling ever so slightly. "Prenuptial jitters, of course, Deborah," she said through lips so stiff they barely moved, the drawl that usually softened her speech nowhere to be heard.

"Stop chattering and play." Chester told the two women, then puffed on his cigar.

Hear, hear! Claire thought. They were one hand away from being done for the night.

Wrinkling her nose, Deborah waved cigar smoke out of her face. "I can't believe Ruby lets you smoke those things in her house. Not only do they stink, but look how they've made the ceiling all yellow. Disgusting."

Chester threw his cards face-down on the table. "Deborah, bid, or I'm going to shove this cigar up your—"

"Chester!" Gramps interrupted from where he sat sideways at the other card table with Manny, Kate, and Jess. He adjusted the bag of ice draped across the bare ankle he'd twisted earlier when trying to step over Henry; it now rested on a cushion-covered, upside down bucket.

"What? I was going to say, 'nose.'"

"Patience is obviously not on your list of virtues," Deborah said.

"I gave up virtues along with cigarettes years ago; now pass or pick a number between one and six so that we can finish getting our butts kicked and move on to the next round."

Manny chuckled. "Someone sounds like a sore loser."

"Kiss my loser ass, Carrera."

The two men had been at each other's throats since Manny found out Milly had shared Chester's two-timing tale with Rebecca, who in turn told Manny that she'd sooner French kiss a rattlesnake than go on a date with him.

"Nice language, two-timer," Manny said. "Kiss your girlfriend with those lips, or are you too busy screwing around with her sister?"

Chester flipped Manny the bird. "Now bid, Deborah!"

"Keep your pants on, you old grouch." She shuffled her cards around some more.

"That's impossible for Chester when there are females in the room." Manny jabbed again.

"Knock it off," Gramps said. "You two—"

Deborah let out a loud, fury-filled shriek.

Claire almost fell out of her chair and knocked over her bottle of Corona while trying to keep from crashing butt-first to the floor. Cool beer ran over the side of the table and landed in her lap, soaking into the crotch of her jean shorts. "Shit!"

"I'll grab a towel." Ruby rose from her chair.

"What the hell is wrong with you?" Gramps asked Deborah.

Deborah shot up from the table so fast her chair flipped over. "Your rotten dog has my boot!"

She ran toward Henry, who stood at the base of the stairwell with one, well-chewed, not-so-shiny red boot.

As Deborah made a grab for the boot, Henry hopped sideways, just out of reach. Deborah let out a very unlady-like curse. She turned and grabbed again, catching just a pinch-full of dog hair as Henry ducked and weaved and zipped across the room. He slid to a stop at Gramps's feet and dropped onto his belly, the boot still firmly clamped in his jaws.

Claire's chest bubbled with laughter. Ruby handed her a towel. Glancing up to thank her, Claire saw Ruby's first true smile of the night.

Jess let out a loud, hiccupping laugh.

"You think this is funny, do you?" Deborah snarled as she tromped toward the other table. "We'll see how much you laugh when you have to pay me back for my boots."

Jess sobered quickly, her smile flattening out. "Why me?"

"Yeah, why her?" Gramps asked. "He's my dog."

"She's the one who let him in and didn't shut him in the bathroom like her mother told her to." Deborah whirled on Ruby. "Your inability to keep a clean house is superseded only by your inability to control your daughter."

Ruby gasped.

"Mom!" Kate grabbed Deborah's forearm. "You're overreacting. Sit down, put your head between your knees, and take a couple of breaths."

"I am not, and you keep out of this!" Deborah's neck was now blood red, almost the color of her precious boots. "Those boots weren't cheap. They're made of alligator skin."

Claire snickered as she mopped up the last of her spilled beer with Ruby's towel.

"What are you laughing at, Claire?" Deborah's voice rose even louder. "Maybe you should help Jess pay for the boots. You've been jealous of them since I brought them home. I've seen you eyeing them more than once."

Claire ignored her one-screw-loose mother.

"If you'd manage to keep a job for more than two weeks," Deborah continued, spouting sparks like a Roman candle, "you could afford your own pair of alligator boots."

Clare handed the beer-soaked towel to Ruby. "That's not alligator skin, Mother. It's alligator lizard skin. If you'd stopped blowing hot air and listened a little, you probably would've heard the salesman tell you that."

"How do you know what the salesman said?"

"Kate told me." Claire dragged her sister into the fire. It was only fair, since they both came from the she-devil's womb.

Deborah reeled on Kate, who slunk down in her chair while nailing Claire with a pissed-off glare.

"You knew they weren't real alligator, Kathryn, and you let me buy them anyway? Why? To share a laugh with your sister behind my back?"

"Mom, stop it." Claire stood, intending to snuff out this wildfire before it spread any further.

Deborah held out her don't-talk-back hand to silence Claire. "You've said enough."

Years of conditioning stopped Claire in her tracks.

Kate lifted her cards in front of her face and frowned at them. "Mom, sit down and chill. We can get new boots tomorrow."

"Don't you placate me!" Deborah snatched Kate's cards from her hand and threw them on the floor. "I know how Claire and you are. You two get a big kick out of laughing at me."

Kate shook her head. "That's not—"

"Oh, shut it, Kathryn. I heard you two whispering the first night we got here, wondering how your father ever managed to stay with me as long as he did."

Grimacing, Claire could've kicked herself. She should have known better than to complain within a mile radius of her mother. Deborah's hearing rivaled most species of bats.

"Well, I'll tell you something neither of you know. Your *perfect* father was having an affair with another woman for the last two years of our marriage."

Silence suffocated the room. Henry buried his snout in the end of Deborah's boot.

Huffing, Deborah stood in the center of the room, her eyes wide, like a cornered coyote.

Claire dropped into her chair, feeling like she'd played chicken with a wrecking ball and forgot to duck at the last minute. Surely Deborah was lying. Claire's dad would never …

Ruby stepped forward first. "Deborah, honey, I'm so sorry." She reached for Claire's mom.

"No!" Deborah batted Ruby's hands away. "I don't want pity, especially not from you. You're no better than the hussy who stole my husband."

Ruby jerked back as if she'd been bitten.

"Deborah!" Gramps shot out of his chair.

"You should know better than to marry a man old enough to be your father. How long before you start lying about where you've been all evening, or hopping from one bed to another? When the money runs out? Or right after you get that gold band on your finger?"

"My God, you sure are one miserable woman." Ruby crossed her arms over her chest.

"Ruby, don't." Gramps limped toward the two women, who circled each other like a pair of rutting buffalos. His twisted ankle barely slowed him up.

"Sit down, Harley." Ruby shot him a fiery glare. "You shouldn't be putting weight on that ankle."

"God damn it, woman, I told you to quit coddling me. I'm not an invalid."

Deborah's smile was full of razor-sharp teeth. "Not yet, anyway. You better sit down, Dad. You don't want Ruby throwing you in a nursing home right after you say, 'I do.'"

"You self-righteous bitch!" Ruby leered at Deborah.

Deborah lifted her chin. "Gold-digging whore!"

"You're a bossy old hag!" Jess told Deborah, her eyes burning two holes in Claire's mom's back.

"Jessica Lynn, you stay out of this."

"But, Mom, she called you—"

"It's none of your business."

"Yes, it is!" Jess's voice reached a shrilling level. Much louder and beer bottles would start breaking. "Least it should be my business since you're replacing me with Harley!"

"Jessica!" Ruby turned toward her daughter. "Not now."

"When then? After I move to Ohio?"

Claire blinked, frowning at Jess, surprised the girl chose this venue to reveal her plan to run away from home. The kid needed to work on her timing.

"I know all about your Ohio plans," Ruby said, "and this is not the time or place to discuss them."

Jess shot Claire a look brimming with hurt. "You promised you wouldn't tell! You're just like all of the other adults around this place."

"Jess, I didn't—" Claire started to explain that she hadn't told Ruby.

"If you're going to tell my secrets, I'll tell yours."

Claire's breath caught. Which ones? "No, Jess wait—"

"Like how you found that mummy hand in Joe's office."

All eyes turned to Claire, except for Kate who was eyeing the back door.

"Did she say 'mummy hand'?" Gramps frowned at Claire.

"I think she said, 'Rummy hand.'" Chester clarified.

"You need to flush the wax out of your ears again, you deaf fool," Manny said.

"And how you paid me to dig up dirt on Porter on the Internet," Jess added.

Kate glared at Claire. "I told you Porter is innocent."

"And how you told me not to tell that Porter snuck—"

"Jessica Lynn Wayne!" Ruby interrupted with a resonance that comes only with having pushed a child out through the birth canal. "Up to your room, right now!"

The wind billowing Jess's sails stilled. "But Mom—"

"Now!"

"Fine! I'm so outta this shithole town." Jess kicked a table leg.

"If you even try to leave this house, I'll personally hunt you down and make you wish you'd never shoved your curly red head out into the world." Ruby's chest rose and fell quickly. "And watch your mouth!"

Tears threatening, Jess raced out of the room.

"Damn it, Claire." Gramps spoke up after Jess was out of sight. "What have I told you about snooping around?"

"Gramps, you don't understand, Porter is—"

"Not guilty of anything other than showing you kindness." Kate finished for her. "Would you just leave the poor man alone?"

"Yeah, sure, as soon as you leave Butch alone," Claire said.

"Butch who?" Chester asked.

"The bartender at The Shaft." Manny grinned. "I saw them driving off together yesterday morning."

"They were on a date," Ruby explained to Chester.

"A date?" Deborah gaped. "Why are you wasting your time with the owner of some rinky-dink bar when you have a handsome author coming around? I swear, Kathryn, you've been spending too much time in the sun. You act more like Claire every day."

"Can it, Mother." Claire was sick of being the butt of all of her mom's comments.

"And you act more like your father every day." Deborah looked at Claire as if she'd grown feelers and preferred to scuttle about in dark, wet places.

"You mean rational and intelligent, Mom?"

"Unlike me, you mean?"

Claire smirked. Her mother was the world champion at turning insults around and crying "poor me."

"Hey, if the shoe—or chewed up boot—fits."

Deborah clenched her fists. "You call shacking up with some guy you barely know rational and intelligent?"

"Mac is not just 'some guy,' and quit trying to drag him down with you."

"Mac is just like all of the other men—out for a free roll in the hay. Why pay for sex when you can get it for free?"

"Drop it, Mom." Talking about her sex life in front of Gramps and his buddies made Claire feel like someone had dumped worms down her shorts.

"You don't just hop into bed with a man because he looks nice in a pair of pants. You never think of the long term, Claire. Ever since you were toddling around the house, you've been foolish and impulsive. And now you've rubbed off on your grandfather. I hope you're happy."

Kate stood. "Mom, you need to go to bed."

"No, she needs to go home." Claire rubbed her temples, wishing someone would ring the bell and call an end to this cage match.

"I'm not leaving this place until your grandfather comes to his senses and puts a stop to this wedding."

"Let me get this straight," Ruby said. "If Harley doesn't marry me, you'll leave?"

"Correct."

"Fine. The weddin' is off." Ruby pointed at the stair. "Now go pack your bags."

Kate gasped. Claire's jaw hit the floor.

"Wait a second." Gramps held a hand out toward Ruby.

"No." Ruby turned on him. "I've had it with your inability to control *your* daughter. Call and cancel the cake, because I'm not marrying anyone this weekend, especially not you."

Without another word, Ruby stalked out of the room, her head held high. The bedroom door slammed behind her.

Gramps grabbed Deborah's forearm. "Pack your shit, right now. You leave first thing in the morning."

She shook her head. "Not without you."

"You don't understand. If you're not gone by sundown tomorrow, I'll drag your ass to Tucson and leave you at the airport myself." He limped over to the back door. The windows rattled with his exit.

Spinning around, Deborah pointed at Claire. "If I leave, you're coming with me." She climbed the steps to her room without a backwards glance.

Feeling like she'd caught a fastball with her gut, Claire looked at her sister, then Chester, then Manny, and then Henry, who lay on the floor chewing on the boot that broke the camel's back.

She could use a cigarette about now. Hell, they all could.

"Euchre, anyone?" Chester picked up Deborah's cards and frowned. "She should have passed."

Chapter Fourteen

Friday, August 20th

"Here we are." Butch slowed his pickup to a stop.

Here where? Kate stared through the bug-splattered windshield at an aluminum gate bearing a No Trespassing sign. Utilitarian rather than ornate, the gate barred the end of a gravel drive that crested the top of a small hill covered with orange-brown dirt and patches of scrubby green bushes.

"Be right back." He grabbed a set of keys from his coin-filled ashtray. Kate watched from his air-cooled truck as he unlocked a padlock that secured the gate to a post, opened the gate, and then blocked it open with a large stone.

"What is this place?" she asked when Butch crawled back behind the wheel and shifted into gear.

"It's where your sister got shot."

As they rolled up the drive, Kate sent several sidelong glances Butch's way. Why did he have a key that opened the padlock on Sophy Wheeler's gate?

Butch cut the engine in front of a gray, single-story, cinderblock house. Kate followed him out of the pickup, shielding her eyes from the mid-morning sun.

She spun slowly, taking in the surrounding, mostly-barren hills that hid the place. Behind the house, a string of violet mountains outlined the mounds of orange-brown dirt. Wind chimes hung from the porch roof, dinging in the warm breeze winding up through the small canyon. Dust salted the back of Kate's throat. The place felt barren, full of ghosts.

The drive dead-ended at a shed with a rusty, corrugated steel roof that creaked with each draft of air. A coat of green paint had been slapped on the walls—somewhat recently, Kate guessed, judging from the dried paint splashed on the ground edging the building. On the door, a padlock that was identical to the one securing the gate kept the public out.

Kate turned to Butch, who leaned against the front quarter panel of his truck and watched her with an amused expression that made her feel like she'd been caught stepping out for the morning paper in her robe and curlers.

"So that's the shed where Claire and Sophy had their showdown?"

"Yep. Do you want to go inside?"

He had the keys to the shed as well? Kate grew more suspicious with each grasshopper that bounced past. "Is Joe's old car still stored in there?"

"Nope. Just a handful of tools. It's mostly empty."

"I'll pass then. Do you have the keys to the house, too?" She tried to sound flippant, but her voice held a slight tremor in spite of her efforts.

"Uh-huh, but I can't let you inside. You can peek in the windows, if you'd like."

Kate shook her head. "That's okay." Sweat beaded on her lower back.

"You ready to go?"

"Sure." She scuttled back to his truck. As Butch turned the ignition key, she wiped her damp palms on her thighs. "So, why do you have the keys to this place?" She hoped she sounded inquisitive instead of accusing.

"I'm taking care of it while the owner is away."

Why hadn't Sophy sold the place? The woman wasn't likely to be back here for a long time, if at all, from what Claire had been told.

Kate waited while Butch turned the pickup around. She adjusted the vents so the blast of air hit her in the chest. "Did you know Sophy well?"

"Sure." He coasted down the drive. "Jackrabbit Junction isn't exactly a sprawling metropolis. It doesn't take long to meet all sixty-seven inhabitants."

"Was she friendly with you?"

"She was friendly with most everyone, especially if you were a functioning male." He smirked. "If you know what I mean."

Dear Lord! The idea of Butch sleeping with Sophy had never crossed Kate's mind—until now. Her stomach dropped at the thought. She watched a lone poppy bobbing in the wind outside her window. "I didn't realize you'd, uh, been intimate with her."

Butch coughed out a loud laugh. "Sex with Sophy? Hell, I've never been that desperate."

Removing her hiking boot from her mouth, she grimaced at him. "Sorry. I thought … Gramps told me Sophy is 'a looker'."

"She is easy on the eyes, especially considering she's pushing sixty and has lived in the desert all of her life." Butch parked the pickup just outside the gate. "But that doesn't mean I want to take her to bed. She's not exactly my type."

"What kind of woman is your type?" The question slipped off her tongue like it'd been slathered with butter.

Her forehead heated as Butch stared at her.

"Kate Morgan, are you asking what I think you're asking?"

The wicked gleam in his gaze made Kate's body hum. She knew better than to get mixed up with yet another man who had a barred window and a urine-stained cot in his future, but that didn't stop her from fantasizing.

"I'm not sure." Her voice came out husky sounding.

Butch reached across the cab and captured the tail end of one of her blonde tresses in his fingers.

"Kate," he whispered.

"Yes?" she whispered back, her limbs heavy with anticipation. The spicy smell of his aftershave drifted over her, making her hungry for more than just sweet-nothings.

"How was your date with Porter the other night?"

She blinked, trying to make sense of his words. "How do you know I went out with Porter?"

"Ruby's daughter was on the front porch this morning when I came to pick you up."

Damned Jess and her mouth!

"It wasn't really a date. Porter is just a friend."

Butch raised his brows. "So you give goodnight kisses to all of your male friends?"

Shit! Kate had thought she'd seen some movement from the upstairs curtains after waving Porter off. She was going to nail two-by-six boards over Jess's window.

"No, of course not. Porter is just ..." she paused in the midst of explaining that Porter was just a mark that she was playing for Claire's sake. Claire would kick her ass if Kate leaked any more secrets.

"Porter is just what?" Butch pressed, letting go of her hair and running his finger down her arm, stroking the inside of her wrist.

"He's just, uh ..." she scrambled to come up with an answer, but Butch's touch had turned her brain to a consistency somewhere between coarse grits and cornmeal mush.

"Yes?" Butch leaned closer, his warm breath bouncing off her cheek as she stared straight ahead.

Kate gulped down a coconut-sized lump in her throat. All she had to do was turn her head and kiss him to find out what he tasted like.

"He's just what?"

"Using me."

His finger stilled. "He's using *you*? Why?"

"I think he has a thing for Claire." She tried to be slightly vague in her response to give her wiggle room if it got thrown back at her later.

"So he's using you to get closer to Claire?"

"Possibly. He's trying to make her jealous."

"But isn't she with Mac?"

"Mostly, and it's breaking poor Porter's heart."

"Mostly? How can you be 'mostly' with … Wait, wasn't she dancing with Porter the other night at the bar?"

"I believe she might possibly have been." Uh, oh, this little white lie was mushrooming.

"Does Claire know Porter is interested in her?"

Kate hesitated, fanning herself, weighing the possible fall out of however she answered. "Not completely."

Her forehead practically on fire, she lunged for the door handle, wanting to put some space between her and Butch before she combusted and melted a big hole in his pickup seat.

"I'll get the gate," she hollered on her flight out the door.

Cursing at her inability to control her hormones, she kicked aside the rock, pulled the gate closed, and locked the padlock. She needed to come up with another interrogation strategy. Her plan to seduce answers out of Butch kept backfiring in her face.

Butch's grin greeted her as she climbed into the pickup. "Cute blondes with pink cheeks," he said as he shifted into gear.

"What about them?" Kate flipped the air conditioning on high and directed the middle two vents toward her face. She glanced in the mirror on the back of her visor and winced. She looked like a red-faced spider monkey.

"They're my type." He punched the gas, spewing gravel in their wake. "Buckle up. Things are going to get bumpy from here on out."

* * *

"What are you going to do about her?" Claire asked Gramps.

She leaned back in Ruby's leather office chair, which squeaked out its two cents on the subject of Gramps swallowing his pride and crawling back to Ruby on his hands and knees.

"I don't know." Gramps paced in front of her. "What do you think? Roses? Chocolate? Jewelry?" He paused to eye the mummified hand sitting on the desktop. "Where do you think Joe got this thing?"

Claire shrugged and took a bite of one of the molasses cookies Ruby had baked earlier in the morning. Gramps needed to fix this mess before Claire grew too big for her britches from all of Ruby's stress-fueled baking.

"I'm still working on that," she told him.

"How old do you think it is?"

"I'm not sure."

"Come on, girl. After all of the college classes you've wasted money on you must have an educated guess or two."

"Well, Mr. Wise Ass, I have been reading about some of the ancient cultures around this area and I do have some thoughts on the subject—but nothing concrete."

Gramps stared at her. "And?"

"I'm almost positive it's older than the Hohokam and Mogollon cultures."

"You're speaking to a layman, Professor."

"Sorry. I'm talking B.C. era here."

"What makes you think that?"

"The early A.D. cultures cremated their dead. I'm still working on this stick figure piece, though." She pointed at the sculpture. "Between the library's Internet time limit and Jess doing my leg work, the research is slow. But yesterday she grabbed some books on ancient cultures that I'm hoping will shed light on the figure or that handmade bag."

A crooked grin formed on Gramps's lips. "They still won't let you in the library, huh?"

"I'm on six months' probation."

"You'd better not get Jess in any trouble."

"How can surfing the Internet get Jess into any trouble?"

"Just talking to you most days can land any poor sucker ass-deep in a rat's nest."

"Thanks for the kudos, Gramps. You just better hope I'm not in charge of what words are carved on your tombstone."

Gramps waved her off and returned to pacing. "So, how am I going to get Ruby to marry me?"

Claire caressed the soft leather of one of the custom-made cowboy boots Gramps had found a half-hour ago (along with a box of expensive cigars) while searching under Ruby's bed for Henry's squeaky wiener chew toy. Claire and Harley had come to the same conclusion about the boots and cigars: wedding gifts from Ruby.

"I think you need to start with talking to her. Go somewhere Mom won't find you and try to interfere. Where's Ruby right now?"

"She's running the store." Gramps snapped his fingers. "I know. I could borrow Carerra's Airstream for a bit, have him on surveillance duty."

"Good idea."

"Better yet, you take your mother to the airport in Tucson and ship her out of here."

Claire would rather eat a cow pie. "Mom's afraid to fly."

She didn't know why he didn't just put his foot down and kick her mom's ass out of Arizona.

"That's just a ploy so she doesn't have to travel alone. I'll call the airlines, see if they have any flights to Rapid City today, and book her a seat."

Claire figured this idea had about as much of a chance of flying as a one-winged rhino. However, if it would save the wedding, it was worth a try. But she'd be damned if she was going to catch and transport her mother with her sharp talons on her own. "Is Kate back yet?"

"No, but she should be in an hour or so."

"Wait until she's here before you say anything to Ruby. Between Kate and me, we can figure out a way to convince Mom to climb on that plane alone."

"Just tell Deborah I meant what I said last night." Gramps snapped his fingers again. "That gives me another idea."

The sound of footfalls on the steps made both of them look at each other.

Claire mouthed, "Mom," and pretended to zip her lips closed. She dropped the boot in her lap and leaned forward to hide it from view.

Gramps tiptoed out of view from the crack under the door.

Someone knocked lightly on the door.

"Claire?" The door muffled Jess's voice.

Whew! Just Jess. "Yeah?"

"Can I come in? I need to talk to you."

Claire raised her eyebrows at Gramps.

"We'll reconnoiter in an hour." He pulled open the door.

Jess jumped at the sight of Gramps standing in the doorway. "Oh! Um, hi, Harley. Can I talk to Claire alone for a moment?"

"Sure, kid." Gramps ruffled Jess's hair as they switched places.

After shutting the door with a quiet click, Jess leaned against it, her gaze glued to her pink toenails.

Claire slipped the boot next to the other one in the box, then kicked it under the desk.

Lacing her fingers, she rested her arms on the desktop and waited for Jess to speak. When the girl remained silent for several seconds, Claire prodded her. "What's up, Jess?"

It wasn't like Jess to be so quiet.

"Mom told me you didn't tell her my secret." Jess's eyes still drilled holes into her toes. "She said she got a call from my dad a couple of weeks ago, and he read her the letter I sent him—the one where I told him I'm moving up there this fall."

Claire winced. "Wow. That really sucks."

"Yeah. I can't believe Mom's known all of this time and never yelled at me about it."

Claire could. Ruby was no idiot. She had to handle Jess like old TNT. One wrong word and Jess would blow the roof off the place.

Over the last fifteen years, Jess's dad had made an ugly habit of stepping on Jess's heart. From the start, he hadn't wanted to take responsibility for Jess and only paid child support after Ruby dragged the courts into the ring for a tag-team match and put a

Full Nelson on his sorry ass. Now that he had a whole new family, including a couple of kids, he'd added razor wire to the wall he'd built to keep Jess out of his life.

"I'm sorry, Jess." Claire pushed back from the desk.

Jess shrugged. "It's no big deal. He just got confused and thought I wanted to live with him again, but I don't. I'm just going to live in the same town."

Claire took a breath, releasing it slowly out her mouth. The girl refused to see the truth, and it wasn't Claire's job to take off her blinders. "Are you still searching for the money?"

"Yeah. Why? Have you found it?"

"No."

Jess's shoulders slumped even lower. "Anyway, I came down here to tell you that I'm sorry I yelled at you and told everyone your secrets. That was really stupid of me. I should have known you wouldn't blab."

"No worries, kid."

"If there is any way I can make it up to you, let me know. I'll even do your research for free from here on out."

That was big of Jess, considering she was scrambling for every penny these days. "Cool. Thanks."

"Just don't tell Kate. I charged her double the research fee you paid."

Claire grinned. "I'll keep my lips sealed if you fill me in about what was on that paper you slipped Kate yesterday after we returned from Yuccaville."

"Oh, that?" Jess meandered over to the bookcase and pulled out one of Joe's first editions. "Nothing major. She had me look up Butch in the Yuccaville Yodeler archives. The only thing I could find was a picture of Joe and him."

"Together?"

Jess nodded, flipping through the book pages, glancing up at Claire. "They teamed up for some kind of fishing contest and won. At least I think that's why they were holding up all of those dead fish. It was pretty gross."

Working to keep her face unreadable, Claire smiled blandly. She hadn't thought about Butch being buddies with Joe, but with

Butch being in Jackrabbit Junction for close to a decade, it made sense.

Although Kate probably looked at the picture, added two and two together, and came up with nine again. She just didn't have good instincts. She never had.

Kate needed to stick to questioning Porter. He was the rotten apple in this bin. Jess's search for him on the Internet yesterday had turned up absolutely nothing, as in: *We did not find results for Porter Banks.*

That in itself made Claire's shooting hand twitchy. Something wasn't quite right about Porter, and it wasn't just that his teeth were too white.

"What's this?" Jess asked, turning the book upside down.

"What's what?" Claire joined Jess in front of the bookcase, catching the fruity scent of the kid's perfume—or gum.

"This." Jess held the book out to Claire.

Claire stared down at the faded, messy pencil scrawls jotted on a yellow Post-it, her brow tightening. Those were Joe's chicken scratches. She'd scrounged through enough bits and pieces of paperwork in his office to know his sloppy slant.

She flipped to the spine ... *Treasure Island.* Her eyes narrowed. This was the book Jess had caught Porter reading.

Turning back to the page with the writing, Claire moved over to the desk and clicked on the lamp. She noted the page number in case it played some significance before pulling the Post-it free, leaving the first edition's page unmarred.

"What does it say?" Jess whispered when Claire handed the book back to her.

"Claire?" Ruby called from the top of the stair.

Jess froze, giving Claire a "we're-busted" look.

Cracking open the office door, Claire answered, "Yeah?"

"That damned toilet is floodin' again. I know you're busy, but can you run on over there and fix it? I don't want anybody slipping and breaking a hip."

"I'm on my way." Claire pocketed the piece of paper. She'd have to decipher Joe's hieroglyphics later.

She made a shushing gesture at Jess.

After crossing her heart, Jess followed Claire up the steps.

* * *

Mac opened the General Store's front door and stepped into the cool interior.

His aunt looked up from the paperback she'd had her nose buried in and smiled wide. "Hey, darlin'. Boy-howdy, am I glad to see you."

Skirting the counter, she hugged him tight, like he had just returned from the moon. She smelled sweet, like cookies, which explained the white dust on her shoulder.

"Where is everybody?" he asked as she stepped back.

His lunch meeting had been rescheduled at the last minute, so he'd jetted out of work early only to get bogged down in typical Friday traffic, which had thinned to a trickle as soon as he reached the city limits.

As he'd sped over the asphalt toward Jackrabbit Junction, his thoughts had bounced around, from Ruby's predicament with the Lucky Monk mine to his own sticky situation with Claire, which included dealing with her mother.

"Oh, here and there." Ruby said, flippantly.

Mac's stomach growled loud enough to draw his aunt's gaze. In his haste to get back to Claire, he'd skipped lunch.

Ruby grabbed the jar of beef jerky strips from the counter and held it out. "Hungry?"

"Thanks." He ripped open the plastic. "How are the wedding plans coming? Is the bachelor party still on for tonight?" He tore a bite from the beef strip.

Her smile wavered. She set the jar back on the counter. "There isn't going to be a weddin'."

Mac froze mid-chomp. "Come again?"

"I called it off."

"When?"

"Last night."

The last time he'd talked to Claire, shit had hit the fan, but the wedding was still on. "Why?"

She shrugged and rounded the counter, sliding onto the bar stool. "Things just weren't workin' out."

Mac chewed on her words and the beef jerky for several seconds, noticing that Ruby still wore the engagement ring Harley had bought her. "What happened last night?"

"I realized a future with Harley wasn't in the cards for me."

"Then why are you still wearing his ring?" Mac nodded toward the ring on her left hand.

Ruby glanced down, then crossed her arms over her chest, hiding her ring finger under her right forearm. "It doesn't matter why. I've made up my mind."

Mac shot her a squinty-eyed glare. "What did Jess do?"

"Jess didn't have anything to do with my decision."

Then it had to be Claire's mom. "What did Deborah say to you?"

Ruby's cheeks reddened. "Nothing she hasn't been saying since Harley and I got engaged."

"You want me to take her to the mine and shove her down a shaft?"

That earned a laugh from his aunt.

"What can I do to help you?"

"Ah, honey. You've always been my knight in shinin' armor. Thanks, but I have to handle this one all by myself."

If he couldn't find the paperwork proving she owned the Lucky Monk, his knighthood status would be revoked.

Glancing at the curtain, Ruby leaned forward and whispered, "What've you found out about the lawyer? I've tried to get some news from Claire, but her lips are sealed up tight."

"Nothing." Which unfortunately was pretty much the truth.

"Damn." Ruby sat back. "Well, now that I'm not going on a honeymoon, I guess I'd better take over from here and get me a lawyer. I appreciate you fixin' to help me on this."

No! Not a good idea. "Why don't you let me work on this over the weekend? Do you know where Joe kept the records on the mines?"

"What kind of records?" Ruby's gaze was sharp, searching.

Trying to hide the truth behind a smile, Mac answered, "Maps, claims, patents, permits. That kind of stuff."

"I'll have to go up in the attic. Joe was a pack rat, and there are a bunch of unlabeled boxes up there that I haven't had a chance to look through." She raised an eyebrow. "Why do you need those records?"

"I just—"

The bells over the door jingled. Mac looked over his shoulder as Kate and a gust of hot air swept into the room.

"Hey, Ruby." Kate did a double-take when her gaze landed on Mac. "You're back, good. You need to do something about Claire."

He grinned. What was Slugger up to now?

Out the plate-glass front window, he saw the taillights of a familiar Chevy S10 pickup as it rolled out of the R.V. park.

"Was that Butch's truck?" he asked Kate.

"Sure was," Ruby answered. "Kate's datin' him."

"I thought you were dating Porter."

"She's datin' him, too." Ruby said.

Kate's forehead reddened.

"Wow, two men in one week." Mac chuckled. "What did you do? Tape your business card to the condom machine at The Shaft?"

Kate jabbed Mac in the ribs as she walked past him. "That's none of your business. You just worry about Claire."

Again with Claire. What kind of trouble was she in now?

Gramps walked out through the curtain just as Kate reached for the fabric.

"Katie, you're home. Good." Harley grabbed her by the wrist. "I need to talk to you for a minute." He glanced over at Ruby, who was suddenly busy inspecting her nails, and then Mac.

"Welcome back," he said, and dragged Kate through the curtain.

"What was that about?" Mac asked his aunt.

"Beats me." She avoided eye contact. "Now finish telling me why you need those records."

"I want to—"

"Why can't Claire do it?" Kate's raised voice came from the rec room.

Mac couldn't hear Harley's reply, just some low-toned murmurs.

"Fine! But you two keep forgetting that I already served my time when I drove her down here." The sound of footfalls bounding up the steps followed.

A look at Ruby earned him a shrug. "Family problems, I guess," she said.

Harley stuck his head through the curtain. "Mac, will you come here a second?"

"Uh, sure."

Harley stood by the bar where Mac joined him.

"What the hell is going on around here?" Mac hoped Harley would fill in the gaps in his aunt's cryptic story.

Sighing, Harley rubbed his bald head. "Ruby called off the wedding."

"She mentioned that. Why?"

"Because I didn't do what I should have."

"Which was what?"

"Lock Deborah in the tool shed until after the—" Harley paused at the clomp-clomp of footfalls across the wood floor in the upstairs hall. Holding his finger to his lips, he motioned for Mac to join him in the kitchen.

As soon as he crossed the threshold, Mac asked, "Where are Claire and Jess?"

"In the men's bathroom." Harley nudged Mac aside and peeked out through the kitchen doorway. "Did you bring my package?"

"It's in my pickup. Why are they in the men's bathroom?"

"It's complicated," Harley whispered over his shoulder, then stepped back quickly. Muffled footfalls followed.

Peering around the doorframe, Mac saw a glimpse of Deborah's blonde hair before Harley grabbed him by the arm and yanked him back.

Two seconds later, the back door slammed.

"Listen, Mac, I need a favor from you."

"What?" he said warily.

"Gramps?" Kate called from the rec room.

"We're in here, Katie."

Kate appeared in the doorway. "It's all clear."

"Good."

"You owe me for this."

Harley's brows lowered. "You're forgetting about those speeding tickets I found under your dresser when I helped move it."

Kate sighed. "Christ. Will you ever forget about those?"

"Probably not."

"Whatever. I'm going to get Claire." She turned to leave.

"Don't forget about Jess."

"I won't," she called over her shoulder and then followed her mother's path out the back door.

"Get Claire for what?"

"Operation Ditch Deborah."

"What?"

Harley dug a piece of paper and a wad of bills out of his front pocket. "Here's a list." He grabbed Mac's hand and slapped the paper and money in his palm. "When you get back, dump the goods in the tool shed. Claire will make sure it's unlocked."

Hold up. He'd just arrived. "Where am I going?"

"Yuccaville. Now hurry up before Deborah sees you leaving."

* * *

The waxing moon shed silvery light on the tool shed's aluminum roof. Claire's shoes crunched over the dry grass as she snuck behind the shed and peeked around the back wall at Gramps's car.

Mabel's bonnet was open, the flickering under-hood light casting a sallow glow over the engine block. An upside-down quart of oil jutted from the engine.

Claire squinted in the darkness, noticing the passenger side door was also slightly ajar, but the dome light turned off.

Thunder rumbled from the northeast—the last goodbyes from the storm that had skirted the valley earlier. Lightning flickered, flashing behind the cluster of clouds as they rolled over the horizon.

"Mac?" Claire hailed quietly, listening for a reply.

A warm breeze trickled over her skin and threaded through the cottonwoods overhead, stirring the leaves into a whispering twitter. An owl hooted twice from the canyon behind the campground, its call echoing off the walls.

"Mac?" Claire said again, a little louder this time. He had to be around here somewhere.

She crept over to Mabel and pulled the passenger door open wide. She popped the glove box, digging through the paperwork.

Ah, sweet Mother Mary, she thought as she pulled a wrinkled pack of Virginia Slim cigarettes from the box, just where she'd stashed them months ago.

All day, all she'd wanted to do was hide in Ruby's office and figure out what those scrawls on that Post-it note meant, but between that damned toilet and Gramps's crazy plan, she hadn't had a single moment to herself.

Until now.

She tapped a bent, undoubtedly stale cigarette from the pack, and held it under her nose, inhaling that old familiar bouquet of tobacco. Damn, she missed smoking.

After spending half of the afternoon driving Deborah and Kate to Tucson International Airport in Ruby's old Ford (sans air conditioning) only to find out at the ticket counter that Deborah had "accidently" forgotten her wallet with all of her identification at Ruby's place, Claire needed nicotine as much as oxygen.

Her mother hadn't stopped crooning her nobody-loves-me sad song until they were half way home. But then she'd changed her tune, and Claire's ears still burned from her fiery rant.

She stuck the cigarette butt between her lips, tasting the stale tobacco, pulled a book of matches from her back pocket, and struck a match. A burst of flame lit her palm, the sharp smell of sulfur an aphrodisiac.

"Rough day, Slugger?"

She dropped the match. "Jesus, Mac! You scared the shit out of me."

"You better put that out."

Crap! She stomped around in the grass and dirt.

He plucked the cigarette from her mouth. "What's this for?"

"I'm a little stressed."

"Your mother's been here a week now and you're only a 'little' stressed?"

"You have no idea." Satisfied there'd be no middle-of-the-night wildfires, she stopped taking her frustrations out on the flattened weeds.

Mac grabbed the pack of cigarettes from her hand, stuffed the bent cigarette back in it, and tossed it in the front seat.

"Come on, Mac. Just one."

"You don't need it."

"You weren't there on the drive back from Tucson. If you had been, you'd buy me a new pack and smoke half of it with me."

He leaned against the back quarter-panel and caught her hand, pulling her toward him. "Come here. I have something that will relieve your stress."

Claire liked the sound of that. "You promise?"

"Oh, sweetheart." He caught her by the belt loops on her shorts and tugged her close. "I guarantee it."

She wrapped her arms around his neck, inhaling the warm, desert-fresh scent that was Mac. "I missed you."

"I bet." He groaned as she pressed against him, rubbing. "How do you manage to live without me?"

"I carry your picture in my locket and moon over it day and night."

He brushed his mouth over hers. "Please tell me you're not wearing anything under these shorts," he whispered as his lips feathered along her jaw.

"Why don't you see for yourself?"

"Claire." His hands spanned her hips. He nuzzled the crook of her neck, his beard stubble rasping her skin. "I missed you."

She slipped her hands under his shirt, dragging her fingernails down the center of his chest. He shuddered under her touch. "You know what I want you to do to me?"

"Tar and feather you?" He nipped her collar bone, his hands drifting northward.

"Kinky, but no." She gasped as his thumbs worked some magic.

"Lock you in an iron maiden?" His breath warmed her inner ear as his lips grazed her earlobe.

"Too S-and-M-ish. Try again."

His fingers slipped beneath her underwire. "Tie you to the rack and give you a good stretch."

"I've always wanted to be a couple of inches taller, but not quite." Pulling her hands free of his shirt, she ran her palms up his forearms and biceps, trailed her nails over his shoulders, and then sank her fingers into his hair.

"I want you to do that trick you do, Mac."

"Which one?" His gaze dipped downward, watching his fingers move under her top.

"The one you do that makes me scream." Claire covered his lips with hers, her tongue teasing, tasting.

"Mmmmmm." The sound rumbled up from Mac's chest.

Drawing back to catch a breath, she said. "Come on, let's get in the car."

Mac glanced through the back window. "In there?"

"Mabel has a big backseat."

"Not big enough."

"Come on, where's your sense of adventure?"

"I lost it down a shaft. How about the shed?"

"No way. It stinks like oil and gas in there, not to mention that colony of scorpions I've been battling."

"Why not right here."

"Against Gramps's car? What if somebody comes?" Claire didn't relish Manny or Chester walking up on them, or watching them through their binoculars. They probably had night vision on those things.

"They won't. Harley has it all planned out. They're leaving early to go out to breakfast before heading to the courthouse." He kissed her again, turning her knees to Jell-O. "Come on, Claire. Where is *your* sense of adventure?"

Mac unbuttoned her shorts and slipped his hands inside the cotton, cupping her hips. "Hmmm, you *are* wearing panties."

"I can change that if you'll join me in Mabel's backseat."

"No way. I'm not getting caught in that car with your hands in my pants again. It took months for the ornery old goats to let me live that down."

Mac's fingers found their way inside her satin underwear.

She groaned, rubbing against him. "So you'd rather get caught out here with your hands in *my* pants?"

His mouth covered hers, kissing her long and slow, exploring every corner of her mouth while his fingers kneaded her.

Claire dissolved against him, giving in to his onslaught. When his lips moved south, down her throat, his tongue licking the hollow at its base, she gasped and grabbed his wrist, moving his hand around to the front of her shorts.

"Touch me," she whispered in his ear, then nipped his earlobe.

"Oh God, Claire. You make me want to—"

"Damn it, Claire!" the sound of Gramps's voice scared a yip out of her. "What did I tell you about sex in Mabel?"

Mac yanked his hand out of her shorts, but when she tried to step away from him, he held her in place, blocking him from their unwanted visitor's view.

"Don't move yet," he said under his breath.

Claire zipped up her shorts. "For your information," she said over her shoulder, "we were not having sex in Mabel."

"I think they were going to have sex *on* Mabel," Manny clarified. "We should have waited a little longer before interrupting, then we could have really gotten a show."

"I should have brought my night vision goggles," Chester said and wheezed out a laugh.

"From now on, no sex in or near Mabel, period," Gramps snapped.

"Well, there's nowhere else we can go to get a little privacy around here." Claire turned around, still shielding Mac.

Ruby appeared next to Gramps in the moonlight. "You can use my bedroom. Harley and I have decided to elope."

Chapter Fifteen

Saturday, August 21st

"What do you mean they're 'gone'?" Jess asked the next morning as she trailed Claire out the General Store's front door and down the porch steps.

"Gone, as in they eloped to Vegas last night and won't be back for a few days." She glanced back to catch Jess's reaction.

Barefooted and dressed in her pink pajamas, still blinking away the remnants from sleep, Jess stood there in the sunlight with a frown so big even her ears seemed to droop. "I can't believe my mom left without telling me."

Deborah hadn't taken the news nearly so calmly.

Last night, after Ruby and Gramps had rumbled off into the night, Claire and Mac had snuck into the house, planning to finish what they'd started. But Claire's excitement had wilted at the sight of her mother, standing in the rec room, with lips pinched tighter than fat toes crammed into a pair of stiletto heels.

Her mother had heard the sound of Mabel's muffler, noted the fact that Gramps and Ruby were nowhere to be found, and come to the correct conclusion that she'd been duped. It turned out the only heavy breathing done last night was by Deborah, who ranted at Claire and Kate for their deception.

By the time Deborah ran out of wind, Mac lay passed out on the couch, where Deborah insisted he stay for the night. Too tired to object, Claire claimed Ruby's king-sized bed, which she had to share with Kate since Mac had monopolized the couch.

Way too soon, sunlight had poked through the curtains, reminding Claire that she had to do Ruby's dawn duty of cleaning the campground restrooms.

Now, six hours, a raspberry jelly-filled doughnut, and two bottles of Coke later, Claire's eyeballs felt like she had dipped them in hairspray.

On top of that, she had yet to sit down and figure out what Joe's scrawls on the Post-it note meant.

Shielding her eyes from the glaring sun, she crunched across the drive toward Mac's pickup. Jess followed, picking her way through the stones.

Claire opened the passenger door and leaned inside, looking for the manila envelope that he'd said was full of information regarding the Lucky Monk. A wave of hot air with the faint smell of Mac's cologne rolled over her.

Jess caught up with Claire. "You'd think Ruby would've at least told her kid she was leaving. Do you think she took the money with her?"

Her back to Jess, Claire rolled her eyes. "Think about it, Jess. Why would she take all of that money with her?"

"Good, that means it's still somewhere around here."

Silence followed as Claire bent the back of the bench seat forward and searched through the gadgets, tools, and geology-related books Mac had neatly packed back there.

"What are you doing?" Jess asked.

Out of the corner of her eye, Claire could see Jess peering over her shoulder. "Looking for something for Mac."

After breakfast, Mac had disappeared up the attic ladder. Claire suspected he was searching for proof of Ruby's ownership of the Lucky Monk, but she hadn't asked, since Deborah had been circling in vulture fashion since emerging from her lair wearing curlers, a silk robe, and bright red lipstick.

Muffled thumps overhead had been the only sign of life from Mac all morning until a few minutes ago when he'd hollered down to ask Claire if she'd run out to his pickup and grab the envelope.

"You should look in the glove box." Jess offered unsolicited help.

"Thanks," Claire said with a dose of sarcasm.

She clicked the seat back into an upright position, pulled open the door to the glove compartment, and screamed.

* * *

Mac looked up from the box of Joe's old tax returns he'd been sifting through. He frowned at the web-clogged mesh covering the attic vent. Was that a scream?

Several seconds passed, filled with the whirring of the attic fan. He shook his head. It must have been his imagination.

Specs of dust twirled and tumbled through the air, illuminated by the 100-watt halogen floodlight Mac had dragged up into the sweltering loft. The scent of dry-rotted cardboard and baked insulation surrounded him. He mopped his face with his sweat-soaked T-shirt and bent back over the box of returns.

A high-pierced shriek rang out.

Jess! He'd know that eardrum-bursting scream anywhere.

Springing to his feet, he dashed down the attic ladder, and took the steps three at a time. The rec room and store were nothing more than a blur.

He raced down the porch steps. "Jess?"

"Mac, no! Freeze!" Claire said from where she leaned inside the passenger side of his pickup.

He skidded to a stop a couple of feet behind her. "Where's Jess?"

"I'm up here," Jess said from the porch.

On his flight out of the store, he'd zipped past where she stood, plastered against the wall, trying to become one with the house.

He turned back to Claire. "What's going on?"

"I have a little problem." Claire said, still with her back to him.

Then he heard it—a dry, rattling sound, like a tiny pair of maracas.

He crept up behind Claire and peered over her shoulder.

A diamondback rattlesnake sat coiled, tail shaking, on the open glove box door, not a foot from Claire. Its head was raised and poised to strike.

"Fuck." He licked his dry lips.

"That's my line," Claire said.

Easing back, Mac rubbed the back of his neck.

Rattlesnakes could strike in under a second. His chance of pulling Claire away fast enough to avoid a bite didn't look too good.

"It's not hissing." Mac observed.

"It looks plenty pissed off to me."

"You should've slammed the door on it as soon as you saw it." Before it had time to prepare to strike.

"Yeah, well, I sort of froze. Snakes freak me out."

"You might be able to move out of its range if you take it slowly." He peered through the open window at the snake.

The snake opened its mouth and hissed.

"He disagrees," Claire whispered. "And I'm with him."

"What are you going to do? Stand there all afternoon until you pass out from the heat?"

"Maybe he'll go to sleep."

Mac thought about going around to the other side if his pickup and trying to distract the snake, but worried he might scare it into striking Claire instead.

Reaching out slowly, he placed his hands on the door panel, the metal almost too hot to touch. "Claire, I want you to take a very small, very slow step backward."

"Uhhhh, no."

Mac heard the screen door squeak open. "What's going on?" Kate asked.

"Claire is about to get bitten by a rattlesnake." Jess informed Kate matter-of-factly.

Mac shot Jess a shut-up glare. Her candid play-by-play wasn't helping.

"There's a snake out here?" Kate's voice was high and squeaky, like she'd channeled Minnie Mouse. She opened the screen door and slipped back inside, watching through the mesh.

"My sister's support is amazing," Claire muttered under her breath.

"Claire." Mac focused on the snake again. Its head had lowered slightly. "Whether you meant to or not, you've cornered the snake. You have to make the first move."

"Easy for you to say. You're not face-to-face with a set of fangs."

"Trust me."

Several seconds passed, the rattling of the snake's tail filling the void.

Claire's shoulders lifted and dropped as she took a deep breath. "Okay."

She took a tiny step backward.

The snake's tail rattled harder.

"Mac?" Claire's voice shook.

"It's okay, Slugger. Take another step." Two more and she'd be clear of the door.

She followed his instructions.

The snake hissed, its fangs threatening.

Claire froze. "If he bites me—"

"He won't."

"—I'm gonna bite you and pass on the poison."

"I love it when you talk dirty to me."

"You're twisted."

"One more step to go, baby."

A butterfly flitted in front of Claire's eyes. She jerked and stepped back. Mac shoved the door, catching sight of the snake throwing itself up and forward as the door closed.

"Shit! Shit! Shit!" Claire brushed off her arms and stomach, shuddering visibly. "That was close."

"Are you okay?" Mac reached for her.

Jess shrieked from her spot on the porch.

"What now!" Mac whirled to scowl at his niece.

She was pointing at the pickup door, where the head of the rattler hung next to the door handle by a thick thread of flesh.

"Damn." He scrubbed down his face. "That was way too close."

"What in the hell are you doing with a rattlesnake in your glove box?" Claire was still rubbing her forearms.

Dragging his gaze from the blood dripping onto the gravel, he stared at Claire. "That was in my glove box?"

She nodded.

Mac grabbed the door handle.

"What are you doing?" Claire stumbled back several feet.

"That's where I had the envelope." He opened the door. The dead snake slid out onto the ground, its tail still twitching.

"Ewww!" Jess made a great audience.

Mac kicked the carcass under the pickup, then leaned inside the hot cab and rifled through the glove box, which now stunk like snake piss thanks to his dead visitor.

"Well?" Claire asked from over his shoulder.

"It's gone."

"Are you sure that's where you left it?"

"One hundred percent." He slammed the truck door shut. All of the information he'd gathered to date on the Lucky Monk was gone, stolen. A week's worth of research wasted. Son of a bitch!

Claire cursed along with him, doing a much more thorough job of it. Then she asked, "Is there anything else missing?" Like Gramps's mysterious package?

Mac shook his head.

"Who would steal that envelope?"

"Somebody who knows I'm digging for proof on the Lucky Monk. I shouldn't have left my windows down yesterday when I was picking up stuff for Harley in Yuccaville."

"Did you see anyone suspicious?"

"No, just a few kids on skateboards and that dickhead Rensberg heading into his bank."

"Rensburg. You mentioned that name before."

"He's the vice president who gave Ruby grief a few months ago."

"But why put a snake in your glove box?"

Despite the late morning sun blazing a trail across the sky, a chill prickled Mac's spine. "As a warning."

* * *

"I need to visit the little girl's room," Kate heard Claire yell over the roar of The Shaft's Saturday night crowd.

She nodded, waiting until Claire had weaved through the throng of bodies before turning to Gary, the bartender. "Is Butch around?"

She fanned herself with a cardboard coaster. If the smoke-filled air didn't choke her by the end of the night, she'd surely keel over from the heat. The place had to be spilling over the maximum occupancy level. Who knew there were so many people hiding under rocks around these parts.

Gary shook his head. He leaned over the bar as he dried a shot glass. "He had to run to Yuccaville, but he'll be back in— oh, shit! Not again."

Throwing down his towel, he dashed out from behind the bar.

Whistles, catcalls, and hoots of laughter erupted from a table near the dance floor. Kate spun on her bar stool and watched, her mouth gaping, as a lanky young redheaded cowboy proceeded to perform a striptease for his well-soused buddies and anyone else interested in watching. His jeans ringed his ankles before the bartender managed to part the sea of drunks and flag Mr. Tighty-Whities's attention.

Kate's window of opportunity slid open. With a glance toward the bathroom to make sure Claire was out of the picture, she hopped off the stool and stole to the door leading to the kitchen.

The hinges creaked as she inched it open and peeped into the florescent lit room, the air hazy with grease and thick with the scent of fried meat. Across the room, a man stood at the stove with his back to her while he flipped burgers and whistled to Johnny Cash's, *Walk the Line*, which blared from the radio perched nearby.

Kate checked over her shoulder to make sure nobody had noticed her. The stripper had managed to shuck his shirt in spite of Gary's attempt to wrestle him down off the table. The group of cowboys and cowgirls watching the show cheered at the sight of the kid's pale, bony chest.

Slipping through the door, Kate tiptoed across the kitchen and down the hall on the other side. Three doors lined the corridor—one on the left, one on the right, and one at the end. A mop and yellow bucket filled with sudsy water leaned against the wall near the last door.

The door on the left had a window in it, but the light was off inside. Kate doubted this was Butch's office, but she reached for the doorknob anyway. A flick of the light switch revealed a large storage room, filled with metal shelves lined with warehouse-sized bags of flour and hamburger buns, among other sundries. Kate peeked through the window to confirm the coast was clear before easing back into the hall.

The door on the right had an EXIT sign above it. It led out behind the bar next to the dumpster, a grease bin, and a small section of the parking lot all bathed in an orange glow from the overhead nightlight.

That left the door at the end of the hall.

Her heart sank at the sight of a deadbolt lock and a keyhole in the doorknob, but it twisted freely in her hand. She knocked lightly, just in case the bartender had been wrong about Butch's whereabouts, and pushed the door open. Shadows greeted her.

With one last glance behind her, she darted into the room. She closed the door and leaned against it, catching her breath. Breaking and entering had always been Claire's forte. Kate usually just ran interference.

A feeble orange smear of light leaked in from the small window across from her. She fumbled along the wall and flipped on the light switch, expecting florescent lights to buzz to life overhead. Instead a desk lamp flickered on, along with a couple of recessed lights overhead, casting a warm glow over the room and Butch's antique-looking desk.

As she waited for her heart to stop racing to win the Kentucky Derby, she studied the room in which Butch undoubtedly spent many hours. Well-polished, fine grained oak lined the floor. On the other side of the antique desk, a red leather chair—the high back dotted with brass tacks—rested against the wainscoting covering the bottom half of walls that were painted cactus green.

Oak filing cabinets lined the wall to her left, a shiny black stereo system sitting on top, the LCD display emitting a dim blue light. A 42" flat-screen TV hung on the wall.

Wow! How much did bar owners make around these parts? The faint clattering of metal pans coming from the kitchen reminded her that she wasn't there to admire Butch's furniture.

Kate tiptoed across the wood floor and rounded the desk. Four short stacks of papers covered most of the blotter. Deftly, she began sifting through the first stack, scanning beer vendor bills, grocery store receipts, and quarterly tax statements.

The second and third stacks held mainly catalogs selling all sorts of bar and restaurant accessories, several issues of a magazine for small business owners, and last week's copy of *The Yuccaville Yodeler*.

She dug into the fourth pile. Part way through a bunch of invoices for some company named V.C. Enterprises, Kate found a bill from the same repair shop where her car was being patched up. She scanned down the paper, expecting itemized costs for fixing Butch's pickup, curious how much her insurance company had forked out for her little mishap. Her eyes stopped at the words bench seat foam.

What in the hell? His seats hadn't been anywhere near her front bumper. She held the paper closer to her face. The next line read: cherry red leather upholstery for bench seat.

Lowering the bill, she frowned at the television. "He's committing insurance fraud."

Someone knocked on the door.

Kate almost peed her pants. Her gaze darted around the room, her ears ringing as she sought somewhere—anywhere—to hide. The small window beckoned.

The second knock came as Kate unlatched the window lock. She looked at the doorknob and froze at the sight of the metal turning.

The door inched open.

"Butch?" A familiar voice called softly.

Claire stepped into the office. When she saw Kate, her eyes narrowed. "I knew it." She shut the door behind her and locked it.

"Jeez, Claire!" Kate's breath whooshed from her throat. Her face burned as she dropped into Butch's chair, feeling like she'd leaned too far out over the rim of the Grand Canyon. "You scared the shit out of me."

"Good! What do you think you're doing in Butch's ..." Claire's voice trailed off as she glanced around the room. "Nice flatscreen." She walked over to the TV, then noticed the stereo and let out a low whistle. "Butch sure knows how to outfit an office." She ran her hand over the filing cabinets. "Hey, that looks like a French, Louis XV partners desk."

"How do you know?"

"Because I saw one just like it last spring in an old newspaper photo of Joe's antique store ..." Claire trailed off again, frowning down at the desk.

Kate pushed up out of Butch's chair. "Do you think—"

"We need to get out of here." Claire stepped backward, rubbing her hands together. She turned to Kate. "You shouldn't have broken in here."

"I didn't break in. The door was unlocked."

"Quit splitting hairs. You've been sniffing around Butch for days now."

Claire's righteous attitude when it came to Butch made Kate's ears steam. She leaned over the desk and snatched the repair shop bill from the top of the fourth stack, shoving it under Claire's nose.

"Explain this, then."

Claire glanced down at the bill. "Explain what? It's a bill from the repair shop, undoubtedly for his pickup, which you so kindly T-boned."

"I remember the turn of events, thank you very much." Kate held up the paper, reading aloud. "Cherry red leather upholstery for bench seat; custom paint touchup: midnight blue; custom—"

"Midnight blue?" Claire grabbed the paper from Kate's hand. "Is he having his pickup painted?"

"It's insurance fraud, I'm sure of it." Kate crossed her arms over her chest.

Claire's read down the page. "Holy shit."

"I know. It's this kind of thievery that makes all of our premiums shoot—"

"He bought Joe's El Camino."

"—through the … huh?"

She handed the paper back to Kate. "Butch bought Joe's El Camino from Sophy." When Kate just continued to stare at her, she clarified, "That's not his pickup they are fixing up, dingbat, it's Joe's old El Camino. Look at the date on this bill. It's a month old."

Kate noticed the date in the upper left corner for the first time. Damn. She tossed the bill on Butch's desk.

So he bought Joe's car. What was the big deal? Why was Claire suddenly looking around Butch's office as if tarantulas were crawling out of the woodwork?

"We need to get out of here now." Claire made for the door.

Kate grabbed the drawer handle to one of the filing cabinets. "You go. I'm not finished yet."

"Kate." Claire's tone warned. She twisted the doorknob and pulled it open a crack. "If you don't exit this room immediately and plant your ass back on that bar stool, I'm going to tell Mom that you were the one who spilled the wine on her great-grandmother's silk wedding gown."

"Fine. Tattle away, but she'll never believe—"

"Hi, Butch." The cook's voice carried through the crack in the door.

Kate's tongue glued itself to the roof of her mouth. She locked wide eyes with Claire.

"I told you so," she mouthed.

Footfalls crossed the linoleum, coming their way.

"Hey, can you come look at this?" the cook said, and the footfalls stopped, then faded.

Claire raced over and grabbed Kate by the forearm. "Get out there and distract him."

"What! How am I going to do that?"

"I don't know. Use that brain of yours and figure out a way to keep him from coming in here."

"No! You go out there. You've known him longer."

"Yeah, but you're the one who's been going on picnics with him."

Claire, who'd always managed to beat Kate in arm wrestling, leg wrestling, and any other sport where extra pounds offered an unfair advantage, dragged Kate across the room. "Now, work your magic."

She shoved Kate out the door.

Kate whirled around in time to hear the deadbolt click. She closed her eyes, imagining seven different ways she was going to kill Claire as soon as this door didn't separate them.

She glanced toward the kitchen. Butch was nowhere to be seen, but she could hear his low voice as he spoke to the cook. Turning back, she rapped on the door lightly with her knuckles.

"Claire!" she whispered. "Open this damned door before I—"

"Kate?"

She froze at the sound of Butch's voice, knuckles hovering.

"What are you doing?" He came up behind her.

Forcing a smile, she turned around. "Looking for you. I need to talk to you."

Butch's gaze drifted down the front of her pink cotton tank top and red shorts, dipping clear down to her white ankle-wrap sandals before cruising back up to her face, his blue eyes suddenly dark, intense. "About what?"

Ignoring the fluttering in her lungs, Kate made a point of looking toward the kitchen. "It's kind of private."

She stalled while her mind raced, trying to come up with something.

He closed the gap between them with two steps and reached around her, his arm brushing her hip. "Let's go in my office."

"No!" She fell more than leaned back against the door, barricading it with her body.

"Why not?" His grin surfaced. "I promise I won't bite you."

He nudged her hip aside and twisted the knob.

"Huh," he said under his breath, twisting the knob again. "I swear I left the door unlocked." His grin faded. "I know I did, because I forgot my keys at home."

"Maybe one of your employees locked it for you, thinking you'd forgotten to when you left."

"Yeah, maybe. Hold on, I'll go see if Gary brought his spare key."

"Wait!" Kate grabbed Butch's arm.

Butch looked at her with raised brows.

Still holding his arm, she dragged him down the hall to the supply room door. "We can talk in here."

"But it'll just take me a second to get the key."

"Trust me, this can't wait."

She flicked on the light and closed the door behind them.

"What in the hell is so important that you can't wait two minutes for me to get the spare key?"

From where Kate stood, she could see Butch's office door out the window in the supply room door. As she watched, Claire stepped out into the hall.

Unfortunately, from where Butch stood, he would see Claire slip past them into the kitchen. Her heart in her throat, Kate grabbed Butch by the shoulders and shoved him back against the door.

Butch frowned down at her. "Did you forget to take your pills tonight, Kate?"

"No." She laughed him off with a rattling cackle. Evil witches sounded more sane.

"All right." He crossed his arms. "You have me in here. What do you need to tell me?"

Opening her mouth, she paused, her mind fishing for lies and hauling up nothing but empty nets.

The sound of the mop handle sliding down the wall and smacking onto the floor made Butch look toward the window.

No!

"I need to … uh …" *Think of something, moron.*

His focus returned to her. "You need to what, Kate?"

She had an idea. Standing on her tiptoes, she slipped her hands around the back of his neck.

"I need to kiss you." She pulled him down to her and covered his lips with hers.

So the on-the-fly plan was to kiss him long enough for Claire to slip by unnoticed. There'd be no tongue action, no extraneous touching. And in spite of how good Butch smelled and tasted, Kate ignored all other temptations and stuck to the plan.

She pulled back after a count of five—well, maybe it was more like seven—and smiled up at Butch, feeling rather pleased with herself. Miss Marple would have patted her on the head.

Butch stared down at her with a furrowed brow. "What was that?"

Tucking a loose blonde tendril behind her ear, she said, "A kiss."

"Not really."

What? "Yes, it was."

"Who taught you how to kiss like *that*?"

"Like what?"

"Like a 1940's movie starlet, all pursed lips and stiffness, no mess and no heat."

Kate sputtered. "Well, that wasn't a real, *real* kiss. I mean I know how to kiss, trust me. I've had my share of practice."

"If that's the end result of all your practicing, your lessons must have really been boring."

Her mouth gaped. "Boring? I can assure you that the last thing I've ever been called is boring."

"I don't doubt that. Most guys would be happy just to have your lips touching them, even if you are a shitty kisser."

A shitty kisser? Kate jammed her hands on her hips. "I am an excellent kisser, Butch Carter, especially when I involve more than just my lips."

One of his eyebrows lifted. "I don't believe you."

"Ha! You're just trying to get another kiss out of me."

"Not really. I'd rather go get a burger. I skipped dinner."

Kate shoved him back against the door. "Liar."

"All right then, Kate. Show me what you got."

This time, she went way off plan. She tugged him down to her, pressing against his full length, going in for the kill.

His lips parted without hesitation when she ran her tongue over them, then she followed with a nip and suck and a tickle. Her tongue found his, coaxing him to play along, which he did with a skill that stole her breath and made her ache for more.

She let her hands explore his shoulders and arms as she rubbed against the wall of his chest, losing herself in the scent of his cologne, the heat radiating off his skin, the feel of his mouth seducing hers.

Wait! She was supposed to be running the show. His hands smoothed down her ribs, yanking her hips against his. She moved against him, encouraging, wanting, forgetting where she was and why she was even there for several heavy breath-filled moments.

Then he groaned against her throat. "Kate, you win."

She pulled away, panting, yearning to keep proving him wrong until she'd removed all of their clothing and finished what she'd started.

"See?" she said between breaths. "That was better, right?"

He shrugged. "Sure, I guess. I'd give it a six-point-five on a scale of ten."

"What?"

"Okay, maybe a seven."

She glanced down at his fly, confirming what she'd thought she'd felt a moment ago. "Just a seven, huh?"

"Yeah, but if you want to try for a higher score, I'd be happy to oblige."

"You are such a—"

"Butch!" the sound of Gary's voice leaked through the door. "Phone."

With a wink and a tweak of her chin, Butch said, "Let's try again another time."

He left her there in the storage room, her curiosity piqued about "another time." Then she remembered where she was and why and took off to find her damned sister.

* * *

"A shot of Southern Comfort, please," Claire told Gary as she waited at the bar for Kate to finish dilly-dallying in the store room with Butch.

She blew out a breath of relief and tossed back the whiskey, gasping as it burned a trail down her esophagus and slammed into the bottom of her stomach.

That had been too damned close. If Kate was going to insist on playing a role in her own *Murder, She Wrote* episode, she needed to learn how to break-and-enter properly.

Gary refilled her glass.

"Good evening, Claire," said a voice from behind her that she wasn't in the mood to deal with right then.

Whiskey sluiced over the edge of the glass and dripped down her fingers. Claire lowered her shot back to the bar, drying her hand on her pants.

"Hello, Porter." She faked a smile.

"Do you know where I can find Kate?"

Making out with Butch in back. "Umm, no, I sure don't. I haven't seen her since I went to the ladies' room. But she must be around here somewhere."

"Do you mind if I sit next to you?"

Hell, yes, she minded. Now that Claire had found the clues in Treasure Island, more than ever she needed Kate to spy on Porter.

If Kate and Butch walked through the kitchen door together, Porter would probably figure out that they'd been up to some hanky panky, especially since Kate had never been able to keep guilt from advertising on her face.

"How about a dance instead?" Claire slid off the stool. "I've always loved this song."

For a split second, Porter's trademark, white-toothed smile seemed flash frozen on his face; then he blinked and his cheeks relaxed into his usual charming grin. "Sure."

Claire led Porter to the far corner of the crowded dance floor where there was no way he could see the kitchen door through all of the cowboy hats.

Once there, Porter pulled her into his arms.

"Have you heard from Mac?" he asked in that smooth Texas drawl, his green eyes drilling into hers.

She'd almost forgotten that as far as Porter knew, Mac had left her high and dry on the side of the road.

"Yes, actually. We're trying to work things out."

She decided to tell the pseudo truth in case Porter ran into Mac over the weekend—that was, if Mac took a moment away from the Lucky Monk, which was where he'd run off to this evening with a load of two-by-fours, a can of paint, and a long cardboard tube.

"Really?" His smile didn't quite reach his eyes. "That's too bad."

Claire wasn't sure what to make of his reply. Instead of asking, she just stared at his smooth, tan chest exposed by the V-neck of his shirt.

They circled in silence for several seconds, Claire trying to catch a glimpse of the bar, hoping that Kate was sitting there when the song ended so that Claire could escape Porter's arms.

Porter cleared his throat. "I've been meaning to talk to you about our last conversation."

Alarms whooped in Claire's head. Their last conversation had been the one where she'd found out his knowledge of classic literature could fit into a thimble and she'd caught him lying through his movie star teeth.

"What about it?"

"Kate told me you don't believe I'm really writing a book."

"She did?" Claire envisioned stuffing a pair of Chester's dirty boxers down Kate's throat.

"I hadn't realized at the time that you were quizzing me on classic lit. I'd just assumed we were having a conversation."

Claire's cheeks warmed, but she held her tongue. Short of admitting he was correct, there was nothing else to say.

"I'd like to apologize for my ineptness. I'd had too many drinks that night, and I found having you so near, after hearing you were free and single again, distracting."

That made Claire pause. She pulled back and frowned up at him, not sure she heard him right. "You did?"

"Of course. Surely, you must remember that it was you I first approached, not your sister."

Claire blinked, twice. Could he be serious? Although, he had turned to Kate only after Mac had made an appearance.

"You take my breath away, Claire." He grabbed her hand and held it against his chest. "Feel how fast you've made my heart beat."

His heart thudded against her palm, but didn't seem any faster than hers, which happened to be busy drumming out a heavy metal music solo in her ears.

He pulled her tighter against him. His belt buckle dug into her belly button. "Of course I know that Robert Louis Stevenson didn't write either Jungle Book or Gulliver's Travels, but when you're pressed against me like this, all I can think about is taking you to my place and showing you Mac's shortfalls."

Okay, first of all, Mac didn't have any shortfalls when it came to the bedroom. Second, she needed another shot of whiskey.

She stared longingly at the bar.

"Claire, look at me." He caught her chin.

"What about Kate?"

"Your sister is a lovely woman, but she's not you."

Claire held his gaze, trying to read his eyes as sparkles rained down from the disco ball. He had to be playing her.

"Listen Porter, thanks for the dance and for being so nice to my mother, but—"

Before she could finish with her brush off, Porter leaned down and kissed her.

Chapter Sixteen

"Jeez, Claire, I can't believe you kissed Porter," Kate said to her sister, who sat in the passenger seat of Ruby's old truck.

A warm breeze blew in through her open window, tearing at her hair that she'd fixed in the ladies' room after Butch got her all flutter-pated.

"Like I told you in the bar," Claire said, "I didn't kiss him. He kissed me." She white-knuckled the dashboard. "Damn it, Kate, would you slow down! I'd like to make it home un-mangled."

"If you wanted to drive, you shouldn't have slammed those four shots." Kate let up on the gas pedal, the scrub bushes at the side of the road no longer just a blur.

Visibly gulping, Claire stuck her head out the window.

"He's supposed to be my boyfriend, you know," Kate yelled, so that Claire could hear her over the wind.

Claire pulled her head back inside. "Did I or did I not see you swapping spit with Butch in the supply room tonight?"

"I was distracting him." At least that was what Kate kept telling herself.

"It looked to me like you were using your tongue to measure the inside of his mouth for braces."

Her lips tightening at Claire's smartass remark, Kate swerved unnecessarily to avoid a small pothole. Claire scrambled partway out the window again, where she stayed until Kate parked the pickup in front of Ruby's place and turned off the ignition.

"What was it like?" Kate asked as she shut the truck door. Stones crunched under her shoes as she rounded the pickup.

"What was what like?" Claire stumbled from the cab. "Ugh. Shit." She leaned back against the side of the truck bed and bent over, her hands planted on her thighs. "I shouldn't have eaten that whole basket of fried mushrooms."

"When you kissed Porter."

Had his mouth delivered all that his good looks promised? Did his lips melt her knee joints, make her head float, and leave her clinging to him like a faux leather catsuit—like Butch's kiss?

Kate shivered in the warm evening air at the memory of Butch's touch, goose bumps prickling her arms and neck. She pinched her forearm, dragging her thoughts back from the stars.

Somehow, she had to get a grip on this foolish crush that had her daydreaming about strolls on the beach and rolls in the hay with the man bent on stealing Ruby's mine. If she could just find some physical proof ... and the brunch he'd invited her to tomorrow morning at his house was just the opportunity she needed to search his home turf.

"I told you," Claire said with a smile, "I didn't kiss him."

"Fine, what was it like when Porter kissed you then?"

Claire peered up at Kate with one eye open. "What are you talking about? You've kissed the guy several times already."

"Porter has never kissed me *that* way. All he's done so far is given me a peck on the lips."

"Well, it wasn't as bad as when Danny Timberman drooled down my chin." Standing upright, Claire gripped the door handle with one hand and held her stomach with the other. "Let's just say Porter has had plenty of practice perfecting the art of kissing, but ..." She looked up at the stars and sucked in a couple of deep breaths.

"But what?" Kate grabbed Claire's arm as her sister staggered forward and led Claire toward the porch.

Claire plopped down on the top step and listed until she came to rest against the rail. "But he's not Mac."

Groaning, Kate dropped onto the steps next to Claire.

"Even drunk you can't stop blathering about Mac. You might as well hang up your rope and spurs for good, cowgirl, because you've done tamed your last stallion."

A mooning smile spread across Claire's face. "Have I told you what Mac can do with his tongue?"

"No!" Kate covered Claire's mouth with her hand. "I don't want to hear the details of your love life and then have to sit across from Mac at the dinner table."

"I do." Manny said.

Kate jerked in surprise, then whirled around and squinted into the shadowed porch. A match flared to life. "What are you doing out here?"

"Eavesdropping." Chester answered for Manny. The red butt of a cigar glowed for a moment, the smell of cigar smoke reaching her. "Now let Claire talk. I could use some new tricks. My arthritis hasn't reached my tongue yet."

Kate winced at the image that popped into her head.

"So, let me get this straight." Manny's chair squeaked as he leaned forward. "Claire and Porter kissed?"

Claire moaned and flopped back onto the porch floorboards.

"That's none of your business." Kate frowned down at Claire.

"I thought he was your boyfriend," Chester said.

"Claire must be trying to steal him away from Kate, *si?*"

"Ah. Cat fight." Chester meowed. "Are you going to tell Mac?"

"Of course not." Kate glanced at Claire. "Are we?"

Claire rolled her head back and forth on the wood boards. "Not on purpose."

Squinting at the two old men, Kate said, "You two had better keep your mouths shut about this, or I'll tell Ruby about that hidden video camera."

"*Ah, mi amor.* I told you we weren't really filming, just testing out a new lens."

"Promise or I'll tattle."

Chester grunted. "You sure know how to piss in an old man's punchbowl."

"We promise." Manny sat back. "But we can't speak for *Señorita* Jess."

Kate heard a muffled, high-pitched giggle from just beyond the end of the porch. "Crap!"

"I'm think I'm gonna be sick." Claire groaned, leaned over the porch rail, and heave-hoed the contents of her stomach onto Ruby's bed of desert lavender.

* * *

Sunday, August 22nd

Claire stared down at the yellow Post-it note, her eyesight blurring.

After spending most of last night draped over the toilet rim, she'd dragged her hung-over ass to each of the park's bathrooms at the butt-crack of dawn. Hours of scrubbing God-knows-what from the stall floors left her wanting to curl up in a dark closet and just practice breathing until the juggernaut in her skull stopped swinging his sledgehammer around.

"What are you doing down here?" Mac's deep voice snapped her out of her trance.

Blinking several times, she looked up from where she sat behind Ruby's desk in the basement office.

Mac stood with his shoulder resting against the doorjamb, wearing a faded red T-shirt and a pair of jeans worn white on the knees and thighs, the ends of his hair curled with dampness. His hazel-eyes dropped to the Post-it note and then the open pages of *Treasure Island.*

There was no use lying. Besides, her brain hurt too much to even attempt a fib. "Trying to figure out what Joe meant by these clues."

The chair creaked as she leaned back and rubbed her eyes, which felt like she'd buffed them with steel wool.

Claire heard the door click shut. She opened her eyes as Mac rounded the desk, leaned over, and dropped a kiss on her lips. He tasted minty and smelled shower-fresh, whereas she felt like something wrung out of a dirty mop.

"You doing okay, Slugger?" He moved behind her and started massaging her shoulders.

"I feel like I've been kicked in the head by a mule."

"Kate said you spent the night riding the porcelain bus—her words, not mine."

Kate or anyone else for that matter had better not have mentioned anything else about last night, or Claire would string them up, slather them with honey, and let the yellow jackets have at 'em.

Another memory from last night flashed in her mind. "I thought Kate had a date this morning."

"So did she, but the phone rang while I was eating breakfast, and Jess informed everyone in the room Butch had to cancel. Something about him having an emergency in Phoenix and he wouldn't be back until tomorrow. I left the kitchen in the middle of your mother's anti-Butch tirade."

He squeezed the knotted muscles at the sides of her neck, making her wince slightly. "What brought this on?"

"Mom's tirade or Kate's date?"

"Your hangover. You know your limit."

"What time did you get in?" Claire skirted that question.

"Changing the subject?"

"I'm tired of thinking about puking."

"A little after three."

Claire's head drooped as his hands worked on the tension in her neck. "Were you up at the Lucky Monk all that time?"

"Most of it."

"What were the boards and paint for?"

"Somebody broke through the barrier I put up at the entrance to Socrates Pit mine, so I boarded it up again and painted No Trespassing warnings on the wood. Then I checked the warnings posted on the barriers for the other mines and nailed up a few more Private Property signs."

"What was in the tube?"

Mac chuckled, his fingers massaging her scalp. "You don't miss a thing, do you?"

"Not when it comes to you." She did her best to keep from sliding to the floor, landing in a pile of flabby flesh. Mac's talent with his fingers rivaled his tongue most days … and nights.

"I found the tube in the attic yesterday with some old maps of Two Jakes, Rattlesnake Ridge, and the Lucky Monk."

"How old?"

"Early 1900s."

"So you spent half of the night traversing the Lucky Monk, comparing reality to paper?"

"Pretty much, yep."

"And?"

"There were a few variances."

"And?"

"And I still have more evaluating to do."

"I want to come with you."

"You have an R.V. park to run."

"Kate can take over for the day."

"You're in no shape to traipse through a mine, Claire. Not with that hangover."

He had a point there. "I don't like you going up to the Lucky Monk alone."

"I'll be fine."

"What if someone follows you up there?"

"I'm careful."

"They could slit your throat and shove you down a shaft."

He worked his way down her shoulders to her upper arms. "I appreciate your concern, Claire, but trust me, I take precautions now. I learned a memorable lesson last spring."

Claire looked up at him. "But what if—"

Mac tilted her chair back and covered her mouth with his, effectively ending her rebuttal. Claire let him work his magic on her, moaning as he increased the pressure and deepened the kiss. He pulled away way too soon, leaving her winded and wanting, aching deep inside with anticipation for the relief she knew he could deliver.

"Now tell me about these clues." He stood upright, pointing at the Post-it note.

Claire hesitated. Knowing Mac, he'd find a way to logically explain every clue, and she wanted to dally in her kooky world of maybes and what-ifs a little longer. "What's in the package Gramps had you bring back from Tucson?"

"Claire." Mac's eyes narrowed as he sat facing her on the desktop, his leg brushing her arm.

Unable to resist, she reached out and ran her palm up his thigh. Maybe just a touch or two would ease her …

He grabbed her wrist, barring her entry into the fun zone. "No distractions, siren. Now spill."

She sighed. "Fine. Tell me about the package and I'll tell you about the clues."

"Swear?"

"Every chance I get."

His grin surfaced. "I don't know what's in the package. I didn't open it."

"Where did you get it?"

"He sent it to me at work."

"Why?"

He shrugged. "I don't know."

"Who's it from?" Claire asked.

"Someone named R.L. Goebel from Phoenix."

Who was that? Claire needed a Phoenix phone book. Damn that library warden for barring the only access Claire had to the Internet. "Is the package heavy?"

"Not really."

"How big is it?"

He indicated the size with his hands—a mid-sized package.

"That could be anything. "Was it hard or soft? Where is it?"

"I don't know; I didn't treat it like a Christmas package. Harley happily took it off my hands the night they eloped."

"Shit." Another road block.

"My turn." Mac picked up the Post-it note. "Explain this."

Claire stared at the note, now clearly able to read it after deciphering Joe's messy scrawls. She wasn't sure where to start.

"I found this note in Joe's first edition of *Treasure Island.*" No need to mention Jess or Porter at this point. Both names would land her in one form of trouble or another.

"And you think they are clues to what?"

She might as well just say it. "A treasure."

Mac stared at her, the dimple in his cheek almost showing. "What makes you think these lead to a treasure?"

At least he hadn't laughed aloud at her … yet. But this was where things got sticky. It was Porter's actions that had led her to this, but telling Mac that her reason for suspecting Porter had to do with gut instinct would go over like a concrete blimp.

"Well, Kate has a theory," Claire fibbed.

"Kate does, huh?" Mac played along like a good boyfriend.

"Yeah." Claire continued. "She thinks that the artifacts we found in that wall safe are more clues."

"You're referring to the mummified hand, right?"

Claire nodded.

"And why does Kate think the artifacts are clues?"

"Because why else would Joe have that stuff hidden in his wall safe? Where did he find it?"

"Maybe he bought it from somebody."

"It smells like a mine."

Mac's eyebrows rose. "You ... I mean, Kate, thinks the bag of goodies came from one of Ruby's mines?"

Claire nodded again.

"Just because of the smell?"

"No, because of the smell and this clue here." She pointed at the first line on the note and read it aloud in case Mac couldn't read Joe's scribbles. "Shiver my timbers."

Mac eyed the words. "So the timbers refer to those that shore up the mines."

"Yep."

"Maybe the hand was just buried in dirt somewhere else."

"I thought that very thing, but this clue links the hand even more to the mine." Claire pointed at another line on the note. "Flint's pointer."

"Flint was the dead pirate who buried the treasure on the island, right?"

"Yes. Do you remember the actual name of the island?"

"Skeleton Island."

"Exactly."

She grabbed the book and flipped to the page number she'd noted on the Post-it note next to the clue.

"And Flint's pointer refers to the skeleton of a man Flint killed and then used as an indicator to where the treasure was hidden. Right here it reads that the man lay 'perfectly straight—his feet pointing in one direction, his hands, raised above his head like a diver's, pointing directly in the opposite.' And then a little further down, 'The body pointed straight in the direction of the island, and the compass read duly E.S.E. and by E.' Long John Silver goes on to say that the skeleton is a pointer that leads to the 'jolly dollars.'"

His brow furrowed, Mac pointed at the next line on the note. "What's this say? Pieces of what?"

"Pieces of Eight. It's the treasure."

His eyes narrowed slightly. "So, you think Joe hid a bunch of Spanish silver dollars somewhere in one of the mines?"

"Maybe." When left alone to ponder the clues, it all made perfect sense, but having her suspicion voiced aloud by Mac made it sound like she'd been sniffing glue again.

He nodded down at the note. "And that last line?"

"It says, 'Pipe up and let me hear it.'"

"How is that related to the treasure?"

Claire leaned back in the chair. "I have no idea. I was just sitting here trying to figure that one out when you walked in."

"If it said 'pipe down,' I'd guess it referred to a mine shaft."

It was Claire's turn to raise her brows. "You mean you actually believe this theory of mine?"

Mac faked a surprise gasp. "I thought you said it was Kate's theory."

"That was before you heard me out and didn't laugh when I finished."

Taking her hand, he traced the lines on her palm, his fingertip calloused, scratching lightly.

"Claire, I'm not going to deny that this whole thing sounds a bit far-fetched, but I thought your theories last spring were off the deep end, and look how that all turned out."

She closed her fingers around his, then rose from her chair. "It's times like this when all I can think about are the nefarious, sweaty, naked things I'd like to do with you."

Chuckling, he pulled her snug between his thighs. "So, what are you going to do?"

"Find the body. The treasure must be close to it."

He lifted the hem of her Sylvester the Putty Tat T-shirt and slid his hands under it. "I meant with my body. Let's explore your naked thoughts."

His fingers skimmed her stomach, making her inhale and lean into him for more. "Here? Now?"

"Claire, I'm not sure if you've been picking up on my signals since I walked in that door, but I came to see you for one primary reason." His gaze was filled with R-rated intentions which she really wanted to see him follow through on.

What about the others upstairs? Her sister? Her mother?

Mac's fingers inched northward, brushing away all of her hesitations.

Cocking her head to the side, she asked, "You think I'm easy or something, Mr. Garner?"

"I think you can be quickly persuaded with the right technique." Pushing her hair to the side, he nibbled on the sensitive skin running from her ear down her neck.

She shivered under his mouth. "Is this your 'right technique'?"

"It's part of it." His thumbs skimmed the undersides of her breasts. "Tell me what you want, Claire."

"You inside of me, coinciding with some mutual moaning," she whispered, closing her eyes to imagine the scene. "Maybe a bit of muffled screaming." She took a shaky breath. "Definitely multiple moments of muffled-ness."

His chuckle warmed her ear. "You taste salty today."

It was called sweat. "I should shower first."

"There's no time for that." His fingertips made her quiver clear down to her ankles. "Shut up and kiss me, woman."

She obeyed, sinking into him as she teased a groan from his lips with some strokes of her tongue and a few well-placed rubs.

Enough was enough. Patience was never on her list of virtues. She reached for the waistline of his jeans. "Take your pants off."

His hands stopped hers. "You first."

She wasted no time. Pants tossed aside, she waited in her underwear, watching as Mac pushed down his jeans.

"Don't forget these." She tugged at the waistline of his boxer briefs.

"I'll get to those in a minute. Your shirt needs to go."

He helped her remove it, his hands getting preoccupied with her breasts as she unclasped her bra.

Covering his hands with hers, she held him still. "Your shirt now," she ordered, and helped him pull it over his head.

Tossing his T-shirt aside, she hopped up on the desktop. "Come here." She reached for him, breathy with excitement for all that she knew he had to offer.

But he held back, staring with an intensity she could almost feel.

She leaned back on her hands, pulling her shoulders back in hopes of adding a tantalizing little lift to her girls. "What's the hold up? Did you forget how this goes?"

"No, I've been thinking about it for days, but my version doesn't involve the desk." He grabbed her arm and tugged her to her feet.

"Oh, yeah?" Running her finger down the middle of his chest, she paused just above his navel. "Tell me more."

"How about I show you?" Spinning her around, he pinned her against the wall next to the door, shoving her back against the cool surface. "Wrap your legs around me."

She hesitated. "I'm not exactly a featherweight fighter, Mac."

"We already had this conversation in the shower weeks ago, remember? If I can handle you when you're wet and slick, I think—"

She stood on her toes and covered his mouth with hers. While she wooed him with her lips and tongue, she captured his hand and led it down to where her body throbbed and ached. "Handle me again."

His fingers slipped inside the elastic of her underwear, teasing, making her writhe and moan.

"I want you," he breathed in her ear.

"Please, Mac," she said between gasps, moving against him to build more friction.

He dropped to his knees, yanking down her panties, his lips feathering down from her belly button.

Her knees threatened to buckle.

All it took was one perfectly placed kiss and touch and she fell to pieces around him, her body pulsing. She squeezed his shoulders as her world tipped on its side.

"Damn." She tugged him upright when her head returned from the moon. "I *really* missed you."

He flattened her back against the wall, lifted one of her legs, and pressed against her.

"Show me," he said and shoved into her.

She shifted her hips, encouraging him further. "When you imagined doing this to me the last few days, did I tell you how great you feel and then bite your earlobe like this?"

When she bit, his body trembled in response. He shoved harder.

"Did I scratch you here?" She clawed down his back.

He moved faster. "Do that again, Claire, and I'll be finished before we even get rolling."

"Did I tell you that I want more of you, harder and faster?"

"Yes." His words blended into a groan as he buried himself fully, then pulled back, slamming her up against the wall again and again.

Panting, her own body tightening again, she leaned her head back. The scent of Mac and sex filled her, winding her up higher. "Did I cry out your name when I peaked?"

"Yes!" he said, his voice raspy.

She slid her fingers into his hair, pulling his lips toward hers. "Mac?"

"What?"

"Here it comes. Kiss me now."

As soon as his mouth covered hers, her body began to convulse around him, this second time stronger, more core shaking. His mouth absorbed the sound of her cries of pleasure.

As soon as she finished, he dragged his lips away, muttered something incomprehensible along with her name, and thrust into her a few more times before shudders rippled through him.

When his breath slowed, he said, "Holy shit, woman." He leaned his forehead against the door over her shoulder. "When you say that kind of stuff to me, I lose it."

"Why do you think I say it?" Knowing she could make Mac lose control was a turn on all on its own.

Claire clung to his shoulders until both feet were firmly on the carpet again. Her legs felt shaky, her body spent.

"Next time we do this," Mac said, "I want to—"

Someone knocked on the door.

She froze.

Mac stared down at her, his finger over her lips.

The knock came again, harder. "Claire?"

Claire winced at the sound of her mother's voice.

Grabbing his jeans from the floor, Mac tossed Claire's clothes at her. He yanked on his skivvies and was buttoning his jeans before Claire managed to slip on one pant leg.

Deborah knocked again. "Open this door, Claire. I know you're in there."

Sweating, Claire pulled up her pants.

The doorknob twisted back and forth. "Claire Alice, what are you doing in there? You'd better open this door right now."

Mac slipped into his shirt and sat down in Joe's chair, pulling on his boots. Claire scrambled into her shirt, took a couple of deep breaths, and ran her fingers through her hair.

Ready? she mouthed to Mac.

He nodded, leaning back, looking relaxed.

Claire unlocked the door and pulled it open.

Her mother stood there, her fist raised to knock again, her cheeks red.

"What took you so lo—" Deborah's eyes narrowed as her gaze fell on Mac. "Oh. I should have known." She stepped into the room, sniffing. "What's going on down here?"

Seriously, she had to sniff the air? Claire felt a blush blooming in her cheeks.

"Would you look at the time?" Mac rose from the chair. "I need to get going." He rounded the desk and paused long enough to drop a kiss on Claire's mouth. "Stay out of trouble, Slugger."

After giving her fingers a quick squeeze, he nodded toward Claire's mom and walked out of the room.

Deserter! Claire scowled at Mac's back as he disappeared up the steps.

"What were you two doing down here?" Deborah asked, her nostrils flared, her lips pinched tighter than the end of a sausage. "It smells like—"

"None of your business." Claire's face baked. She slipped around the desk and flopped down in the chair.

"You're being extremely rude."

"You're being extremely nosey."

Deborah harrumphed. "I'm not being nosey. I'm interested in what you do because you're my daughter and I love you."

Claire crossed her arms over her chest and glared up at her mother. Deborah had been using her "love" to manipulate Claire since the womb. "Why is it that when people say they love you, they really just want to control you?"

That earned Claire another pinched glare.

"Ever since you started dating Mac you have had nothing but attitude with me."

"We're doing much more than dating, Mother."

"I don't want to hear about that."

Fine. "What do you want, Mom?"

Deborah closed the door.

Uh, oh. That couldn't be a good sign.

Approaching the other side of the desk, Deborah said, "I want you to stay away from Porter."

"What?" Claire was surprised to hear Porter's name instead of Mac's.

"I overheard Kate and you talking last night."

"You mean you eavesdropped on our conversation."

Her mother just smiled. Acid might have dripped from the corners of it; Claire wasn't one hundred percent certain. "Stay away from Porter. Your sister needs a nice, respectable man, not some bar owner." She wrinkled her nose at those last two words.

"What if I don't?" She still needed to figure out what he was up to, because writing a book was a definite cover.

"Stay away from Porter or I'll tell Mac you kissed another man."

Chapter Seventeen

Mac stood high up on the hillside just outside of the Lucky Monk mine, shielding his eyes from the afternoon sunshine. Across the valley, two black turkey vultures circled, sailing on the thermals rising from the desert floor, waiting for the Grim Reaper to call on some unlucky creature.

Boom! The percussion raced across the desolate earth.

A gust of oven-hot air thick with the scent of baked greasewood ruffled his hair and plastered his shirt to his ribs, where it stuck to his sweaty skin.

His gaze followed the valley's left flank north as it skimmed along the base of the water-rutted foothills of the Sierra del Gato Loco Range. The view before him quivered as heat rose from the fried landscape.

Boom!

The ground beneath his boots quaked just enough to make him question if he'd really felt that one. Pebbles clattered down from the crust of reddish-brown rock perched above the mouth of the mine and littered the cliff ledge.

Mac frowned into the distance, unable to catch sight of dust from the Copper Snake Mining Company's blasting efforts. They'd started early in the pit today, and by the sound of it, they weren't wasting time scratching around on the surface.

Boom! Boom!

So much for Sunday being a day of rest.

Mac retreated from the cliff's edge. His plans today didn't include cartwheeling down the steep hillside.

He faced the shadow-filled mine opening, hesitating. The earth-shaking effect of Copper Snake's blasts made his legs reluctant to lead him into the Lucky Monk's rock-lined intestines. As he stood there, a packrat scuttled out of the mine and nearly brushed his boot as it raced past him and dashed down the hillside behind him.

"That can't be good," he said under his breath.

Slinging his backpack over his shoulder, he drew one last breath of fresh air and then ducked his head and walked into the mine's dark throat.

* * *

Claire sat behind the counter in Ruby's store, examining the figurine made of bound twigs that she'd found in Joe's safe.

Kate leaned against the other side of the counter. "I thought you said it was a horse."

"I did, but after doing some research, I've decided it's a deer. Or a mule." Claire glanced at Kate, wondering why her sister was wearing all black on such a toasty afternoon. "What's with the Johnny Cash look?"

Kate shrugged. "I'm in mourning."

"Why?"

"My sister stole my boyfriend."

Claire snickered. "As if you hadn't already wadded him up and tossed him aside."

"Mom doesn't know that."

"Ahhh, I see. This is all for her benefit."

"You'd do it, too, if Mom had bitten a chunk out of your ass this morning." Kate strolled over to the candy aisle and plucked a package of red Twizzlers from the shelf. "She really doesn't want me spending any more time with Butch."

What would Deborah say if she found out Kate had been playing tongue tag with Butch last night?

"Why are you wearing those?" Kate nodded at the yellow, rubber, dish-washing gloves Claire had donned after realizing just how old Joe's stick figure might be.

"Precautionary measures." She grinned at Kate. "Something you should try practicing the next time you feel like breaking and entering at The Shaft."

Flipping Claire the bird, Kate stuffed a Twizzler in her mouth and tromped toward the coolers at the back of the store.

Gingerly placing the twig figurine on the countertop, Claire scanned the pages of *Ancient Southwestern Cultures in a Nutshell*, one of the books Kate had checked out of the library for her last week after Claire had wrestled with that old dame.

Could this toy-looking-thing really date back over four thousand years? According to the author, the people who made these animal figures had lived in and around the Grand Canyon prior to the Anasazi's occupation. Constructed of willow twigs, the effigies were used in hunting ceremonies.

Kate placed a bottle of diet soda on the counter, along with a couple of bucks. "So, what's the big deal with this stick deer? Besides Joe stashing it with the mummified hand."

"Others like it have been found only in caves." Claire shoved Kate's money in the cash drawer and pushed it closed.

"Hey, what about my change?"

"Consider it my tip."

"For what?"

"Not telling Mom you were mauling Butch last night when she prodded me for details."

"Oh. Thanks." Kate stuck another Twizzler in her mouth. "So you think Joe found that in a cave?"

"Or one of his mines." Claire tucked the figurine in a Ziplock bag and peeled off her gloves, her hands wet with sweat.

"But those mines are only a century old. If this thing is as ancient as you say, how would it have ended up in a mine?"

"Maybe somebody found it and stowed it in the mine."

"That sounds pretty flimsy."

"I know." Claire stole a piece of candy from Kate. "But it was with the mummy hand, which I think came from one of the mines, too."

"What about the sandal and bag?"

Claire paused mid-chew. "What do you mean?"

"What have you learned about them?"

"Nothing yet. I'm still searching for similar-looking designs in these books for the bag, and I haven't read a thing about footwear."

Kate opened her soda pop. "Speaking of footwear, can I borrow your tennis shoes again?"

"Why? What's wrong with yours?"

"They still reek of skunk, remember?"

"Fine, but watch where you step or you'll be scraping the dog shit out of the grooves this time."

"You're the one in charge of taking care of Henry while Gramps is gone, including scooping up his parting gifts."

Claire sat back, her arms crossed. "You know, I'm getting pretty damned tired of cleaning up after everyone's shit. How is it you've managed to avoid any tasks requiring even the least bit of crap-work yet again?"

Kate shrugged. "Just good karma, I guess." She opened the latest copy of a scandal rag and scanned a page while chewing on her candy. "Oh, I also need a ride to town tonight."

"Ask Mom to drive you."

"You know she doesn't drive after dark."

"We're not going to the bar again." Claire's stomach heaved at just the thought of tossing back more alcohol.

"No, this is for something else."

"What?"

Jess shoved through the curtain. "Claire, what's this?" She raced up to the counter and held out a couple of pieces of paper, her breaths quick, her cheeks pink, and one side of her hair still damp. Obviously fresh out of the shower, she smelled like her favorite coconut-scented shampoo.

Claire took the papers. "One is a receipt for a general delivery post office box at Creekside Supply Company."

Make that a twenty-five-year-old receipt, according to the date scrawled on the receipt. The box must have been Joe's originally, since Ruby hadn't even lived in town for a decade. Claire laid the receipt on the counter.

"I didn't know this place even had a post office." Kate leaned over to take a look at the receipt.

"The hardware store rents out the back corner of the store to the government." Claire explained.

"What's the other?" Kate asked.

Claire read the faded words and numbers. "It's another receipt covering the cost of the post office box through next year."

"Is this the key for the box?" Jess pulled a small, brass key from the front pocket of her red shorts.

"It might be." Claire wondered what Jess was up to.

"Do you think Mom might be keeping my money there?"

Ah. Claire caught the caboose of Jess's train of thought. "There's a slim chance." But she doubted it. If Ruby didn't trust the bank, she surely wasn't going to trust the good ol' U.S. Postal Service to keep her money safe.

"But there is a chance."

"Sure." There was also a chance that Bigfoot really roamed the forests of the Pacific Northwest.

Clapping her hands, Jess said, "Let's go see."

"We can't. The post office is gated off on Sundays."

Jess's face fell. "Crud." She started to turn toward the green curtain and then stopped. "Oh, yeah." She dug in her back pocket. "What's this?" She placed a small, rectangular, black box on the counter along with the post office box key.

"Looks like a jewelry box." Kate offered some candy to Jess as she stared at the box with a slightly furrowed brow.

Claire picked up the box and gave it a slight shake while loosening the lid. As she lifted the top off, she gasped, gaping down at the slice of shiny gold.

"Holy shit!" Kate leaned close to Claire, breathing sweet-scented warm air on her. "Is that what I think it is?"

Claire raised her gaze to Jess. "Where did you find this?"

Jess shrugged and smiled wide—too wide. Red bits of candy laced her white teeth. "I can't remember."

"Think harder then." Claire didn't feel like playing games.

The girl's smile faltered. A dark pink blush climbed her neck and spread across her cheeks. "Umm, it might have been in the floor of Mom's closet."

* * *

The layers of earth surrounding Mac muted everything but the sound of his footsteps on the dirt and rock floor as he traipsed further into the depths of the Lucky Monk. His hard hat light bounced along the craggy rock walls and ceiling. Shadows nibbled at his boot heels as he followed the rusted, half-buried tracks that ran down the middle of the adit, the avenue through which all copper had found its way to the surface.

The cool air trapped under the earth made his sweat-dampened T-shirt feel like a cold, wet sheet. He paused near a wide-mouthed tunnel that drifted off to the right and lowered his pack to the floor. First things first—a dry shirt. He peeled off his wet shirt and fished out the clean one he carried with him for times like this.

Next, he unfolded the eleven-by-seventeen inch copies he'd made of Joe's old map of the mine and spread them on the floor in front of him, lining up the edges. While exploring yesterday, he'd marked some of the side tunnels with orange spray paint, but not enough to go skirting willy nilly through the mine without consulting the map every few hundred feet.

His stomach growled for some dinner. He dug in his pack for his flashlight and the protein bar he'd picked up at Biddy's Gas and Carryout on his way to the mine. As he chewed, he scanned the underground roadmap.

Unlike Rattlesnake Ridge, which followed a mostly-vertical vein deep into the ground, the Lucky Monk spread out along a horizontal wave of copper, with three relatively shallow shafts sunk into the earth—although, there were only two noted on the map in front of him. Side tunnels branched off from the main adit, and more branches spread from those, making the map look like a lopsided tree, with twice as many branches on one side.

At some point in history, the Lucky Monk had been a prosperous claim. And from the clues Mac had found so far in the walls and ceiling, with enough capital, it could flourish again.

In addition to the slew of tunnels shown, there were several X's marked on the map. But there was no explanation for each X—a casualty of many old mine maps, especially ones that had passed from hand-to-hand over the years.

The first X Mac had sought out had led him to a solid wall jagged with scarred rocks—a dead end.

The second X turned out to be the third, unlisted shaft: a hole, four-feet in diameter, dug straight down into the earth. Rusted remnants of ladder anchors were all that remained of the past. Mac had scooped up several pebbles and dropped them down the dark shaft, expecting a splash as they hit water, which often filled old shafts around these parts. Seconds later, he'd heard the clatter of the pebbles bouncing off solid rock.

Not only was the shaft shallow, but dry too. One of these days, he'd have to bring his climbing equipment and slip down there to see if any drifts spliced off from it.

The third X represented a small chamber where a prospector had been digging out some copper ore mixed with tiny glints of silver that zig-zagged along the wall, up the ceiling, down the other wall, and into the floor. A square shovel and broken pickax had been left behind to rust together in the dark.

The last X he'd had the time to seek out turned out to be another dead end, almost half a mile back in the mine. This time, a pile of rocks—the results of a cave-in—blocked any further travel. There was no telling how long ago the beams holding up the walls and ceiling had submitted to the god of gravity.

Stuffing the last of the bar in his mouth, Mac scooped up the maps. He glanced back the way he'd come. His nerves waged a campaign to head for sunshine and Claire, to inhale fresh air instead of the musty breaths from the Lucky Monk's dusty lungs.

But his sense of duty didn't suffer quitters well. He'd made a commitment to his aunt, not to mention the gut feeling he couldn't shake that there was something yet to be found in this mine that made it worth stealing out from under Ruby.

He shot one last look behind him as he slipped his arms into his pack, and then hiked deeper into the mine.

* * *

"How did you find this?" Claire asked Jess.

They stood in Ruby's closet staring down at a trap door in the floor that lay open. A 40-watt light bulb dangled from the ceiling. The parquet-style, oak floor boards creaked under Claire's feet as she stepped over the carpet Jess had pulled back from the wall. The long, skinny room smelled faintly of jasmine, no doubt due to the two packets of fragrant beads hanging from a nail next to the accordion-style closet door. Shoe boxes lined the shelf above Ruby's clothes.

Jess popped her gum. "I was in here looking for my money yesterday, and the floor kept squeaking when I'd step right here." She pointed at the trap door.

With her back to the bedroom, Claire squatted next to the trap door cleverly disguised in the floor's triangular design. The handle lay flush with the wood, visible only under scrutiny, and accessible only after removing a triangle piece.

"Then today, when I was in the shower, I was thinking about you and that loose board in the tool shed last spring and it hit me—maybe the boards squeaked because Mom hid the money under it."

Claire lifted a small box from the hole in the floor, the metal cool in her palms. Listening with half an ear as Jess prattled on about why Ruby should just share the money with her now instead of waiting two more years, Claire opened the lid.

A Browning 9mm lay diagonally in the box, taking up most of the available real estate. Claire glanced up at Jess, glad she wasn't the kind of kid who got off on playing with guns.

Ruby had made a point of teaching Jess all about firearms long ago. She'd once told Claire that living with Joe Martino made gun familiarity a necessity, since the man had them stashed all around the house. He'd claimed collecting guns had been his hobby—a rather creative way of hiding his true sleazy profession, in Claire's opinion.

Carefully lifting the handgun from the box, Claire made sure the safety was on and set it down behind her, the barrel pointed toward the outer wall. She turned back to the box. A greeting-card-sized envelope, yellowed in the corners, lay at the bottom of it.

"What do you think?" Jess's question drew Claire's gaze. The girl wore a pair of Ruby's silver, three-inch heels and held a white satin dress under her neck. "Mom wore this when she married Joe."

"It's a pretty dress." Claire picked up the envelope. It was sealed.

"I wonder if Mom still has those diamond earrings Joe bought her the Christmas before his stroke." Jess brushed past Claire and clomped into the bedroom in Ruby's heels.

With Jess off digging through Ruby's jewelry box, Claire picked at the envelope seal. The glue was so old that the flap tore open easily. She pulled out a handful of pictures, squinting at the top one in the dull light.

A quiet gasp slipped from her throat. She gawked down at a naked blonde woman, who could give Dolly Parton a run for her money, posed on all fours on a bed.

But it wasn't the chesty blonde that had Claire's jaw hitting the parquet-floor, it was the guy behind her playing Rin-Tin-Tin. Joe Martino had been quite a looker in his youth, prior to eating too many sour-cream-and-onion flavored potato chips. The shock of black hair partially blocking one eye, the square chin, those dark piercing eyes—Joe definitely had the rebel-without-a-cause look down pat.

Claire stood, moving closer to the light bulb. While the blonde seemed lost in Candy Land with her eyes half-closed, Joe stared straight into the camera lens. The cold hardness of his smile held Claire's gaze for several more seconds.

Shuddering, she tucked that picture behind the others and moved to the next.

She gasped again.

The woman in this picture had curly red hair. The walls were covered with pink, flowery wallpaper, the bedspread matched and hadn't even been turned down. The woman's bra hung from her arm—she'd been short on time, apparently. Knocking on the woman's back door was Joe, grinning around a cigarette, focused on the camera.

Claire's hands felt dirty as she flipped to the next photo.

The third picture had a short-haired brunette, small chested, caught in mid-scream, her eyes rolled back. Joe was winking at the camera this time.

The fourth picture had another brunette—her hair long and straight. A wire-mesh Tiffany's table lamp, red poppies decorating the glass, sat next to the bed. A Victorian era, curved head frame provided a romantic backdrop for yet another one of

Joe's campy smiles. He either liked that particular mattress-romping position, or he preferred that camera angle, because the brunette and he were again on their knees.

"Jesus!" Kate said from over Claire's shoulder. "Where did you find those?"

Claire jumped and almost dropped the bunch of photos. She'd been so lost in Joe's sordid little world she hadn't heard Kate walk up behind her.

"Where did she find what?" Jess stood in the closet doorway, trying to peek over Kate's shoulder.

Claire shoved the pictures back in the envelope. Her face burned as if she'd been busted ogling her aunt's *Playgirl* magazines again.

"Did you look in this?" she asked Jess, holding up the envelope.

While it had seemed sealed shut, Claire didn't put it past Jess to peek and then glue the flap shut again.

"Oh, I forgot about that. I saw it under the gun, but then I saw the receipt and key and came to see you." Jess pushed past Kate. "Why? What's in it?"

"Nothing." Claire shoved the envelope in her back pocket. She wiped her hands on her pants, wondering if bleaching her palms would remove that icky feeling.

"Whose gun?" Kate asked as she stared down at the Browning.

"Joe's." Claire squatted and packed it back in the box. Then she lowered the box back in the floor. "You're supposed to be minding the store, Kate."

"Manny's standing guard. I had to use the bathroom."

"Jess," Claire said, "will you go take over the register?"

"But Manny is already doing it."

"It's not Manny's job." The teenager opened her mouth to argue. "Please, Jess."

"Fine!" Jess kicked off Ruby's heels and hung up her mom's wedding dress. She muttered something about "slave labor" and left.

"What are you going to do with those pictures?" Kate asked after Jess was safely out of earshot.

Claire finished rolling the carpet back into place and stood up. "I don't know. The guy in all of them is Joe."

"Yuck!" The expression on Kate's face looked like she'd bitten into a rotten apple filled with worms.

"Tell me about it. That's almost as bad as finding those pictures of Mom and Dad having sex." Claire shuddered again and walked into the bedroom.

"Do you think Ruby knows about that box?"

"No. Nothing in it belonged to her. It's one of Joe's stashes."

"So that's his kilo of gold?"

Claire grabbed the little black box from Ruby's dresser and popped the lid off again, frowning down at the slice of gold. "Definitely. Ruby would have cashed this in last spring if she'd known about it."

"Deutsche Reichsbank," Kate read aloud the stamped words on the bar. "That's German, you know."

"I wasn't born yesterday, knucklehead. Besides, there's no missing that Nazi symbol. I remember learning about missing Nazi gold in one of my history classes. It's kind of trippy to think that we may be holding a bit of that treasure." Claire ran her finger over the smooth, shiny surface. "I wonder ..." Her words trailed off as cylinders in her head clicked.

"What?" Kate leaned against the dresser.

"If this is the treasure Porter was looking for."

"What's going on in here, *Señoritas*?" Manny asked from the doorway, making them both jump. Grinning, he ambled into the room.

Claire thought about closing the lid on the box, but instead, held the gold bar out toward Manny. "What do you make of this?"

Taking the box from her hand, Manny took a long look at the slice of gold, then let out a low whistle. "You got you an expensive piece of history here, *mi amor*. That's Hitler's gold. Reichsbank was the bank of the Third Reich."

Manny confirmed Claire's suspicion. She could only imagine how Joe had gotten his hands on this little trinket.

"What are you going to do with this?" Manny handed the box back to Claire.

Sighing, she dropped the item in question on the dresser. "Shit, I don't know. Hand it over to Ruby, I guess."

"Oh, speaking of shit," Manny's said, "the toilet is overflowing again in the men's restroom."

"God damn it!" Growling in her throat, Claire stormed out of the bedroom.

If that toilet clogged one more time, she was going to use a stick of dynamite to clear the sucker once and for all.

* * *

A half-mile back in the Lucky Monk, Mac tipped his canteen and sipped some lukewarm water, washing the coat of mine dust from his throat. Hours had slipped by while he'd been busy spelunking and charting, hours that he'd rather have spent most anywhere, but in the bowels of a mine.

Suddenly, a rumbling sound, born from deeper within the mine, rolled over him.

"Fuck," he whispered, knowing the sound of a cave-in all too well.

Goosebumps raced up his arms and across his shoulders, making his hairline tingle. He lowered the canteen, gulping down the last swallow still pooled in his mouth.

Fighting the urge to get the hell out of there, he screwed the lid on his canteen and tucked it away in his pack.

With that cave-in, his plans changed course. Before continuing with his surveying, he wanted to know where the cave-in had occurred and see if any new rooms had been opened or drifts sealed off.

He hoisted his pack onto his back and hiked further into the mine, watching for a cloud of dust, sniffing the stale air, listening for the sound of more rocks crashing to the floor.

Twenty minutes later, at the fourth X he'd sought out yesterday, he hit pay-dirt—the previous cave-in had crumbled further. This time, several feet of rock from the ceiling had given way, most of it appearing to have cascaded down over the pile of rocks already there.

Mac coughed, small particles of dust still flurrying in front of his hard hat light. He squinted up at the now steeply-arched ceiling, searching for further stress fractures or veins of minerals, finding neither. The blasting from Copper Snake was taking a toll on Ruby's old mines, shaking loose the at-risk sections for better or worse. The ceiling looked as stable now as the rest of the mine, which didn't say much.

As his light flitted over the rock pile, he caught sight of a small, dark hole between the ceiling and the top of the mound of rocks. Dust drifted through the hole toward him.

He pulled his high-watt flashlight from his pack and shined the beam at the hole. The light pierced it, disappearing into the darkness.

What was on the other side? His instincts told him there were answers there waiting for him, something important. But were they important enough to risk his life to find out?

Rubbing his neck, Mac weighed his odds. He scanned the ceiling, wondering how long it would hold before giving way again. He lowered his pack to the floor, the voice of reason in his head trying to talk him out of doing something foolish. He was too old to flirt with death, had too much to lose for it to be appealing. But what if ...

He squelched the thought, cursing its source—Claire. Without a doubt, he knew that if she were here, she'd already be up there trying to wiggle through the hole.

But he wasn't Claire.

He walked away from the cave-in, telling himself there was nothing wrong with using some common sense. Fifty feet or so later he stopped and cursed at the ceiling.

Turning back, he returned to the rock pile and carefully climbed it, his breath shallow and fast. At the top, the hole was just big enough to squeeze through if he felt ballsy enough to try it. He settled for just peeking through with his flashlight.

The first thing his light bounced off was a boarded up wall, not thirty feet from the other side of the rock pile. He frowned, his flashlight lowering slightly as he wondered what someone had wanted to keep out … or in.

Something shiny reflected the light, catching his eye. He shifted his beam to the floor several feet in front of the wall and almost lost his grip on the flashlight.

Leaning against the rock wall, covered in a layer of dust and rags, sat a dead man.

* * *

"Make a right," Kate told her sister as they pulled up to the stop sign at the only intersection in Jackrabbit Junction. The two overhead streetlights cast an orange glow on the night.

Kate resisted the urge to glance over at The Shaft as the old Ford rumbled onto the main highway. A lukewarm breeze fresh with the smell of damp earth puffed through the passenger window as Claire accelerated.

To the northeast, lightning flashed behind the thick bank of clouds that had dumped dime-sized drops on the valley around sunset, an hour earlier.

Kate clasped her hands together to keep them from shaking. This whole sneaking-around-looking-for-clues routine made her armpits clammy.

"Quit driving like a grandma. I'd like to make it there before sunrise."

Claire turned down the radio, muting Jeannie C. Riley singing about telling off the Harper Valley PTA. "Exactly where am I taking you?" She sounded annoyed.

Kate ignored her sister's glare. "I'll tell you when we get there. You'll need to make a turn at Gila Monster Road."

She'd memorized the route this afternoon, not wanting to carry a map or written address around in case Claire figured out what she was up to before they reached the destination. "It should be right up here … there it is. The dirt road on the left."

Muttering under her breath, Claire slowed the pickup and made the turn, then pulled to the side of the road and shifted into park. "You haven't answered my question. In fact, you've been dancing around it since we left the R.V. park."

"I don't know what you're talking about." Kate glanced over her shoulder as an eighteen-wheeler whooshed past on the main highway. "Come on, let's get moving. We're almost there."

Claire turned off the engine. "We're not going anywhere until you tell me where 'there' is."

With a sigh, Kate stared at Claire in the shadows. "You're acting like Mother."

"And comments like that make me want to turn this truck around and head back to Ruby's."

"Okay, okay. I'll spill. I arranged a meeting with Porter tonight," Kate lied.

"In the middle of the desert at night … alone? That's real smart, Kate. And I suppose you brought Joe's Browning 9mm as a gift for our host. Better yet, Ruby's big ol' butcher knife."

"Jesus, Claire. You need to stop reading Stephen King. Porter is just a writer. All he did was kiss you, not bite your neck and drink your blood."

"What reason did you give him to meet us?"

Kate gulped. Slipping a lie past Claire meant giving an Oscar-winning performance.

"To apologize in person for you sucker-punching him last night after he kissed you."

"What? I'm not apologizing for that. He went too far too fast."

Kate ignored her. "And I'm coming along because you're too nervous to face him on your own." Proud of her stellar fib, Kate smiled.

"Why would you tell him *that*?"

"To get him to invite us to his place so you could see for yourself there's no reason to suspect him."

"It's not that simple, you know."

"Sure, whatever." But Kate could hear the interest in Claire's voice. She reached over and turned the key. The engine sputtered to life. "Can we go now? We're already late because you kept dinking around back at Ruby's."

After another dirty look at Kate, Claire shifted into gear. "I wasn't dinking around. I was scrubbing the smell of that freaking clogged toilet off my skin."

They rode in silence for a couple of minutes. Kate's heart beat harder and louder with each passing mesquite tree. After winding up a short canyon, they came to a fork in the road.

"Take the left one." Kate checked her side mirror for any followers. The night cloaked them in darkness, the radio and the Ford's headlights the only illumination in the shadows.

"How much further is it from here?" Claire asked.

"Another mile." That was her guess, anyway. Kate sat forward and watched for a driveway. The road turned to washboard for a quarter mile, making her teeth rattle … at least she told herself it was the road.

Claire swerved to miss a scraggly looking coyote, and Kate's stomach roller-coastered. She needed a stiff drink, one that would burn all the way into the pit of her stomach. She didn't know how Claire pulled off this Inspector Gadget routine without popping antacids like Tic Tacs.

Up ahead, Kate saw a drive and a mailbox. "There it is."

The numbers on the box matched those she'd memorized.

Claire turned the steering wheel and cruised up the smooth, paved drive. "Are you sure this is it?" They ascended a small hill. "The place looks dark."

Pitch black was more like it. With the moon recently set, the stars too far away to help, and no outside nightlight, they could be driving off the rim of the Grand Canyon for all Kate could see.

"Hit the brights. I can't see anything."

They crested the hill and Kate gasped.

Claire hit the brakes and skidded to a stop. "Holy shit."

Kate shoved open her door and stepped outside so she could get a better look without trying to peer through the bug guts splattered on the Ford's windshield.

Standing there, under the milky spill of stars, she crossed her arms and let out a very definitive, "Humph!"

How in the hell could the owner of a two-bit bar in a spitwad of a town afford something like this?

In front of her sat a huge, Pueblo-style house. Two stories high, headlights reflecting in all umpteen windows that stretched from floor to ceiling on both floors, the place looked like a five-star resort. Homes like this went for a million-plus in Tucson, according to the real estate channel Deborah tuned to day after day since arriving in Jackrabbit Junction.

After killing the engine but leaving the headlights on, Claire joined Kate under the Big Dipper. "We're too late, huh?"

"We're not late."

"You just said back there—"

"I lied. We're not meeting Porter here. We're not meeting him at all."

"Damn it, Kate!" Claire pinched Kate's arm hard. "What in the hell are we doing here then?"

"Ow!" She rubbed her bruised flesh, glaring at Claire. "We're here to find proof."

From her back pocket, Kate pulled out a pair of cotton gloves she'd found in Ruby's tool shed and slipped them on.

"Shit," Claire said, watching Kate slip on the gloves. "Please tell me this isn't Butch's house."

"Okay. It's not Butch's house." Kate climbed the steps leading to a pergola-covered patio. Lights in the walls lining the steps kicked on, illuminating the stairs in a soft glow. Kate smirked. Motion sensor lights, those couldn't be cheap. "It's Butch's desert palace."

A string of curses flew from Claire's lips.

"Your mother would be so proud," Kate told her potty-mouthed sister.

On the top stair, Kate pulled a penlight from her shirt pocket. More motion-sensor lights flickered to life, revealing an immense patio covered with a jungle's worth of potted plants and patio tiles made of travertine limestone—the kind imported only from Spain or Portugal.

Turning back, she shined the penlight on Claire's face. "By the way, we're not leaving until we find proof that Butch is trying to steal the Lucky Monk, so start digging."

Chapter Eighteen

Mac stared at the dead man, unable to drag his gaze from the withered corpse—especially its empty eye sockets.

Tucked away deep in the Lucky Monk's dry innards, Father Time and Mother Nature's creatures had been kind to the body. Tuffs of hair still clung to the skull, along with patches of leathered skin, stretched tight across both cheekbones. The right ear lobe was half chewed off. The left ear was missing entirely, no doubt a tasty meal for one of the mine's past residents.

His flashlight beam reflected in the unbroken lenses of a pair of wire-rim glasses that sat askew on the man's face. The nose was nothing more than two holes, not even a hint of cartilage remaining. The mouth gaped open, frozen in a silent scream, lips peeled back to expose crooked, brown teeth.

As he watched, a spider crawled up the piece of loose, dried flesh hanging from the chin, scuttled over the bottom set of teeth and disappeared in the shadow-filled mouth.

Something touched the back of Mac's neck.

He jerked back, scraping his elbow and forearm on a serrated rock edge. The flashlight slipped from his grip, the beam cartwheeling through the air before it clattered between two small boulders at his feet.

Then the world went black.

Mac brushed frantically at his neck in the darkness, his breathing ragged, his heart a juggernaut in his chest.

The rock he stood on wobbled underfoot, then rolled out from under him. He stumbled, reaching out to catch his balance and busting his knuckle on another sharp edge. He landed on a pointed chunk of rock, his hard hat tipping to the side.

"Fuck me," he said in the darkness. Pushing to his feet, he rubbed his throbbing ass cheek and coughed on the dust he'd stirred up.

From the other side of the hole, he heard a scratching sound.

The blackness surrounding him seemed to grow thick, choking. He flicked on the light on his hard hat and stared at the hole.

With his breath locked in his chest, he heard the sound of toenails—*or bones?*—on stone. Rocks clattered to the floor on the other side.

Something was climbing the other side of the rock pile.

In a blink, Mac jerked into action. He scrambled down the remaining rock pile, grabbed his backpack, and rocketed toward the main adit.

Minutes later, he leaned against the wall next to the place where he'd spread out the maps earlier that afternoon. His lungs ached; sweat rolled down his forehead.

Glancing back toward the direction of the cave-in, he shook his head, disgusted with himself. With distance between him and the dead man, his common sense had reclaimed its position at the helm.

Sure now that what he'd heard was a packrat or some other critter who had also been exploring the cave-in's leftovers, he debated his next course of action. Should he wrap up his work in the Lucky Monk tonight and head back to Ruby's? Or should he head to Yuccaville first and report the dead guy to the sheriff's office?

He sipped from his canteen, still mulling what to do as he swished the warm water around, washing the dust from the back of his throat as he swallowed.

That dead man had sat in the mine for a long time. What was another night? Mac would hit Yuccaville in the morning.

A thought hit him—he hadn't checked to see if the dead man had both hands. He shoved off the notion. That wasn't important right now.

Claire's words about *Treasure Island* and Flint's Pointer replayed in his head:

> *And Flint's pointer refers to the skeleton of a man Flint killed and then used as an indicator to where the treasure was hidden ... the skeleton is a pointer that leads to the "jolly dollars."*

Mac looked back in the direction of the cave-in again, trying to remember details about the dead man's body and if an arm or leg had been pointing in a particular direction.

Unfortunately, he'd been so mesmerized by the tattered remains of the guy's face that he couldn't even picture what the dead man had been wearing other than glasses.

Without a doubt, he knew that as soon as he told Claire about the body, she'd insist on coming up to the mine with or without him and seeing the dead guy for herself, risking her life in a very unstable section of the mine.

Damn.

He rubbed his forehead. Maybe he shouldn't tell her about the remains.

Right, and when she found out about the skeleton—and she undoubtedly would somehow—and realized he'd skipped her and gone to the police without even checking to see if the skeleton had two hands, she'd be pissed as hell.

"Shit." Mac sighed.

That left just one option—go back and take another look at the dead man tonight.

But if he was going to pay another visit to the dead man, he wasn't going to do it from this side of that hole. He needed the pry bar and some of his other tools he'd stashed behind a greasewood bush near the mouth of the mine.

This time, he'd get some answers to a few questions of his own, like how the guy died, if he'd been a miner, and if he had any kind of identification on him at all.

Blocking out the fear that tingled up from the base of his spine at returning to the cave-in, he squared his shoulders and tried to mentally prepare himself for his up close and personal meeting with the dead man.

* * *

"You're doing it wrong," Claire said from where she sat in a plush patio chair while she watched Kate dash from window to door to window, searching for a way into Butch's fortress.

Kate's obsession with Butch being Darth Vader's evil twin had "therapy" written all over it.

The desert's creatures of the night kept Claire company. A giant crab spider scurried across the partially lit terrace while crickets chirped from shadows over by the potted palms surrounding a small pool with a fountain in the center of it. A warm breeze, carrying the scent of damp earth mixed with pungent greasewood, blew wisps of her hair across her face.

"Would you stop saying that?" Kate wiggled both handles on the second set of French doors that led out onto the patio.

"Well, you are. And you already tried those doors."

"Just shut up!" Kate scared the crickets into silence.

"If wearing all black is your idea of coming prepared to a breaking-and-entering party, you haven't learned a thing from me over the years."

With a brush-off wave that incorporated the use of her middle finger, Kate strode across the patio, away from the house, and down the steps leading to a large pole barn with three garage doors fronting it. Butch seemed to be into super-sizing his dwellings.

Claire lifted her feet, making way for a beetle on its route across the patio tiles toward one of the motion sensor lights. "Kate, where are you going?"

Kate didn't answer her. Claire looked over to find her sister shining her penlight in one of the pole barn's windows.

"Can we go back to Ruby's now?" Claire asked. Her voice sounded tired even to her own ears.

Now that she'd calmed down about being tricked into driving to Butch's place, she felt like a deflated party balloon. She wanted nothing more than to sit in front of Ruby's TV with a mixer bowl full of cereal in milk while she waited for Mac to come back from the mine.

Some nicotine wouldn't hurt, either.

The idea of driving off alone and leaving Kate for the scorpions and coyotes to fight over tempted her. That would teach Kate a lesson for lying to her.

"Claire?" Kate's nose was still pressed against the window.

"What?"

"What color was Joe's old El Camino?"

"Midnight blue, why?"

"I'm just wondering if the El Camino I'm looking at is one and the same."

Claire sprung from her chair, her flip-flops flapping as she raced to the pole barn window.

"Let me see that." She grabbed Kate's penlight and shouldered her sister aside.

"Hey! Pushy." Kate knuckled Claire's shoulder hard. "This is my breaking-and-entering shindig. Go find your own light."

She reached for the penlight, but Claire held it out of her reach.

"Just give me a minute, would you?"

Claire turned back to the window, ignoring her throbbing shoulder, and shined the bright light through it.

Sure enough, there sat Joe's old El Camino, shiny and overflowing with muscle, parked in the center of the oversized garage. The custom red leather bench seat glowed next to the midnight blue hand-rubbed paint job.

She directed the beam of light along the car's sleek lines, wondering why it was sitting in Butch's garage. The last Claire had heard, Sophy Martino's name was on the title. A prison sentence shouldn't have changed that.

"Has Butch ever talked to you about Sophy?" Claire asked her sister.

When she received no answer, she looked over her shoulder. Kate was nowhere to be seen.

"Kate?" She shined the light into the grove of mesquite trees behind her. "Where are you?"

Still no answer.

Claire shrugged. Kate had probably gone back up to the house to nose around some more.

Turning back to the window, she shined the penlight back in at the El Camino, memories of Sophy's deadly threats and shotgun blasts dancing through her head.

For the first time since she'd met Butch last spring, uncertainty about his character made her tense. What did she really know about the guy, besides the fact that he'd been tending bar at The Shaft for close to a decade? How could he afford such an elaborate house, not to mention the set-up in his office at the bar? How well had he known Sophy? Did their relationship go deeper than fellow Rotary Club members?

The tinkling sound of glass breaking snapped Claire back to the present. Something moved in the garage, off to the right of the El Camino's front bumper.

She redirected the beam of light. The sight of Kate standing next to the car, brushing her hands on her jeans made Claire snarl.

"God damn it." She pounded on the window, snaring Kate's attention.

"What?" Kate mouthed, blinking in the beam of light.

"I'm leaving right now!" Claire yelled. "And you are, too!"

* * *

Kate crossed her arms and shook her head. She shielded her eyes from the penlight's beam and held a silent stare-down with Claire, even though all she could see of her sister was the black outline of her head.

She was not leaving, not after finally finding a way into Butch's fortress—okay, forcing her way in. And while the garage didn't exactly open up to a secret room in his house, it was a start.

Besides, she wanted to see what he was hiding behind those black-painted windows around the back side of the garage. The moldy, stale, humid smell leaking out through the myriad vents interspersed below the windows had filled her head with a new suspicion, one that involved the Mexican border, oodles of cash, and a little plant called "Mary Jane."

Claire shined the penlight on the pickup keys she was holding, then Kate, then the direction where the pickup waited.

Kate smiled and waved, calling Claire's bluff. Her sister would never leave without her, not with their mother waiting for them back at Ruby's.

She skirted the El Camino and unlocked the door leading to the outside, in case Claire came to her senses and decided to join her.

Ignoring Claire's loud raps on the glass, Kate headed for the room at the back of the garage only to find the door locked. She should've anticipated that. Glancing around, her gaze landed on a tall tool chest against the wall. A screwdriver would make short work of the lock.

She heard the flap of flip-flops behind her as she picked up the screwdriver.

"Give me that thing." Claire snatched the screwdriver from Kate's hand.

"I thought you were leaving."

"I should have. I'm sure I'll regret this." Claire pocketed the screwdriver and held out her hand. "Give me your Visa card."

"What makes you think I have a Visa card on me?"

"Please, Kate. You're a shoe-a-holic. You never travel anywhere without a credit card."

Pulling her platinum card from her inside jacket pocket, Kate dropped it in Claire's palm. "I'm not a shoe-a-holic. I just like to be prepared for unforeseeable, necessary purchases."

"You're hopeless." Claire slid the credit card along the edge of the door. Kate tried to watch over Claire's shoulder, but her sister was too quick. Within seconds, the door popped open.

Standing back, Claire ushered Kate forward. "After you."

"I want my credit card back." Kate snatched it from Claire and then pushed open the door, walked into the room, and blinked in the bright overhead lights. A wave of humid heat made her breath stick in her throat.

"Well, would you look at this?" Claire joined Kate. "It looks like we've stumbled upon the Great Cactus-Napper's headquarters. Where's your camera, Lois Lane? This is all the proof we need to convince the police that Butch is the evil master-mind behind that illegal cacti trading ring."

"Cactus?" Kate rubbed her forehead, staring around the large greenhouse. "Why the dark windows then?"

Clare walked over to one of the tables filled with hundreds of baby cacti sprouting from the small containers of pebble-covered dirt.

"Who knows? Maybe he likes to control how much sunlight these puppies get." She looked back to Kate, her arms crossed. "Now, can we go back to Ruby's?"

Damn. Wrong again.

Her shoulders sagging in defeat, Kate nodded.

She'd thought for sure she'd find a room full of marijuana, which would explain how Butch could afford such a lavish house. The Shaft might be busy most nights, but not enough to support all of this.

Claire locked the greenhouse door behind them, dropped the screwdriver back in the tool chest, and led the way around the El Camino. She held the outside door open for Kate.

"I don't understand where Butch gets his money." Kate said as she stepped outside.

"Neither do I." Claire closed the door. "I wonder why he—"

"Hold it right there!" a familiar voice commanded from the darkness in front of them. A blinding light blasted them.

Behind Kate, Claire groaned. "Oh, shit. We're busted."

Busted? Nausea gripped Kate. "I'm going to throw up," she said, bending over, wheezing.

"I said don't move!" Sheriff Harrison hollered. "You're both under arrest for breaking-and-entering!"

* * *

Monday, August 23rd, 2:37 a.m.

Hard, jagged edges scratched Mac's shoulders through his T-shirt as he squeezed through the hole into the dead man's tomb. All of his sweating and swearing had paid off. With the help of his pry bar, he'd managed to widen the gap a few crucial inches without bringing the ceiling down on his head.

Directing his hard hat light at the skeleton, he realized why he hadn't noticed whether both hands were present and accounted for when he'd first peeked into the tomb. A large boulder sat in front of the skeleton, blocking the lower half of the dead guy's body.

Stones and pebbles clattered to the floor below him as he crawled forward on his hands, sliding his hips, legs, and boots through the hole.

He half-rolled, half-stumbled down the rocks; the slope was less steep on this side of the cave-in. The smell of dust filled the tomb, thick in the small, enclosed space. The scent of decayed flesh was not even a memory anymore.

Brushing off his shirt and jeans, Mac tiptoed across the floor toward the skeleton, as if his footfalls might wake the dead. As he approached, he realized that the large boulder that had been blocking his view was actually sitting on the lower half of the dead guy's left leg. He grimaced at what must have happened and scanned the concave section of the ceiling. Gravity could be so cruel.

He walked around to the left side of the body, squatting next to the boulder. A rusted canteen leaned against the wall within the skeleton's reach, a pickaxe lay a couple of feet beyond, out of reach. An antique brass Davy safety lamp, tinted green with patina, lay on its side next to the canteen.

So far, all signs pointed to this guy being the missing mine owner he read about when researching the history of the Lucky Monk.

He tried to budge the boulder with his shoulder, but it wouldn't move.

What a miserable way to die: alone in a dark mine, trapped under a chunk of ceiling. Had the miner bled to death? Or had the rock acted as a tourniquet and allowed him to live until the water in his canteen had run dry and then some? The mine floor was too dark and dust-covered to show traces of dried blood in this light.

Leaning over the body, Mac admired the Lucky Monk's preservation handiwork. Dried flesh, the color and texture of turkey jerky, clung to the skull and hung in strips from the jaw bone. A dusty, holey shirt draped awkwardly on protruding shoulder bones. The right forearm dripped dried skin, but the left arm was bare, the bone bearing chew marks. Both hands were present, frozen in claw position. Flesh shrink-wrapped the fingers, nails still visible on the digits not gnawed down to the knuckle.

Mac sat back on his heels. He'd hoped to find a hand missing, making this imprudent trip into the tomb worth his time and energy. Maybe even tie together two pieces of the puzzle upon which Claire had stumbled. Instead, he'd just added another piece that didn't seem to fit anywhere.

A tingling in his toes drove him to his feet again. He skirted the boulder and approached the dead man from the right.

Careful not to disturb the body, Mac trailed his fingers over the pants pockets, wondering if the old miner had carried a leather wallet or anything that would confirm his identity. But he felt nothing, just worn cotton over pelvic bone.

As he rose to his feet again, his boot bumped against the dead man's right hand, knocking it forward a couple of inches and turning it palm-side up. He bent down to return the hand to its original position and noticed a short piece of thin rope trailing out from the palm.

With a light tug, Mac freed the rope from the miner's hold. The piece was slightly frayed at both ends and braided in an unusual pattern. It reminded him of the sandal Claire had found in the same bag as the mummy hand.

He unbuttoned his shirt pocket and pulled his small flashlight free. Under closer inspection with the halogen light, he was fairly sure this was the piece missing from the heel portion of the sandal, but he couldn't be sure until he got back to Ruby's. He stuffed it into his front pocket.

The sound of claws scratching on wood boards made Mac flinch in surprise. He stared at the wall of boards, his skin prickling. Something on the other side of those boards wanted to pay its respects to the dead man sprawled at Mac's feet.

After several seconds, the scratching stopped.

Mac remained frozen, staring at the powder gray nail heads dotting the slabs of pine. He waited for the ruckus to start up again, telling himself it was only a rat or porcupine or some other desert creature.

Silence reigned.

With one last glance at the dead man, he started toward the rock pile, but stopped two steps later and spun back around. He again focused his light on the boarded up wall. Except for a small spot of rust here and there, those nail heads looked new, unmarred by time. But if this was the missing mine owner, this guy must have died over a hundred years ago. Iron nails should have rusted by now.

Mac crept over to the wall and shined his flashlight on several of the nail heads. They were definitely not one hundred-year-old nails.

He examined the boards, realizing they didn't have that cracked and aged appearance of century-old wood either. He shined his light on the end of one board where it abutted the timber beam, looking for signs of wear, and instead found a price tag stapled to the rough end. Faded, but still visible, were the words: Creekside Supply Company.

Somebody else had been in this part of the mine before, and within the last couple of decades at that. Somebody who had ignored the dead man lounging just feet away while hammering up boards.

Had it been Joe? He'd owned the mines for a little over a decade before dying. It could have been the owner before Joe too, or even the owner prior to that guy based on how long the hardware store had been in business.

And why had someone wanted to block off the remaining section of the tunnel?

The scratching started again down near his feet, louder, more determined. Mac stumbled backwards, almost landing on his ass for the second time that night.

Regular old packrat or not, there was something about standing next to a dead man while listening to the sound of something wanting to get into the tomb that made Mac's upper lip sweat in spite of the mine's cool temperature.

His curiosity about what was on the other side of the blockade ebbed, his bones and joints aching. Besides, he needed the crowbar from his truck to break through the wall; the pry bar was too long. He stuffed his flashlight into his shirt pocket and crawled up the pile toward the hole without looking back.

Tomorrow, he'd return, crowbar in hand, and find out what was hiding behind those boards. He ducked through the hole, carefully wiggling through. His pack sat on the floor on the other side, rumpled and dusty, a mirror of himself. He rubbed his burning eyes. As he bent over to lift his pack, his small flashlight slipped out of his shirt pocket and bounced on the stone floor. The battery cover broke open and the two AA batteries spilled out, rolling in different directions across the floor, disappearing into the shadows.

"Shit." Mac dropped onto his hands and knees next to his pack. He pulled off his hard hat, searching for the escapees with his hat light. One battery lay in a crevice along the base of the wall. Mac stuffed it in his pocket and clambered toward the rock pile. Half way there, he noticed a footprint.

It wasn't his.

He sat back on his heels, staring down at the wavy-lined imprint. It hadn't been here earlier when he'd climbed through the hole to spend some quality time with the dead miner.

He shined his light across the floor toward the main adit. Several more prints with the same tread design headed to and from the edge of the rock pile. They were too big to be Claire's or Jess's, and nobody else at the R.V. park had a clue how to get up to the mine. That meant one thing—while he'd been messing around on the other side of that hole, he'd had a visitor.

Shit! Blood roared in his eardrums.

He shoved his hard hat back on his head, his gaze darting around the shadows that wavered at the edge of the beam of his hat light. Sweat beaded on his skin.

Who had come for a visit and why?

Adrenaline pumping, Mac scooped up his pack and ran toward the main adit.

There was one thing he was certain about: Tomorrow, when he came back to the mine, Ruby's Smith and Wesson would be keeping him company.

Chapter Nineteen

Morning sunlight shone through the cell window, the bars striped the glowing square onto the concrete floor.

Kate rubbed her eyes, which felt like they'd been dipped in Tabasco sauce, and struggled to her feet. Her body ached. Between the floor and the cell's single cot, she'd opted for the unforgiving concrete.

She would've needed to be vaccinated and flea dipped before even sitting on the stained mattress, which reeked of sweat, urine, disinfectant, and a hint of something she didn't want to decipher.

She glanced at where her sister slouched in the corner of the cell. Early this morning, sometime between when the crickets stopped chirping and the mourning doves started cooing, Mr. Sandman had whopped Claire on the head with a sandbag. Kate's mind, on the other hand, had been too full of whirling dervishes to catch any shut-eye.

Wrapping her hands around the cool bars of her cage, she stared out through the open steel door that divided the jail cells from the civilized section of the police station. From where she stood, she could see three oak desks and a tall reception counter. The glass entry doors, front window, and waiting area were hidden from her view.

Sheriff Harrison sat behind the largest of the three desks, his fingers clacking away on a computer keyboard. His dark hair curled slightly over his forehead, his jaw clean-shaven. Arizona ruggedness in the flesh.

The spicy bay rum scent of his aftershave wafted through the doorway on air-conditioned currents.

Kate shot him full of holes with her eyes. It wasn't fair of him to come in this morning looking as if he'd slept on clouds, showered under a Costa Rican waterfall, and floated to work on a magic carpet.

She cleared her throat, wishing she had a gallon of mint-flavored mouthwash. "Excuse me, Sheriff?"

The clacking stopped, but the sheriff's gaze remained fixed on the computer screen.

Kate added several scoops of sugar to her tone before continuing. "I'm sorry to interrupt, but I was wondering if you'd heard back from Butch yet?" Miss America had never sounded so sweet.

The sheriff squeezed the bridge of his nose. "It's only been twenty minutes since the last time you asked."

"Yes, well—"

"And you can see from your cell that I've been sitting at this desk, typing away for every single one of those twenty minutes."

"That's true, but—"

"Have you seen me pick up my phone even once?"

"No, however—"

"As I told you the last three times you asked, I will let you know as soon as I—"

A buzzing sound from the front door sensors cut him off.

He looked up from his computer and a smile spread across his craggy face. His chair scraped on the linoleum as he stood. "It's about goddamned time!"

"Well, good morning to you too, my little ray of sunshine." Butch's voice filtered into the cell room.

Kate's pulse ramped up. She ran over and kicked Claire's flip-flop. "Get up! Butch is here."

Claire jerked awake, knocking the back of her head on the cinderblock wall in the process, and rattled out a string of colorful curses.

Back at the bars, Kate strained to catch a glimpse of Butch's face. But short of squeezing her head through the bars, he remained just out of sight.

"What took you so long?" Sheriff Harrison asked Butch.

"The speed limit. Some idiot posted 55 mile-per-hour signs every other mile from Safford on."

The sheriff's grin widened even further. He meandered over to the reception counter. "Real funny, Valentine. I'll be sure to remember your sense of humor the next time you ask me to let you off with just a warning."

Valentine? Kate frowned. That had been the name on the fake license that had fallen out of Butch's wallet a couple of weeks ago.

"What's with the frown?" Claire stepped up next to Kate. "We're about to get sprung."

"The sheriff just called Butch 'Valentine'," she whispered.

"So. Maybe that's Butch's nickname."

"Or his birth name. That was the name I saw on his license." Her gut churned. If she had been wrong about something as basic as the man's name, what else was she wrong about?

"Jesus." Claire leaned her head against the bars. "Don't tell me you based your Butch-Is-the-Bad-Guy theory on something as flimsy as a different name on his license."

"It could have been a fake I.D."

"Damn it, Kate." Claire shoved away from the bars and paced to the other side of the cell and back. "Let it go. Butch is not Dr. Evil. He's just a bar owner—and some kind of cactus dealer."

Shit. If Claire was right, Kate would need a crane to remove her foot from her mouth.

"You'd better fix this mess you made," Claire said, "because I like going to The Shaft."

The jangling of keys sounded like a chorus of angels to Kate's ears.

"Well, girls, it's your lucky day." Sheriff Harrison shot Kate a cockeyed grin as he swung open the cell door. "Remember, darlin', third time's a charm. If I get you in here again, you may be leaving in shackles."

Avoiding his stare, she stepped past him through the doorway. Kate scanned the room for a certain blue-eyed bar owner. The waiting area stood empty.

Claire pushed past her and beelined for the women's restroom.

Kate approached the reception desk, familiar with the sign-for-her-valuables routine after her last performance of the Folsom Prison Blues in Sheriff Harrison's Read-'Em-Their-Rights Resort. She couldn't wait to go home and steam herself clean under Ruby's showerhead.

The men's room door on her right creaked open. She glanced over. Butch strode toward her. Besides the muscle twitching in his jaw, he gave her no hint as to the depth of the hole she'd dug for herself.

"Hello, Butch." She offered a slight smile.

"Kate," he replied with barely a nod.

Wringing her hands, she stammered, "Umm, thanks for … for not pressing charges against us, uh … you know, for last night."

The sheriff chuckled from behind her. "I told you that new security system would work better than a pack of Dobermans. These two had no idea they'd even tripped the alarm."

"Whew!" Claire stormed out of the women's restroom. She glared at the sheriff. "You need to explain to Deputy Droopy that giving me a bottle of Coke and then not allowing me to use the restroom is cruel and unusual punishment. It's no wonder your jail cells stink like piss."

The sheriff's lips twitched. "I'll talk to my deputy about your concern." He pushed a piece of paper across the desk toward her and held out his pen. "If you'll just sign here, I'll give you back your personal items."

Claire signed the paper, handed the pen to Kate, and then turned to Butch. "I'm sorry about all this." She gestured toward the jail cells. "Did Kate explain why we were at your place?"

Kate busied herself with signing on the dotted line, her forehead and neck roasting. "Not exactly."

The door buzzer rang again. Kate looked up from the paper and found Chester's shit-eating grin. Manny followed on Chester's heels, his smile even toothier. A groan escaped her throat before she could swallow it.

"We've come to transport the convicts back to Jackrabbit Junction," Chester announced to the sheriff.

"Did we miss the strip search?" Manny asked.

Claire grinned and lightly punched Manny on the shoulder. "What are you guys doing here already? We just got cleared not five minutes ago."

Plopping down in one of the green vinyl waiting room chairs, Chester answered, "Butch stopped by on his way back from Phoenix to let us know you'd need a ride home."

Kate's stomach took another turn on the Tilt-O-Whirl. If only she had the ability to spontaneously combust at will. Suffocating under a hippo-sized mass of mortification, she mouthed *thank you* to Butch.

He gave another hint of a nod in return, his gaze dogged.

"Please tell me Mom isn't waiting in the car." Claire peered out the front window.

Kate's head throbbed at just the thought of listening to her mother's high-pitched rebuke all the way home.

Without looking away from the Wanted pin-ups hanging on the bulletin board, Manny said, "She planned on riding along until Chester mentioned that we were stopping for some booze and condoms on the way."

"Here you go." Sheriff Harrison slid two boxes across the desk.

"What kind of booze are we talking about?" Claire snatched up her grandmother's ring and slipped it on her finger.

Kate could use a little liquid courage of her own, especially with Butch standing mere feet from her. She clipped on her earrings and stared out at a passing station wagon to avoid his gaze and her guilt.

"Hey, Chester," Manny said. Papers rustled. "Isn't this the *señorita* who could do that trick with peppers? The one who tied you to the bed and then ran off with your wallet and autographed Willie Nelson bandana?"

"That's her all right." Chester sighed. "What I wouldn't do to see her pepper trick again."

"On that note," Butch said, heading for the door. "I'll see you tomorrow morning, Grady."

The buzzer hummed and Kate watched the door close behind him.

"Go after him, Kate." Claire nudged her toward the door.

"I already apologized."

"But you didn't explain anything." Claire grabbed Kate by the elbow, her fingers punishing, and dragged her over to the doors. "Go clean up the mess you made."

She shoved Kate outside.

The sun's rays, hot and bright, made Kate feel like she'd landed under the burger warmer at McDonald's. The outside world stunk of heated tar and diesel exhaust, which was like exotic perfume after that jail cell.

She shielded her eyes and looked across the street to where Butch was opening the door of his pickup.

"Butch, hold on!" She jogged across the street.

He waited, leaning against the side of his truck, his expression unreadable.

She skidded to a stop in front of him. "Listen, I need to talk to you." She moved closer to him as a cement truck rattled by behind her.

For the first time since he'd stepped out of the men's restroom, his lips curved upwards. But the grin didn't reach his eyes. "What's there to talk about? You tried to sneak into my house, tripped my alarm, busted out one of my garage windows, broke into my greenhouse, and ended up in jail. Seems pretty cut and dried to me."

"Don't you want to know why I did any of those things?"

He shrugged. "Sure, I'm curious. But I figure anything you say will just piss me off more."

Kate held his stare in spite of her face blazing.

"The way I see it," he said, "the best thing for me to do is say '*adios*' to you and the frustrations that come as part of your packaging." His eyes drifted south. "No matter how much I like the packaging."

"Surely, you don't mean to—"

"Goodbye, Kate." With a mock salute, he climbed into his pickup and started it up.

"Butch, wait!" She pounded on his window.

He rolled down the window. "What?"

"Give me just fifteen minutes. We could go get a coffee—you drive and I'll talk." She clutched the windowsill of his truck. "Please."

For several silent seconds, he stared straight ahead, his forehead crinkled. Then he blinked and looked down at her. "No, Kate. We're done." He shifted into gear. "Take care of yourself."

Her hands shaking, Kate stepped clear of his tires as he slowly rolled forward. The sun pummeled the top of her head as she watched his taillights until he turned left and slipped out of sight.

Oh, God, what had she done?

A horn blared behind her. She looked over her shoulder. Manny's Chevy Tahoe sat idling in the middle of the street, the back door open. Head hanging, she sulked toward the Tahoe—her ferry to Hades.

* * *

"I hope you're happy!" Deborah's voice dragged Mac from a shallow slumber.

He opened one eye. Claire's mother stood scowling down at him, her lips pinched tight. Mac groaned and rolled away from her onto his side, pulling the cool cotton sheet up over his head.

"MacDonald Garner, don't think you can turn your back on me and pretend I'm not here." Deborah yanked the sheet down. "This is all your fault."

Growling, Mac glared up at her. "What in the hell are you talking about?"

"Your bad influence on Claire."

He sat up, all hope of catching another hour of sleep washed away by Deborah's senseless ranting. "I don't know what you're talking about, nor do I care."

Thank God, Claire took after her father.

He stood, adjusted his boxer-briefs, and strode toward the kitchen in nothing but the thin piece of cotton covering his ass. Modesty be damned—he needed some caffeine to keep from saying something he shouldn't to Claire's mother.

Deborah trailed him into the kitchen, her gaze steadily northward, two rosy spots dotting her cheeks. Chiggers were less irritating.

"Well, you should care." Deborah's said. "You're the one who told her you love her."

Mac froze, coffee pot in mid-air. Christ! Had Claire bought a one-page ad in the *Yuccaville Yodeler*? Everyone around here knew that he'd told her how he felt.

"Now she has it in her head that I'm out to run her life when all I'm trying to do is steer her in the right direction," Deborah continued.

Filling his coffee cup to the rim, Mac rolled his eyes. "Maybe she doesn't need anyone steering her anywhere. She is old enough to make her own decisions, you know."

He gulped several swallows of the black liquid.

"Mornin', Mac." Jess bounced into the kitchen, bopping to some tune only she could hear. "You forgot your pants," she added, giggling as she opened the fridge, and grabbed the pitcher of orange juice.

"Claire always has and always will need guidance." Deborah frowned at Jess as the teenager twirled around with the glass pitcher in her hand. "She floats on the wind, drifting here and there, unable to settle down and make something of her life."

Mac took another gulp of coffee to bide some time and form a reply that didn't involve swearing or shouting. How could she be so oblivious of how insulting she was to her own flesh and blood?

"Until you came along, I was making progress on getting Claire to toe the line."

Mac slammed his cup down on the counter harder than he'd intended, coffee sloshing over the rim onto the yellow Formica top. "Whose line, Deborah? Yours?"

Her chin lifted. "Of course. I know what's best for her."

"Isn't it time you stop trying to live vicariously through your daughters and focus on fixing your own mess?"

Deborah's eyes widened, her cheeks reddening even more.

Jess placed the orange juice on the table and dropped into a kitchen chair, watching the jousting match.

"Fixing my mess? I don't know what you mean."

Mac crossed his arms. "Really? Oh, right, that's because you've been so set on interfering with everyone else's business around here, trying to control everything down to who shares whose bed, and making everyone miserable in the process."

"Control everything …" Deborah repeated, sputtering. Her breath came in huffs, the tendons standing out in her neck above the strand of pink pearls resting on her collarbone. "You're one to talk, Mr. Garner! Claire said the only reason you told her you love her is because *you* want to control her."

"What?" Mac took a step back. Deborah's words hit him like a sucker-punch below the navel. She had to be making that up. "I don't believe Claire really said that."

Her face pinched, Deborah snorted. "Well, she did, and that makes you a hypocrite."

Speechless, Mac stared into Deborah's kohl-lined eyes. Claire wouldn't have said that, would she? No. Or would she? And if so, why would she run and tell her mother, of all people, her feelings rather than come to him? It didn't make sense.

He shoved away from the counter. "Stay away from me, Deborah."

Fists clenched, he strode out of the kitchen, away from the frosty bitch.

"I'm not done talking to you!" Deborah followed on his heels as he headed for the bathroom.

"Yes, you are!" Mac kept his head down. He hastened his pace, grateful for the lock on the bathroom door.

"What are you going to do about Claire?" she asked.

"I can't see where that is any of your business."

"Of course it's my business, especially when her bad influence is affecting Kate's future."

Mac walked into the bathroom and slammed the door shut behind him, twisting the lock on the knob.

"If anyone back home catches wind of this," Deborah hollered through the door, "Kate's chance of landing a job as a principal at a good school is history."

What? The woman was talking in tongues. Mac unlocked the door and yanked it open. "What in the hell are you talking about now?"

"I'm talking about my daughters spending the night in jail all because Claire coerced Kate to break into that bartender's house."

Mac blinked several times, speechless yet again.

Then he slammed the door in Deborah's face.

The world had gone mad.

* * *

Claire raced down the basement steps. After Kate's admission to their mom of total responsibility for their rendezvous at Butch's place, Claire wasn't going to wait around to see what else her mom might try to blame on her instead.

After the last twelve hours of jail cell merriment, followed by Chester and Manny's slammer-jam, comedy road show, and then Deborah's dance of the ass-flogging fairies, Claire wanted to hide under Joe's desk for the rest of the day.

She shoved open the office door and stopped short at the sight of Mac sitting behind the desk, pouring over a map that spilled across the desktop.

He looked up. The frown wrinkling his brow deepened.

"Hi, stranger." Claire's shoulders relaxed at the sight of him. She'd missed him, and if he didn't mind her prison-issued, Pepé Le Pew eau de perfume, she'd like to show him just how happy she was to see him.

He leaned back and crossed his arms over his chest. "So, is it true that everybody in the whole cell block was dancing to the jailhouse rock? Or were Kate and you the only jailbirds wiggling your tail feathers last night?"

"Cute. You should go on tour with Manny and Chester."

She closed the door and sauntered over to the desk in her best attempt at a sexy stroll down the catwalk.

The map on the desk caught her eye. "Is that the Lucky Monk mine?" She cocked her head to the side as she stared down at the map.

"It sure is." A frown still creased his forehead as he stared up at her.

Claire wiped the back of her hand across her mouth, wondering if she had MoonPie crumbs on her face.

"What?" She took a step back from the map. "Why are you giving me that look?"

"What look would that be?"

"Your old-time-western, gun-slinging outlaw, 'I'm-pissed-as-hell' glare. Landing in jail wasn't my fault, you know."

"Really?"

She nodded. "Kate tricked me into taking her to Butch's house. She's the one who broke the window in Butch's garage." Claire crammed her hands in her back pockets. "Sure, if you want to get technical, I was the one who actually broke into Butch's greenhouse. But I had to, or Kate was going to ruin the door jamb with a screwdriver."

Mac's lips twitched, but the thunderclouds still hovered over his eyebrows. "You spending the night in jail is not what has me 'pissed as hell' with you right now."

"Oh." Claire chewed the inside of her lip, replaying the last twenty-four hours to figure out what she'd done wrong. Then she remembered the incident on the way to the tool shed yesterday while trying to fix that damned toilet.

"If this is about the little accident I had with your cell phone, your warranty probably covers theft."

Mac sat forward. "Accident?"

"Yep, an accident." She tried to chuckle, but it came out sounding like a hyena. "What was I supposed to do? I needed to get into the shed and that damned rattler wouldn't budge. If only my aim had been a little better."

"You threw my GPS-enabled cell phone at a snake?"

Claire nodded. "The Twinkies were too soft to do any damage. How was I to know the snake would actually eat the thing? I told you not to get one of those super slim phones. It was only a matter of time until somebody lost it."

"Or somebody fed it to a snake."

"Exactly." Moving back to the map, she pointed at a section he'd circled in pencil. "What's this?"

"It's where I found the dead man," Mac said, matter-of-factly. "The phone is not why I'm pissed at you, Claire."

"What dead man?" She gaped at him, wondering if she'd heard him right.

A vein next to his eye pulsed. "Some things are meant to remain private."

Shit. She sighed. Kate must have run her mouth about Joe and his Kodak moments.

Claire had spent several hours during her long night behind bars trying to tie those pictures in with Joe's other not-so-legal hobby and had come up with zilch. If whatever waited in that post office box didn't offer some answers to all of her questions, she'd be hanging up her magnifying glass and trench coat and taking up crocheting.

"I didn't mean for anyone to see the naked pictures of Joe and all of those women. I promise; nobody is going to say a thing to Ruby about them." Especially not her. Ruby had had her heart broken enough times by Joe over the last year.

Mac sat frowning for a moment in silence. "What naked pictures?"

Crap. "You mean you don't know about the pictures?"

"Not a clue, until now."

"Criminy! Then why are you mad at me? And what do you mean you found a dead man? Freshly dead?" The image of Flint's *pointer* popped into her brain. "Or is it a skeleton?" she whispered, leaning over the map, her pulse speeding up.

"It's mostly a skeleton." Mac stood and rolled up the map.

Claire stepped back as though her hands had been smacked.

"Okay, spill." She'd been hit with enough of his frowns this morning.

"You told your mother that I said 'I love you.'"

"Oh, right, that." Claire grimaced.

"Yes, that." He tapped the rolled-up map against the desktop. "Why did you tell her?"

"I didn't exactly 'tell' her."

He lifted an eyebrow.

"Not on purpose, anyway."

"Damn it, Claire." He yanked open one of the desk drawers and pulled out a rubber band. "Is nothing I say in the bedroom sacred to you? Everyone in this whole fucking house knows now."

"Not everyone," Claire lied before she could bite her tongue. If only Mac would just start yelling or throwing things like the rest of her family. This quiet, calm rage made her feel off kilter, like a moose on ice.

"Oh, really? Who hasn't heard the news?"

Claire gulped, choking on her lie. "Ummm, Henry."

"That's not funny."

"Mac, I'm sorry."

"Yeah, I am, too." He snapped the rubberband around the map. "Sorry I ever told you how I felt. I should have known you'd make a joke of it, just like everything else in life that makes you uncomfortable." He walked past her.

What? Wait! "Where you going?" She caught his arm.

"Anywhere but here." He pulled free and grabbed the doorknob, then paused, his head lowered. "I've been thinking. Maybe you should move out for a while."

Dumbstruck, Claire stood there trying to find her breath while a tornado ripped through her. He was kidding, right?

"I'd hate for you to continue suffering under my controlling personality." He glanced back at her, his jaw taut. "I'm sure Ruby would like to have your help here full-time now that she has a husband to occupy her time."

He opened the door.

"Hi, Mac." Jess stood at the foot of the steps, her hand in the air, ready to knock.

"Hey, Jess." He ruffled her hair, but the gesture looked stiff.

Jess peered around Mac. "Claire, Porter's here to see you."

"Me?" Claire's voice squeaked. "Don't you mean Kate?"

Mac stepped to the side to allow Jess into the room.

"Nope. Just you."

Claire stared at Mac's back as he started up the steps. What did he mean by his "controlling personality"? He was the first guy to come into her life who hadn't tried to slip a collar and leash on her and chain her to one place.

"You must be great at snogging," Jess continued, totally clueless, "because ever since you kissed Porter, he doesn't want anything to do with Kate. I want to learn how to kiss like that."

Alarms blared in Claire's ears. Mac stopped halfway up the steps, his body visibly flinching. Then he shook his head and climbed out of sight, two steps at a time.

Jess danced over to Claire. The kid's cheeks glowed, her eyes wide. "I found the money," she whispered.

"Money?" Claire echoed, still shell-shocked from Mac's suggestion. Did he really want her to move out?

"Yeah, my money. You know, the dough Ruby was hiding."

Blindly, she stared down at Jess. Claire's heart twisted, her stomach cramping. She didn't want to live somewhere else.

"I'm thinking that I'll leave before Mom gets back. It'll be easier that way."

Stumbling sideways, Claire dropped into Joe's chair. Nobody had warned her that the sky would be falling today. She needed a cigarette. No, make that a pack of them.

"But first—" Jess started.

"Claire!" Chester yelled from the top of the steps.

She jerked back to the present. "What?"

"Get your ass up here! That toilet in the men's room is overflowing again, and some old geezer slipped on the floor and hurt his hip."

"God dammit!" Claire slammed her fist on the desktop.

Chapter Twenty

"Are you sure you don't want to go to the hospital, Manny?" Claire asked.

"*Sí, querida.*" Manny smiled at her as Porter towed him out from between the toilet and wall partition where he'd ended up wedged after he fell. "It's just a bruise. I'll be back to sowing my wild oats in no time."

Chester snorted. "What wild oats? Your crop has been frozen in a mid-winter blizzard for the last twenty years."

As Manny limped out of the stall, using Porter's arm for support, Claire backed out of the way, her hands ready to help.

Jess sat on the counter between the two sinks. "Phew!" She pinched her nostrils closed. "It sure stinks in here."

Porter glanced at Jess. "Will you get the door, Jessica?" Sweat spotted his gray T-shirt.

In spite of the fan sucking in air through the open window, humidity had transformed the room into a Turkish bathhouse. Outside, the noontime sun scorched the topsoil into a hot, crusty coating. A doozy of a monsoon loomed on the southwestern horizon, its tell-tale bloated clouds swelled before the eye. Helios had thrown Southeastern Arizona in a microwave and hit High.

Sweat rolled down Claire's spine, tickling. "Take him to Ruby's," she told Porter. "He can wash up in her tub."

Porter nodded as he led Manny toward the door. "You feel up to a short hike?"

"Sure. Just don't go too fast. We'll be passing by Rebecca's R.V. on the way, and she may feel like playing Florence Nightingale if she sees I'm injured."

Claire chuckled under her breath. For the first time since she'd raced into the men's room and found Manny on the floor next to the toilet with his pants soaked from the water spilling over the rim, the worry squeezing Claire's lungs loosened its hold.

Chester moved up beside Manny, offering his shoulder as another crutch. When Manny waved him off, Chester's eyes narrowed. "Quit being such a hard ass, Carrera."

"You just want to steal the show and play the superhero in front of those two stacked *señoritas* parked next door."

"Just use my shoulder, you rotten geezer."

As Manny touched Chester's shoulder, he wrinkled his nose. "You're all sweaty."

"Yeah, well, you smell like piss," Chester said as they shuffled toward Jess and the open door.

"Maybe I can convince Rebecca to come along and sponge me off."

Chester's laughter trailed after the three stooges as they escaped into the blistering sunshine.

After sending Jess to the supply room for a mop and bucket, Claire scanned the flooded floor. She gave up. The toilet had won. She waded through the mess, slipped into the stall, and shut off the water supply at the valve.

The only thing left to do was post an Out of Order sign on the stall door and call in a professional. But she'd leave the latter task to Ruby, who'd phoned last night and told Deborah she'd be home in two days, in time for Jess's sixteenth birthday. Claire couldn't wait to hand back the reins.

The clatter of the mop bucket on the concrete floor announced Jess's return. "I grabbed the bleach, too," she said as Claire exited the stall.

"Thanks." Grabbing the mop, Claire set to work pushing the excess water toward the floor drain in the center of the room. The reward of an ice cold Corona with a hint of lime juice drove her onward while sweat poured down her arms and dripped from the tip of her nose.

Jess's chatter about all of the nail polish and lip gloss she planned to buy with "her" money droned into a high-pitched hum while Claire tried to figure out what had pushed Mac over the edge. There had to be more to it than just Deborah knowing he'd uttered those three words.

She gritted her teeth. What had possessed her mother to raise that subject with Mac anyway? It's not like they were even on speaking terms most days.

"… that gold you found?" Jess's question cut through Claire's ruminating.

"What?" Claire stood up straight and stretched her back.

"I asked what you're gonna to do with that gold you found."

"Give it to your mom."

Her stomach churned a bit at that thought since it would probably involve showing Ruby where Jess found the gold and lying by omission about Joe's porn pictures.

"That's good, I guess. Mom could sure use the money to keep this place going."

Now was as good a time as any to call Jess's bluff. Claire leaned on the mop handle. "What do you care if she keeps this place going or not? You're not going to be around anymore after tomorrow, right?"

"Tomorrow?" The word came out sounding like a croak, as if Jess had swallowed a bullfrog.

"You said you plan on leaving before Ruby gets home."

"Oh, yeah. Right."

"Well, your mom will be back on Wednesday, so that doesn't leave you much time to get out of town."

"Mom's gonna be here for my birthday?" Jess's eyes lit up.

"That's the plan. Too bad you'll be halfway to Ohio by then. It's going to be weird celebrating without you here."

Staring down at her sparkly orange nails in silence for several seconds, Jess's forehead creased. "Maybe I'll hang around a little longer then."

"Bad idea." Claire fought to keep her tone solemn.

"Why?"

"School will be starting soon over there, and you need to establish a residence and register at the local high school."

Jess's frown furrowed even more. "What's a residence?"

"It's proof that you aren't just drifting through town. A permanent address or a driver's license, for example."

"Maybe I'll skip school this year."

"And spend day and night hiding from the truant officers?" Claire wasn't even sure there were such things as truant officers anymore, but it didn't hurt to throw some into the mix.

"What are truant officers?"

"Kind of like the police. They check up on kids who are skipping too much school." That's what she'd heard, anyway. Claire crossed her fingers behind her back.

Jess's mouth dropped open. "Will they throw me in jail for not going to school?"

With a shrug, Claire stared at the drain in the center of the floor for several seconds, struggling to smother a grin before looking back into Jess's wide eyes.

"Ohio laws may be different, but I've known kids who ended up in juvie court for lesser crimes." If she'd been strapped to a lie detector, the needle would have painted the graph paper black by now.

"What was jail like?"

"Imagine this bathroom with bars on the window and door."

"Were you scared last night?"

"I was too mad at Kate to be scared."

"Your mom really yelled at Kate after you guys got home." Jess shook her head. "She isn't very nice sometimes."

Claire guffawed. "My mom isn't very nice a lot of times."

"You should've heard what she said to Mac this morning."

"Yeah, he mentioned something about that."

"I thought he was going to punch her in the nose when she told him that you're unable to settle down and make something of your life."

Claire had lost count how many times she'd heard her mom preach that. She shoved more water down the drain.

"But then he got all still and quiet when she told you think he said he loves you only because he wants to control you."

It took a few seconds for Jess's pronoun-filled sentence to sink into Claire's broiled, tired brain.

"Say what, now?" She grasped the mop handle in a death grip.

"Did Mac really tell you that he loves you?"

Claire's vision clouded, fury tunneling her vision. What happened earlier down in Joe's office made sense now.

"She's gone too far this time."

Throwing down the mop, Claire strode toward the door. Deborah was going to be on a plane out of here by tomorrow morning, even if Claire had to drag her by the hair all the way to Tucson.

"Hey, wait up." Jess followed.

Claire barged out into the bright sunshine and rammed right into Porter's chest.

He grabbed her by the shoulders. "Whoa. Where's the fire?"

Huffing, she yanked free of his grasp. "I'm about to light it."

* * *

Halfway up the hillside to the Lucky Monk mine, Mac paused to drink some water from his canteen. Dripping with sweat, he shielded his eyes from the noonday sun.

Shimmers of heat blurred the surrounding mountains, while a heavy mantle of humidity suffocated the valley. The cumulus clouds building on the horizon threatened.

Hell was on its way.

Distant booms echoed across the desert floor, each one making Mac wince. It was only a matter of time until the ceiling in the dead man's tomb gave way again, and the Copper Snake's blasting efforts would only speed the process along.

Capping his canteen, he hefted his pack on his back, then grabbed his duffel full of tools and trudged onward and upward. As he reached the mine's mouth, he remembered the map was still in his truck. With his shirt plastered to his chest and heat stroke knocking, he decided to trust his spray paint directions on the walls.

The Lucky Monk's chilled, musty breath feathered across his skin as he hiked down the main adit toward his mummified pal. Now that he'd escaped the sun's rays, he had time to think of things besides not keeling over in the heat. Things like why in hell did Claire kiss Porter?

Mac paused long enough to dig a T-shirt from his pack and shuck his sweat-soaked one.

Had it just been one kiss? Like the kind she'd give an old friend? Or a new lover?

Flicking on his hat light, he tucked his flashlight in his back pocket. Shadows fluttered at the edge of his vision, dancing, celebrating his humiliation, doubling his chagrin. He marched deeper into the mine, his thoughts growing more tangled and knotted with every step.

Deborah's words echoed in his mind ... *the only reason you told her you love her is because you want to control her.*

Had he driven Claire to Porter? Pushed her away by letting those three words slip out before she was ready to hear them?

Damned woman! He kicked at a golf ball-sized pebble. It bounced and clattered into the darkness in front of him.

Most of the women he'd dated in the past had fished for those three words, baiting him with everything from lace teddies and fur-lined handcuffs to pot roasts and homemade cherry pies. Then along came Claire, with her purple toenail polish, crazy T-shirts, and watermelon-scented shampoo.

All it had taken was just one drunken kiss.

He rounded the last corner before the cave-in and noticed a fresh layer of dust covering his footprints from yesterday. His steps slowed. Part of the ceiling had crumbled further. He pulled his flashlight from his pocket and shined the beam at the rock overhead. Fractures road-mapped the jagged, concave surface.

What he needed was some rock netting.

Or a bigger set of balls.

Unfortunately, he had neither on him at the moment.

He dropped his duffel to the floor. The crowbar, hammer, chisels, and small pick axes clanged against each other inside the leather casing.

He had two options: give up or dig.

The first meant never finding out what was behind those boards, and he'd been hanging around Claire for too long for that choice to settle easily in his gut.

The problem with the latter, though, was the possibility of spending eternity with a dried up, eyeless miner. That was not Mac's idea of resting in peace.

Dust floated in front of his hat light as he debated.

Hell, he'd come too far to turn back now. Besides, he needed to finish the job he'd set out to do for Ruby.

He unzipped his duffel and pulled out the crowbar. Slipping off his pack, he rooted out Ruby's Smith and Wesson, checked the safety, and stuffed it in the back of his jeans.

This time, he'd be ready for any visitors.

After a glance over his shoulder to make sure he was still alone, he dug in.

* * *

Claire slammed into the General Store with Jess on her heels and Porter bringing up the rear. She scanned the room, huffing like she planned to blow the house down.

"Where's Mom?" she asked Kate, who sat behind the counter, filing her nails.

"In the kitchen. Why?"

Jess's pattering footfalls followed Claire as she marched across the room. "Claire's pissed at her," she told Kate.

Claire found her mother sitting in one of the kitchen chairs, her nose buried in a paperback novel. A half-empty glass of lemonade sweated on the table in front of her.

"I hope you're happy!"

Grabbing the book from her mother, she threw it across the room. It hit the refrigerator, knocking off Ruby's set of Lucille Ball magnets, and fluttered onto the linoleum.

Her mouth agape, Deborah stared at Claire.

She leaned down into her mother's face. "I want you out of here today."

In a blink, Deborah snapped out of her stupor. Her lips compressed into a tight, glossy pink bow. "How dare you—"

"I've had enough of your meddling. Pack your bags!"

Her cheeks sporting two dark, rosy spots, Deborah pushed to her feet. "I will do no such thing."

"Fine! Then I'll pack your shit for you and drag you to the airport. One way or another, you're leaving."

"Claire?" Kate teetered on the threshold, as if she weren't sure whether to stay for the rest of Round One or hide until the dust settled. "What's going on?"

"Mac wants me to move out."

"I heard, but what's that got to do with Mom?"

Jess had the decency to blush when Claire speared her with a pointed glare.

Grabbing Deborah by the arm, Claire forced her to face Kate. "Tell Kate what you told Mac. Go on; show her your forked tongue."

Deborah wrenched free. Her blue eyes sparked as she whirled back to Claire. "Good! I'm glad Mac is finally coming to his senses. That man is nothing but trouble for you."

"You don't know what the hell you're talking about."

"Don't you use that language with me, young lady."

"Oh, kiss my ass. You no longer get my respect." Claire threaded her fingers through her hair, tugging, barely containing the urge to wrap them around her mother's neck. "It's a wonder Dad didn't leave you years ago."

Deborah gasped, holding her hand over her chest.

Shit. She probably shouldn't have said that aloud.

"Claire," Kate started, stepping into the kitchen.

"Oh, zip it, Kate."

Jess dropped into one of the kitchen chairs and propped her chin on her hand, her eyes wide.

"How can you say such a horrible thing to me?" Her mother's watery eyes only fueled Claire's anger.

"Horrible thing, huh? How about all of the horrible things you've said to me? All of those snippy comments about my hairstyle and choice of clothing? All of the times you've held Kate's achievements over my head and mocked my lack of a degree? Or how about your attempts to set me up with men who would 'straighten me out' or 'fix me,' so that I'd meet your expectations of success?"

"I've never said anything so cruel."

At her mother's denial, Claire's head nearly popped and showered them all with Twinkie dust and MoonPie crumbs.

She leaned into Deborah until their noses almost rubbed. "Those lies just slide off your tongue like it's made of butter, don't they? How about yesterday, Mother, when you told Mac that I'm unable to settle down and make something of my life?"

Jess blushed again, this time under Deborah's glare.

Deborah shoved Claire back several steps and stomped over to the refrigerator. She scooped up her Nora Roberts paperback, along with Ruby's Lucille Ball magnets which she stuck back on the fridge before turning to frown at Claire.

"Maybe I have mentioned your lack of stability a time or two, but it's with good intentions."

That made Claire laugh—a harsh, grating sound.

"And as for Mac, I was only repeating what you told me."

"When I said that people only say they love you so they can control you, I was talking about *you*, not Mac."

Again, Deborah held her hand to her chest. "You think I don't love you?"

"Oh, I'm sure in your own twisted way you do. But it's a possessive kind of love, as if I were a tarnished piece of silver you bought at an antique store."

"That's not true." Her mother lifted her chin. "I just want what's best for you."

"Your 'best,' not mine. If you'd been paying more attention to your own life instead of trying to run mine and Kate's and Veronica's all of these years, maybe Dad wouldn't have left you for another woman."

"Don't you mention your father to me again!" Deborah advanced on Claire with one pointy red fingernail extended. "You've been Daddy's little girl since day one. I should've known you'd take his side. You always liked him better."

"Jesus! This isn't about who's more popular, you or Dad. It's about my future with Mac." Claire knocked her mom's finger away. "I swear on every single piece of your Tiffany jewelry collection, Mother, if you do or say one more thing to try to interfere with our relationship, I'll never ever talk to you again. We will be done."

Deborah tittered. "You don't mean that."

"Oh, believe me, I do. I'm also serious about you leaving. I'll give you until tomorrow. If your bags aren't packed by then, I'll ship your clothes to you."

"You can't make me get on a plane." With her jaw thrust out and her arms crossed, Deborah looked like a bratty eight-year-old who sorely needed to spend some time in the corner.

"No, but I can drop you off in the middle of Tucson with nothing but the clothes on your back."

"You wouldn't!"

She poked her mom in the sternum. "I want you out of here before Ruby and Gramps get back."

Shaking with fury, she shot a glare at Kate. "She goes with or without you, understand?"

Claire didn't want her sister to leave, but there'd be no debating the subject of their mother's departure.

Marching out of the kitchen without a backwards glance, she found Porter hovering next to the rec room bar.

Her cheeks warmed. "Sorry you had to witness all that."

He shrugged. "Family business is always messy. I need to talk to you."

Oh, yeah, she still had to figure out a way to brush off Porter's newfound affection. "How about lunch at The Shaft?"

That was as safe a venue as anywhere, and she preferred crowds when it came to doling out rejection.

"Sounds great. I'll drive."

"Okay, but I need to stop at the hardware store afterward and pick up some of Ruby's mail."

Or rather, Joe's mail. It was time to see what he'd stashed in that post office box.

* * *

The sight of the dead miner reminded Mac that thanks to Deborah's warm and fuzzy wakeup call this morning, he'd forgotten to compare the piece of braided rope he'd pulled from the skeleton's hand to the sandal Claire found in the wall safe. He'd have to take a look before he left for Tucson later tonight.

A glance at his watch showed one o'clock had come and gone. Busting through the cave-in had taken him longer than he'd expected, but slow and easy was the name of the game. No need to bring the mountain down on his head. With time working against him, he hefted the crowbar to his right hand and tore into the wall.

Minutes later, the first board fell to the floor, landing with a dull thump.

Mac leaned over and shined his flashlight through the opening he'd made.

The tunnel curved not ten feet from where he stood, disappearing out of view. Silence greeted him, his labored breathing the only sound to be heard. Maybe it was just his imagination, but the air smelled fresher on the other side of the wall, the dust still undisturbed.

Several more minutes passed before he'd made a space large enough for himself. He shoved his pack and duffel through first, and then with one last check to confirm the skeleton was his only audience, he climbed through the wall.

His breath shallow with excitement, he rounded the bend and hiked along the tunnel. His trouble with Claire was now just a burred nugget that poked him periodically as he scanned the walls for signs of copper and silver. He skirted another bend and stopped so fast his toes smashed into the steel front of his boots.

"You've got to be fucking kidding me," he whispered, staring at the pile of rocks and wood debris blocking his path. Apparently, Lady Luck was pissed at him today.

He dropped his tools to the floor and leaned against the wall.

Shit.

His back ached at just the thought of sifting through the mess, trying to find a path to the other side. He tipped back his canteen and washed the dust from his tongue.

A breath of air brushed across his damp forehead.

Where was it coming from?

Mac crawled over to a triangular crack between a stack of mid-sized boulders. He splashed some water on his palm and held it in front of the narrow opening. A cool draft dried his hand.

He pulled out his flashlight and inspected the walls and ceiling of the tunnel. Both looked relatively stable. The air was free of fresh dust. A wave of his light over the numerous critter footprints on the dirt floor confirmed that this cave-in most likely happened some time ago.

A scratch with his fingernail over a splintered piece of timber found the wood weakened by rot.

Curiosity breathed a second wind into his tired muscles. Maybe this would be easier than it looked.

Returning to his duffel, he drew out his small pickaxe and rolled his shoulders to loosen them. Ruby's gun rubbed against his lower spine.

There was no stopping now. That air was leaking in from somewhere on the other side, carrying humidity along with it— enough to rot the timbers in this section of the tunnel, anyway.

Mac had a feeling he'd found another way out of the mine.

Gritting his teeth, he swung the pickaxe.

* * *

"I'll be right back," Claire told Porter, then closed the passenger side door of his pickup.

The pavement rippled with heat in front of the Creekside Supply Company's windows, the scent of roasting tar heavy.

She hurried across the parking lot, shielding her eyes from the searing sun. The chicken-fried steak and chilled Corona— food that was supposed to make her feel better about having Alice's Queen of Hearts for a mother—sloshed in her gut with every step.

Lunch had gone smoothly. No crying in his beer on Porter's part when she'd made it clear Mac hogged her head and heart, leaving no room for anyone else.

But in spite of Porter's easy acceptance of her rejection, the intensity in his green eyes throughout lunch had made Claire squirm in her seat. She couldn't wait to get back to Ruby's.

The store's door handles were warm to the touch. Even the buzzer announcing her arrival sounded weary, burned out.

Dust-covered aluminum blinds blocked the sun from Aisle One's row of pickaxes, shovels, garden hoses, and post-hole diggers. A tinny version of June Carter and Johnny Cash singing *Long-legged Guitar Pickin' Man* crackled out of the speakers mounted in the ceiling.

Claire paused for a second under the ceiling vent, wafts of air drying the sweat from her upper lip.

"Can I help you find something?" A silver-haired sales clerk seemed to appear out of nowhere. With her electric blue eye shadow and bright red blush, the lady looked like she'd been playing dress-up over in cosmetics.

"Uh, no. I'm just here to pick up some mail." Claire smiled as she side-stepped the clerk and boogied down Aisle Eleven: Pesticides, Hunting Supplies, and Greeting Cards—typical first date material in Jackrabbit Junction.

The post office occupied the back corner of the store. The pony-tailed old dude behind the counter didn't even glance up from his guitar-covered magazine as Claire zipped past.

Joe's post office box anchored the bottom right corner of the cluster. It was one of the bigger boxes—eleven inches squared. Claire squatted in front of it.

The lock turned as if it had been WD-40'd recently. The small door creaked when she opened it.

Her fingers shook slightly as she pulled out a thick, padded package sealed shut with reinforced packing tape.

She peeked at the guy behind the desk, who was still glued to his magazine, and then checked behind her to make sure Porter hadn't followed her inside.

The coast was clear.

She tried to tear open the package, but the tape wouldn't give.

Shutting the door, she slipped the key back in her pocket and scanned the aisle signs until she zeroed in on Aisle Three: Plumbing, Wiper Blades, Fire Protection, and School Supplies.

Scissors hung in a line above boxes of crayons and stacks of notepads, next to rows of baskets filled with P traps and pipe fittings. She cut open the end of the package and peered inside.

Reaching inside the package, she hauled out a handful of photos. She flipped the first picture over, wincing in anticipation.

Ruby's dead husband didn't disappoint.

Joe wasn't smiling at the camera this time. He was too busy bonking some curly haired blonde, whose ankles circled his neck. It was a profile view of the lovers this time with a blurred white stripe along the left edge.

Claire shuffled to the next picture. A blush toasted her cheeks, followed by a gag.

This photo had a touch of sleaze to it that would make most porn-lovers smile. The setup was the same, including the white strip along the side, but Joe had flipped the blonde over. The camera caught a full-on shot of her face—pouting red lips open in mid-gasp, as well as a crystal clear view of Joe Jr. at full mast, pre-thrust.

The third photo was a close-up, vignetting a tattoo of a green and blue snake slithering across the blonde's boney hip. Unfortunately, Joe's bare ass cheek, including a saucer shaped birthmark, shared the focal point.

Claire started to turn to the fourth picture and stopped, looking back at the third. Wait a second. This was a close-up.

Holy shit! Somebody had taken these pictures of Joe and the blonde. The photos Claire had found in Ruby's closet could've been shot with a camera that had a timer on it, but not these.

Glancing again at the first two photos, she realized the white strip at the edge of each was a curtain. Joe's paparazzi poser had been peeping in the window.

The fourth picture made her wince. This close-up showed a portion of the blonde where the sun didn't shine much, and, unfortunately, it wasn't her armpits.

The fifth was yet another close-up, this time of Ms. Blonde's face, her emerald eyes open, her tongue reaching out to touch Joe's—Claire flipped to the next, her greasy lunch churning, bubbling up her esophagus.

She fanned through the next five shots, grimacing the whole time.

Sweat framed her forehead by the time she reached the last one. Digging in the package, she fished out three more photos from between several pieces of paper.

The first photo was just another profile shot with the white strip at the side. She'd seen enough of these types of shots by now that the sight of Joe's naked flesh didn't even make her blink.

But the last two pictures made her pause. All clothes were on in these shots. One had Joe holding open the motel door, the number seven visible next to his head, as the blonde stepped out of the room, a wide smile on her lips as she stared right into the camera eye.

The other picture showed the blonde in the forefront climbing into a black Jaguar, her long, bare legs visible under her fire-engine red dress. In the background, Joe watched from the doorway of room number seven. The motel's neon sign was legible over his right shoulder—The Sundown Inn.

Claire remembered hearing about that very motel from Chester months ago, who considered himself the Robin Leach of southwestern Arizona's Lifestyles of the Lewd and Depraved. The Sundown Inn reigned as one of the seediest in his opinion, and he'd been there three times, so he knew.

Claire chewed on her lower lip, wondering who'd been the photographer, and if he or she had been attempting to blackmail Joe, the blonde, or both.

Then again, maybe Joe just got off on keeping pictures of his ex-lovers.

She dumped the pictures back in the package and pulled out one of the pieces of paper. It was a yellowed newspaper picture of the blonde with a man in a three piece suit. A young boy, probably ten years old or so, held the blonde's hand. Claire read the caption below the picture.

Richard Rensberg II and his wife (Bianca) brought their son along to watch Yuccaville's 85th anniversary parade.

A banner in the background spelled out, "Congratulations, Yuccaville!"

Digging in the package again, Claire drew out another piece of paper. This was just an article—no pictures—with the headline, "The Copper Snake Goes Public."

She scanned the print, finding the news about the Copper Snake Mining Company now trading on the New York Stock Exchange, along with details on the company's profits for the last few quarters, all quite boring after Joe's X-rated exhibit.

Another piece of paper showed the lovely Bianca Rensberg sitting in front of a handful of little kids, reading a Dr. Seuss book as they stared up at her.

The next article covered the history of the Copper Snake Mining Company, with a picture of three generations of Rensbergs standing in front of the company's office building. Richard the second was there, along with the young boy from the parade picture. An old man with a handlebar moustache stood next to them—the first Richard Rensberg, according to the caption.

Claire stuffed the papers back in the package, noticing something squishy in the bottom of it. She fingered past the papers, touched something satiny, and weeded it out.

Red panties.

"Ew!" She dropped them like they were alive and wriggling.

As she squatted next to them, she'd realized she'd seen those panties before in one of the pictures—Joe had been removing them from the blonde with his teeth.

Shuddering, she used a pair of scissors to lift the satin undies for a closer inspection without touching them. Joe must have kept them as some kind of memento, the sick bastard.

"There you are," Porter said from the end of the aisle.

Claire squeaked in surprise, teetered off balance, and fell onto her ass. Luckily, her back blocked the panties from Porter's view.

She managed to stuff them back in the package before he saw them. "I thought you were going to wait in the pickup."

"You've been gone for ten minutes. I came to see what happened to you." Porter eyed the package. "Did you find what you were looking for?"

She'd found way more than that.

"Uh, yeah." She glanced toward the front of the store. "I'm ready if you are."

She wanted to get back to Ruby's and lock herself in Joe's office while she took a closer look at the package's contents. Why had it been locked up in a post office box for years?

Porter nodded at the package she held against her chest. "You want me to carry that for you?"

"No!" She clutched it tighter, then smiled, every centimeter of it as fake as her mother's hair color. "I mean, no thanks. It's not heavy."

As Claire crossed the parking lot under the wilting heat, movement across the street in The Shaft's parking lot caught her attention. She watched as Butch crawled out of his pickup with a briefcase in hand. He walked around the back bumper and opened the passenger door.

A brunette in a pair of pink cowboy boots, Daisy Duke shorts, and a white halter top crawled out of the cab. A wide smile on her face, she draped her arm around Butch's waist. Side by side they strolled around the back of the bar.

Who in the hell was that? A girlfriend?

Poor Kate. This was going to burn, no matter how much she denied her feelings for Butch.

"Claire?" Porter hesitated at his door.

Shrugging off the veil of bewilderment, she reached for the pickup's door handle.

She had a mystery to figure out, a boyfriend to win back, and an R.V. park to run. This was no time to get mired in another one of Kate's messes.

"Let's go."

* * *

Mac's stomach growled as he stood at the base of the rock pile, catching his breath. The beef jerky he'd gobbled up a short time ago had barely eased the panging in his gut. But until he knew for certain that he would be seeing the sun again, he needed to save his food.

He glanced at his watch—three-thirty.

Sweat soaked his T-shirt, the wet cotton clinging to his skin. He'd busted through the rubble a half hour ago, and then cleared a V-sized slit along the left wall wide enough to slip through. It was time to find out why there was air movement on the other side, and why someone had boarded up this section of the tunnel.

He squeezed through the slit, slipped his pack over his shoulders, and shifted his duffel to his left hand. Adjusting the Smith and Wesson in his waistband, he inched along the tunnel, which narrowed quickly. Less effort had gone into carving out this part of the tunnel for some reason.

The ceiling suddenly lowered ahead, forcing him to hunch. Around the next bend was another bend, and then another, until he lost count.

His lower back began to throb from stooping, his shoulders scraped walls closing in on him. His stomach growled with enough gusto to wake the dead man sleeping off eternity behind him.

Mac rounded yet another bend and slowed as the walls and ceiling drew together ahead, leaving just a narrow rectangle carved out of the rock. The tunnel breathed around him, the air still musty, but alive with dust particles.

He slipped off his pack and slid along the walls, the rocks scratching him as he inched between them.

A strip of blackness loomed ahead, so dark his light didn't even pierce it. He took a deep breath and stepped into the darkness.

Only the darkness turned out to be a cavernous room, so large that it swallowed his light. Pulling his flashlight from his pocket, he shined it across the room.

Rudimentary paintings covered the opposite wall halfway to the ceiling.

Rocks clattered behind him. He turned, his light pointed at the floor where he expected to see a critter.

Instead, he found a pair of dusty black cowboy boots.

He jerked his flashlight upward, and coughed in surprise. "What in the hell are *you* doing here?"

Then pain exploded from the side of his head and someone flicked off the lights.

Chapter Twenty-One

Kate chanced a glance away from the wet road in front of her to frown across the old Ford's front seat at her sister. "What did you just mumble?"

"I didn't mumble," Claire yelled to Kate over the hammering of rain on the pickup's metal roof. "I said I still think this is a bad idea."

Kate's grip on the steering wheel tightened as she fought the urge to reach over and flick Claire's ear.

It was the second time Claire had voiced her lack of support for Kate's plan since they'd left Ruby's not five minutes earlier.

"And as I told you the first time you said that," Kate yelled back, "I'll be careful. Contrary to what everyone around here thinks, I'm a perfectly good driver."

Dime-sized raindrops smacked against the windshield, blurring the road and surrounding valley under the afternoon gloom. The monsoon that had been brewing on the horizon since before lunch had finally graced Jackrabbit Junction with its presence a half hour ago, dispensing rations of billowing winds, fierce lightning, and curtains of rain that had soaked everything below. With the dark clouds blocking out the sun, it looked more like twilight than just four o'clock.

"I'm not talking about your driving. I'm talking about you bursting in on Butch right now. Maybe you should sleep on this."

"You, of all people, think I should sleep on this? Aren't you the same girl who on a whim streaked buck-naked across our high school stage during *The Taming of the Shrew*?"

"I was making a political statement about women's rights. Quit trying to change the subject. This is a different situation. There's something you don't know about Butch."

Kate did a double-take. "You've got to be kidding me. Now you're going to start spouting conspiracy theories about Butch? So, what is it? He's a secret agent for the CIA? He has some itchy, infectious rash? He wears women's underwear?"

"You really need to work on your sarcasm." Claire shifted in her seat, nosing closer to the window.

"Kiss my ass."

"And on your comebacks, too." Claire smacked down Kate's middle finger. "Anyway, this afternoon, when I was leaving the hardware store, I saw Butch pull into The Shaft's parking lot."

Claire paused and pointed at something in front of them. "There's the road up ahead. Take a left there."

Kate tapped the brakes and eased the Ford onto the dirt road—now mostly mud with a spattering of gravel.

"Finish your story about Butch."

"He wasn't alone." Claire flipped up the hood of her yellow checkered raincoat.

Kate drummed her fingers on the steering wheel while she waited for the other shoe to drop. "Well, who was with him?"

"A woman."

"Old or young?" Maybe his mom was paying a visit.

"She was wearing a pair of Daisy Duke shorts, a halter top, and pink cowboy boots."

"Oh." Kate's sails fluttered and flapped.

"Exactly." Claire pressed her nose to the windshield again. "There's Mac's truck, off to the right."

Rolling onto the edge of the road, Kate braked.

Claire grabbed the flashlight she'd brought along and tucked it inside her raincoat. "If you go to the next dirt road and turn right, it will take you back around to the main road. Watch out for flooding on your way back to town. It can be deeper than it looks. You don't want to get caught in a fast-moving current, dragged into a dry wash, and end up floating down to the Gila River."

"Okay."

"If something runs out in front of you, don't slam on the brakes. This old tin can doesn't have ABS or power steering."

"Gotcha." Kate had already realized those facts.

"And if it stalls when you—"

"Claire! Go already. Leave the nagging, older-sister routine to Ronnie."

"Fine." Claire reached for the door handle. "See if I help you the next time you come to me with gum in your hair."

"You were the one who threw it there in the first place."

"Good luck, wacko."

"Same to you, knucklehead."

After slamming the door shut, Claire jogged over to Mac's truck. She squatted next to the back wheel-well, reached under the bed, and pulled out a little black key box. She waved at Kate, then unlocked the passenger door and slipped inside.

Kate shifted into gear. Bumping her way along, she rolled back toward Jackrabbit Junction, The Shaft, and the man she planned to beg to give her another chance. Somehow, she'd managed to fall for one of the good guys, which hadn't happened since her gradeschool crush on Rambo. Now if she could just convince Butch that she wasn't some nutcase.

The windshield wipers cheeped and thumped as the rain slowed to a drizzle. Kate cracked her window, inhaling the scent of wet dirt mixed with noxious whiffs of what Claire said was wet greasewood trees. The cool breeze teased her hair, lifting her spirits in spite of Miss Pink Cowboy Boots.

As Kate swung into The Shaft's parking lot, her stomach barrelrolled at the sight of Butch's pickup. She needed a stiff shot of Jack Daniel's to up her courage a notch. Ignoring the chicken clucking inside her head, she parked and raced across the lot before she had time to change her mind.

Gary nodded at her from behind the bar. The neon beer lights hanging in the windows reflected in his glasses. "What can I get ya?"

She peeled her tongue from the top of her mouth. "I need to speak with Butch."

"He's busy right now."

He'd better not be busy bonking Miss Pink Boots.

Kate flashed Gary one of her top-five, most charming smiles—the one she usually reserved for traffic cops and highway patrolmen. "This will only take a minute."

Or ten. Maybe twenty, if Butch was in a better mood than this morning.

"Sorry. He said he didn't want to be disturbed. Why don't you come back later this evening?"

"Hey, sweetie." A long-legged, redhead sidled up to the bar, her dry goods almost spilling out of her low-cut tank-top.

Gary's glasses practically fogged over. "Hi, Mindy. I didn't know you were back in town. What can I get for you?"

Kate didn't wait to hear the redhead's answer. While Gary's eyes were glued to Mindy's headlights, Kate dashed through the door into the kitchen. The cook paid her no mind while he cleaned the grill and whistled along with Marty Robbins's tune about falling in love with a Mexican girl from El Paso.

The door to Butch's office was closed, but the knob turned easily in her hand. Head held high, Kate marched into the room, only to falter at the sight of a jaw-dropping brunette sitting behind Butch's desk.

"Oh!" Kate gritted her teeth. Claire forgot to mention that Butch's arm candy made Charlie's Angels look like last week's meatloaf. "I was looking for Butch."

"You found him," Butch said from behind her. "Kate, say hello to Lana. Lana, this is Kate."

Lana's grin accentuated her killer cheekbones. "Ah, the infamous Kate. It's good to meet you."

Infamous? Kate wrestled with the urge to run screaming from the room.

"You, too," she said to Lana, remembering the woman's name from the phone call Butch had taken the other day.

She took a deep breath and faced Butch. "I'm sorry to interrupt, but could I have a moment of your time?" She glanced at Lana out of the corner of her eye. "Alone."

Butch's face didn't give away anything. "I'm kind of busy."

"Let me get out of your way." Lana stood. "I could use a beer." Pink cowboy boots clomped across Butch's carpet. "Come and find me when you're finished, Valentine."

Valentine? No *Butch* for Miss Lana and her sexy boots. Kate's teeth were going to be nubs if she ground them any harder.

She waited until the door clicked closed. "Why didn't you ever tell me your real name?"

Butch shrugged. "It didn't seem important." He sat on the corner of his desk. His gaze traveled down over the front of her rain speckled shirt and red jeans, his eyes telling no secrets when they met hers again. "To what do I owe the honor of your presence this afternoon, Kate?"

Now that she stood in front of him, her well-practiced speech lodged in her throat. "I came to ... umm ... apologize."

"You already did this morning. If you're looking for an official acceptance, you have it. Is there anything else I can do for you?"

His cold tone froze her tongue.

He stood and passed her on his way to the door. "If not, I need to get back to work."

"Wait!"

She hadn't spent hours this afternoon on her nails to be blown off so quickly. Beating him to the door, Kate leaned against the hard slab and grabbed the door knob before he could.

"I'm not leaving until you hear why I tried to break into your house."

A muscle twitched next to his left eye. "Fine. But make it quick. I have a lot to do and an early dinner reservation in Yuccaville."

With Lana? Kate blinked, trying to evict the brunette from her thoughts for the time being.

"Okay, here's the deal. Somebody is trying to steal one of Ruby's mines out from under her and I thought ..."

Butch raised his brows. "And you thought it was me?"

"Well, yeah. Kind of."

He crossed his arms over his chest. "What in the hell would I want with a mine?"

"I don't know. It just seemed like all of the clues I found pointed to you."

"What clues?"

"Well, your driver's license for one thing. It has Valentine on it, not Butch. For all I knew, you were using an alias when making your crooked deals."

"Of course, my crooked deals."

Kate ignored his smirk. "Then there's that Copper Snake Mining Company business card in your wallet."

Butch fished his wallet from his back pocket and flipped it open. Leaning forward, Kate pointed out the suspicion-causing card tucked into one of the narrow pockets.

He drew the card out and flipped it over, showing her the address and phone number on the back. "It's from one of the miners. The guy brews his own beer and wants me to try selling it here." He handed her the card. "It's just a generic business card."

Sure enough, the mining company's name and address were the only words printed on the front. Kate's forehead and nose roasted. Why couldn't she blush like a normal person?

"Then Betty Boop asked how the takeover was going and you stated your lawyer said it would be all wrapped up by the end of this month, which correlated with the attorney's letter Ruby received listing a similar court date for when the mine's ownership would be determined."

"Betty Boop?"

"Yes. She also mentioned something about contacting her when it was all over and you two could play with some numbers."

"You must mean Sally, my accountant."

"Sure, if your accountant likes to ogle your ass when you're not looking. I figured you were probably sleeping with her, too."

A grin surfaced on Butch's lips. "Too? Who all do you think I'm sleeping with, Kate?"

"Never mind." Kate returned to the task at hand. "Then Lana called and you dropped everything to talk to her."

His grin spread wider. "You don't know Lana."

"So, as far as I could see, all signs pointed to you being the one trying to take Ruby's mine from her." Kate blushed harder when she noticed the mirth flickering in his eyes, but continued in spite of it. "Claire told me I was crazy, but then we saw your beautiful house and Joe's old El Camino in your garage, and even she admitted that it was odd for a bar owner to have so much money. Why do you have Joe's car, anyway? I thought Sophy owned it."

"Sophy needed the cash and I wanted the car."

"Oh. So what takeover were you talking about?"

"The one involving my business back home."

"You mean VC Industries?"

Butch's eyes widened for a split second. "Wow, you really did your homework on me."

"Jackrabbit Junction doesn't offer a lot of distractions."

"Yes, VC Industries. The company my brother heads up is buying me out at my request. The paperwork should be finalized by the end of August, and then I'm free."

"So you didn't buy that house with income from The Shaft?"

"Hell, no. This place is more of a hobby than a business."

"And that greenhouse in your garage?"

"I like plants. If I can make a buck or two selling them, even better."

Kate stared at him, speechless. She decided not to bring up her suspicions about the mummified hand, his black market alliance with Joe, or her conclusions about why he had a key to Sophy's place.

"So, am I cleared of all of my fictional crimes?"

She nodded.

"Good. Now, if you don't mind …" He grasped the door knob.

"Butch." She clamped her hand over his. His knuckles felt rough against the soft skin of her palm. God, he smelled good enough to eat.

His gaze dipped to her lips for several heartbeats. When he raised his eyes back to hers, the intent smoldering in them turned her knees to Play-Doh.

"Yes, Kate?"

She took a deep breath, plugged her nose, and dove off the high dive. "I like you."

"Gee, that's swell, Peggy Sue."

She ignored his sarcasm. "I mean, I really, really like you. If you'd give me another chance, I want to make up for all of my craziness by showing you how much I really like you."

He leaned in so close Kate could feel the heat radiating off his skin. "Define 'showing.'"

Licking her suddenly parched lips, Kate gulped. "Dinner, maybe some dancing, maybe something else."

"What else?" He leaned lower, his mouth hovering over hers.

"Sex," she whispered, waiting with every tingling nerve in her body to taste him. Instead, a cool breath of air conditioning swept across her fevered skin as he stepped back. "Or not."

"You'd have sex with me just to make up for accusing me of trying to steal Ruby's mine?"

"Yes," she breathed, her heart still rattling.

His forehead creased.

"I mean, no. Butch, it's not like that."

"Forget it, Kate. I don't want pity sex from you."

"That's not what I meant. I'd have sex with you because I like you."

"That's right, you 'really like' me. I wonder what you do to the guys you just kind of like."

This was not going well at all.

"Look, Butch, I know I probably give off crazy-girl vibes, but I'm not like that. I'm just an ex-school teacher who came to town for my grandfather's wedding and ended up falling for a guy who owns the local bar."

She closed the distance between them, grabbing his hand, needing some kind of connection to continue. He didn't pull away.

"When I'm not doing a horrible job of playing Nancy Drew, I'm really boring and spend most of my days trying to figure out what I want to do with my life."

His silence squished all hope.

She squeezed his hand and got nothing in return.

Damn.

It was time to get the hell out of there with what little pride she had left. "I'm sorry for being such an idiot and causing you so many problems. But I'm even sorrier for blowing any chance I had with you."

She let go of his hand and headed for the door. Her stupid tears threatening, she reached blindly for the doorknob.

The kitchen was just a blur as she raced for the main entrance. It wasn't until she yanked open the Ford's door that she was able to breathe under the weight on her chest.

Kate climbed into the cab, slammed her door shut, and burst into tears. Then she pounded the steering wheel and kicked the dash a few times for good measure.

God, she needed a drink.

She started the pickup and drove across the highway to Biddy's Gas and Carryout. A stiff Bloody Mary—or four—would soothe her bruised ego and patch up her fractured heart. If not, she'd just crawl under Ruby's bed and never come back out.

* * *

"Mac?" Claire called as she stepped into the mouth of the Lucky Monk mine. Then she remembered the thousands of tons of rock overhead and clapped her hand over her mouth.

She stood still, the latest downpour dripping from her raincoat, her breath puffing out her nose in short bursts of steam, and listened for any sound other than her pulse clamoring in her ears. The stitch in her side ached.

Silence urged her deeper into the mine. Drawing her flashlight from the inner pocket of her coat, she crunched across the loose pebbles strewn just inside the threshold.

"Mac?" This time, she used her inside voice.

Still, nothing but the smell of stale, earthy air greeted her.

She glanced back at the entrance, debating whether to head back to his pickup and wait for him.

The rain drizzled over the valley, and after slipping and sliding her way up to the mine for the last half hour, she wasn't in a rush to battle the muddy trail again. Besides, she had the map— albeit waterlogged and mud-speckled—that Mac had left in his truck to steer her in the right direction. She also had the package she'd found in Joe's post office box to show Mac.

No More Secrets! That was her new policy.

Her decision to stay made, Claire unrolled the map and spread it out on the floor. With her flashlight, she traced the adit back to the circle where Mac had told her he'd found the skeleton. She counted the side tunnels branching off from each side of the main adit and tried to convince herself that finding the dead guy would be a piece of cake.

She rolled up the map as she stood. Convincing Mac to let her back in his bed might not be so simple. But if it came down to it, she could always start removing her clothes. She wasn't above using whatever weapons she had in her arsenal to her advantage.

Her flashlight guiding the way, Claire moved deeper into the Lucky Monk. The shadows flickered, brooding at the edge of her peripheral vision.

Every five minutes or so, she called Mac's name, then paused and listened, straining to hear any sound that confirmed she wasn't the only one rattling around in the belly of the mine.

By the time she reached the tunnel that led to the dead man, she was beginning to have serious doubts about her decision to go searching for Mac. For all she knew, he'd taken another trail down to the pickup while she was on her way up to find him and was on his way home to Tucson. She was also getting hungry for dinner. It had to be getting close to six by now.

She turned a corner and found a huge pile of rocks looming ahead. Claire's heart thumped in her chest. What if Mac were trapped on the other side of the rocks? How much oxygen did he have? Should she try to dig him out or go get some help?

Then she noticed the hole up near the ceiling and scrambled up the pile, shining her light through the opening.

"Mac?" she whispered.

Her flashlight lit a wall of boards, a few of which were missing from the center. She lowered the beam and flinched at the sight of a dead man staring blindly at the opposite wall.

Wow! She'd anticipated a replica of Mr. Bones, her anatomy class's mascot, not a desiccated body covered with scraps of leathered flesh.

She shined her light back on the gaping hole in the boards. Had Mac gone through there? What was on the other side?

Rocks clattered as she scrambled headfirst through the hole, scraping her kneecap on a protruding rock along the way. Cursing, she limped up to the skeleton, curiosity urging her on, and shined her light into the empty eye sockets. Something moved in amongst the shadows.

Claire screeched and jumped back.

The mine's silence suddenly seemed ominous, suffocating—giving her goose bumps.

She peeked through the hole in the boards.

"Mac?"

Boot prints littered the floor. Were they Mac's?

A waft of musty air slid past her cheeks. She blinked in surprise. Why would there be a breeze hundreds of feet under the earth?

After one last look at the dead guy to make sure he had both hands, she climbed between the boards and tiptoed further down the tunnel, following the boot prints in the dust-coated floor. She'd rounded a couple of bends when a second pair of footprints split off from the first.

She stopped, squatting. If one set of the prints were Mac's, then either he'd been carrying someone on his back until this point, or somebody else was in the mine.

Claire's skin tingled. She whipped her light all around, half-expecting the creature from the Black Lagoon to rush at her from out of the shadows. Fear locked her legs at the knees. She listened and heard what sounded like heavy breathing, then pinched herself for freaking out at the racket of her own breath rushing in and out of her open mouth.

Her logic stepped up to the microphone. Maybe Mac had actually brought somebody else into the mine—Sheriff Harrison, for example—to show him the skeleton.

Of course! Mac probably had already contacted the police about the dead man he'd found.

She chewed on her knuckle as she stared down at the prints. Damn, he must really be pissed to include the cops before her.

Uncertainty lingering, she inched further along the mine walls. Even if the prints belonged to the sheriff and not some Ted Bundy wannabe, it didn't hurt to be cautious.

Several bends later, she came to another cave-in. This one had a V-shaped clearing along the left wall.

The air back here was murkier, as if it'd been stirred up. Her lips tasted like she'd been blowing raspberries on the tunnel floor. Dust tickled her nose, and she pinched it to hold back a sneeze.

As she tried to sneak through the cleared section, one of the rocks wobbled loose under her weight and rolled down to the floor with a loud clackity-clack-clack-clack.

Rooted in mid-wince, Claire waited until silence again surrounded her, then edged along the wall to the other side of the cave-in.

Still, the only sign of human presence was the footprints.

Further ahead, the tunnel narrowed quickly, the walls jagged and uneven, the ceiling much lower. Claire felt like Alice, getting closer and closer to that little door. Too bad she didn't have any blue or red pills in her pocket; she could have used something to distort her reality at the moment.

As one bend turned into the next and the walls contracted around her, Claire's leg muscles began to quake and burn. Her raincoat scratched over the rocks as she slid through a narrow gap toward a rectangular opening ahead that glowed with light.

A shadow flickered across the gap. She froze, her heart sharing real estate with her tonsils.

Mac?

After several seconds of willing her legs to move, she shut off her flashlight and crept forward, peeking into a cavernous chamber.

Across the room, Mac leaned against a wall half-covered with crude drawings of what looked like deer, or maybe horses. His eyes opened and closed in the battery lamp-lit room, his wrists and ankles bound with red climbing rope.

Claire's mouth opened in a noiseless gasp.

Mac's gaze seemed to land on her for several seconds, then he groaned and tried to sit up, only to fall back against the wall, his eyes shutting, his head lolling to the side. Blood trailed from his temple and stained his cheek.

For half a minute, Claire sat there, every cell locked in uncertainty. She listened for the sound of Mac's captor, and for another half a minute, the only noise she heard was an occasional groan from Mac, along with her own pulse banging in her ears like a Tommy Gun.

Her gut told her to go to Mac, untie him, and drag him to safety.

Her head warned her to race back to Mac's pickup and go get help in the form of a badge and licensed firearm.

Her feet and legs voted to just stay there in the crook of the mine's intestines until she woke up from this nightmare.

Claire decided to go with her gut. It had served her well most of the time in the past. Moving with her version of sniper-like grace, she snuck into the chamber.

Three clicks of a revolver hammer stopped her a few steps in.

"Move and I'll pull the trigger," an unfamiliar voice said from behind her.

Fuck! Shit! Damn!

Her gut had been wrong.

* * *

The bottles of vodka and hot sauce clinked against each other in the small paper sack sitting in the passenger seat as Kate rumbled toward the R.V. park.

On the bright side, the rain had finally stopped, and sunshine glistened on the wet rocks and shards of broken glass littering the shoulder.

On the not-so-bright side, Butch hadn't changed his mind and come chasing after her.

Up ahead, someone walked along the shoulder carrying an orange suitcase. Kate let off the gas as she neared the pedestrian, swerving into the middle of the road to give plenty of space as she passed.

A familiar pair of green eyes met Kate's through the windshield. She slammed on the brakes, the Ford's tires skidding on the wet roadway as the pickup spun one-hundred and eighty degrees before stopping.

Her fingers still white-knuckling the steering wheel, Kate rolled forward to where Jess stood on the shoulder with her mouth gaping, her ponytail blowing in the breeze the storm had left in its wake.

"What are you doing, Jess?"

Jess walked over to Kate's open window. "Did they teach you how to do that in driver's ed.?"

Kate ignored Jess's question. "What's in the suitcase?"

"Nothing."

"Where are you going?"

"To Yuccaville."

Jess's stony expression clued Kate that she needed to step carefully. "What's in Yuccaville?"

"A bus." Jess shifted the suitcase to her other hand. "I'm going to Ohio."

Shit! Talking sense into Jess's head was Claire's job. Kate had agreed only to helping out at the store.

"Does Claire know about this?"

Jess nodded. "She's the one who told me I needed to leave by tomorrow, since Mom's coming home on Wednesday."

What in the hell was Claire thinking? Kate chewed on her lower lip. There was no way she could let Jess leave on her watch. If she could just stall Jess for the evening, she could dump this problem on Claire's lap tomorrow morning. But how?

"Why don't you hop in? I'll give you a ride to Yuccaville."

Her eyelids narrowing, Jess took a step back. "How do I know you're not going to kidnap me and take me back to Ruby's?"

Okay, so Plan A was a bust. "You have my word."

When Jess hesitated still, Kate said, "Come on, Jess. It's a long way to Yuccaville. It'll be dark before you even reach the halfway point, and trust me, you don't want to hitchhike at night. Climb in and let me drive you to the bus station."

The kid stared Kate down for several more seconds. "Okay, but you'd better not try to stop me. I'm going to Ohio and nothing you say or do is going to change my mind."

"I won't," she lied.

As Kate stuffed the paper sack from Biddy's under the seat, Jess jogged around the front of the pickup and pulled open the passenger side door.

"You're kind of weird," she said to Kate and crawled into the cab, smelling like grape bubblegum and fresh desert air. "But I still like you. You should visit me sometime in Ohio."

Maybe she would.

Kate hit the gas.

Maybe she should even save Jess the bus fare and drive her to Ohio. There certainly wasn't any reason for Kate to hang around here now that Butch had kicked her to the curb.

Wait a second! She was supposed to be figuring out a way to keep Jess in town, not daydreaming about a Thelma-and-Louise road trip to the Buckeye state.

"What are you going to do after you arrive in Ohio?"

"Get my license."

"You have someplace lined up to stay?"

"No." Jess patted the orange suitcase. "But I have plenty of money, so I'll probably just live out of a hotel for a while."

Crap! Jess must have found that stash of cash Claire mentioned Ruby had hidden somewhere around the house. So much for scaring the kid into sticking around. If Jess had that much cash, she'd be set for a few months without a problem.

Kate avoided looking over at The Shaft as she paused at the highway junction.

"Does your dad know you're on your way?"

She turned onto the main highway.

"Nope. I want to surprise him on my birthday."

Wincing mentally, Kate glanced over at Jess. The girl stared out at the passing scrub, chewing on her sparkly fingernails. Kate whipped her gaze back to the road as Jess looked over at her.

"Kate?"

"Yes?"

"Do you think Claire is really going to drag your mom to the airport tomorrow?"

Knowing her sister, probably. "I don't know. It depends on Mac, I think."

"What do you mean?"

"Well, Claire's mad at Mom because Mac is mad at Claire. If Mac forgives Claire and changes his mind about kicking her out, Claire might let Mom stay."

"What's it like to have a big sister?"

Kate shrugged. It had been a way of life since birth, so she hadn't put much thought into it. "It's okay, I guess. Claire is usually pretty fun to hang around."

A large orange diamond sign whizzed by, warning of road construction ahead, followed shortly by a green sign stating Yuccaville was just fifteen miles away. She was running out of time. How was she going to keep Jess from climbing on a bus?

"What about your other sister, Veronica? What's she like?"

"Ronnie? She's fun too, most of the time. Every now and then she gets pretty bossy, but she's not as bad as Mom."

Jess sighed dramatically. "I wish I had an older sister."

"You do, kind of."

"I know, I have your mom. But that's not the same. She's just a stepsister, and not very nice most days."

"I wasn't talking about Mom. I was talking about Claire— and me. We're kind of like big sisters, don't you think?"

"Yeah, I guess. I just wish you lived closer."

"Me, too." But Jackrabbit Junction wasn't big enough for Butch and her. She didn't think she could stomach running into him off and on, smiling like she didn't care who was sharing his bed, waving as if they were just old friends. "Maybe you'll find some more big sisters in Ohio."

"Probably not." Jess sounded like someone had torn the arm off her favorite teddy bear.

"You can always—" A loud bang interrupted Kate in mid-sentence. The steering wheel jerked hard to the right. She jammed her foot down on the brake pedal.

Jess screamed as they skidded across the asphalt toward the ditch.

Chapter Twenty-Two

A steel gun barrel jabbed into the side of Claire's head.

She stood frozen, her jaw clamped tight, her breath whistling through her teeth.

Shit-criminy! She'd been around more guns in the last few months than she had her whole life. They must hand out guns with birth certificates in Arizona.

"Who are you?" the man at the other end of the revolver asked, his voice a steady baritone with a slight rasp.

"Avon calling?" Claire tossed out the first thing that came to mind.

"Real funny." He planted his free hand in the middle of her back and shoved hard.

She stumbled forward, falling, her palms and wrists taking the brunt of her weight. Joe's package of porn spun across the dirt floor in front of her, pictures sliding out of the envelope and fanning in several directions.

"Leave her alone." Mac's vocal chords sounded rusty, as if they'd weathered under the desert sun and rain for too many years.

Claire looked across the room at him, relief spreading through her at the site of his hazel eyes wide open.

"Shut up, Garner." The gunman placed his cowboy boot on Claire's hip and pushed, rolling her onto her back. "Get up!"

Scrambling to her feet, Claire stared at her attacker in the low light of a battery-powered lantern, finally able to see who'd been holding the gun to her head.

He looked vaguely familiar, with his silver sideburns and salted black hair greased back off his forehead. His ruddy face and jowls were stretched taut in a menacing grin. His eyes shifted back and forth like windshield wipers between Mac and her.

"Now get over there next to Garner." He used the gun to motion Claire toward Mac.

How did he know Mac's name?

She licked the dust from her lips, wondering what in the hell this guy was doing in Ruby's mine and how they could get away from him without losing any blood. She needed a distraction. Something to sidetrack him long enough for her to get that gun from him. But what?

As she walked toward Mac, she glanced at the drawings covering the wall over his head. Were those actual petroglyphs? Did Joe know about those? Did they have anything to do with the mummy hand, sandal, and twig animal?

Claire slowed as she neared the package she'd dropped, bending over to scoop it up.

"Leave that alone. Get moving."

Johnny Ringo could use a little work on his manners. Claire stepped over one of the bawdier shots of Bianca and Joe, then stopped and spun around to study the gunman again.

Holy Little Smokies! "Richard Rensberg," she said.

"What?" Rensberg raised the gun.

"You're Richard Rensberg—the Third." He looked a bit thicker in the face than his father, and very little like the young boy in the newspaper photos, but add a handlebar mustache and a cane, and he was a dead ringer for his grandfather.

"And you're about to get a bullet in the teeth if you don't move your ass, lady."

"Claire." Mac's tone practically vibrated with tension. "Would you please get over here next to me?"

Hesitating, she eyed the photo at her feet. But what if Richard saw the photos of his mom and Joe? He might …

Claire's pulse kicked into a buzz-roll that would make any jazz drummer envious. That was it! Her distraction, front and center, courtesy of Kodak. If she could get Richard to take a look at the photos, the sight might set him off his game enough to offer her the opportunity needed to get that gun away from him.

She joined Mac, squatting instead of sitting so that she'd be ready to pounce when the time came.

Mac frowned. "Whatever you're thinking, don't do it."

Ignoring Mac's warning, she focused on Richard.

"How's your mother doing, Richard?" Claire tried to keep her tone light and happy, like old friends catching up.

Richard's face crinkled. "Shut up."

Bingo. There was that nerve. Too easy!

"Claire," Mac whispered, "stop poking the bear."

"Is red still her favorite color?"

"I said shut the fuck up." Richard's ruddy complexion deepened to a nice purple hue as he aimed the gun at her head.

"Calm down, Richard." Rising to her full height, Claire held out her hands palms-up. "I'm just curious how that snake tattoo on her hip looks now that she's eligible for Medicare."

"Oh, shit." Mac didn't hide his struggle to free his wrists.

Richard's nostrils flared, his mouth white around the edges. "How do you know about my mom's tattoo?"

Scanning the pictures spread across the floor in front of her, Claire pointed at the close-up of Bianca's hip. "I saw it in that picture right there."

"You lie!" The revolver trembled, but stayed locked on her.

"Claire, please shut up." His wrists still bound, Mac reached for the rope tethering his ankles together.

"Look for yourself," Claire continued. "It's right there in Kodak color."

Richard angled over to the picture. Keeping the gun on Claire, he glanced at the floor. His brow scrunched as he peered at the shot of his mother's hip, along with Joe's bare butt cheek. "Where did you get that?"

Claire ignored his question and pointed at another photo. "Check out that one over there. It's a great profile shot of your mom." And Joe, in the middle of tearing off Bianca's red panties with his teeth.

Richard followed her advice, the gun drooping a little as he eyeballed the second picture.

"She sure has long legs. Was she a dancer before she married your dad?" As in the pole-hugging, bump-and-grind kind?

His eyes were rimmed with red when he focused on Claire. "Where did you get these?" he asked again. A vein throbbed in the center of his forehead.

"I found them. That one over by the wall is particularly interesting." Especially if he enjoyed seeing close-up views of his mother in the process of orally satisfying Joe.

"Your mother's lipstick seems to be the exact same shade as her panties—which you'll find in the bottom of that package, if you're interested in keepsakes."

A pain-filled groan rose from Mac.

Claire tried to keep an eye on Richard as he tore into the package, while sneaking peeks at Mac, who'd paused to lean his head against the wall. His chest rose and fell rapidly, his face chalky white except where dried blood stained it dark maroon.

"Are you okay?" She spoke low, for Mac's ears only.

"I'd be a hell of a lot better if you'd stop trying to get shot."

"Trust me."

He grimaced. "You're playing with fire."

"I'm a licensed pyromaniac. Besides, I have a plan." Well, she kind of did. Some parts were a bit murky.

"That's what worries me."

Richard roared and threw the package across the room. "I should've known."

"Should've known what?" Claire prompted him. If she could get Richard talking, maybe he'd forget about his revolver.

"He blackmailed her."

"Joe Martino or whoever took the pictures?" She'd bet the farm on Joe, but that left the question of who took those shots.

"Yes, Joe. The mother fucker!" Richard's breath mimicked an old steam engine. The gun dangled from his fingers.

Claire needed to get that gun, but her intentions got tangled up in her curiosity. "Why would Joe blackmail your mom?"

He sneered at her. "For money, of course. And revenge."

Her ears perked up. "Revenge? What did your mom do to him?"

"Not revenge on her. On my father."

Claire checked on Mac, who was now sitting forward again. She breathed easier at the return of color to his cheeks.

Behind him, she noticed a pointy, softball-sized chunk of rock lying on the ground, undoubtedly making a painful cushion for his lower back.

With an almost audible pop, an idea formed in her brain. Stealing a small step backwards, she tried to act as if she were casually leaning against the petroglyph-covered wall.

She needed to keep Richard swimming in the past for a bit longer. "What did your father ever do to Joe?" She tried to sound disgruntled on behalf of the Rensberg clan while stretching her foot behind Mac.

"Killed his dad."

Say what! Claire paused in the midst of using her heel to nudge the rock toward her.

"Your father murdered Joe's dad?" She hadn't expected that.

"No. My father bought some low-end equipment for the mining company that turned out to be faulty."

When Mac noticed what Claire was up to, he pressed back against her foot, pinning it to the wall.

Richard was fixated on the photo in his hand, his face blotchy. "The cause of the mine fire that killed Joe's dad was listed as 'human error,' but the bastard blamed my father."

"So, he blackmailed your mom to ruin your dad's marriage?" She purposely confused the situation to keep Richard's tongue greased.

Meanwhile, she tried to pull her foot free, shooting Mac a knock-it-off glare.

"Don't you get it?" Richard snorted, crumpling the photo in his palm. "Screwing my mother was only part of that asshole's revenge."

"I'm confused." With a grunt, she extracted her foot from behind Mac's back. "How would blackmailing her with these photos exact revenge on your dad?"

"Joe knew my father would do anything for my mother. He must have used her to convince my father to sell off what company stock he still owned in the Copper Snake."

"So that's how the Rensberg family lost control of the mining company." Mac sounded as if an itch had been scratched.

Richard's laugh was ragged, harsh. "And the money-hungry bitch still left him. A year later, he blew his brains out."

Claire grimaced. Young Richard must have been in his early teens then. And she thought living with Mommy-dearest had been rough.

"Did your father have any idea that Joe played a part in his demise?"

"No, but I did. I'd caught Joe in bed with my mother once. After she left us, I figured she'd run off with him. Years later, when he came back to town, I wanted to kill him for what he did to my family. I even followed him up here one night, planning to leave him to rot at the bottom of a shaft, but I lost him in the mine. When I finally found him, he was standing in front of that boarded up wall, lighting a stick of dynamite. After the explosion, when I finally found my way out of here, he was long gone."

Richard stared at the wall above Claire's head. "I tried to come back and see what he'd been hiding, but I ended up lost again and gave up. Now, I understand why he wanted to keep this place hidden."

"Because of these petroglyphs?" Claire indicated overhead.

"No, because of the mummified bodies lining the walls in that side chamber." Richard nodded his head toward the shadows hovering in one of the corners of the room.

Mummified bodies?

That would explain the stick-figure deer and the sandal, answering several of the questions that had plagued her over the last two weeks. Joe had stumbled onto some kind of ancient burial chamber. But he wouldn't have wanted anyone else to find it and risk the authorities sniffing around the Lucky Monk, especially with his practice of stashing stolen goods in his mines.

"Unfortunately, there's a lot of copper and a little gold in this mine." Richard pointed the revolver at a shimmering vein that ran down one of the walls. "Ore that the Copper Snake could profit richly from over the next decade."

"Maybe so." Mac struggled with the rope around his wrists, trying to pull one hand free. "But once word gets out about the archaeological remains here, there's no way the state will allow anyone to touch this hillside."

"Unless nobody finds out it's here. Which is why you two have to die."

"What?" Claire's legs wobbled. According to her addition, one plus one did not equal them dying. "Are you sure about that?"

"Huh," Mac said. "Now it all makes sense."

"No, it doesn't." She slid down the wall, squatting next to Mac once again. "Why do you care about the Copper Snake, Richard? Your father sold out."

"I know some people with deep pockets. People willing to lend cash for a high return. I've bought back forty percent of the company's stock, and I want more."

Mac bumped Claire to get her attention. "He hired Leo Scott to help him steal the Lucky Monk from Ruby."

"And Leo says I'll have it in another week. With you out of the picture, it will go even smoother." His smile widened, his eyes taking on a freaky, Cuckoo-for-Coco-Puffs glaze.

Richard aimed the gun at Claire's chest, then Mac's, then back at her head. "The only question now is who dies first?"

"Him." Claire pointed at Mac while watching Richard.

"What!" She could feel Mac's glare.

With a shrug, Richard turned the gun on Mac.

"Hey, Richard," she said, "you forgot about this picture over here."

Claire scooped up the rock from behind Mac and fast-balled it at Richard's head.

Richard was slow to react and dodge. The rock slammed against his kneecap with a loud thwack.

Oops! Her aim wasn't what it used to be.

Howling in pain, Richard doubled over, the gun clattering onto the floor behind him.

"Was breaking his kneecap part of your brilliant plan?" Mac asked.

"I'm improvising as I go."

Claire ran toward the gun. Midway there, she changed course and instead charged straight at Richard, who was reaching for his gun.

"Claire, no!"

Mac's words caught up with her as she nose-tackled Richard, who'd just grasped the revolver.

Richard stumbled backward, off-balance. His heel caught on a small jut of rock, and they tumbled to the floor, arms and legs tangling, gun flying free and sliding out of reach.

Somehow Claire ended up on the bottom. She wiggled one arm free and tried to poke him in the eye. He blocked her and grabbed her hand, twisting her wrist until tears blurred her vision.

She tried to move her legs and realized her right leg was free. With all the strength she could muster, she jammed her knee into his crotch.

Richard grunted, his eyes bulging as he gasped in her face, showering her with stale breath and spittle.

Yanking her wrist free of his loosened grasp, she brought her elbow down on the tender spot between his neck and shoulder blade.

He wheezed and curled sideways, half off her.

Shoving him further onto his side, she squirmed out from under him and scrambled toward the gun. Her fingertips brushed the polished wooden handle at the same time his hand clamped on her ankle and wrenched her backwards.

"Come back here, you bitch." He caught her by the knee and hauled her closer. "You'll pay for that cheap shot."

Claire rolled onto her back, swinging her free foot around, and smashed the heel of her tennis shoe into his nose.

Something crunched. Blood gushed from his nostrils.

He roared, tipping his head back, cupping his nose.

Flopping back onto her stomach, Claire lunged for the gun. But it was gone, replaced by a pair of ostrich-skin cowboy boots.

What the …?

Claire looked up. "Porter!"

She could have danced a jig at the sight of his green eyes. Then she remembered where they were.

"What are you doing here?"

"Looking for you." He held the revolver steadily on Richard, who lay there whimpering, dripping blood.

"Oh. How did you find me?" She stood, her legs quivering so much that she clung to a nearby wall to stay upright.

"I followed you after your sister dropped you off."

Porter walked over to where Richard lay. He pointed the gun at Richard's head, smiled at Claire with his pearly whites, and pulled the trigger.

Claire screamed as the gunshot boomed through the chamber, turning away at the spray of blood and brains across the floor. Her ears ringing, she clutched her stomach, fear mixing with revulsion to produce instant nausea, and gagged several times, barely managing to keep her supper down.

"We didn't need him slowing us down." Porter's voice sounded different, more clipped, even while slightly muffled by the lasting effects of the gunshot explosion in her ears.

Then it hit her—his drawl was gone.

"You should thank me," Porter said. "He was going to kill you."

Claire looked over at Mac.

Run, he mouthed, nodding toward the narrow exit. He held up his hands just enough to show her he'd managed to free his wrists, but his legs were still bound.

"Where are the goods, Claire?" Porter asked.

Next to Porter's boots, Richard's foot was still twitching.

She snapped her lids shut and spoke between gasps. "What goods?"

"Don't fuck with me, darling." His boots clomped across the room. She opened her eyes in time to see him point the revolver at Mac. "Tell me where the goods are, or I'll blow out your boyfriend's brains next."

Mac nudged his head toward the exit again. Then his face spasmed, his body jerking in pain, and he paled even more.

There was no way Mac could take on Porter, not with what was probably a concussion slowing him down.

Claire stood up straight, focusing on her newest nemesis. "Which goods?"

"The ones I heard Jess talking to you about while you were mopping up the bathroom floor earlier today."

Claire replayed the scene with Jess in her head. "You mean the money she mentioned?"

"No, I mean the gold."

The gold? Oh, yeah, Jess had asked her what she was going to do about that piece of gold they'd found. "Oh, that gold."

"Yes, *that* gold. My dad didn't spend the last few years of his life in prison with his lungs rotting in his chest to die for nothing. That gold belongs to me. It's my inheritance." He pulled a crumpled piece of paper from his pocket and threw it in Claire's direction. "There's the note to prove it.

Claire limped over to the wadded up paper, her body aching like she'd slid down the whole length of the Olympic bobsled track on her stomach.

Smoothing out the note, she read aloud:

If you find this, you know where to find me.

The handwriting was Joe's. She'd become an ace when it came to nailing his penmanship.

"I don't understand what this means."

"Last year, my dad called to tell me he was dying and that a 'treasure' was waiting for me in a safe deposit box in a Vegas bank. But instead of any money, I found this note from Joe."

What was it with the father-son stories today? Claire let the note fall to the floor. "How'd you know it was from Joe?"

She wasn't surprised that Joe had gotten into a safe deposit box that didn't belong to him. After learning as much about his past as she had in the last few months, she figured that breaking into a safety deposit box was probably child's play for him.

"He was the only other one who knew about this so-called treasure, according to Dad."

"You're the one who broke into Ruby's office." Claire had been right to suspect Porter from the start. She couldn't wait to make Kate eat her words—providing she made it out of this mess free of bullet holes. "I knew that writer from Texas routine was a bunch of bullshit."

Porter shrugged. "People here don't trust outsiders. But throw on some cowboy boots and slur your words a little, and they'll spill their guts for a free beer."

She needed an answer to something that had been bugging her since Jess told her about it. "What prompted you to look in *Treasure Island* for clues?"

"Dad always used the word 'treasure' when referring to the safe deposit box contents. But Joe's notes in the book didn't make any sense to me."

Welcome to her world.

"Turns out it didn't matter in the end." He pulled back the hammer, aiming squarely at Mac's head. "Now, where's the gold?"

"Well ..." Panic paralyzed her brain.

"I'm going to count to three, Claire. That's it."

Oh, fuck!

"Claire, don't." Mac's eyes drilled hers.

"One."

"Don't what?" she asked, her whole body trembling. She had to do something, think of something.

"Don't do it."

"Two."

"Mac, I'm sorry about the whole mess with my mom."

"Damn it, Claire!" Mac shifted forward, as if to stand.

"Three."

"No!" Claire yelled, holding out her hand to stop Porter. "I'll show you where I hid the treasure ... I mean gold."

She needed to get Porter away from Mac.

Porter raised his brows. "Why not just tell me where and save yourself the trouble?"

"Because I've stashed it in a spot that's not easy to explain where." It was a bell-ringer of a lie, but she kept a straight face and managed not to pee her pants. "Besides, you'll just kill us like you did Richard if I tell you now."

"Fine. Have it your way." He directed her toward the exit with the revolver. "You lead the way."

Fear glued her feet to the floor. "You're not going to shoot Mac when I turn around, are you?"

Porter chuckled. "I don't need to shoot either one of you, unless you force me to. I just want what's mine, and then I'll disappear and be gone for good."

Her shoulders clenched, Claire walked stiff-legged toward the narrow tunnel. She glanced at Mac once more; worry lined his face as he tugged at the ropes around his ankles.

"Come after us, and I'll shoot her," Porter told Mac, and then nudged her along the narrow corridor, the gun pressing against her spine.

She wondered if he'd allow her a cigarette along with a blindfold before standing her up against the wall and firing.

By the time they reached the skeleton, her back felt bruised. She climbed through the hole at the cave-in first, his threat to turn back and kill Mac if she tried anything funny kept her hands at her side as he wiggled through after her.

"Hold it," he said as she started toward the main adit. A gunshot rang out, followed by a deep rumbling.

Her ears clanging again, Claire watched as the ceiling rained down over the pile. Dust coated them, choking her and burning her eyes. When the roar stopped and it had cleared enough for her to see the pile, the hole was gone, filled with rubble, leaving Mac on the other side—trapped.

"On we go." Porter dug the gun into her back again.

Sweat coated Claire's skin as he prodded her out of the mine.

What was she going to do? She couldn't take him back to Ruby's place. That would endanger everyone back there.

Somewhere, between the Lucky Monk and Jackrabbit Junction, she needed to find herself a treasure.

* * *

Kate shielded her eyes from the sun. The rain seemed to have washed the air, leaving it crystal clear. Across the valley to the east, she could practically count the sage brush and little trees dotting the hillside.

"I thought you said hitchhiking was dangerous." Jess sat in the driver's seat of the pickup, leaning out the window, watching Kate, who was trying to flag down someone without ending up as road kill.

"It is. That's why I'm doing the thumbing and not you."

A pair of headlights from the direction of Jackrabbit Junction crested the small hill about a half-mile away.

"Boy, Kate, we really caught air when we left the road, didn't we?"

Jess had recovered from their short flight over the shallow ditch and touch down onto the desert's soft dirt, but now she seemed determined to turn it into a big-fish story. The distance they cleared kept growing longer and longer.

Kate was just grateful that she'd been able to get the old Ford to limp back to the road's edge, blown tire and all. But her luck had screeched to a halt when she crawled under the truck bed, freed the spare tire, and found it flat as a crepe.

Inching onto the road, Kate held out her thumb and stared at the approaching vehicle, the growl of its engine now audible.

"You look pretty scary with that blood on your forehead." Jess sure had a way with compliments. "I bet you're going to need stitches. You should have been wearing your seatbelt."

"I told you, it's broken." Kate spoke through gritted teeth. Her forehead still throbbed from the impact with the steering wheel upon landing.

"Oh, yeah. I guess Mom better get that fixed. Hey, maybe you should lift your shirt and flash this car when it's close enough for them to see you."

"Thanks for the advice, Dear Abby, but I think I'll try my method for a little longer." Squinting as the vehicle came closer, its daylight running lights shining in her eyes, Kate leaned out as far as she could without falling.

The whine of the engine lowered, the vehicle seeming to slow as it neared. She pasted a smile on her lips, hopeful the bloody gash on her forehead didn't make her look like a cast member of *The Hills Have Eyes*.

The vehicle pulled to the side and braked to a stop. The flashers came on.

Behind the headlights, Kate made out the shape of two people in a pickup cab. She held her breath as the driver's side door opened and a pair of long, jean-clad legs ending in a pair of cowboy boots touched the ground.

"You're bleeding," her Good Samaritan said as he walked around the front bumper of his truck.

At the sound of Butch's voice, Kate closed her eyes and groaned. How much humiliation would she have to choke down today?

"Hi, Butch!" Jess shouted. The squeak of the old Ford's door meant the teenager would be joining them shortly.

"What happened to your forehead?" The warm touch of Butch's hands on each side of Kate's head surprised her into opening her lids.

He frowned down at her, his fingers gentle as he inspected her gash. The smell of fabric softener and his musky cologne made her hungry for more than his feathery touches.

Jess bounced up next to them. "We wrecked again, but this time Kate didn't hit anyone."

Kate's face burned with all twenty-four shades of Crayola's red at once. If she'd had any spare clothing, she'd have crammed it in Jess's mouth.

"Jess," Butch said while looking at Kate. "Will you do me a favor and grab the first aid kit out of my glove box."

"That's not necessary." Kate pulled his hands away from her face. "I'm fine. It's just a little cut."

But Jess was already rounding the passenger side of his truck.

"Maybe so, but Jess needs to keep busy." He stared at Ruby's Ford. "You're having a bad day. What happened?"

He didn't know the half of it. Kate rubbed her eyes. "A tire blew."

"You're lucky you didn't roll it." Butch walked past the driver's side door and around the front of the old Ford, pausing to free a thatch of brownish-purple tufted grass pinched between the bumper and the grill. "I take it you head-butted the steering wheel when you landed."

Nodding, Kate followed him. "Luckily, Jess made it through without a scratch."

The spare tire leaned against the shredded remains of the blown-out front tire. Butch kicked the spare. "Flat—nice. My spare might fit."

"No!"

That came out sharper than she'd intended, but the last thing she wanted was to be indebted to the man who'd freed her from jail this morning and then rejected her this afternoon.

Butch raised his brows.

"If you'll just give us a ride to Yuccaville, I can take care of things from there."

Jess jogged up as Butch asked, "What's in Yuccaville?"

"The bus station," Jess answered, smiling as she held out the first aid box toward him. "There's a lady in your pickup."

Knowing exactly who that lady was, Kate's chest ached.

"Is somebody going somewhere on a bus?" He looked at Kate for an answer.

Kate shrugged. What did he care if she flew to the moon tonight? He had Lana to keep his sheets warm. "Maybe."

"I'm going to live with my dad in Ohio." Jess ruined Kate's ploy. "Have you ever been to Cleveland?"

He turned to Jess. "Nope. Is your mom back from her honeymoon now?"

Jess lowered her gaze. "Um, no."

Butch shot Kate a suspicion-filled glance.

Shrugging again, Kate kept silent. She had to be careful what she said in front of Jess or risk alienating the kid completely.

"Will you do me another favor, Jess?" Butch asked.

"Sure."

"Go ask Lana to help you find the tire patch kit stuffed behind my seat."

Jess set off toward his truck with a skip.

"What's going on?" Butch popped open the first aid kit.

"I found her walking along the road. She's determined to leave for Ohio before Ruby returns. The only way she'd crawl in the truck was if I promised to take her to Yuccaville. I was working on a plan to delay her when the tire blew."

He pulled a small pouch from the box and tore it open. "Does she really want to live in Ohio, or is this some kind of game she's playing with her mom?"

"Ow!" Kate jerked back as he touched the square swab of cotton to her head, her gash stinging. The scent of alcohol drifted between them. "I don't know. Jess usually spills her guts to Claire, not me."

"Where is Claire?"

"With Mac." With Mac's truck, was more likely. "Somehow, I have to convince Jess to stick around, at least until Claire has a chance to talk to her."

"Maybe I can help." He touched the pad to her head again.

Kate held still as he finished cleaning the wound. "I doubt your girlfriend would appreciate you missing dinner to hang out with us any longer than necessary."

"Stop grimacing. You're making it bleed again."

"Sorry." Kate smoothed out her forehead as he dabbed some clear goop on her skin, determined to be a good little patient so he'd hurry up and finish playing doctor. Holding up the flimsy wall she'd erected between them while standing this close made her palms clammy.

"Lana isn't my girlfriend, Kate."

"She's not?" She stared at his Adam's apple, wondering what that meant.

"Nope. She's my brother's wife. She's here to help me with some of the takeover paperwork."

Her face warmed in all of the usual places.

Once again, she'd jumped to the wrong conclusion and landed head-first in a puddle of mortification. If only she could crawl away and lick her wounds.

Butch grabbed a bandage from the kit. "Somehow you seem to have acquired this image of me as some kind of cheesy Don Juan, screwing anyone with shaved legs and painted toenails."

She opened her mouth to disagree, then closed it. He was right. Jealousy had a psychedelic way of distorting her sanity.

He tore the bandage free from the wrapper. "To be honest, I haven't had sex with anyone for quite a while."

She gulped at his admission. How long was a *while*?

"And for the record …" He lifted her chin so his blue eyes could lock onto hers. "I really wanted to have sex with you."

"Oh." His admission made her hot and sweaty in all the right places.

"I still do, even though you seem to have such a shitty opinion of my character."

"Then why didn't you stop me from leaving back there in your office?"

"You're trouble, Kate. Sex with you would only make matters worse."

"Gee, thanks." She felt like the cover girl for Pariah Monthly.

"Think about it. You're only here on a temporary basis, and I'm building a life in Jackrabbit Junction. You wear designer clothes and I prefer holey T-shirts. You teach kids for a living, and I provide alcohol to the masses. We're sailing toward different horizons. Not to mention that you tend to think the worst of me at every turn."

"That's not true."

His smile was crooked. "Prove me wrong."

"I think you're an excellent driver."

"Even though I don't use my blinker when backing up?"

"*Touché.*"

He laid the bandage against her forehead, smoothing it out and then trailing his fingers down the sides of her face. "You and I are just not meant to be."

Several more pieces splintered off Kate's duct-taped heart.

"Besides, your mother scares me a little."

A chuckle escaped through her frown. "Medusa often has that effect on people."

Kate stepped back at the sound of Jess's tennis shoes crunching toward them on the gravel shoulder.

"Here you go, Butch. Lana says you better hurry or you're going to lose your reservation."

"Thanks, Jess." Taking the aerosol can of Fix-A-Flat from Jess, he squatted next to the spare tire.

Kate backed away as Jess dropped cross-legged onto the ground next to Butch and started giving him second-by-second details of their latest crash.

She needed some distance from Butch as he worked on the flat spare. Some time to repair the new cuts and scrapes he'd delivered to her already bruised and battered sensibilities.

She lollygagged along the shoulder, pausing here and there to watch the ants rebuild after the flood, monitor the slow progress of a tarantula ambling across the sand, and breathe in the stinky bouquet of some pinkish-purple flowers.

Jess's voice droned behind her, Butch's occasional deep tone interjecting as Kate tried to figure out where to go from here. The crossroads she'd reached had no signs pointing out towns or mileage. She felt empty with nowhere to go.

"Kate!" Jess ran up beside her. "Kate, guess what?" The teenager bounced like she was trying out for Tigger.

Shaking herself out of her self-pity party, Kate forced a smile. "What?"

"I'm not going to Ohio."

No shit. "Why not?"

"Because I got a job! Butch wants me to work for him."

A picture of Jess behind Butch's bar made Kate pause. "You're too young to work in a bar."

"I don't need her at The Shaft." Butch walked around the front of the truck, wiping his hands on his jeans, staring at Kate as she and Jess approached. "I need her at my greenhouse."

"Oh." Kate wanted to curl into a ball and hide under the nearest mesquite tree. Butch had saved the day, and yet still managed to crush her heart into fine, red powder in the process. "That's great news, Jess." She tried her hardest to sound happy for the girl and included Butch in her smile.

"You're all fixed," he said.

No, she wasn't. She felt very broken.

"Now we can go home and you can drink that vodka you bought." Jess had a knack for finding Kate's humiliation button and jumping up and down on it with both feet.

"I'll see you Friday, right?" Butch said to Jess.

Jess nodded and stuffed a new piece of grape-smelling gum in her mouth.

Looking at Kate, Butch reached out to touch her cheek, but stopped inches from her skin. He shook his head and stuffed his hands in his pockets. "Take care, Kate. You should probably have that cut checked out."

"Yeah, maybe I will." Somehow, she managed not to wrap her arms around his leg and beg him to give her just one more shot. She still had her pride, even if it dangled by a single thread.

Without a backward glance, Butch walked back to his pickup and climbed inside.

Kate climbed into the old Ford and started it up.

With a honk and a wave, Butch drove off toward Yuccaville. She watched his taillights fade into the distance and out of her life.

Chapter Twenty-Three

Mac squeezed out through the crevice in the rock face, tugging his pack out with him, and gulped a couple of breaths, the warm, clean air scrubbing the mustiness from his lungs.

The sun sat on the western horizon, so it had to be close to seven o'clock, giving him about an hour of daylight left to find Claire. The desert floor panned out below, motionless.

Where was Claire?

He scanned and then scanned again, searching the valley's growing shadows for some sign of life. She must be a little further around the side of the mountain.

In the sun's fading light, he slipped on his backpack and slid twenty feet down the slope, then jogged along the side of the mountain on a narrow deer trail.

The side of his head ached where Richard had used his skull for batting practice. He still couldn't believe the bank vice president was dead, even though he'd checked for the man's pulse before finding his way outside.

His thoughts slipped back to the burial chamber and the darkness that had ensued after Claire had led Porter away almost an hour ago.

He had freed his legs within seconds and hurried along behind them, following the sounds of their footfalls. He reached the wall of boards and the dead miner in time to see Porter's ostrich-skin cowboy boots wiggling through the hole.

When the gunshot rang out, his stomach had dropped. After the rumbling quieted and the dust had cleared, the skeleton and he were roomies in a sealed tomb.

Ten minutes later, he'd raced back to the burial chamber, grabbed his backpack, checked on Richard, and searched the side room where rows of burial mounds lined a floor littered with painted gourds and tiny rudimentary stone statues—what Mac guessed were ceremonial artifacts.

A corridor split off and led to a small storage room, cluttered with baskets, clay pots, remnants of what he guessed used to be corn cobs, hand-carved tools, and worn grinding stones. Here, he found a sliver of an air hole in a crumbling wall laden with roots and melon-sized rocks.

Digging his way to freedom through several feet of earth and stone and squeezing out that narrow crevice had taken almost forty-five minutes—enough time for Claire and Porter to make it out of the mine and down to the valley floor if they hadn't stopped for any reason and had made it out alive.

He picked up his pace, jogging faster, mindful of the uneven surface and slippery spots where puddles had formed and drained within hours.

His headache chiseled away at the inside of his skull. Dizzy spells tag-teamed with the nausea racking his body, but he had to keep moving.

Time raced along, faster than his feet. Ten minutes later, across the hillside, the mouth of the Lucky Monk finally came into view—a gaping black hole against the brown rock.

Mac stopped to catch his breath, digging out his canteen, thirsty as hell. He took a couple of sips of warm water, and then fished his binoculars out and searched the shadowed valley floor.

There!

He moved back a hair and focused on Claire, leading Porter along the edge of the dry wash about a half-mile away.

If only he could let her know he was there, signal her to stall while he snuck up on Porter.

A flickering of light to the northeast caught his eye. A bank of clouds, black in the dusk sky, stacked up against the horizon. Lightning illuminated the clouds like the finale of a Fourth of July fireworks show. Even without his binoculars he could make out the dark curtains of rain.

Another check on Claire before he started his race down the hillside made his breath catch.

She and Porter had dropped into the wash, their shoulders and heads barely visible now.

Mac watched their progress for several seconds.

Damn it! She knew better than to walk in a dry wash, especially with it still raining up north.

Mac visually backtracked, following the twists and turns of the dry wash as it zigzagged upstream.

Then he saw it.

A fist of water that filled his binoculars sped toward them. It couldn't be more than two miles away from them.

His heart jackhammering on his ribs, he yelled, "Claire!"

On a still evening, the valley might channel his echo down to her, but the breeze interfered, muffling him.

Claire and Porter continued along inside the wash, oblivious that a wall of water was about to slam into them.

"Oh, God, no," he whispered, then ran and slid down the hillside as fast as his feet would carry him.

He was already too late, though. He knew it.

There was no way he'd reach her in time, but he prayed that Claire would hear the roar of the water coming.

That she'd have enough time to make it out alive.

* * *

A trickling stream wound its way through the blend of sand and gravel covering the floor of the dry wash. This hint of life in an otherwise barren world, along with the congregation of flash-filled storm clouds crowding the northeastern horizon, had drawn Claire into the ravine.

Lucky for her, Porter had played right into her hand and followed her lead down the steep bank without question. He apparently hadn't read much about the desert before visiting Jackrabbit Junction.

Her ears tuned to catch every little sound, Claire stuck to the edge of the wash, her muscles tense and ready to scramble up the bank on cue. She knew better than to think she could outrun Mother Nature's septic system, especially in this section of the dry wash where the sheer walls channeled rain runoff into snarling waves five to six feet high.

With each crunching step, she fought the urge to glance over her shoulder and check upstream. Fear that her auditory sense would fail her and send the run-for-your-life signal too late had her heart fluttering. The snap of a twig underfoot nearly sent her careening down Coronary Infarction Avenue.

As plans go, this one fell into the "Totally Insane" category, but desperation and reason didn't usually run hand-in-hand in her head.

If it worked, she might shake Porter long enough to go help Mac out of the mine, and possibly even make it back to Ruby's in time to warn everyone and call Sheriff Harrison.

If it didn't work, and she ended up full of bullet holes or drowned and spit out in some muddy desert backwash, she'd haunt the crap out of her mother for the rest of Deborah's mortal life. Maybe even pester her for eternity.

Paybacks were hell.

A quiet, crackling sound, like the static-filled black holes in-between the stations on an AM radio, drifted into the ravine. Her pace slowed, her knees stiffened. She shot a quick glance over her shoulder.

"Quit dragging your feet, Claire." Porter poked her in the kidney with the revolver's barrel. "There's a beach chair with my name on it south of the border, and I want to be sitting in it by morning."

So that's how he figured on escaping the long arm of the Arizona law after all was said and done. Mexico had a lot of beaches—South America, too, for that matter—along with plenty of other places to disappear.

Her thigh muscles trembling, she forced her feet to continue the trek along the wash. The crackling noise swelled, clearly audible in the hushed, shadow-filled land of dusk. Her fingers and toes began to tingle.

"What's that?" Porter had stopped.

Claire continued forward several more feet, putting some distance between them, before halting. "What?"

"That sound?"

Run! A panicky, squeaky voice shouted in her head.

Claire held her ground, her fists clenched.

Just a little longer. "I don't hear anything."

"You don't hear that?" Porter waved the gun in the air.

The stream at her feet no longer babbled, its volume doubling before her eyes. The sand and gravel around her popped and snapped as air bubbles made their escape.

A deep rumbling started, so muffled that she wondered if she was imagining it.

"Must be the Copper Snake." She swallowed to keep her voice from trembling along with her legs. "They do a lot of blasting in the evening."

"That's not blasting. It's more like …" Porter stood on his toes to peer over the rim of the dry wash. "Wait. Now it sounds like a caravan of tanks rolling toward us."

That was pretty close to the mark.

"You think?"

She inched toward the bank while he had his back to her.

The rumbling surged, throbbing around them. Pebbles tumbled down the banks, the ground seemed to quiver in anticipation. A puff of air, thick with the scent of wet earth, breathed over the beads of sweat dotting Claire's face, toying with her bangs.

Porter whipped toward her. "What's going on?" he yelled over the growing cacophony.

His eyes darted to where her hand clung to an exposed root sticking out of the bank. He pointed the gun at her chest.

"Where do you think you're going?"

She had no time to answer. Fifty yards upstream, the beast emerged from around the bend, roaring, rushing and churning toward them in the pre-twilight shadows. The wave leading the flood frothed and splashed over the bank as it slammed into the wash's inner elbow.

Now! A voice inside her skull shrieked, or maybe she screamed it aloud—she couldn't tell in her panic.

She used the root to hoist herself partway up the bank. Her feet slid backwards in the crumbly earth, but she plowed forward and upward, grasping and tearing at the earth.

Her upper torso crested the top with seconds to spare. She threw one leg over the edge, letting the other dangle as she dug her fingers into the earth to keep from sliding backward, and hoped like hell the bank didn't collapse under her weight.

Sparing a glance upstream, Claire gasped at the sight of the muddy wall of branches and tumbleweeds, boards and rocks tearing toward her. The flood was swallowing everything in its path. She'd made it just in time.

A hand grasped her ankle that dangled over the bank.

Shit!

Then another hand clamped onto her shin.

Frantic, she clawed at the ground as Porter's weight dragged her backwards, downwards, both legs now back over the edge.

"Let go!" she screamed over the bedlam, trying to kick free of the hands towing her into the path of the raging monster that was just a breath away from swallowing her whole.

"Pull me up, damn it!" Porter's weight suddenly seemed to triple, dragging her hips over the edge.

Her fingertips stung as she scratched at the hard, gritty desert floor, trying to cling to it. Her breath wheezed as the bank's rocky edge dug into her abdomen. "I can't—"

The wall of water crashed into them.

Porter's grip on her leg slipped, his scream melting into the roar of the water.

Claire struggled against the pull of the water to heave herself over the bank before the crest of the water reached her. She pulled one leg up onto dry land and started to lift the other when the bank crumbled under her.

In a gasp, the water dragged her down, its muddy fingers tearing at her.

She tumbled amidst sharp branches and blunt rocks, quickly disoriented in the swirling and spinning darkness.

A current slammed her even deeper into the maelstrom.

Her back scraped along the gravel floor as the water towed her along. An arsenal of debris bounced off her tangled limbs and torso. Her lungs ached and burned.

She pulled her feet under her and pushed to the surface, breaching with a gasp, coughing and spitting in the muddy water. She tried to point her feet downstream and float on her back, but the current tugged her under again, twirling her around and around.

Her muscles weakening, wobbly at best, Claire quit fighting and let the water shove her this way and that. She bobbed to the surface again and choked in more oxygen while the current wove her between a pair of boulders.

Something under the water snagged her leg, biting into her flesh. She moaned as claws scraped down her knee and calf, then jerked her to a jaw-snapping stop as teeth locked on to her ankle.

She fought to keep the rushing water from swirling over her face while rocks and boards ricocheted off her. She tried to kick free.

The water spun her around then, just in time to see something big and black surfing toward her.

Her arms felt leaden as she lifted them to shield her face, but the tire came hard and fast. It bashed into her forearms, knocking them into her chin and cheek.

Stars floated behind her eyes for a second.

Then time stopped.

* * *

"Claire!" Mac raced along next to the ravine, his light's beam bouncing over the churning water.

It'd taken him a good twenty minutes to sprint down the hillside and across the valley floor. Twenty agonizingly long minutes filled with dread and panic. His chest ached from the run and the fear that he hadn't raced fast enough.

The scent of wet dirt saturated the air. He'd passed the point where he'd found her and Porter's footprints leading into the dry wash a quarter-mile back. With the torrent still rushing, he had no way of knowing if either of them had made it back out.

"Claire!" he yelled between gasps.

On the opposite bank, his flashlight skimmed over what looked like a muddy, gnarled tree trunk snagged on several branches of a mesquite tree.

A hand bobbed in the current next to the trunk.

Mac skidded to a stop, his heart throbbing in his throat, his burning lungs constricting with fear.

"No, no, no," he whispered.

He inched up to the wash's edge and squared the beam on the hand, then followed along the arm to where it met up with the trunk—a torso floating face-down, feet directed downstream. The mud and debris obscured the rest of the body.

Mac dropped to his knees. *Claire?*

In spite of grinding pain in his chest, he had to know for certain. He examined the torso again, searching for any definitive sign. A tumbleweed caught in the current bumped against the mud-covered shoulder, then caught on the body and blocked his view.

He moved the beam down, following where the legs should be but were under water.

Then he saw a boot heel floating above the surface as water rippled around it.

A boot heel.

The memory of Porter's ostrich-skin cowboy boots wriggling through the hole flashed through his mind.

Claire had been wearing tennis shoes.

Mac closed his eyes, running his shaking hand down his face. He swallowed his heart back down into his chest.

She was still out there somewhere.

He sprang to his feet and jogged along the bank of the wash again, slower this time as he studied every clump of matted roots, tumbleweeds, and tangle of branches.

As the bank flattened, the wash spread out and grew shallower. Over the next quarter-mile, he counted three rats, one coyote, and the front half of a deer.

Then he found another body—this time human.

It lay face-down along the bank closest to him, the hips and legs still submerged in the brown water.

Stumbling over a broken wooden gate, he crashed through a thicket of brambles and landed on his knees next to the outstretched arm. Claire's grandmother's ring glittered from the middle finger on the pale-skinned hand.

"Claire?" He croaked, his voice clogged in his throat.

He flipped her over, mopping the mud from her skin with trembling fingers. He shined his light on her face. Her lips were tinged blue, her eyes closed. He patted her cheeks. Dirty water drooled out from the side of her mouth. He turned her head to the side, forcing her mouth open to clear it. More water seeped out.

"Sweetheart, come on, open your eyes."

His fingers found a pulse in her neck, still strong.

Quakes of relief racked him from head to toe. He grabbed her under the armpits and tried to pull her free of the water. She slid about half a foot and then something tugged her back into the wash.

A moan escaped from her lips.

"Claire?" Mac gave up on pulling her free and returned to trying to rouse her. "Come on, baby. Come back to me."

She gurgled, then coughed and rolled her head to the side. When he turned her on her side to help clear any mud or water from her lungs, another moan crawled up from her chest.

"Claire, wake up!" He used a hard, stern voice this time.

Her mud-caked eyelashes fluttered against her ashen cheeks, then opened, instantly closing again.

Mac moved the beam of the light to the side, and she lifted her lids partway.

The urge to squeeze her against him and never let go coursed through him. Instead, he cleared the wet strands of hair from her face and smiled down at her.

"Welcome back, Slugger."

A wave of coughs rang from her, followed by retching. After it passed, she lay limp in his arms.

"Mac?" Her voice sounded raspy.

"Yeah, baby."

"Something's chewing on my ankle."

"Come again?"

"It keeps biting me."

"I'll look." His boots sank into the mud as he stepped carefully into the shallow bank of the fast-moving, dark waters. He tested his footing and the current before focusing on Claire's leg. He ran his hands down her right pant leg and found nothing.

"The other one." Her voice barely carried over the rushing sound of the water.

Around her left ankle, Mac found the offender—a strip of barbed wire.

She cried out as he lifted her foot.

"Sorry." He followed the strand down, digging it out of the soft sand until his fingers bumped into something solid that wouldn't budge from the earth. He needed his wire cutters, damn it.

He stood, noticing that since he'd found Claire, the water had climbed further up the bank and now lapped at her upper thighs. Shit, the water was still rising. He had to get her out of there.

"You're caught in part of a barbed-wire fence, Claire. I'm going to have to unwrap it from around your ankle." He found her ankle again. "This is going to hurt."

She gasped as he started working the barbs free, but kept silent as he struggled with the tangles and worked to free her.

"Got it," he said several minutes later. "I'm going to carry you out of here, Claire."

He hated to move her, but he needed to get her to higher ground in case another swell came along.

"Can you tell me if anything feels broken?"

"Just my head."

"That's too hard to break, sweetheart."

Her chest rumbled with a half-cough, half-laugh.

Squatting next to her, he slid his arms under her.

"Wait!" She grabbed his arm.

"What?"

"I need to tell you something."

He frowned down at her pale face.

"I think there's a good chance—" She sneezed, twice, into his chest.

"You were saying?" His knees were too old to hold this position for long, especially after his flight down the hillside.

"I think that I might possibly love you back."

He stared into her dark eyes, and then burst out laughing.

Only Claire could take those three short words and jumble them into such a noncommittal sentence.

"Mac!" Claire tried to sit up and failed. "Mac, stop."

"I can't ..." He laughed, all of the fear and worry tumbling away. "I can't help it."

He tried to swallow the rest of his chuckles, and sputtered behind closed lips.

Her attempt at a glare fell short. "You should be kissing me, not laughing."

Looking away from her, he took a deep breath before turning back.

"I'm sorry," he said and dropped a kiss on her forehead. "You taste like mud pie."

"That's not very romantic."

"Mud pie?"

"No, kissing my forehead."

"I'll kiss you properly after I get you to the hospital and the doc says you're okay."

She sighed. "Fine."

He scooped her up in his arms.

"Wait!" Her gaze darted around.

"Now what?"

"Porter."

Mac glanced upstream. "He didn't make it."

Her lids lowered. "Oh."

Handing Claire the flashlight to guide them, he asked, "Can we leave now or would you like to go skinny dipping first?"

"Funny. You've been hanging around Chester and Manny too long. Next you'll start talking about hooters."

"Yours are often on my mind," he said, heading away from the wash.

"Good. How's your head?"

"It's still attached."

She leaned her head against his shoulder. "There's no way you can carry my fat ass clear to your pickup."

"Watch me. And don't insult your butt. It happens to be one of my favorite parts of your anatomy, along with your hooters."

She pressed a kiss into his jaw. "Mac?"

"What, Claire?"

"I love you."

He grinned. "Yeah, I know."

Chapter Twenty-Four

Wednesday, August 25th

The noonday sun cooked the tar-streaked pavement at Biddy's Gas and Carryout at a slow, smelly boil.

Kate fanned herself with a credit card pamphlet as the gas pump chugged beside her, spewing high octane fumes as it took its sweet time filling her tank. A blast of heat from a passing semi-truck plastered her shirt against her damp skin.

The engine of her newly repaired Volvo ticked along with the numbers on the pump's LCD display.

Across the street, Creekside Supply Company's flag fluttered and flapped in the cross-breezes, sagging in the humidity every time the desert paused to take another breath.

Kate tapped the edge of the pamphlet against her chin. Good ol' Jackrabbit Junction spread out before her in all its dusty, heat-rippling glory. In less than twenty-four hours, she'd watch it disappear in her rearview mirror.

After receiving a call from the repair shop yesterday that her Volvo was ready to roll, it hadn't taken Deborah much hot air to convince Kate to leave a few days earlier than originally planned. Monday's chain of events had Kate wanting to run for the hills—the Black Hills. Back to square one.

She was tired of being hung out on the line to dry only to end up caught in another August gale.

Claire's injuries had kept them from escaping before Ruby and Gramps returned earlier today, much to Deborah's chagrin. But with Ruby home, Kate no longer needed to hang around to mind the store. They were free to flee tomorrow at first light.

If it weren't for Jess's birthday party tonight, Kate would have pushed to make their exit this afternoon.

An all-too-familiar, almost brand new, red pickup, its tailgate down with a couple of two-by-fours sticking out, rolled into the carry-out's parking lot.

Kate avoided looking in Butch's direction as she heard his pickup door open and then slam shut. She breathed a sigh of relief at the sound of the store's electronic door buzzer. Her mother was right, some places were meant only to be passed through—preferably at sixty miles per hour.

The gas pump clicked off. Kate hung the nozzle back in its holder, fidgeting with her keys while she waited for her receipt to print. She wanted to escape before Butch came out and saw her.

Finally, the machine spit out her receipt.

"Hi, Kate."

Her shoulders pinched together.

Damn!

Planting a smile on her face, she faced Butch, who stood just outside the glass doors with three packs of hamburger buns and two loaves of bread in his arms.

"Hey, Butch."

"How's Claire? Grady said she looked like she'd gone a couple rounds with Muhammad Ali after her dip in the wash."

Which was nothing compared to Porter, according to what Mac had told Kate after returning from the county morgue where he'd had to identify his body.

The truth about Porter's reason for courting both Claire and Kate still took her breath away. All of those times she'd spent alone with him in his pickup and he'd turned out to be a cold-blooded killer. She shivered in spite of the heat searing her skin.

"Claire's moving pretty slow and has a big bruise on her chin, but she was up and limping around the place this morning." In spite of Mac's protests.

The friction that had caused all of the sparks between Claire and Mac last weekend seemed to have smoothed out, which was another reason Kate couldn't wait to leave. She'd had enough salt rubbed in her wounds lately. Watching those two lovebirds made her want to jab pencils in her eyes.

"Good to hear. Your car looks brand new again."

"Yep." Kate patted the roof, fighting back a grimace as the sizzling black metal burned her hand.

Several seconds ticked by way too slowly, Kate glancing everywhere but into Butch's blue eyes.

"I heard Ruby and your grandpa made it home this morning."

She gaped. Who had told him that? This town was way too small.

"Jess called to say her mom gave the 'okay' on her working for me."

Ah, Jess. Of course.

"She also told me you're heading home early." His expression remained fixed, his grin nothing more than polite.

Kate's throat stung. He didn't even care, the bastard.

"The time seemed right." Her voice creaked, dang it.

Butch nodded, staring at her like he was evaluating her as a Botox candidate.

More long, empty seconds passed.

Then he cleared his throat. "Well, I should be going."

"Right. Me, too."

"Take care, Kate. I'm going to miss you."

Her heart twisting, Kate watched Butch climb into his truck and drive off with a wave in her direction.

A sledgehammer to her gut would have hurt less.

His truck crossed the highway and rolled into The Shaft's lot, parking in the usual spot. Sunshine glinted off his side mirror as he stepped out onto the gravel.

A dust devil swirled to life on the highway separating them, snatching up a couple of plastic bags and a paper cup from the ditch, twirling them faster and faster.

Something inside of Kate snapped.

She couldn't go on like this, all sappy and sad. Enough was enough. Butch liked her. She liked him. One of them needed to do something about it.

Yanking open her door, she slid into the driver's seat, keyed her Volvo to life, and shifted into gear. Her tires squealed as she peeled out of Biddy's parking lot.

His arms loaded with the buns and bread, Butch had almost reached The Shaft's front door when she cranked her steering wheel and slid into The Shaft's parking lot.

Before she could chicken out, Kate punched the gas, sending gravel airborne. She gritted her teeth, pushed back against her seat, and aimed for the back of his pickup.

Metal screeched and crunched as she plowed into his truck, her new airbag going off in her face.

She turned off the engine. Steam billowed from under her hood.

Shoving open her door, she stepped out under the cobalt sky and wiped her damp palms on her shorts. A walk around front to assess the damage revealed the tailgate sticking out from her radiator. She'd torn the whole sucker free. Damn.

For the first time today, she smiled.

"What the hell!" Butch yelled.

She watched him stride across the lot, the buns and bread in a heap by the door.

He paused to gawk at his rumpled, scraped bumper. When he turned on her, his neck glowed as red as Deborah's fancy boots. "You did that on purpose!"

"Yes, I did." Kate crossed her arms over her chest.

Was it just her or did those yellow poppies lining the ditch seem brighter, dancing in the breeze with more gusto than usual?

"Are you insane, woman?" Butch was still yelling.

"I have my moments." She took a deep breath, soaking up the homey scent of sun-baked earth.

He marched around to the front of her Volvo and the chunk of metal piercing her grill. "Look what you did to my tailgate!"

She walked over next to him, shaking her head at her hissing radiator. "Hmmm. And to think my insurance company dropped me after that last accident."

"What!?"

"It looks like I'm going to need to wait tables or help Jess in your greenhouse to pay this off. What's your starting wage?"

"My starting wage …" He peered down at her, his eyes narrowing. "Ahhh. I get it now. You're a real professional, Kate Morgan, but it's not going to work."

"Of course it will." She played dumb, fluttering her eyelashes a little. "I used to be a waitress in college."

He growled. "You know I'm talking about you and me."

"How can you be sure unless you give us a chance?" She inched closer, licking her lips for extra measure.

He glanced down at her mouth for a split second. "You're heading home tomorrow."

"Well, I'm not going anywhere now, am I?"

"You don't like Jackrabbit Junction."

"It's growing on me." She captured his hand.

"I won't wear those fancy, designer clothes." He tried to tug free, but Kate held tight, drawing him toward her.

"You don't have to wear any clothes at all as far as I'm concerned."

His Adam's apple bobbed. "What about teaching school?"

"I've been thinking about finding a new career."

She wrapped his arm around her and trailed her fingernails down his T-shirt, scraping his chest. His muscles flinched under her touch.

"Really?" His voice sounded low and husky, the anger slipping away.

She squinted up at him. His blue eyes bored into hers, measuring, questioning, hesitating.

"What other objections do you have for me, Butch?"

"I'm thinking."

"Think on this," she whispered and pulled his mouth down to hers.

He tasted salty, smelled woodsy, and lit a fire inside her that scorched her inside and out. Her hands snuck under his T-shirt, palms rubbing over his damp skin.

He groaned and teased her tongue with his, making her quiver and mold her body tighter against his, leaving her tied up and twisted, hungry for more.

With a gasp for breath, he broke contact, and then trailed his mouth along her jaw.

"Does that mean you're done objecting?" She dragged her nails down his back.

"Christ, Kate." His breath came in soft huffs, matching hers. "You've been driving me crazy since you crashed into my pickup—the first time."

"You sure haven't acted like it." She shuddered as his teeth nipped her collarbone.

"Come into my office and I'll try harder." His hands spanned her hips, his body offering promises of its own.

Cravings rippled through her. "Is that a guarantee?"

"Only if you swear to stop playing demolition derby with my truck."

She directed his mouth back to hers.

"Deal." Her lips brushed his as she spoke. "I want you, Butch."

"Damn, you are such a crazy, hot mess."

He crushed her mouth under his, making her head spin. She wrapped her arms around his neck, hanging on as he bent her backwards.

When he came up for air, he smiled down at her. "I'm glad you're sticking around."

The blast of a horn made Kate look around. She pulled away from Butch, shielding her eyes, and gazed across the road.

Mac's pickup sat idling in front of the Creekside Supply Store. Claire hung part-way out the passenger-side window, a huge grin plastered on her black-and-blue face.

"Mom is gonna kick your ass when she finds out what you've done!" she yelled loud enough for the whole damned valley to hear.

Kate stuck out her tongue at Claire, then turned her back on the world and grabbed Butch's hand. "Let's go inside and finish this."

"Oh, we're just getting started, Kate."

After a wave to Claire, he led Kate out of the heat and into the fire.

* * *

"Hey, Mac." Ruby stood at the kitchen sink, up to her elbows in sudsy water, washing the dishes from Jess's birthday dinner. "I thought you were playing Euchre."

"Jess is sitting in for me," he explained.

Grabbing a clean dishtowel from the drawer, he started drying plates. The kitchen still smelled like chocolate. The sight of the carved-up birthday cake with fudge frosting called to him, but he had something to clear up first.

"I need to talk to you, Ruby."

"Uh, oh." Ruby's smile didn't hide the flicker of worry behind her green eyes. "That sounds serious, darlin'."

Mac didn't smile back. No need to sugarcoat the truth. Ruby liked her bad news straight, without sweetener.

"The Lucky Monk is worthless," he told her.

Ruby paused in mid-scrub. Lines wrinkled her forehead. "You mean there's no more copper in it?"

"No, it's rich with minerals."

"Honey, you're not makin' any sense."

He decided to skip all of the finer details for now. "There's a burial chamber in it."

"Burial chamber? Are you talking about the room where you found that old miner?"

Shaking his head, he grabbed another wet dish. "Further back. I found an ancient burial chamber—possibly from the late B.C. or early A.D. era. It's full of graves."

Ruby dropped her sponge. "Really? In my mine?"

"There's no way the state will let you dig up there now. The site needs to be thoroughly studied."

"Have you reported it already?"

"I didn't have to. Sheriff Harrison and his men had to go into the chamber to collect Richard's body." Earlier in the day, Jess had given Ruby the low-down on Monday's excitement. "The sheriff has to let the state know."

"Of course." She fished her sponge from the suds. "I mean, if there are ancient bodies up there, then the state should be involved, right?"

The cake plate she scrubbed on didn't merit the extra attention she was giving it.

Mac grasped her wrist and gently pulled the plate from her grip before she broke it in half. "It probably has great historical significance."

Sighing, she threw the sponge back in the water and stared down at her hands. "I know. I'm just tired of having Harley use his own money to put out my little fires. It's just an old mine, but it was *my* mine. Something I could have sold."

"Just because you can't extract the minerals from it doesn't mean you can't make a profit on this."

He handed her the damp towel and nudged her aside, plunging his hands in the warm water. "Who knows? This could bring you even more business in the future. Archaeology-related tourism is becoming more and more popular."

Ruby walked around him, grabbed a wet glass from the dish rack, and started to towel it dry. The grin she shot him was cockeyed. "Claire's optimism is rubbing off on you."

"No comment." Ruby didn't know the half of it when it came to Claire's influence.

His aunt chuckled.

Then again, maybe she did.

Rinsing a plate, he returned to his previous train of thought. "You should probably contact the university in Tucson and give the anthropology department a heads-up. I have a feeling this is going to be a big deal."

"Okay." She paused, her lips pursed. "It's kind of exciting, you know. And to think, Joe had been sittin' on this for years and never knew it."

Mac grimaced, hating that he had to burst another of her bubbles. "Joe did know about it, Ruby. He tried to hide it by walling off the tunnel and then causing that cave-in to seal off that section of the mine."

Joe must have taken the sandal from the dead miner's hand around that time, unknowingly leaving behind a piece of the braided rope. He was probably going to see what kind of price it would fetch on the black market. Whether he nabbed the mummified hand, stick figure, and bag from the skeleton or the burial chamber would probably never be answered.

Two red spots formed on her cheeks. "Of course he did."

The dish she had in her hands clattered louder than necessary on the stack of dry plates. "I should've known the bastard had tainted this, too."

She didn't know the half of it. Claire and Mac had agreed that Joe's lewd photo collection didn't need to become public information and hid them before Sheriff Harrison and his crew got to them.

"Hey, Mom." Jess slid into the kitchen in the new pair of fuzzy pink slippers Claire had given her for her birthday. "Dad's on the phone. He wants to talk to you."

"He is? I didn't even hear the phone ring."

"Oh, I called him. You know how he always forgets to call on my birthday."

Ruby's lips thinned. "He forgets, right."

She dropped a kiss on Jess's forehead as she left the kitchen.

"Aren't you in the middle of a card game?" Mac asked Jess as he rinsed the last plate.

"Chester had to go to the bathroom." Jess shoved the stack of plates her mom had dried onto a shelf in the cupboard. "And Manny went outside with Harley to smoke a cigar."

"Why'd they go outside?"

"Claire's mom refused to finish the game if they didn't."

Ah, good old Deborah. Mac dried his hands on the damp towel. He couldn't wait to wave goodbye to Claire's mother. Unfortunately, with Kate's car out of commission again, his plan to take the rest of the week off so he could stay and take care of Claire had backfired. He was counting the days until Sunday, when they'd return to Tucson together.

"Jess." Claire stood in the doorway. "The boys are back and waiting for you."

"Cool." Jess bounced toward the doorway.

"Hey." Claire caught Jess by the arm as she passed. "Did you put the money back?" she asked in a low voice.

Jess's ponytail bobbed. "I did what you said and put it exactly where she'd hidden it. Mom won't know I touched it."

"Good." Claire let Jess's arm go. "Now go kick your new stepsister's butt. I hate it when Mom gloats."

Giggling, Jess zipped into the rec room.

Claire joined Mac, leaning her hip against the counter. "I'll have to tell Ruby she needs to find a new hiding place."

"Are you going to let her know Jess almost hopped a bus to Ohio?" Mac grabbed a Coke from the fridge, offering it to her.

"Not if I can help it." She stared at the can like it had been sprayed with DDT. "I'd rather have a Corona."

"Doc said no alcohol until you're off the meds."

"Fine, spoilsport." But her grin was flirty as she cracked open the can. "So, what do you have that will take the edge off another evening with my mother?"

"Oh, I can think of a thing or two." He let his gaze linger on her baby blue, *Zombies Love Girls with BIG Brainnnsssss* T-shirt. "If you feel up to it."

Zombies Love Girls with BIG Brainnnsssss

"That depends what you have in mind."

Mac took the can of Coke from her hand and set it next to the sink, then lifted her onto the counter. "Nothing too strenuous on your part." He ran his hands up her bare thighs. "I'll do all of the work. You can just lie back and watch."

Her husky laugh rippled through him. "We need to rent a motel room. This place is packed."

"Ruby's office will do." He trailed his lips over the purplish-yellow bruise on her jaw, his fingers exploring through her T-shirt. "Besides, there's something I've been wanting to try in that chair."

Claire shivered as he nibbled on her earlobe.

"Oh, jeez, you two! Enough already."

Mac pulled back at the sound of Kate's voice.

Standing just inside the kitchen doorway, her arms crossed, Kate smirked at them. "Can't you find some closet to do the wild monkey dance in? This is a public place, you know. And I eat off that countertop."

"You're one to talk." Claire grabbed Mac's hand and placed it back on her thigh. "Remind me again who gave that porn-star exhibition in The Shaft's parking lot earlier today."

Kate's forehead reddened as she shushed Claire and glanced into the rec room.

"I can't believe you smashed Butch's pickup again." Mac leaned against the counter next to Claire, shaking his head.

Kate shrugged. "A girl's gotta do what a girl's gotta do."

"The poor guy has no idea what he's getting into with this family."

Claire pinched Mac's arm.

"How did Mom take the news?" Kate asked Claire just as Deborah waltzed through the doorway.

"How did I take what news?"

Kate winced and turned, her smile extra wide. "Hi, Mom."

"Don't you 'Hi, Mom' me, Kathryn Lynette." Deborah prodded Kate further into the kitchen. "What were you thinking? That man is a bartender, for God's sake. What future can he offer you?"

Here they went again. The six-pack of Coors in the fridge screamed Mac's name.

Claire slid off the counter. "Mom, don't—"

"No, Claire. This is my problem." Kate held her mother's stare. "What Butch does for a living is none of your business. All you need to be concerned with is my happiness, and he makes me happy," she paused and chuckled at what must have been a private joke, "very happy. So I'm staying here."

"Look on the bright side, Mom." Claire crossed her arms over her chest, apparently unable to keep quiet. "At least Butch isn't a killer—unlike your first choice."

"Or a thief." Mac couldn't resist adding that tidbit, referring to the office break-in that started this whole mess.

Deborah shot them both a scowl before continuing with her scolding. "You're not thinking straight, Kathryn."

"No, you're the one who's confused. You were wrong about Porter, and you're wrong about Butch. For the first time in my life, I like a guy who has his shit together, and I'm not going to let you screw this up for me. That's why you're flying home without me tomorrow."

Mac had been the second person to volunteer to drive Deborah to the airport, right after Chester.

Deborah turned to Claire. "Look what you've done."

"Don't blame me. Kate's a big girl. She hasn't taken any of my advice since I convinced her to moon our high school football team for good luck."

Kate's pointed glare said Claire wasn't making that up.

"All right, Kathryn." Deborah gave in. "You stay and have your fun. But I won't be one bit surprised to have you knocking on my door by Labor Day."

"We'll see," Kate said with another little chuckle.

Pointing at Claire, Deborah said, "And you! Stop sticking your nose in where it doesn't belong. In case you haven't noticed, the people around here aren't real friendly to strangers, and my heart can't take another near-miss on your life. I didn't endure nine months of morning sickness and a slew of stretch marks for you to just throw it away on some Angela Lansbury fantasy of yours."

A grin surfaced on Claire's lips. "I love you too, Mother."

"As for you." Her manicured finger now pointed at Mac. He braced himself for her stinger. "Take care of her. She says she doesn't need a keeper, but a bodyguard might serve her well."

Mac blinked in surprise. "Uh ..."

"Not that you've done the best job of keeping her out of harm's way so far." Deborah walked toward the rec room.

That was more like it. Mac's world tilted back into place.

"Oh, Kathryn." Deborah paused in the doorway. "Be sure to close the door when you come to bed. Ever since your grandfather returned with his new wife, this place stinks like some cheap Vegas card room."

"I'm staying at Butch's place tonight, Mom."

"Really?"

Mac nudged Claire and winked. They'd figured that would be the case when they saw them in Butch's parking lot.

Deborah's sniff was full of disgust. "Where did I go wrong with you two girls? Haven't you heard of playing hard-to-get?"

When neither Claire nor Kate responded, Deborah shook her head. "Fine. Have your little fling with Butch. But you tell him that before I leave for the airport, I want to have a talk with him."

With a flounce of her hair, Deborah exited the room.

"Shit." Kate raced after her. "Mom, no. Not yet."

"Poor Butch." Mac chuckled. "First Kate, then your mother. The guy should have fled the state while he had the chance."

"Maybe he's into masochism." Claire grabbed his hand and tugged him toward her. "Come here. If you're going to be guarding my body, I should give you a thorough tour so you don't overlook anything."

His pulse jump-started at the wicked gleam in her eyes. He pinned her against the counter and tilted her chin up. "Are we talking clothes or no clothes?"

"No clothes, definitely." She rubbed against him, all soft skin and curves. "What do you say, tough guy? You up to the task?"

"Maybe."

He lowered his mouth to hers, breathing her in. She smelled like chocolate and all things Claire.

"Where's your tool belt?"

* * *

Thursday, August 26th

"Ruby found your tool belt in the office again," Gramps told Claire as he tore another chunk of sheetrock from the wall behind the faulty toilet that had been giving Claire fits since she'd arrived at the R.V. park two weeks ago.

"Sorry about that." Claire fanned her sweaty T-shirt in the sweltering, concrete block room.

The perfume of newly weed-whacked grass filtered in through the open window, along with fat, black flies and a steady stream of humid air, to add to the lovely aroma of ammonia-based disinfectant. A monsoon swelled on the southern horizon, building another gully washer under the white-hot sun.

Henry sprawled nearby on the floor, snapping at any fly that buzzed too close to his drooping ears. He hadn't left Gramps's side since Ruby and he returned from Vegas, nor was he acknowledging Claire's presence anymore. The freaking mutt acted as if he'd spent the last week receiving daily canings instead of slipping free of his collar each day to chase butterflies and grasshoppers, eat handouts from campers, and shit and piss wherever he damn well pleased.

"Mac and you need to sell tickets to your tool belt shows." Manny grinned so wide his moustache curled at the corners. He sat on the sink counter next to Claire, sharing her bag of barbecued pork rinds. "You could advertise at The Double D strip joint, especially on Wednesday nights."

"What's so special about Wednesday nights?" Claire crunched on a piece of fried barbecued pork fat.

He waggled his eyebrows at her. "Nude mud wrestling."

Chester crushed his empty beer can and tossed it in the trash. "That depends on whether she or Mac wears the tool belt."

Gramps aimed the crowbar he was using to strip the drywall at Manny and then Chester. "Stop talking about my granddaughter and sex."

Manny chuckled and winked at Claire. "He's so easy."

"Hey, Gramps." Claire remembered something that had been bugging her for days now. "What was in that package you sent to Mac at work?"

Gramps snorted. "None of your damned business, girl."

A belch rattled from Chester's throat. "Who jammed a stick up your ass today, Harley?"

"He's just suffering from a case of penis envy."

Claire shot Manny a *huh?* look.

"*Sí.* Ruby kicked his ass in the Euchre tournament. It's pretty obvious his new wife wears the pants in his casa."

"Keep flappin' your lips, Carrera," Gramps said, tearing off more sheetrock, "and I'll be jamming this crowbar up your—"

"Hey, what's that?" Claire hopped off the sink counter and walked over to the stall where Gramps stood sweating.

A small piece of wood bridged the pair of two-by-fours Gramps had just exposed that ran parallel up the wall on the right side of the sewer vent pipe. On this makeshift shelf sat a small jewelry box, like the one Claire had when she was seven, including the frilly pink scrolls.

Tossing the chunk of drywall he'd freed onto the pile in the middle of the room, Gramps lifted the box from the shelf.

Chester peered into the stall over Claire's shoulder. "It looks like something of Jess's."

"Move your block head, Thomas." Manny said.

He tried to nudge Chester aside with the cane he still used after his quarrel with the flooded toilet last weekend. Unfortunately, his plight had had no effect on Miss Rebecca, who'd motored out of the park yesterday without an *adios* or backward glance.

"Hit me again with that cane, you old geezer, and I'm going to wrap it around your testicles."

Gramps opened the box's hinged top. A blonde ballerina circled on a pink satin ledge while mechanical-sounding music twanged and dinged. Claire leaned closer, mesmerized by the glitter on the dancer's tutu. The steely scent of Gramps's Aqua Velva merged with the smell of beer from Chester's warm breath as his chin brushed her shoulder.

Henry barked twice, breaking the spell, making Claire jump back—right onto Chester's toes.

"Yowch!" Chester limped out of the stall.

Crunching on more rinds, Manny laughed. "That's what you get for wearing argyle socks with open toed sandals."

"Sorry, Chester." Claire turned back to the music box as Gramps pulled a chiseled arrowhead out of it.

"Looks like a piece of flint." He held it up under the sixty-watt light bulb overhead. "Why would Jess put a flint arrowhead in the wall?"

Flint arrowhead. Claire stared at the chipped stone, something sparking in her bruised brain.

Arrowhead.

"Gramps, what did Kate call arrowheads when we were kids?"

His brows wrinkled as he glanced at her. "Pointers, why?"

"That's it!" She snatched the arrowhead from his hand and cupped it in her palm. "This is Flint's pointer! And all along I kept thinking Joe was talking about that dead guy in the mine."

Gears spun in her head as she stared at the vent pipe running up the wall.

"And that explains what he meant with the 'pipe up and let me hear it' quote."

She pushed past Gramps and gripped the pipe, wiggling it.

"Of course!" she continued. "'Shiver my timbers'—this pipe always rattles against the wall when the toilet is flushed. But what about 'pieces of eight'? Where did that fit into this?"

She turned around and looked to the guys for help.

All three men stared at her like she'd morphed into the one-eyed, one-horned, flying purple people eater.

"Have you been smoking doobies again, girl?" Gramps asked.

Chester grunted. "Maybe she has leftover water on her brain."

"I bet that tire knocked some wires loose upstairs," Manny added. "Have you noticed her one eye keeps ticcing, especially when her mom is around?"

"Gramps, remember what I told you yesterday about Porter flipping through Joe's first edition of *Treasure Island*?"

"Yeah. So?"

Claire waved all of them off, shoved the arrowhead in her pocket, and focused on the vent pipe again.

"Would one of you smartasses hand me that saw?" She knocked on the pipe next to where the music box had sat. It sounded hollow just like the rest of the pipe.

"Move aside." Gramps squeezed in next to her. "And show me where you want me to cut."

"Just give me the saw."

"No way. If Mac finds out I let you do any work today, he'll have my hide. You're supposed to be sitting on that sink and taking it easy, remember?"

"Oh, yeah." She'd forgotten about Mac's threat to have Deborah play nursemaid instead of him if Claire didn't cooperate. "Mom's definitely flying out tomorrow, right?"

"Yep. Ruby and I need some time to settle in without your mother's big nose around. The two of them are barely speaking as is. A couple of more days together and blood will spill. Now where am I cutting, Sherlock?"

Pointing out two places a couple feet apart on the pipe, she backed out of the stall and joined Manny on the sink counter. Her fingers drummed on her thighs as she watched Gramps saw through the black PVC pipe. Sewer gas seeped from the open pipe and filled the small room, making her eyes water.

"Woo wee!" Chester moved to the open doorway as Gramps pulled the chunk of pipe free. "That smells like Carrera's breath in the morning."

Gramps chuckled as he stuffed a grease-smeared rag from his back pocket into the bottom part of the open vent pipe.

"All the better to kiss you with, lover." Manny puckered his lips and wiggled his index finger at Chester. "Come over here, big boy."

"I have something you can plant those lips on, Carrera." Chester reached for his belt buckle.

"Never mind. I wouldn't want to put Tilly or Milly out of a job. Which one are you seeing tonight, anyway?"

"Tilly. Tuesday, Thursday, and Saturdays are her nights. Milly gets me on Wednesday, Friday, and Sunday."

"What about Monday?" Claire asked, amazed that the twins were so desperate for a man they'd be willing to share Chester.

"That's Chester Jr.'s day of rest. A man can't live on Viagra alone, you know."

"Well, lookie here." Gramps peered into the piece of pipe. "No wonder this toilet kept backing up over the last few years." He banged one end of the pipe in his palm, peeked again, and then shook the pipe until a roll of paper in a plastic bag stuck out the end. "The air vent was partially clogged."

"What is it?" Claire hopped down off the counter, unable to sit still any longer.

Handing her the empty pipe, Gramps pulled the roll of papers out of the bag and smoothed them out. He whistled and offered one of them to her.

"What's the Copper Snake's stock worth these days, you think?" he asked.

Claire stared down at the paper—a Copper Snake Mining Company stock certificate for one hundred shares made out to Joe Martino.

Ah, ha! Here it was, Joe's "pieces of eight," otherwise known as "treasure" by Long John Silver and his greedy men.

An image of Richard Rensberg waving a gun at Mac and her flashed in her head. Were these the shares his father had sold? The reason Joe blackmailed Bianca with those X-rated pictures?

"Who's Will Banks?" Gramps asked.

She leaned over to see what had Gramps frowning. "Banks was Porter's last name."

Claire stared down at what she guessed was Porter's father's name printed on the certificate Gramps held. "This must be the 'treasure' Porter's dad told him about."

Why had Joe taken Porter's dad's share of the stocks? What exactly had Joe's relationship been with Porter's dad? Had they had some kind of falling out or did crooks always turn on each other over time?

She glanced back at the stock certificates in her hands and put two and two together, whispering, "I'll bet you Porter's dad is the one who took those pictures of Bianca."

"What pictures?" Manny asked.

Chester followed with, "Who's Bianca?"

Biting her lip, Claire struggled to figure out a way to cover her *faux pas*. She'd forgotten they didn't know about the blackmail photos. If she had her way, they wouldn't find out about them anytime soon, either. The last thing she needed was Ruby catching wind of those pictures.

The chunk of Nazi gold that she'd stashed in the wall safe next to that mysterious antique pocket watch of Joe's was another story she probably should share. But that would hold for another day or two, until she came up with a good lie as to why she and Jess were digging around in Ruby's closet floor.

"Uh, it's not important." She ignored the squinty-eyed glare coming from Gramps. "How many of these are there?"

Gramps fanned the pile. "If they're legitimate, enough to make Ruby a good-sized chunk of money."

Claire would bet her mom's Elvis-autographed poodle skirt the stocks were legit. Porter's dad had been right. There was enough here to set someone up for a long time, especially if Porter had managed to get his hands on Joe's portion, too.

Poor Porter, robbed of his father's legacy by a dead, blackmailing scoundrel.

"Claire?" Mac stepped into the men's room, then coughed and covered his nose and mouth. "Christ, it reeks in—hey, what are you guys looking at?"

Manny stepped aside so Mac could squeeze into the stall. He took the certificate Claire held out to him, his eyes scanning down the paper.

"Holy shit!" Lowering his hand from his face, he looked at the stack Gramps still held in his hands. "Holy goddamned shit."

"It looks like your aunt is a rich woman." Gramps didn't sound very happy about it either. He seemed to be allergic to any wealth Ruby accumulated through her dead husband.

"Cheer up, Ford." Chester finished off his beer and let out another belch. "Maybe she'll buy you a new R.V., since yours still stinks even after that thousand dollar detail job."

Claire looked up at Mac. "Did you need me for something?"

"Oh, yeah." He still stared at the stocks. "It's about your family."

"Jeez, what's Mom doing now?" The woman seemed bent on making life hell for all during her last twenty-four hours on site.

"Not your mom. Your sister," he said distractedly. "She called."

"Isn't she back from Butch's yet?"

Chester snickered. "She didn't crash again, did she?"

"Not Kate," Mac said. "Veronica."

That grabbed Gramps's attention. "What did Ronnie want?"

Mac looked up with a slight frown. "She said she's leaving her husband because he's in jail for some kind of money fraud."

Claire gaped at him. "You're kidding."

"And she's coming down to Tucson to stay with us."

"What?!" She leaned against the stall wall, dread filling her. "For how long?"

Anything more than a few weeks and she'd have to start smoking again just to keep her hands busy, or they'd end up circling Ronnie's neck ... again.

"She didn't say."

"Shit!" Gramps and Claire said at the same time.

Mac's eyes narrowed. "I thought we liked Veronica."

"Uh, yeah, we do, but ..." Claire licked her lips, not sure how to explain to Mac what he'd just done by giving Ronnie the OK to cross his threshold with a suitcase in her hand.

"What haven't you told me about your older sister, Claire?"

Claire grabbed his arm and led him toward the door. "Mac, honey, remember how you said you love me, and I told you that I love you, too?"

He yanked her to a stop. "Claire." His tone rang with warning. "What's wrong with your sister?"

Gulping, she shrugged and tried to smile. It felt more like a grimace.

"Nothing her shrink can't fix … I hope."

The End … for now

Connect with Me Online

Facebook (Personal Page):
http://www.facebook.com/ann.charles.author

Facebook (Author Page):
http://www.facebook.com/pages/Ann-
Charles/37302789804?ref=share

Twitter (as Ann W. Charles): http://twitter.com/AnnWCharles

Ann Charles Website: http://www.anncharles.com

Bio

Ann Charles is an award-winning author who writes romantic
mysteries that are splashed with humor and whatever else she
feels like throwing into the mix. When she is not dabbling in
fiction, arm-wrestling with her children, attempting to seduce her
husband, or arguing with her sassy cat, she is daydreaming of
lounging poolside at a fancy resort with a blended margarita in
one hand and a great book in the other.

Five Fun Facts about Ann Charles

I'm a big fan of the movie, *Tremors*, with Kevin Bacon and Fred Ward. Ever since I first "met" Kevin's character in the movie, I've wanted to write a story with a guy named Valentine in it. That is how Valentine "Butch" Carter came to be in this book. This movie also inspired my character, Ruby, who has been Heather Gummer (played by Reba McEntire in the film) since I first dreamed up the cast.

* * *

I have been a fan of country music since childhood thanks to my dad and stepfather. I grew up listening to Tammy Wynette, Hank Williams Sr. and Jr., Patsy Cline, Johnny Horton, Waylon Jennings, Dolly Parton, and many more. While I write the scenes in the Jackrabbit Junction Mystery series, I often pick a song from one of these classic country artists and play it over and over in the background, which drives my family nuts.

* * *

The mummy image on the "Mummy Dearest" T-shirt Claire is wearing on the cover of this book is a picture of me dressed as a "pregnant mummy" for Halloween years ago when I was six months preggo with my son. My husband helped me to fashion a mummy costume complete with wraps of linen, creepy makeup, and rotting teeth. Ah, true love.

* * *

I'm a huge fan of westerns and spend many late nights after my family goes to bed watching my favorite westerns over and over—*Big Country*, *Two Mules for Sister Sara*, *The Outlaw Josey Wales*, *McClintock*, *North to Alaska*, *Open Range*, and *Lonesome Dove* to name a few. My husband once made the mistake of cutting out the Western channel from our satellite TV package in order to save money. He still puts up with me grumbling about that.

* * *

When my mother first read this book, she called me, told me she really enjoyed it, and then asked if I had some issues with her that we needed to discuss with a therapist in the room. Ha ha ha!

CPSIA information can be obtained at www.ICGtesting.com
Printed in the USA
BVOW070938270812

298878BV00002B/3/P